When diplomat's daughter Sophie Langley is sent on an errand of mercy to the Channel Island of St Nicolas in order to care for her two elderly aunts, she finds herself trapped in an unenviable position following the German invasion.

In the Battle for France, linguist and poet Robert Anderson, a lieutenant in the Royal Welch Fusiliers, finds himself embroiled in an impossible military situation from which there seems to be no escape.

From the beautiful Channel Islands to the very heart of Nazi-occupied Europe, *Message From Captivity* weaves factual authenticity into the fabric of a narrative where the twists and turns of captivity, freedom and dangerous pursuit have unforeseen consequences; where Robert's integrity is tested to the limit and Sophie needs all her inner strength to cope with the decisions and challenges she faces.

Sally Aviss

Message from Captivity

Message from Captivity
by Sally Aviss

Text © Sally Aviss, 2016
Last verse of *Three Days* by Stephen Spender from *New Collected Poems* by Stephen Spender © 2004. Reprinted by kind permission of the Estate of Stephen Spender.
Front cover photograph of Biberach taken by Frank Hiley, 1945. Other images courtesy of Jeric Santiago, George Hodan and the National Library of the Netherlands.

Published by Ōzaru Books, an imprint of BJ Translations Ltd
Street Acre, Shuart Lane, St Nicholas-at-Wade,
BIRCHINGTON, CT7 0NG, U.K.
www.ozaru.net

First edition published 6 December 2016
Printed by Lightning Source
ISBN: 978-0-9931587-5-9

For my family
with love

Also by Sally Aviss, published by Ōzaru Books

The Cairnmor Trilogy:

The Call of Cairnmor

Changing Tides, Changing Times

Where Gloom and Brightness Meet

Acknowledgements

I am, as ever, indebted to my family, Peter, Tim and Elizabeth for their unstinting support and encouragement; to Annette Vidler and Christine Lord for their astute observations; to Carol Dodd and Jackie Readwin at my local library; to Kenneth Bird for his help with the use of idiomatic German; to Aniela Robinson for her cover art suggestions, to Stephen Matthews and Roger E. Harris for assistance with the cover art photograph, and finally, to Ben Jones of Ōzaru Books for his attention to detail and continued willingness to publish my books.

Contents

PROLOGUE

The English Channel
March, 1943

The night was dark with a just a glimmer of moonlight. Silently, their oars muffled, the canoes cut through the water.

Rocks loomed out at them: strange shapes, alien in the darkness. A strong current took them shore-wards, their uniforms bulky in their backpacks; their weapons resting against their legs, concealed in the front section of each canoe.

Behind them, the submarine disappeared beneath the waves in a sucking swirl of water, leaving them alone in the all-enveloping opacity.

They paddled on through the night, checking the compass, straining to see through the inky blackness as the moon disappeared behind a cloud; making sure in the diminished visibility that they were not about to encounter unexpected and unwanted visitors.

Eventually, there came the welcome hiss of surf, the sound of waves breaking gently on the shore.

This was it.

They headed for the right-hand side of a little cove, beaching their canvas boats and dragging them along the sand to a type of grotto created by an overhanging cliff. Without hesitating, they shrugged off their backpacks and stripped off their wet clothes, rubbing themselves dry before changing into uniforms and strapping on Lugers.

Together, they bundled up their sodden garments and put them into bags, packing these in the front of their canoes. They tied long ropes around both prows, concealing and securing them tightly in the lush vegetation that abounded in and around the grotto. Together, they lowered the canoes over the edge of the wave-smoothed stones, allowing time for them to fill with water, before paying out the ropes as the boats gradually sank into the deep recesses of the pool.

Satisfied that all was as it should be, they left the security of the hidden cavern and covered their tracks.

Everywhere was quiet, save only for the sound of waves upon the sand.

For a moment, one of them allowed his mind to dwell on exactly where it was they had come to and his heart beat faster with something greater than fear and adrenalin.

She might be here – his unknown girl from the past.

PART ONE

APRIL – AUGUST, 1940

CHAPTER 1

Maybury, Oxfordshire

"How utterly, utterly, tiresome!"

Lady Margot Langley, her lips pursed in annoyance, an opened envelope and two thin sheets of pale blue writing paper in her hand, walked across the manicured lawn that radiated from the family's redbrick mansion like a verdant carpet.

Her daughter Sophie, cool and pretty in a white *broderie-anglaise* summer dress that blended perfectly with the small latticework table next to which she was seated, looked up from her book.

"What is it, Mother?" she asked, as Margot came to sit beside her.

"It's your aunt. She's had a fall."

"Which aunt?" enquired Richard, sprawled out in a deckchair, languidly resplendent in his newly acquired R.N.V.R. sub-lieutenant's uniform which he was reluctant to discard, despite the exceptionally warm spring sunshine.

He chuckled suddenly. "*Which-aunt!* Makes her sound like some kind of old hag with hairy warts, a broomstick and a black cat!"

"Neither of them is witchlike in the slightest, you silly goose, and well you know it," said Sophie, gently admonishing her brother.

"Only kidding," responded Richard good-naturedly. "In fact, they're two of the kindest, most generous-hearted old biddies one could hope to meet." He lifted his officer's cap from his eyes. "So, which aunt is it?"

"Edna."

"What's she done?"

"Broken her arm?"

"Her arm!" exclaimed Sophie, all too aware that her redoubtable, capable aunt would be in a complete state of bad-tempered frustration at this misfortune.

"Goodness!" said Richard, unconsciously echoing his sister's thoughts. "Right or left?"

"Right." Lady Margot's brow held a deep furrow. "It's a bad break, apparently. Two places. She's in plaster all the way from her wrist to her shoulder."

"That is bad news. How on earth did she do that?"

"Sawing a branch off a tree, apparently. The ladder slipped and she fell."

Richard couldn't help smiling at the picture this created of his energetic aunt who, even at the age of sixty-five, refused to have a gardener or a maid (having always maintained that servants were for people who were incapable of doing things for themselves) standing at the top a ladder waging war against a recalcitrant branch.

"She was lucky she only broke her arm," he observed. "How's Aunt Mae coping?"

"She's not, I'm afraid. It's all too much for her and that's why she's written. She says she's exhausted and that Edna's driving her to distraction as she will insist on trying to do things and then failing miserably. Mae's having to pick up the pieces as well as looking after everything else on the farm." Lady Margot sighed. "You know she isn't very strong."

"I think she puts it on half the time," remarked Sophie. "Her frailty has become a habit."

"Nevertheless, one can't afford to take that chance. She nearly died of rheumatic fever when she was a baby…"

"And it's left her with a weak heart and a weak chest," chorused Sophie and Richard together.

"Well, mock away you two, but she was very kind when you used to stay with her and Edna during the school holidays while your father and I were stuck abroad in some godforsaken embassy and couldn't get home."

Sophie and Richard exchanged a glance that held a touch of guilt.

"So, what's going to happen?" he enquired. "How does she expect the family to help?"

"She wants me to go there and look after things."

"And are you?" Sophie asked carefully.

"How can I, dear? What with my work at the Red Cross, I'm just too busy organizing everything and everybody. You'll have to go."

"Me?" Sophie looked up in consternation. "There is a war on you know."

"I'm all too aware of that, my dear, but nothing much seems to be happening, does it?"

"Really?" said Richard.

"I mean, there *are* things happening," Margot added hastily, her cheeks warm with embarrassment, seeing her son's reproachful glance, "but not here at home. Apart, that is, from my war work."

Sophie didn't react to this. Whatever was or was not taking place in the outside world, she had no desire to go anywhere and certainly not to uproot her comfortable existence and go gallivanting across the sea to St Nicolas to look after her elderly aunts, especially in wartime.

She enjoyed being at home, surrounded by home comforts. To be in one place for a long time was a luxury and she revelled in it, having spent her early formative years travelling around Europe with her parents to whatever diplomatic posting her father had been given; then, from the age of eleven, at boarding school in England and finally, to university at eighteen. She had sailed through her degree and now that her father had retired from the diplomatic service, Sophie was making the most of just being at *home*.

Of course, before the war intervened, she had had every intention of forging some kind of career for herself but because the precise nature of this had never quite revealed itself to her, she had remained content to amuse herself within a purely domestic setting.

"I'd go if I could…" and Richard brushed an imaginary speck of dust from his brand new uniform and ran his fingers round the peak of his officer's cap.

"You? Even if you weren't in the Royal Navy and could go, you'd be hopeless. Even more than me," said Sophie. "At least I can boil an egg."

"Well, I'm afraid that if you're going to be the saviour of our distressed relatives, you'll have to add other culinary skills to your meagre repertoire," he observed, "because man, or in this case, elderly aunts, cannot live by eggs alone."

Sophie pouted and turned towards her mother. "I really don't want to go."

"You have to, darling. There's no one else."

"What about sending Maisie? She'd cope far better than I would."

"She's just joined the A.T.S."

"Really? I had no idea. When did you find that out?"

"Yesterday morning."

"And Ellen?"

"The same. She told me just now, when she brought me the afternoon post." Margot shook her head in exasperation. "They must have been hatching this for a while."

"Oh Mother, how will you cope without the maids? Surely you'll need me at home to help you?" said Sophie, clutching at straws, hoping to find some reason to persuade her determined parent to allow her to remain at home.

But Margot was not to be swayed. "Cookie and I will manage somehow. Reginald is too old to be called up, thank goodness, so he'll continue to look after your father's needs. If necessary, I can shut off part of the house. I don't suppose I'll be doing much entertaining, anyway – we've hardly seen anyone since the war started, let alone since your father retired."

With her mother's words, Sophie's ordered existence suddenly became one of disruptive uncertainty and the prospect of a sea voyage in wartime filled her with absolute dread. However, she consoled herself with the thought that according to the newspapers and the wireless, everyone had been absolutely flocking to St Nicolas and the other Channel Islands for the Easter break.

"I'm afraid there is no choice, my dear. Someone has to do this and I'm sorry, but it has to be you," and this was Margot's final word on the subject.

Hiding an inner reluctance to send her daughter away, Sophie's mother stood up and went in search of afternoon tea for them all. In a few hours also, her precious son's embarkation leave would be over and he would be reporting to his new ship in Devonport. Goodness knows when she would see him again.

Resolutely, she closed her mind as to what might befall him.

Richard, observing his mother's determinedly straight back as she walked away from them, said to Sophie: "So, when you come home from ministering to our elderly relatives, which branch of the services will you join?"

"None of them. I don't want any part of this wretched war."

"That's very unpatriotic of you, Sis."

"Why? Our grandfather was German and I loved Grandpa very much. He was a dear old man who gave up his country to move to St Nicolas to be with Grandma, knowing that she'd never leave her home. It would be like fighting someone within our family and I want no part of it."

"But Hitler is not like Grandpa."

"And more's the pity. If he was, Europe wouldn't be in the pickle it is now."

"That's true. But look at it this way – Grandma was of French extraction, we are English and as we live in a democracy, thank goodness, an Allied majority in the family wins the day. So there's our justification for fighting for our country.

Sophie sighed. "Maybe."

"In any case, Grandpa wouldn't have approved of what Hitler and his henchmen are up to. He'd have hated it. If he'd still been alive and in his native land, he would have stood up for freedom and justice."

"And found himself in serious trouble."

"Exactly. So we're doing everyone a favour."

"Even if it means that innocent men and women on both sides suffer in the process?"

"We didn't start this war and let's face it, they're all in it together, aren't they?"

Sophie was appalled. "How can you say such a thing? There must be millions of ordinary people in Germany who hate what the Nazis are doing."

"Well, if there are, they're keeping pretty quiet about it. Hitler wouldn't still be in power, would he, if that were the case?" When his sister failed to agree, Richard observed: "Besides, have you forgotten that Grandpa was interned on the Isle of Man as an enemy alien in the Great War?"

"But only for a little while as the authorities soon realized he was no threat to national security. He minded being away from Grandma, though," she added sadly, "even if it was only for a short time."

Seeing her disconsolate expression, Richard smiled and patted her hand. "Cheer up, Soph. Let's not argue about it. While you're on St Nicolas, I'll bring my destroyer into Port le Bac on the way home from convoy duty and wave to you from the bridge. How about that?" Gently, he lifted her chin and touched the tip of her nose. "It'll be all right, you'll see!"

"I'm still not joining up."

Exasperated, he let go of her chin. "Well, do voluntary work with Mother then!"

"No thanks. I'd rather take my chances on the Channel Islands than be under Mother's thumb all day, every day. When she's out being a stalwart in the war effort, which is most of the time, at least I can please myself at home."

"Think about it anyway, will you? It's your duty." Tactfully, he changed the subject. "Now, where's our tea? I could do with cucumber sandwiches and cake. Supper seems an age away."

Richard unwound himself from the deckchair and as he stood up, Sophie held onto his arm.

"You will be careful won't you? While you're at sea, I mean. Promise me. No heroics."

He laughed and patted the top of her head. "I'll be fine. I'll obey orders and be a good officer." He looked at her and then said, in all seriousness, "I promise I'll be careful," before adding, with a twinkle in his eye and the appropriate salute, "Scout's honour."

"Richard Langley, you are incorrigible!"

"It's my middle name!" and he disappeared towards the house in search of Margot and their tea.

6

Her concentration ruined, Sophie laid her book aside and walked down to the lowest level of the terraced garden to where the River Thames lapped against the lawn. Reflectively, she stood for a long time staring into the sun-dappled water as it meandered gently on its course, comparing it to her present directionless existence; seeing in its liquid path, a future that stretched before her without form or substance.

Just like the phoney war itself, she supposed – a strange sort of limbo, rather like waiting in the wings before going on stage.

Suddenly, just as she had felt at the very moment war was declared, Sophie became aware of deeper, external forces leading her, as an individual, into uncharted waters from which there would be no escape and over which she would have no influence or control. The thought made her shudder and with a sigh, she turned and made her way back towards the house, climbing the steps between the terraces slowly and thoughtfully.

"Sophie! Sophie!"

The tall, rangy figure of a young man came bounding down the garden, interrupting her reverie.

Edwin. Her heart sank. She arranged her features into a polite smile as his bespectacled, tweed-jacketed figure reached her. He kissed her cheek enthusiastically.

"Your mother said I'd find you out here. She's invited me to supper. I had a letter today from the powers-that-be and I'm to be sent somewhere hush-hush. Something to do with my doctorate in maths and my chess-playing abilities, apparently. I've no idea what it is but I hear they've recruited some chaps from Oxford as well as me and several mathematical chums from Cambridge. I mustn't reveal to a living soul what I'm to be doing. I've even had to sign the Official Secrets Act!"

"Well, good for you!"

Sophie was genuinely pleased for him. Intuitively, she realized that whatever this was, it would suit him admirably, far more so than being in one of the armed forces where his intellectual abilities would be wasted and his eccentricities render him out of place.

"I could tell them about you and then we could be together for the rest of the war," he said, attempting persuasive ardour.

Sophie shook her head. "That's sweet of you, Edwin, but I hardly think that a degree in English Literature qualifies me for dealing with whatever it is you'll be doing."

"You're fluent in French and German."

"True, but what use would that be? From what you've just said, whoever *they* are, they seem to be recruiting mathematicians."

"I suppose."

He became downcast and therefore, not wishing to hurt his feelings further, Sophie took him by the hand and led him up to the house in search of the tea that had failed to materialize in the garden as planned.

Later, leaving Edwin in full flight discussing politics with her father who had returned early from his club, the St James in Piccadilly, which twice a week provided him with the opportunity to play chess or backgammon with friends and acquaintances from the diplomatic service, Sophie strolled over to the open French doors, staring out across the immaculate garden.

"Edwin is in love with you," said Richard, coming to stand beside her.

She smiled indulgently. "I know, but only in the same way that an overgrown, highly intelligent puppy is with life in general."

"If he asks, would you marry him?"

"He has asked already, countless times." Steadfastly, Sophie looked at her brother. "I always say no."

He chuckled. "Probably wise. Though it'll break his heart one day. He's felt the same way about you ever since you could both toddle."

"So have I." Sophie regarded Edwin standing across the other side of the room. "Although," she added mischievously, "come to think of it, I suppose for a D. Phil. he's quite communicative and not bad looking in a dishevelled sort of way."

"Don't be so disparaging," replied Richard, defending a fellow mathematician and pretending to take offence. "*I* communicate and I'm better looking than average."

"True, but you're exceptional." She stroked his cheek affectionately. "No, when the time comes, I shall marry for love, even if it takes years and years to find the right man. What about you?"

"What about me?"

"Have you asked Caroline yet?"

Richard was silent. Then he said carefully, "No."

"Why? You always said she was the girl for you."

"I do seem to remember saying something to that effect. But the eve of going to sea is not the right time for a chap to propose to his girlfriend."

"Have you discussed it with her?"

"Does one usually?"

"Yes, *one* does." She smiled gently. "It's called *communication*."

"Ah," he said. "That thing."

"She is in love with you."

"I know."

"And you're in love with her."

He nodded.

"So, will you think about it?"

He nodded, again. "But is it fair, I mean? Goodness knows how long I might be away and what if…?"

Quickly, Sophie covered his lips with her fingers. "Don't say it. Please. Just ask her. I'm sure she's been thinking along the same lines as you."

Richard eyed his sister astutely. "You've been talking behind my back!"

She blushed, having been found out. "Actually, she's been talking of nothing else. So do us all a favour and propose, will you? This evening, before supper, before you join your ship."

"To please my exquisitely lovely sister, I shall propose to my even lovelier Caroline and if she'll have me, I shall be the happiest man alive!"

8

Sophie, choosing to ignore the forced brightness in his voice, replied encouragingly, "Good for you and I'll be the chief bridesmaid. After all, she is my best friend. Apart from you, that is," she added quickly, catching Richard's expression. "Well, I want a bath and to change before supper, as we're to be quite a gathering for once, so I'll leave you to concoct whatever it is you plan to say. By the way, Caroline's arriving early, about six-thirty, so if you want to spruce yourself up a bit in order to make a good impression, I suggest you get a move on!"

Whereupon, after kissing Richard lightly on the cheek, Sophie went upstairs and ignoring wartime frugality, indulged herself in a long hot bath, thinking about weddings and trying very hard to keep her mind away from war and the prospect of an inevitable and prolonged stay with her two elderly, but very entertaining, aunts.

CHAPTER 2

St Nicolas

It was with some relief that Sophie arrived in Port le Bac, the main destination from the British mainland to St Nicolas, one of the larger Channel Islands.

Situated some ten miles from the Contentin Peninsula in Normandy and some ninety miles from the south coast of England, the island, in keeping with its neighbours, was staunchly British yet maintained its own system of government, remaining independent both in mind and spirit but, at the same time, fiercely loyal to the Crown.

At one time, Port le Bac had been a tiny fishing village but in the 1860s, the island had been discovered by wealthy upper and middle-class holidaymakers and incomers, both French and English, who expanded the harbour and transformed it into a fashionable and thriving Victorian tourist destination – an identity it still retained.

Having disembarked from the steamer, Sophie was immediately transported into a world that seemed blissfully unaware of the storm clouds gathering force in Europe. The harbour café was open and doing brisk business and the quayside shops thronged with souvenir-hunting visitors making the most of their last few remaining days of Easter escapism.

It took a while for Sophie to adjust to this spirit of optimism, finding in the relaxed wellbeing that surrounded her a stark contrast to the undercurrent of anxiety that pervaded life at home in England. She felt a sense of blessed relief but at the same time a strange sense of unreality.

She stood on the quayside, breathing in the familiar sea-tang of the harbour. Childhood memories came flooding back – of long, carefree summer holidays spent on St Nicolas with Richard and their beloved grandparents and aunts in the rambling, wisteria-covered farmhouse which had been in the family for generations.

She remembered how, when the weather was fine, she and her brother were provided with sandwiches and cake, wrapped in greaseproof paper and placed in a small knapsack, together with a few pennies for lemonade or an ice-cream. They were allowed to roam for the whole day wherever they wished, for Grandpa and Aunt Edna were staunch believers that all young people (they were never referred to as 'children') needed the freedom of the outdoors, enjoying themselves in the fresh air and healthy, summer sunshine.

Even Grandma and Aunt Mae had held no worries for their safety, providing Richard and Sophie stayed together and were "back in time for tea at five o'clock". Sophie supposed they must have done this, as she couldn't recall her relatives ever being anxious or upset.

Given that trust, she and Richard had felt both empowered and carefree, revelling in their independence; enjoying all-day piscatorial expeditions with kindly local fishermen; playing hide-and-seek while exploring the old silver mine workings; climbing up to the ruined Château sur la Colline, which stood proudly atop its granite plinth looking down protectively onto the harbour below.

They made friends with the local children, learning the *patois*, that strange mixture of English and French spoken by much of the population; the boys playing cricket and football on the grass while the girls sat on the swings with their dolls, sharing imaginary scenarios of future homes and husbands.

They explored the bays and inlets, paddling in rock pools, catching crabs and collecting mussels, or swimming in the sea and constructing enormous sandcastles on seaweed-strewn sands before returning home, their hair bleached white by the sun and their young bodies lithe and brown.

Sophie remembered those halcyon days as a perfect paradise and tears pricked her eyes for their passing.

Picking up her two large suitcases and handbag, she walked to the landward end of the jetty and hailed the only taxi waiting on the narrow road beside the harbour wall.

"On holiday, Miss?" asked the driver, putting her luggage into the boot.

"Sort of."

As Sophie didn't recognize him, she didn't elaborate further but when she gave the address of the farmhouse, the taxi driver exclaimed: "Ah, so you're staying with the Wiseman sisters! Miss Edna fell off her ladder a few weeks ago and I had to take her to the cottage hospital. She refused to have an ambulance, said it was 'undignified'. Quite a character, she is! Well, they both are, but Miss Mae's the quiet one. Keeps herself to herself, like. Are you a relative?"

"Yes, I'm their niece."

"So, you're Miss Sophie! They told me you was coming! They've been looking forward to it and Miss Mae's been in a right old fluster getting your room ready. I've been back and forth into town to get this and that. You've no idea! Still, I'd do anything for them if they asked me. Been here before?"

"Yes, many times. But not for some years."

Since just before going to Oxford, she thought. Had it really been that long? Four years, nearly five?

"I'm George, by the way. Came to live on the island with my family three years ago after being here on holiday. The wife fell in love with the place and so we decided to up sticks and move. She runs the little café on the sea-front and I do odd jobs for all sorts of people during the week – run errands, collect the ladies if they've been shopping in the town and look out for the tourists. There's very few cars on the island, so it keeps me busy."

He steered the taxi along the picturesque, upwards-winding road that Sophie had always loved, with its commanding view of the harbour below and the coast of France beyond.

"The island government don't encourage the use of motor transport, so there's very few private vehicles around," continued George conversationally. "We think that's by far and away the best thing. The farmers have their tractors and there are a few delivery vans and one single-decker bus covering the whole island, but that's about it. The roads are narrow and the Consell de Souverain is not prepared to have them widened. Everyone else uses bicycles or a pony and trap."

Nothing changes, thought Sophie, and she was glad; oh, so glad.

She rejoiced in the scenery as the taxi meandered slowly along familiar dusty lanes, shadowed by high hedgerows covered in a profusion of fragrant white May blossom. She wound the window down and closed her eyes, absorbing the delicious sweetness of the scented air.

Once more, Sophie became part of the island's timelessness, part of the unhurried pace of an unchanging existence governed by the seasons and the weather.

She felt comforted knowing that market days would still happen at their set times; that cows would be milked each day, ambling from pasture to cowshed and back again, following well-trod cloven paths; that sheep would still graze contentedly on the lush, green hillsides, lambed or sheared according to the time of year. Sun-ripened crops would be harvested from fertile fields and thanks for their bounty given in the impressive Norman church in Port le Bac or the little Nonconformist Chapel on the western side of the island.

The inhabitants were an eclectic mix of incomers and families of ancient lineage: wealthy landowners and tenant farmers, middle-class professionals and tradesmen as well as those who were fortunate enough to live independently on a modest private income. She knew that there was no public envy of someone else's wealth or status here, only acceptance and respect – an unchanging adherence to time-honoured tradition – and she loved it for its predictability.

Disputes and grievances that could not be settled privately were brought informally before a special subcommittee of the governing Consell de Souverain that sought to be fair and even-handed in these matters. Generally, this was successful and court cases were rare as crime was not prevalent on the island.

The friendly half dozen or so policemen had little to do other than break up a few drunken brawls on Friday and Saturday nights or solve the occasional unexplained disappearance of farm animals. These usually turned out to be innocent and resulted in the offending cow or sheep looking up at the policeman's lamp with ruminant, wide-eyed consternation from the hollow or underground cavern where it had accidentally strayed in search of greener pasture.

There was the odd rash of petty theft but generally speaking, Sophie knew the islanders to be honest and hardworking with a characteristic predilection for indulging in gossip or having a good moan about everything in general and nothing in particular – an outlet that provided those who indulged in its peculiarities with as much entertainment as watching a play or a film at the little theatre-cum-cinema in Port le Bac.

As the taxi drew up outside the farmhouse, slightly more ramshackle than Sophie remembered and the journey much shorter than she recalled, Aunt Edna, the entire length of her arm encased in a plaster cast, came striding out to greet her.

"Darling girl! It's good to see you! I'm so sorry to have dragged you all the way here but thank you for coming to our rescue. Mae has been in such a state of anxiety and relief that I haven't quite known what to do with her." She put her unencumbered arm round Sophie's shoulder. "George, please would you bring Miss Sophie's luggage inside the house and put it at the bottom of the stairs."

"Yes, ma'am."

Edna lifted up her purse which had been placed on the hall table in readiness and, with some awkwardness, extracted the necessary coinage.

When Sophie protested, saying she should pay, her aunt replied, "No, no, my dear. You're here at our behest and the least I can do is pay your taxi fare. You'll earn your keep for the next couple of months or so until I'm out of this wretched plaster, so worry not."

She turned to George and gave him the money.

"Thank you, ma'am," he said, touching his hat. "It was nice meeting you, Miss Sophie. I expect we'll see each other again."

"I'm sure we shall," she replied, with a warmth that concealed her inner anxiety as to exactly what she would be doing to 'earn her keep', as her aunt had so eloquently phrased it. She had thought she was only here to help.

She removed her hat, gloves and jacket and after hanging them on the coat stand in the hall, followed Edna into the sitting room which owed its character and décor to the Victorian era. It was like stepping back in time and from early childhood, Sophie had been fascinated by its myriad *objets d'art* and unusual furniture, its *bric-à-brac* and mysterious boxes containing intriguing relics from the past.

She and Richard had spent many a rainy afternoon happily ensconced within its cluttered and absorbing minutiae, while Grandpa sat comfortably in his chair, puffing away on his pipe and contentedly listening to his wife while she satisfied the children's insatiable curiosity by recounting stories about each and every item. They were allowed to touch anything they liked, as long as they were careful and put everything back in its proper place.

They always did as they were told – for Grandpa's word, for all his affability, was law.

On rainy days and during long winter evenings, she and Richard were taught French and German by their grandparents. However, it was Sophie who had absorbed both languages into the fabric of her being, loving them equally. Living abroad in France and Germany because of her father's work had enabled her to hone and perfect her skills until she could speak, read and write both languages with fluency and ease.

"Do sit down, my dear, and I'll fetch your Aunt Mae," said Edna, who had been quietly observing her niece for some moments. "She's been having a little rest on her bed. Then we'll have a cup of tea."

Once her aunt had left the room taking her considerable, but not insensitive, presence with her, Sophie took stock of her surroundings. The fittings and furnishings appeared more faded than she remembered but the cherished baby grand piano, covered with a cloth upon which were numerous framed family photographs, still sat snugly in the net-curtained bay window.

She crossed the room to study the images more closely: family groups at picnics and weddings; her mother and sisters when they were younger; herself and Richard in various stages of childhood and adolescence and finally, Grandma and Grandpa – she pretty and petite, he tall and broad-shouldered, one arm around the wife he adored and who adored him in return.

She smiled, experiencing in memory the forgotten happiness of uncomplicated childhood.

"Sophie, Sophie! How lovely that you're here! Edna and I have been *so* looking forward to seeing you again. It's been such a long time!"

Mae held out her arms and Sophie was obliged to stoop for her welcoming hug and kiss. Was this merely the illusion of passing years or was her aunt really smaller and more frail?

"It's good to see you, Aunt Mae. I gather you've been having a bit of a rough time."

Mae threw her older sister a meaningful look. "Your Aunt Edna is a headstrong woman, who never listens to advice. I told her not to climb that ladder but to get someone from Port le Bac to cut the branch. But of course, she didn't listen – she would insist on doing it for herself. And then look what happened. She could have been killed!"

Edna took this reprimand in good spirit. "I know, and I remain suitably chastised. You are quite right, of course, my dear, but that wretched branch was a nuisance and half hanging off anyway. It could have fallen on someone's head at any moment and then where would we have been? Up before the Consell de Souverain on a charge of manslaughter!"

"Anyway, I know you won't do anything like that again."

"You're quite right, my dear sister, I shan't. I shall tie the ladder in place next time!"

Sophie laughed at this characteristic exchange and presently went to make the tea with Edna (supervising) before bringing the tray, with its tiered cake stand, teapot and delicate bone china cups, into the sitting room.

"I'm longing to hear all your news," began Mae, stirring her tea. "Your mother writes, but it's usually to do with her Red Cross work. Margot seems to be fully occupied organizing everyone and everything."

"Oh, she is and totally in her element," replied Sophie equably.

"Our little sister always was a bossy-boots."

"Edna! How can you say such a thing?"

"Quite easily."

"Please tell us about your dear father as she rarely mentions him," asked Mae, frowning at Edna. "What's he up to these days?"

Sophie smiled. "Enjoying his retirement. Feels he can say exactly what he means to people without having to worry about whether or not it will cause a diplomatic incident."

"That must be a relief for him," observed Edna dryly. "What else does he do?"

"He spends a great deal of time at his club in London and when he's at home, he exercises the horses. He says he wants to take up polo again but Mother won't let him, says he's far too old. So every time she becomes unbearably bossy, he goes to the tack room, finds his polo stick, sits down in his arm chair and starts polishing it with a duster, muttering about joining in with some all-comer's game to be held at Windsor Great Park. She goes very quiet after that."

Edna laughed. "They've always been the same ever since they've known each other."

"And they enjoy every moment of it," responded Sophie.

"It must be nice for them to be in one place after all their travels. I know I'd appreciate it."

"We all do, Aunt Mae. Father has also joined the Local Defence Volunteers and says that if the Nazis ever invaded, he'd be so rude to them, they wouldn't want to stay."

"Do you believe him?"

"No. I think he'd find it difficult to discard the diplomatic habit of a lifetime!"

"And you are absolutely right, my dear," declared Edna. "However, *I* wouldn't stand any nonsense from that wretched little Austrian upstart and his cronies if they ever came here."

"The merest thought of invasion fills me with abject horror," observed her sister tremulously. "It would be unbearable."

"Let's hope it won't come to that," replied Edna with habitual reassurance.

Taking a deep breath, Mae changed tack. She had no wish to burden her niece unnecessarily with her own private fears. She turned to Sophie again.

"Please tell us all about you and your dear brother. Such a lovely boy."

"There's not much to say about me. I've really enjoyed being at home this past year since leaving Oxford, just reading and generally being able to please myself. I go out riding with Father every day and I've also become quite involved with the local amateur dramatic society. That's been something of a revelation, I must say, as I used to do a lot of drama at Somerville and never thought to find another society that matched up to it."

"Good for you," said Edna, regarding her niece astutely. "But you haven't yet found anything that you'd like to do as regards a career…?"

"Or met some nice young man to settle down with?" added Mae hopefully.

Sophie shook her head apologetically to both enquiries.

"I expect you miss Richard now that he's in the Royal Navy," observed Mae, knowing how close her nephew and niece were.

Sophie sighed. "I do, very much, but at least he was home recently on embarkation leave, so we were able to spend some time together. You do know that he's completed his officer training at H.M.S. *King Alfred* in Hove?"

"So he told us in his last letter. He's a dear boy and we're so very, very proud of him now that he's a sub-lieutenant. But Edna and I do worry about him going off to sea." She hesitated for a moment. "Not that this is important, but how does he look in his new uniform? He's always been such a good-looking boy."

Sophie smiled. "He still is, Aunt Mae. And he looks very smart. It really suits him."

"Does he know what his posting is to be yet?" asked Edna.

"He's been appointed as navigating officer aboard a destroyer and is the envy of all his class mates because R.N.V.R. men usually get corvettes or minesweepers. Richard didn't say much about why he was chosen above the others but, reading between the lines, I think it's because his maths skills are so good. I know he came out top in every exam they had at *King Alfred* and won a special commendation at the end of the course on navigation."

"He always was a clever boy," said Edna, "although I have to say that he wasted his time at university. He was lucky to pass his degree. Perhaps he's acquired some sense at last."

"Anyway," said Mae hastily, not wishing to countenance any criticism of her nephew, even if there was an element of truth in it, "I can't quite believe that he's a serving officer now. But even so, the war still seems distant and unreal, doesn't it?" she observed, trying hard to keep all her illusions intact.

"I only wish it was," replied her sister, the tight line of her lips reflecting a personal deep-seated anxiety that prevented her, on this occasion, from offering any reassurance.

Edna's apprehension was well-founded and any remaining delusions were swept away sooner than anyone could have anticipated when, at breakfast the next morning, in common with most of the population of the Channel Islands and Great Britain, they listened to a news bulletin which, delivered in the solemn and matter-of-fact tones of the BBC announcer, shocked everyone out of their phoney-war complacency.

'The German Army invaded Holland and Belgium early this morning by land and by landings from paratroops. The armies of the Low Countries are resisting. An appeal for help has been made to the Allied Governments and Brussels says that Allied troops are moving to their support.'

The three women looked at each other in consternation. Holland and Belgium were not that far away. France was even nearer and all at once, seemed very vulnerable.

"Perhaps the Allies will be able to stem the tide of invasion like they did in the Great War. Perhaps this time, the Germans will be stopped in their tracks before they even reach France," suggested Mae.

"Perhaps. We can only hope that will be the case. But whatever happens, we are now truly at war and must prepare ourselves for the worst," replied Edna. "And Sophie, my dear, you must go home immediately."

"But I've only just come," protested Sophie. "Besides which, you really do need my help."

Mae looked at her sister. "We do."

Edna pursed her lips. "Unfortunately. Damn this wretched plaster cast."

"Anyway, it seems cowardly to run for home when there's no immediate danger," added Sophie. "What if I stayed for as long as it's safe for me to do so?"

Edna sighed. "All right," she agreed, reluctantly. "But at the first sign of trouble, you must take the next available boat back to England."

"Yes, Aunt Edna."

Mae laid her hand on Sophie's arm in relief and gratitude. "Thank you, my dear," she said.

Edna stood up. "Well," she said brusquely, "we have to get on with our lives despite what is happening on the continent. Invasion or no invasion, the animals still need our attention and care. So, come, my dear. It's time for me to show you round the farmyard and to acquaint you with just a few of the things you'll be needed for. The rest I shall reveal over the coming days."

Purposefully, Edna strode out of the kitchen with Sophie, stumbling over her chair after standing up too quickly, following in her wake.

CHAPTER 3

River Dyle, Belgium
1st Battalion, Royal Welch Fusiliers, 'C' Company

"Lieutenant Anderson!"

"Yes, sir?"

"We have to get the artillery to support our position and I can't get in contact with anyone because the field telephone's as dead as a dodo."

"Yes, sir."

Robert Anderson shared his commanding officer's frustration. As a forward company, they had been subjected to constant shelling and heavy mortar fire from the enemy but holding firm, had repulsed successive German attacks along their section of the river.

He knew they would need reinforcements soon or alternatively, be replaced by the reserves thus allowing his unit to regroup and rearm. In their present situation, with the whole battalion running low on ammunition and suffering repeated casualties, to stay where they were in such an exposed position without further *matériel* support would amount to nothing short of suicide.

The sheer speed and ferocity of the German advance through Holland and into Belgium had caught everyone by surprise and Robert wondered about the quality of the intelligence reports that should surely have forewarned the Allies that the enemy were about to make their move.

Tactically, he knew that it would have made more sense to remain in their well-thought out defensive positions, painstakingly constructed during the long winter months along the Franco-Belgian border, rather than rushing into conflict in a new location without adequate preparations or guaranteed lines of supply.

However, the highly-trained, battle-ready British Expeditionary Force was under the orders of the French generals who had decided that the Allies should meet the invaders head on in Belgium in response to the request from the government of that beleaguered country.

"*'Now is the winter of our discontent,'*" muttered Robert, squatting down beside his commanding officer in the shelter of a hedge covered in snowy white blossom. After a moment of thought, he added his own words: "*But in May, among this profusion of fragrant spring beauty forever tainted by the stench of warfare.*"

"What's that?" said Captain Lewis, anxious to proceed.

"Nothing, sir." *Only a potential poem I might never find time to write*, he thought. Sighing, Robert bent over and studied the map.

"The last known position of our heavy guns was here," and Captain Lewis pointed to a small wooded area on top of a nearby hillock.

"They've been silent for a while, sir."

"I know." Lewis took a deep breath. "Anyway, we need to find out what's happened to them. Tell Divisional H.Q. that the battalion could do with a bit of artillery support. While you're at it, mention that we're running low on ammo, the telegraph's out and although we're holding the line, if we have any further losses,

18

our current situation will soon be untenable. We must get the men out safely before it's too late. Then report back here. I'm sending you rather than a note with one of our despatch riders as I want someone who can persuade the powers-that-be of our need to withdraw and regroup." Captain Lewis knew that this young officer was resourceful and if anyone could succeed, he would be the one.

"Yes, sir. I understand."

"Good man. Better take the map with you and whatever else you think might be appropriate. Be as quick as you can, there's a good chap." He cleared his throat. "Well, good luck, Lieutenant Anderson."

"Thank you, sir."

Tucking the map into the inside pocket of his tunic and keeping low, Robert zigzagged his way to the rear of 'C' Company's position where, having located a motorbike, the mode of transport he deemed most suitable for the job in hand, he filled up the tank with petrol from the stores and after fastening his helmet, kick-started the engine.

As he roared away, Robert glanced back at his unit with the thought that even if he did succeed, there was a distinct possibility he might never see them again.

He attained the main road with some difficulty: his progress hampered by a steady stream of refugees and his own need to seek shelter from a bout of shelling that kept him pinned down by the roadside in a foul-smelling drainage ditch. But, even as he lay prone and partially protected, his mind reeling from the onslaught, he felt shame that he was hiding while refugees continuously toiled past him in weary procession. They paid no heed to the clamour surrounding them, their senses dulled to all danger, their shuffling gait full of exhaustion and resignation.

He watched helplessly as an old man with vacant, sunken eyes plodded by, gripping the hand of a frightened little girl clasping a bedraggled doll to her chest. An elderly woman, struggling with the weight of two enormous suitcases, shuffled along beside a young woman pushing a bicycle with a huge bundle of clothing balanced on the handlebars. A few paces behind came a weary and dispirited man pulling a small handcart filled with his meagre possessions.

For the second time in twenty-six years they and thousands like them had become nomads, outcasts in their own land; forced to flee before an invading army.

Inwardly, Robert railed against man's inhumanity towards his fellow man and his all-consuming lust for power but what upset him the most was his own impotence in being unable, at that moment, to offer help and relief in the face of their suffering.

After a while, there came a lull in the barrage. Cautiously, Robert left the shelter of the culvert and remounted and restarted his bike. Carefully, he threaded his way through the remaining, disconsolate stragglers and when at last he reached his destination, he could see that divisional H.Q. was in the process of packing up.

"We're off, I'm afraid," said the major, to whom Robert had been directed upon arrival.

"Where to, sir?"

"Lord knows. Well, officially, it looks like being somewhere near Brussels. But things are changing so quickly, it's difficult to know exactly where we're going to be. The German advance is a bit like a long snake with its head moving across the Low Countries and its tail into France."

"What about intelligence, sir?"

"None that's any use. And when there is some, it's out of date by the time it reaches us."

"We should have stayed where we were."

"I quite agree with you, Lieutenant…?"

"Anderson, sir."

"Who did you say you were with?"

"'C' Company, 1st Battalion Royal Welch Fusiliers, sir."

"Where did you say you were?"

"Near Ottenburg, on the River Dyle. We're keeping the Germans at bay, but…"

"Ah yes, you said. No radio, no ammo…" The major became apologetic. "I'm afraid the supporting artillery has already been pulled back. The whole B.E.F. has orders to withdraw, Lieutenant Anderson. Starting tonight."

"Tonight!" Robert took a deep breath. "Where to, sir?"

"Let me see. You're part of 6th Brigade, aren't you?"

"Yes, sir."

The major extracted a sheet of paper from a folder in his briefcase. "It's a three-stage withdrawal for everyone – the ultimate goal being the River Escaut where a new defensive line is to be established. I'll show you on your map if you've got one. For some reason they're like gold dust."

Robert duly produced the required item and the major marked the Royal Welch Fusiliers' consecutive destinations. "And if you head for here…" he placed another cross on the map "…there should be some trucks to take you the rest of the way. You can pick up some ammo at the same time. They've had orders to resupply." He regarded the map reflectively. "Your route will take you through the battlefield of Waterloo. Now there's a name to conjure with," and he laughed, harshly, at the irony of a modern British withdrawal through the site of a historic British victory.

"Belgium and France are full of names to conjure with, sir."

"Indeed they are. Mons, Ypres, Passchendaele, the Somme. The list is endless. Who'd have thought it, eh? That we'd be back in Flanders after this short time?" He folded up the map and returned it to Robert. "Well, that's all the info I can give you for the moment. The B.E.F. have held their line magnificently but the wretched Hun are giving the French on our right flank and the Belgians on our left the run-around. They've actually broken through at Sedan in the south and the Dutch army is on the point of collapse in the north. If we're not careful, we'll be caught in the middle with our pants down, hence the need to withdraw. Damn and blast their *Blitzkrieg* tactics. Damn and blast the Belgians for hanging onto their neutrality and not letting us in to help them *before* the enemy invaded. But most of all, damn and blast the French generals for bringing us into Belgium now. We've fallen right into the trap the Germans set for us."

Suddenly realizing he'd said enough in front of this young officer, the major stopped abruptly and cleared his throat, making a pretence of shuffling his papers.

"I understand, sir," replied Robert diplomatically.

"If you wait a moment or two, I'll get your orders typed up."

20

"Is that necessary, sir? I'd like to get back on the road. Things are pretty hot where I've just come from and I don't want to leave my comrades in the lurch."

"Quite right, quite right." The major, harassed and anxious, scribbled a note on a piece of headed paper and handed it to Robert. "Here, this'll have to do. Then there can be no official comeback when you make your withdrawal."

"Thank you, sir."

"Look, I've got an urgent message from my C.O. to his opposite number near Louvain. Be a good chap and deliver it first, will you? They're having a bit of a rough time up there. All our despatch riders are out because the shelling's playing havoc with communications along the entire sector – not just in your neck of the woods. We're trying to reach everyone with the new orders before nightfall." He opened his briefcase again and extracted another sheet of paper, putting it into an envelope. "It's not too far out of your way."

Only the opposite direction, thought Robert. "Of course, sir," he said.

Frustrated and annoyed, he topped up the petrol tank from the stores and set off again. Once more, he had to run the gauntlet of mortar and shell-fire; once more, his progress was hampered by slow-moving groups of refugees.

When at last he did arrive, Robert was surprised to find Louvain a ghostly, shattered town. Unbidden to his mind came the phrase: *Where desolation stalks the empty streets and drags the weary soul within its wake.*

Another line for a potential poem, he thought resignedly; another line that was bound to disappear from his mind before he had the chance to write it down.

How often had this happened to him? How often had ideas come to him since being in France and Belgium when circumstances had not allowed him to record the creative impulse? And how often, when he was at last in a position to do so, had he been unable to capture the original fleeting thought or line intact?

Too many times.

With a sigh, Robert picked his way cautiously through the broken glass and masonry that littered the pavements and gutters, avoiding the upturned cars strewn across the street like gruesome metallic monsters. However, when overhead tramway cables, wrenched from their poles by bomb and shell explosions, drooped their lethal tentacles across his path, he was forced to stop.

His feet on the ground and balancing the bike between his legs, Robert switched off the engine and removed his helmet, deciding upon his next course of action.

Trench mortar explosions and furious bursts of machine-gun fire were coming from the north of the town and after consulting his map, Robert estimated the distance to the front was about a quarter of a mile in the direction of the railway station, an area he imagined as being difficult to defend with its multifarious goods yards, sidings, signal boxes and subway system.

However, as there was no sign of any British troops in the town, he assumed they were all fully engaged defending their portion of the front line and, it would seem, holding it too, as there were no Germans around either.

Unexpectedly, given the condition of his immediate environment, Robert experienced a momentary surge of pride in the B.E.F.'s achievement so far in Belgium. It was an army operating under extreme difficulties but doing so with courage and determination. Instinctively, he knew therefore, that the men involved in the fighting would not react favourably to the order to withdraw. The stoical, dependable British Tommy would only be aware of what he and his fellows were achieving – successfully following orders and holding the line, keeping the enemy at bay. And that was what mattered the most.

However, as an intelligent, regular army officer, given all that he had learned of the current military situation, Robert realized that an organized withdrawal was now the only sensible option.

With these thoughts in mind, he found a way to carefully circumvent the cables and resume his journey but after a few hundred yards, was obliged to stop again in order to remove a hastily erected barricade of brand new wardrobes dragged outside from a nearby furniture shop: their wooden doors swinging to and fro in the wind; their cracked mirrors reflecting distorted images of shell-shocked buildings.

What desperation, he mused, must have prompted the construction of a barrier as ineffective as if it were in a child's playground? Still, at least it was something. *Better to do something than nothing*, he thought.

Having cleared a path, he went to kick-start the motorbike's engine but just as he was about to lift his foot, he found himself unable to move – his eye drawn towards discarded bottles in the gutter and newspapers blowing along the pavement; his senses heightened by an eerie silence.

A crawling sensation up the back of his neck and a distant roar alerted him to danger. Instinctively, he cast around for somewhere to hide.

From out of nowhere, a squadron of *Stukas* appeared, their banshee wailing filling the skies with confusion and dread as they dived. Above the roar of the engines, came the whistling of the first bombs – the air rent suddenly by noise, flying debris and the acrid smell of smoke.

Robert threw himself into the nearest house. The entrance was open to the street; the door, wrenched off its hinges by a previous bombardment, lying carelessly in the hallway.

He glanced at his precious motorbike, marooned and vulnerable in the road and, at considerable risk to himself, ran outside and dragged it into the house, thrusting it under the stairs against the grubby, patterned paper that lined the wall, and heaving the discarded door protectively in front of it.

Nearby steps led down to a cellar into which he quickly descended and there, in the shadowy light cast by a single flickering candle, cowering behind racks of wine and sacks of potatoes, Robert discovered three terrified children huddled together.

They screamed when they saw him.

"Ne tirez pas ! Ne tirez pas !" called out a young voice. *"Don't shoot! Don't shoot!"*

"Je ne vais pas tirer sur vous. Je suis un soldat britannique."

"Ah, Monsieur, Monsieur !" exclaimed the boy, who was no more than eleven years old, his voice full of relief. *"Vous parlez français, Monsieur !"*

"Oui."

"Yet you are an English soldier, Monsieur?"

"I was born next door to England, in Wales."

"But you are still British?"

"Mais oui, and proud of it."

"*We are proud to be Belgian and proud that the British came to our aid,*" said the boy. "*We are glad you are not a German soldier.*" Then very quietly, with a note of pleading in his young voice, he added, "*The three of us, we are alone. Our parents, they are both dead. You will help us, please, Monsieur? There is no one else.*"

How could he refuse?

"*If I can,*" replied Robert, "*but first we must wait until the air raid has stopped. You must all be very brave.*"

"*We shall stay here, Monsieur, with you. We shall try to be brave.*"

"*I feel safe now,*" said the youngest child, who had crept away from the others, coming to sit next to Robert, holding onto his arm with her small hands and looking up at him with absolute trust. "*I think you are a good man, Monsieur. I know you will help us. What is your name?*"

"*Robert.*"

With a gesture of unexpected politeness, given their situation, she offered her hand, which he shook matter-of-factly.

"*I am Aimée, this is Hélène and my brother is called Claude.*"

Solemnly, they greeted Robert in a similarly polite fashion.

Above them, the screaming bombs rained onto the town, shaking the house with the reverberations from each tumultuous detonation.

Hélène and Claude moved closer to Robert until all three children were holding onto him tightly. Protectively, he put his arms around them, calming their agitation as best he could and in the process, trying to keep his own fear at bay.

After what seemed like an eternity, the bombing ceased. For a few moments, there was silence.

"*Has it finished now, Monsieur?*" asked Aimée in a very small voice, her little body still trembling with fear.

Robert shook his head. He knew there was more to come; knew exactly what they were in for. The pattern was familiar to him now and even as he was about to speak, the shelling started just as he had anticipated: strident, relentless.

Even if they survived this onslaught, Robert had absolutely no idea what he was going to do with three children in a deserted town with the enemy virtually on the doorstep and his own battalion waiting for him to deliver the order to withdraw.

There was a whining through the air and an ear-splitting explosion several yards away. Then another and another, each one closer than the last. Instinctively, Robert held the children to him, shielding them with his body.

He knew nothing of the line of houses that collapsed further along the street. He knew nothing of the shell that exploded directly outside the house and reduced his motorbike to a tangle of blasted metal.

All that Robert knew before sinking into unconsciousness, were the screams of the children in his care and being covered in a choking white dust as the ceiling caved in.

CHAPTER 4

St Nicolas

"Rise and shine, girl! It's five o'clock! There's work to be done!"

There was a sharp rapping on her bedroom door and Sophie turned over with a groan and buried her head under the pillow, trying to blot out Aunt Edna's penetrating voice.

"Sophie, dear, time to get up. The animals won't wait."

This was to be her first day of milking the cows; her first day of being up at some ridiculous hour. During the previous week, Sophie had served her apprenticeship under Edna's strict but good-natured tutelage by doing general chores around the farmyard and inside the house but today, she was taking on her full workload.

There had been no opportunity to protest at some of the more odious tasks she had been asked to do, such as cleaning out the pigsties or raking soiled straw out of the stables before transporting it by wheelbarrow to the manure heap ready for distribution to the greenhouses or the fields. Any ladylike reluctance or dilettante pretensions on her part received short shrift from her aunt who brooked no nonsense when it came to the farm or the animals' welfare. When Sophie actually did manage a murmur of dissension, it was merely pointed out to her politely but firmly that these things had to be done and that she was the one to do them.

She didn't mind in the least collecting eggs or feeding the hens or exercising the two elderly horses but Sophie failed to understand why her aunts didn't employ someone from Port le Bac to do the more physically demanding tasks around the farmyard. They must be able to afford it, surely? She wondered if it was because Aunt Edna actually enjoyed doing this sort of work and preferred to do things for herself. Probably, knowing her aunt. She supposed it kept her fit and active.

With great reluctance and feeling slightly rebellious after being disturbed so early, Sophie left the warm comfort of her bed and splashed cold water onto her face from the ewer on the washstand. She dressed quickly so as not to keep her aunt waiting, putting on trousers, shirt and jumper, and went downstairs to join Edna in the hallway.

"Good, you're all ready. Are your hands clean?"

Sophie showed her aunt both sides of her hands.

"I approve. You're dressed sensibly, too. Now, come with me, girl."

"Yes, Aunt."

Sophie followed Edna to the barn where three light brown Jersey cows, loosely tethered in their stalls, regarded them with soulful eyes and very full udders.

"Have you ever milked a cow before?"

"You showed me once, a long time ago. I wasn't very successful at it."

"Hm. I seem to recall the occasion." Edna regarded her niece, her lips pursed in contemplation. "Well, you're older now and needs must…" She put a three-legged, wooden milking stool next to the first cow. "As you can see, she's full of milk and ready and waiting for us. This is Bluebell. She's as gentle and mild-mannered as they come so we'll start with her. Now, sit on the stool there, put your shoulder against her flank and place your hand on her udder, like so. That'll relax her and let the milk down. If you do that, it'll be more comfortable for her and easier for you. I washed her down earlier, so she's nice and clean."

Sophie did as she was asked and wondered what time her aunt had got up that morning.

"Next, you need to place your thumb and first finger like this…" and Edna demonstrated with her free hand. "You can't yank at the udders like they do in these American films, otherwise you'll never get anywhere and will only stretch the teat and make the poor old cow very uncomfortable. Place your thumb and finger like so, just where the teat joins onto the udder. That stops the milk going back up inside. Then wrap your other fingers round the teat and just squeeze."

Sophie did as she was instructed and a tiny amount of milk spurted into the pail.

"That's right. Good. It's the first milking of the day so not much will come out to start with."

"There are more?" Once was surely enough.

"Oh yes. Twice a day the cows need to be milked. Once in the morning and once in the evening. So, carry on, my dear. It takes about half an hour to milk a cow."

"Half an hour?"

Sophie looked at all three cows munching contentedly on their hay, thinking of the three hours daily it would take her to complete this task.

"Now, don't you fret. I'll milk Buttercup as she's very particular. I can manage with one hand, though it will take longer. You will have done the other two by the time I've finished."

Sophie had to be grateful for this small mercy. However, soon she had established a rhythm and admitted that there was something very satisfying about the whole process as the milk swished into the pail.

After they had finished, they took the creamy, frothy liquid into the dairy where Sophie was instructed to decant most of it into a churn ready for collection by the milkman, keeping back as much as they would need for their own use during the day along with some more to turn into cheese and butter later.

"I'll show you how to make butter tomorrow, dear," said Mae, after Sophie had taken their milk into the kitchen. "That's my domain. Papa always said that I made the best butter and cheese that he had ever tasted." She ladled the milk into a jug and turned to Sophie. "Next, we need some eggs for breakfast and I intend to bake a cake for tea today, so perhaps you'll be kind enough to go and collect those."

Sophie liked doing this. The hens were becoming used to her and she was becoming accustomed to their roosting places. She had also come to enjoy the wonderful breakfast that Aunt Mae prepared for them every morning after she and Edna arrived in the kitchen hungry and thirsty, gasping for a cup of hot, sweet tea after completing the first part of the day's labours.

"Has the postman been yet?" asked Sophie, who had not so far received any letters from Richard, Edwin or her mother.

"No, dear," replied Mae. "It's too early in the morning for him to deliver to us here. Port le Bac takes first priority, while we and the other outlying farms have to wait our turn."

"Oh." Disappointed, Sophie sat down at the table.

"Never mind," said Edna. "Have you written to the family?"

"I have, actually. And that's quite something as I hate writing letters. It's such a chore. Well, it's not really so much a chore," she amended hastily, "but as I tend to write a whole essay once I get going, I rather put it off."

"But you're so wonderful at English, dearest, and your letters are always lovely. Edna and I always looked forward to receiving them, didn't we?"

Edna merely nodded and continued to eat her toast.

Feeling guilty, Sophie said, "I'm sorry I haven't written much recently. When I was at Somerville, I had to take lecture notes and do so many essays and dissertations that I was all written out by the end of each day."

"Perhaps you should have studied German while you were at Oxford, then you would have had fewer essays," observed Edna dryly.

"Possibly, but I loved my English course, and studying literature, poetry and plays in great detail was an opportunity I couldn't resist. I do keep up with my French and German, though," she added, wishing to placate her aunt.

"I'm very glad to hear it. We have kept all of Mama's and Papa's books, so that will help you while you're here with us. They're in the library upstairs and you're welcome to read them any time you like. Papa was a great reader of both fiction and nonfiction, while Mama only favoured novels. She had some fairly racy ones too." Edna felt obliged to raise a disapproving eyebrow, yet there was a distinct twinkle in her eyes and she couldn't resist an impish grin. "Mae insisted we hid those away in the attic once you could read French fluently."

Sophie smiled, thinking it best not to reveal that when she was about twelve, her curiosity fuelled by the sudden disappearance of many of the French books from downstairs, she had inadvertently discovered them in the attic and surreptitiously borrowed them, taking her chosen novel down to the little beach near the farmhouse or reading it by torchlight under the bed clothes at night.

"I don't suppose you'd consider getting them out of storage for me now, would you?" she asked sweetly.

Mae looked horrified. "Absolutely not, my dear. Whatever would your mother say?"

"She'd probably say that she wished she could read them as well. Mother is no prude and we were brought up to appreciate a wide range of styles. Besides which, I am over twenty-one."

Edna chuckled. "All the same, they ought to stay packed away in their *box* in the *attic*..." She regarded her niece meaningfully.

"Ah," replied Sophie, blushing slightly. "Er, thank you, I might go up there and explore..." and she had to laugh at Mae's shocked expression.

"Sophie! How could you do such a thing?"

"Quite easily," responded Edna, "especially as she's probably been up there and read most of them already."

"When did you do that?" exclaimed Mae aghast, watching a deep red flush creep into Sophie's cheeks.

"Years ago," replied Edna, amused by her niece's discomfiture.

"I didn't think anyone knew."

26

"You were very discreet. But the attic has creaky floorboards…" and Edna smiled. "Besides, I thought it a good idea. They are beautifully written – Mama was very particular – and it was as good a way as any of learning, shall we say, about the intimacies of life."

"Edna!" Mae was shocked.

"They're very good actually, Aunt Mae," observed Sophie, having recovered from the embarrassment of being found out.

"They are," agreed Edna smiling fondly at both her younger sibling and niece, "but Mae is an innocent where it comes to literature."

"Not completely," muttered her sister, also blushing furiously.

Sophie laughed. "You don't mean to say that *you've* been upstairs and read them as well? Oh, Aunt Mae, how could you?" she teased, good-naturedly imitating the tone of her aunt's earlier words.

Embarrassed, Mae didn't know where to look. "Well…"

"In fact, she spends many a rainy afternoon up there in the loft, sitting in the old armchair."

"Edna, how could you possibly know that?" said Mae, suddenly ashamed of her secret pleasure.

"Ah, well, my dear, as I said just now, the floorboards are very creaky and you are always gone for hours."

"It won't happen again," said Mae in a small voice.

"Why not?" replied Edna. "I think it's good for you."

"You do?" Mae was surprised. She had always imagined that Edna would disapprove.

"Yes. It'll broaden your horizons."

"Broaden my horizons? At my age indeed!" Mae made a face at Sophie.

"Why not? You've led a very sheltered life."

"But that's been my choice and I don't feel I've missed out on a thing," declared Mae. "Besides, I had Charles."

The two sisters looked at each other.

"Indeed you did," said Edna.

"But not for long," replied her sister sadly.

"No."

"At least you had more time with Ralph."

"Yes." Edna sighed. "Our two Fusiliers," she mused, lost in a rare moment of nostalgia.

"I often think of Charles," said Mae quietly.

"I know you do. But I don't give Ralph a thought these days," responded Edna with only a modicum of truth. However, before Sophie could ask the questions her aunt knew would inevitably follow on from this exchange, Edna stood up abruptly. "Now, dear girl, we must take the cows up to the pasture and then speak to Jean le Rouge about our cereal crop."

"Jean le Rouge?"

"Yes. We call him our estate manager."

"You have an estate manager?" Sophie was surprised. How large was the farm? She had never asked or indeed, been told.

"He's getting a bit doddery now and so's Fred, his right-hand man, but you'll not find anyone who knows the job better than either of them. There's also a couple of lads that come in from Port le Bac each day as well." Edna regarded her niece with a smile. "We have over a hundred acres, my dear, which is a sizeable plot and quite a responsibility. We grow mainly barley, oats, potatoes and tomatoes as well as rearing our own cows, pigs and hens. Once local needs have been catered for, we export most of our produce. Our tomatoes are regarded as being the best anywhere in the Channel Islands. Therefore, my dear, today you and I shall take the horse and trap and I'll show you over the whole kit and caboodle."

"As we're one of the largest farms on the island," added Mae, "it means you'll be out for the rest of the day. So I'll prepare a picnic lunch for you both and we can have supper this evening. Then we can listen to the news together on the wireless."

"In the meantime, you can put your feet up. The rest will do you good." Edna thought her sister looked particularly pale that morning.

"That would be lovely. I do feel a little tired today and I can always make my cake tomorrow."

"You could read some more racy French novels in the attic while we're out…" Sophie grinned at her aunt.

"Sophie! How could you say such a thing?"

"Quite easily!" chorused Edna and Sophie together, as they disappeared through the kitchen door.

"Richard and I used to come up here years ago," said Sophie, later that morning, undoing Stargazer's harness and freeing him from the trap, while Edna sat on a fallen tree trunk and spread out their picnic lunch on the little table that Jean had thoughtfully provided before he returned home to his wife and his midday meal. "He always called it the best view on the island."

Sophie removed Stargazer's bridle, replacing it with a nosebag full of oats, upon which he munched away contentedly.

"And he's quite right, too. On a clear day, you can see all the way to France. Sometimes, if the sun is bright enough, you can even make out the cars travelling along the coast road and see the people on the beaches."

"Do you think the Germans will get that far?" asked Sophie, as she came to sit beside her aunt.

Edna took a moment to reply. "If they continue to make the spectacular progress they seem to have done so far, anything is possible."

"And if that should happen what about us, here on St Nicolas? After all, we're only twelve miles from the coast."

"In that scenario, all the Channel Islands will be vulnerable but especially us as we're so close. The islands' capture would make quite a propaganda coup for Hitler, I imagine. However, I shall send you home if there's the slightest whiff of the Nazis coming here."

"But what about you and Aunt Mae? You can't stay here if the island is invaded."

"We can and we shall. It's our home," declared Edna stoutly.

Anxiety for her aunts crept into Sophie's voice. "St Nicolas is properly defended, isn't it? I mean, the British Garrison is very much in evidence in the town and along the coast."

"Yes, but unfortunately without possessing enough men or equipment to keep out a determined invader."

Sophie looked across the sparkling sea towards France, hoping that the allies would keep the Germans at bay on mainland Europe while Edna, as a determined pragmatist, presumed that it would be only a matter of time before the enemy reached the French coast. And if that should happen, her first priority would be to ensure that Sophie was returned safely to England. The rest of what had to be done would follow on from that.

In contemplative silence, both women ate their lunch.

"So, who were Ralph and Charles?" asked Sophie when they had finished, helping her aunt to pack away the remains of their picnic, unable to keep her curiosity to herself any longer.

Edna, removing Stargazer's nosebag and giving him a drink of water, smiled at the anticipated question. "They were two wonderful men that Mae and I loved once upon a time."

"You were both in love?"

"We were. Does that seem so unlikely?" Edna regarded her quizzically.

Sophie was embarrassed. "No, of course not. It's just that I'd never thought of you as having a romantic attachment."

"Well, we did. Several. But, apart from Ralph and Charles, none with whom we wanted to 'settle down', as they say. They were either too tall, short, thin, fat, stupid or too ridiculous for words. I suppose we were much too particular."

Sophie smiled. "Do you mind if I ask what happened?"

"Of course not, although until today, Mae and I haven't mentioned our two Fusiliers for a very long time."

"So, did it not work out? Did something go wrong?"

"Not with the relationships. Those were very strong." Edna sighed, an involuntary action. "You see, they both died in the Boer War."

"Oh, Aunt Edna, I'm so sorry. I shouldn't have asked."

Her aunt shook her head. "Don't worry. It's a long time ago now, and one gets over these things, you know." *Does one?* she asked herself.

"We learned about the Boer War in school," said Sophie gently. "The British fought the Boer farmers in South Africa and eventually defeated them. After this, the two Boer Republics became part of the British Empire."

To Edna, it seemed strange to hear the war spoken of so succinctly, in such a matter-of-fact manner. She had been there, had lived through its horrors; had seen the terrible battle wounds, the devastating effects of enteric fever and dysentery on the soldiers; had witnessed both defeat and victory.

Perhaps, therefore, it was better to try and look at it like that – objectively from a historical perspective.

"How did you meet your two Fusiliers?" asked Sophie.

"At a ball in London."

"London? How come?"

"Mae and I had been there for about a year, trying to earn our living in various ways, having wanted to experience life outside in the wider world. I had become bored and restless here at home and Papa suggested we should spread our wings for a while before we became a pair of *alte Jungfern*."

"Grandpa said that? That you'd become a pair of old maids? Weren't you upset?"

"Yes and no. He'd meant it humorously but there was an element of truth in his words. And it was exactly what I had been thinking." Edna picked up a napkin and absent-mindedly, folded it into a neat triangle. "So, we went to London to seek our fortunes and, for Mae especially, to find our future husbands. Then in 1899, the Boer War broke out and various regiments were stationed at Woolwich before being shipped across to Africa. Through a friend of a friend, we received an invitation to a regimental ball. It was there that I met Captain Ralph Llewellyn and Mae met Captain Charles Griffiths, who were best friends. Mae and Charles fell in love at first sight, but it was only later that Ralph and I came to love each other."

"How long did you know them?"

"Mae knew Charles only for a few months but Ralph and I were together off and on for two years."

"You were with him for two years?"

"Yes, although until the last six months of his life I didn't see a great deal of him once he and Charles had been posted abroad. However, I was luckier than Mae who never saw Charles again. He was killed in action at Frederikstad in October, 1900."

"Oh, poor Aunt Mae. Such a short time."

"She was inconsolable so I took her home to St Nicolas. Ralph and I corresponded and eventually, he wrote to say that he was coming back to England to convalesce as he'd been badly wounded. He was very lucky to have survived." Edna smiled reflectively, remembering her joy. "Anyway, in the same letter, he told me that he loved me and wanted to marry me." She paused and regarded her niece, who was listening intently, wondering how much she should reveal of her past. Edna decided she would keep nothing back. "So, I went back to the mainland and rented a beautiful little cottage just outside Reigate in Surrey, a short tram journey from the convalescent home where it had been arranged that he should stay. Once he returned to Britain, I visited him every day until he was well enough to be discharged. Very discreetly, we set up home together as a married couple. We wanted to make the most of every moment," said Edna, wondering what her niece might think.

Sophie opened her eyes wide with surprise and then smiled. "Good for you, Aunt," she said, doubting whether she would have the courage to defy convention as Edna had done but at the same time, admiring her aunt for doing so.

"You must have cared for each other very much."

"We did and I've never had a moment of regret. We remained secret lovers. It was very romantic."

"Just like a French novel."

"Just like that."

Sophie wondered what her grandparents and Mae, had they known, thought of the liaison. "How long were you together?" she asked instead.

"Three months. And I still remember every moment as though it were yesterday."

"Why didn't you get married straight away?"

"Because we thought Ralph was going to be invalided out of the army and we even set a date on that premise, intending to have a proper family wedding here on St Nicolas. Unfortunately, his regiment found themselves short of good officers so after his medical, instead of being discharged as we had expected, Ralph was deemed sufficiently fit to be sent back into the fray."

"That must have been a terrible blow," said Sophie.

"It was. But I decided there and then that I was going to volunteer as a nurse so that I could be as near to him as possible. Unfortunately, having finished my training and reached South Africa, I didn't see a great deal of him, even though I'd wangled myself into the hospital nearest to his barracks, as his battalion was charged with protecting a munitions line. He used to spend endless days and nights travelling up and down on the trains, sometimes not returning for a week."

"What happened next?" Sophie was almost afraid to ask.

"We'd been out in South Africa together for about three months when, returning from a long spell at the other end of the line, he was rushed into the hospital. He'd gone down with dysentery and unfortunately, was brought back much too late. There was nothing anyone could do for him." She paused, the pain of long-forgotten grief catching in her chest. "I was with him at the end. He died a week before the war ended."

"Oh, Aunt Edna. I'm so, so sorry."

Sophie, with tears in her eyes, touched her aunt on the arm and the two women hugged each other before Edna, straightening her back and standing up, said resolutely, "Well, my dear, we must get on. I can see Jean strolling up the hill. Let's get this harness back on Stargazer and go on with our inspection."

"What did you do after the war ended?" asked Sophie, once they had resumed their tour.

"Went back to London, threw myself into the suffragette movement for a while and various other futile causes before coming home having assuaged my grief."

"Was it really assuaged?"

"No. Nor will it ever be."

"Is that why you've never married?"

"Yes."

"Thank you for telling me all this."

Edna smiled. "Do you know, I'm rather glad I did."

With a new closeness, Sophie and Edna went indoors to supper and the disturbing news from the BBC that the Dutch army had surrendered but, according to a *communiqué* issued by Lord Gort, the commander-in-chief of the British forces in France:

'The B.E.F., after hard fighting have today successfully held serious German attacks and that the air component with the B.E.F. has destroyed at least a hundred and twenty-four German planes.'

"Is it enough?" asked Sophie.

"Probably not," replied Edna.

CHAPTER 5

Beyond the River Escaut
1st Battalion, Royal Welch Fusiliers, 'C' Company

Steadily, the lorries rumbled on their way. Exhausted and footsore, the soldiers inside – officers and non-commissioned ranks together – slept despite the discomfort, despite the overcrowding. For three days the battalion had marched before their promised transport eventually arrived. For three nights they had dug defensive positions along their successive lines of withdrawal and manned them.

Over one period of thirty hours, they covered a distance of forty miles but no stragglers were left behind and they took pride in this small triumph. And now, after taking a stand against the enemy for the past four days along the River Escaut, where casualties had been high on both sides and where many heroic acts of courage and gallantry had taken place, they were on the move again: heading back with tragic irony towards the old established defensive positions on the Franco-Belgian border.

Robert rested his back against the canvas sides of the lorry; his head throbbing yet again with what he hoped would be only a temporary legacy from his concussion. He needed complete rest but there'd been no chance of that – for any of them – but especially for him.

He closed his eyes and drifted off to sleep, his dreams full of disparate images: the battle on the Escaut and before that, Louvain, the air raid, the cellar, little Aimée.

He had to save her; he had to save them all. Claude, Hélène, where were they?

The lorry went over a pothole and jolted him awake. He looked round for the children. He couldn't see them.

"The children…!" he exclaimed aloud.

"It's all right, sir. They're safe. You told us all about them when you and the D.L.I. sergeant got back. Remember?" said a voice close by, gruffly soothing.

He did. Sleep deprivation and battle-fatigue must be making him overanxious. Perhaps if he thought about the children again, it might take his mind away from the horrors he had experienced during the past few days. Robert tried to relax and closed his eyes again.

He remembered the masonry being removed and the blessed sight of another human face. He remembered the strong, kind hands that helped him out of the devastated cellar. He remembered coughing until it felt as though his lungs were about to burst. But most of all, he remembered sitting on the pavement in the ruined street and being given water to drink from a British army-issue canister. It was odd that this should be the thing that stood out most vividly in his mind and offered him the most comfort.

Dazedly, he had looked around. There, sitting on the ground beside him, sobbing quietly and holding onto his hand had been little Aimée.

"Ah, Monsieur Robert ! Nous avons pensé que vous étiez mort !" she'd exclaimed.

"Non, je ne suis pas mort."

32

He'd squeezed the little girl's hand to reassure her he was still alive.

"Hélène et Claude ?" he'd asked.

"We are safe, Monsieur Robert. You saved all our lives. But you are hurt...?" said Claude.

"I'm all right."

Tentatively, he moved his arms and legs. Miraculously, he seemed to be in one piece, but his head hurt like blazes.

"Concussion, sir. You won't 'alf 'ave a bump. Right 'ere, sir." The man, a sergeant, pointed to the back of his head.

Robert remembered his overwhelming sense of relief as he heard the familiar, welcome tones of a Cockney accent.

"Lucky you wasn't killed, sir. Saved the lives of the children though by protecting them the way you did. Your body's took a bit of a battering, though. It was the little 'uns screams that led us to you."

Robert had closed his eyes again. It was almost too much to take in. "Who's us?" he managed eventually.

"Me, sir. Sergeant Ron Smith, 2nd Battalion, Durham Light Infantry."

"You're a long way from home, Sergeant."

"Yeah. We was ordered to shore up the French lines along the River Lasne and then join up with your lot but some of us got lost 'cos some stupid bleeder – beggin' your pardon, sir – left the one decent map we 'ad behind. Twenty-two ruddy miles we'd gone in completely the wrong direction before the officer realized his, sorry, *our* mistake. We was on our way to Holland, I reckon. So I was ordered to go back and get the map. But I only got as far as 'ere before the *Stukas* came. Then I was caught. Same as you. And like yours, my bike's a gonner. So we're both stuck."

Robert felt sick.

"'Ere, sir. 'Ave some more water."

"I have to deliver a message and get back to my battalion."

Robert remembered feeling panic and anxiety and how he had tried to sit up.

"'Ere, sir, take it easy." Sergeant Smith had squatted down beside him and placed his hand on Robert's shoulder.

Robert remembered closing his eyes for a moment, trying to make his mind work, trying to decide what to do next.

"See if you can find us some transport, Sergeant. I have to tell them about the withdrawal."

"The withdrawal?"

"Yes, Sergeant. Tonight. The whole B.E.F."

"What on earth for? We're holding our lines, ain't we, sir? We're doing everything what's being asked of us, ain't we? I've never seen the lads so full of confidence. They won't take kindly to a withdrawal, sir."

"I know, but the French and Belgians are not holding their lines and we could find ourselves trapped in the middle. But first, I have to get a message to the C.O. up here, then tell my battalion about the withdrawal, and then somehow inform your misplaced unit how to get back to the rest of your battalion."

"Complicated, ain't it?"

"A bit. But it has to be done."

Sergeant Smith was thoughtful for a moment before asking, "What d'you want to do with these 'ere children, sir?"

"We can't leave them here, that's for sure." Robert regarded the three grimy, trusting faces looking up at him. "We'll have to take them with us."

"Righty-ho," came the cheerful and accepting reply. Sergeant Smith stood up. "Leave it with me, sir. I'll see what I can find."

Robert closed his eyes again. He heard the children whispering to each other then, a few moments later, felt the cooling balm of a cold, wet cloth on his forehead. After a while, Sergeant Smith returned, an expression of triumph on his face.

"'Ere we are, sir, I found us just the thing. Ta-da!" And expansively, throwing wide his arms, he indicated a civilian car parked beside them, its engine purring.

"You're a miracle worker, Sergeant!"

"No, sir. Just lucky. Now, let's get you to your feet."

He helped Robert upright and into the car. The children climbed onto the back seat, unable to believe their good fortune. They were recovering quickly from their ordeal, as children often do if cared for without being fussed over. To them, feeling safe with Monsieur Robert and the sergeant, the whole thing suddenly seemed like an exciting adventure.

"So, which way, sir?"

Robert consulted his map. "That way first, I think, Sergeant, to deliver my message and then we'll try to find your company, providing you can remember where you left them and providing they're still there."

"I can remember, sir."

"Good man. It's relatively quiet at the moment but even so, we need to get out of here as quickly as we can. I think we'd best avoid the main roads as they'll be choked with refugees and will be a prime target for the *Stukas*."

"Wise decision, sir, if I may be so bold."

"I'm glad you think so, Sergeant Smith, and yes, you may be so bold." He smiled. "I'm Lieutenant Anderson, by the way."

"Please to meet you, Mr Anderson. I won't salute, if you don't mind, sir."

"No, best not to under the circumstances. I appreciate your desire to keep both hands on the steering wheel." He looked across at the dashboard. "How are we off for fuel?"

"Don't rightly know, sir. Gauge doesn't appear to be working. Funny things these foreign cars are. Everything's the wrong way round, if you get my drift."

"Well, we'll just have to see how far we get."

"Indeed, sir."

"Where did you find this jalopy?"

"I liberated it from a garage. Just sitting there on the forecourt, all abandoned it was, with the key still in the ignition. So I put in as much petrol as I could find and, Bob's your uncle!"

"I wish he was, Sergeant!"

After exchanging a grimace, they succeeded, with time-consuming difficulty and no little danger, in delivering their message to the C.O. in Louvain, finally reaching Robert's battalion late that afternoon. Captain Lewis was adamant that the children could not stay with 'C' Company. He immediately ordered Robert to take them somewhere else. He didn't care where, as long they were nowhere near the battlefront.

"Well, we'd better get you back to your company first," said Robert to Sergeant Smith, once they were out on the road again.

"Yes, Mr Anderson." Then Ron hesitated before saying, "Sir, I ought to stay with you. You're in no fit state to drive, if I may say so."

"I know, Sergeant. We'll worry about that later."

"Righty-ho, sir."

They reached the Durham Light Infantry positions just as dusk was beginning to fall. For the moment, the shelling and machine-gunning seemed to have eased.

"I've always reckoned old Jerry's afraid of the dark. He never comes out at night," remarked Ron. "Since we've been 'ere, we've been waking him up every couple of hours with a few rounds of MG fire just to keep 'im on 'is toes and to let 'im know we're still 'ere. Can't let 'im 'ave any beauty sleep now, can we?" he added, with a chuckle.

Robert smiled. Like so many non-commissioned officers with whom he had come into contact since being in the army and for whom he held the greatest respect, Sergeant Smith was cheerful, resilient and totally dependable.

"Now, let's find your C.O.," said Robert.

Fighting his nausea and dizziness and using whatever charm and persuasive powers he could muster, Robert was eventually allowed to take Ron as his driver, providing they were at the prearranged rendezvous before morning.

Ron filled up the petrol tank from the stores, grabbed some food, water and blankets and they set off once again. By this time, the children were fast asleep and Robert covered them up to keep them warm.

"What exactly are we going to do with them, sir? Old Jerry's likely to come this way after we've withdrawn. It'll be as dangerous as the front line and from what we've seen so far, most places are deserted."

Robert sighed. "I know."

His body was aching and his head felt like a lump of rock. But he had to think. Suddenly, the solution came to him.

"A convent would be the best place. The children would be safe there."

"Yeah. Even the Nazis wouldn't hurt nuns. Well, we'll keep a lookout, Mr Anderson, sir."

"Bit difficult in the dark – unless you've been eating a lot of carrots, of course," observed Robert dryly, showing a flash of humour despite the headache.

"I agree, sir. Actually, I did 'ave carrots for dinner."

"When?"

"Last week. Found them in a field and dug 'em up. We was short on veg."

"We've been short on everything."

The two men exchanged a wry smile.

"Brussels would be the most likely place for a convent," observed Robert. "It's about a half-hour's drive."

"Your wish is my command, sir."

"I'm very glad to hear it, Sergeant."

It was Ron's turn to chuckle. "Look, why don't you get some shut-eye, Mr Anderson? I can manage."

"Sure?"

"Yes, sir. I'm good at map reading."

Robert closed his eyes. "In the dark."

"It's those carrots, sir."

"Of course. Look, wake me up when we reach Brussels and I'll find us a convent somewhere."

"Righty-ho, sir."

They had driven on into the strangely silent night and Robert recalled looking up at the stars through the car window and wishing for a safe journey and a safe outcome to their mission.

A short while later, he'd felt his shoulder being gently shaken.

"Sorry, sir, but you asked me to wake you when we reached Brussels. We're on the outskirts now, Mr Anderson."

"Thank you, Sergeant," he'd replied, returning to reality only with reluctance. "God, my head hurts like blazes," he'd muttered, struggling to sit up.

"You really need a proper sleep, sir."

"I know but unfortunately, that's out of the question." He picked up the map. "Now, all we need to do is find a convent. Why have we stopped?"

Ron pointed to a high, whitewashed wall outside which he had parked the car.

"Will that do?" he asked, a smile of achievement lighting his face.

Robert looked out of the window. "Will that do? Sergeant Smith you really are a miracle worker! However did you find it?"

"We was lucky, sir. We was just driving past when I spotted the statue of the Madonna on top of that there pillar. So I stopped the car and 'ad a peek over the wall. I don't know any French, sir, so I've no idea what it's called. But it looked like the sort of place we was after."

Robert read the name painted on the sign above the wall. "*Couvent du Sacré-Cœur,*" he said aloud and shook his head wonder, hardly daring to believe their good fortune. "Are you a Catholic, by any chance, Sergeant?"

"No, sir. Methodist. What about you?"

"Chapel when in Wales and C. of E. when in England. I like the variety."

"Hm. In that case, d'you reckon they might throw us out on our ear?" Ron smiled.

"Hardly. Come on, let's wake the children, who are probably Catholic being Belgian."

"We'll be all right then, sir."

"I think so, Sergeant."

They walked through an enormous metal gate and up to the main door where there was a large bell rope. Sergeant Smith gave it a tug and they heard its sonorous tones resonate deep within the building.

Robert hoisted the still sleeping Aimée higher onto his shoulder, staggering as his dizziness suddenly returned. Ron immediately came to his aid, but Robert insisted that he was all right. Observing his discomfort, Claude and Hélène stood quietly, close by his side, looking up at him.

After a while, the door was opened by a nun, her robes long and flowing, a cross and rosary beads visible within the folds of material. Once Robert had explained their predicament, she merely nodded and indicated, silently, that they should wait outside, closing the door before disappearing back into the convent.

When she reappeared, they were invited to enter the building this time and, amid tearful protest, the three children were immediately whisked away for a bath and a meal, while Robert and Ron were taken to what appeared to be an office, the walls lined with books and religious pictures. Presently, the Reverend Mother entered the room, her imposing presence belying a gentle and courteous manner.

"I speak only a little English," she began, apologetically, after the introductions had been made.

"Je parle français," replied Robert, and once more gave the reasons for their unexpected arrival, describing what had happened in Louvain.

Suddenly, he felt the world spin.

"Excusez-moi, s'il vous plaît. I must sit down."

"Of course, Monsieur. You are unwell?"

"Non, just concussed."

"Then you must rest! You will be found somewhere to sleep."

"Vous êtes très gentille. But we have to get back to our units."

"Monsieur, you must rest, even if it is only for a little while. You will be of greater use to your comrades and to the Belgian people if you are fit for duty."

She rang a small bell on her desk and presently, the young nun reappeared. The Reverend Mother spoke to her in words that Robert could not understand, although he guessed it was probably Flemish and, after giving in gracefully, he was taken along hushed corridors to a tiny, spartan room that contained only a bed, small table and a wooden chair.

"Here you will sleep," said the nun, *"then you shall be given food. It is a long time since you have eaten, non ?"*

"Oui, c'est vrai."

Once he was alone, Robert unbuckled his revolver, removed his jacket and shoes, pulled his braces down over his shoulders and removed his shirt and trousers. Gratefully, he lay down on the bed, pulled the blanket over him and instantly fell asleep.

Meanwhile, Sergeant Smith was asked to remain where he was and very soon was brought cheese, bread and a large mug of milk.

Under the watchful eye of the Reverend Mother seated at her desk, he ate and drank with relish, for he too was hungry and he smiled as he wondered what the lads would think if they could see him at that moment.

Later, rested and fed, Robert re-joined Sergeant Smith and when the time came for them to leave, they made a reluctant and difficult departure. The three children were inconsolable.

Moved by their demonstration of affection for Robert, the Reverend Mother said to him: *"The children will be safe here in our care. You need have no worries for their wellbeing. I shall pray for you all."*

"You must come back for us," said little Aimée, clinging onto Robert's hand. *"Promise me that you will come back to us."*

And he had put his arms around Aimée, Hélène and Claude and promised that he would.

One day.

Whatever it took, Robert knew he would honour that promise to the three trusting children who had come so unexpectedly into his life and whose own lives now appeared to be inextricably linked to his.

Robert also knew that he would never forget the friendship unexpectedly forged with Sergeant Smith but above all, the kindness and compassion of the Reverend Mother.

The lorries continued to rumble across a flat, featureless landscape, past isolated farms and deserted hamlets, winding their way slowly through long columns of refugees that slowed their progress with everyone vulnerable to attack from the air.

Mercifully, none came.

Desperate for sleep, Robert closed his eyes again. Perhaps now, he would be able to rest; perhaps at last he would be able to shut out the horrors he had witnesses along the River Escaut, especially the tragic death of Captain Lewis: killed while trying to reach the members of 'C' Company whom he had mistakenly believed to be cut off across the other side of the river after a bridge was prematurely blown.

This calamity had left Robert temporarily in command of the company with all its attendant responsibilities – the greatest of which, for him, was to ensure the safety of the men in his charge while still carrying out their orders.

He needed to relax and clear his mind. For a brief moment he slept, his head nodding onto his chest; reality and dreams mixed together…

He had to stop the Germans crossing the river and although he kept firing his revolver, it made no difference. The enemy kept coming because the river had dried out as there'd been no rain and the sluice gates had been shut and it no longer formed a barrier.

He opened his eyes briefly. That was real. Very real.

There was no water, yet wave upon wave of enemy infantry paddling inflatable rafts were coming towards him: firing, firing.

He was on his own. Where were his comrades? Why was no one giving him covering fire? He tried to run, to get away, but his legs wouldn't move…

But that wasn't. Surely that was a dream?

He was being given the order to withdraw but his unit were too closely engaged to extricate themselves. Somehow, he had to get the men away…

In sudden panic, he sat bolt upright.

"The men?"

"Safe, sir. We made it, remember?" The voice next to him was reassuring. "You made sure we did."

Had he? He must have done.

"Yes," he said, remembering.

'C' Company had been beaten back across the river by the Germans and were under constant mortar and machine-gun attack from enemy positions sited on the opposite bank. It was a war of attrition which the Royal Welch Fusiliers were in danger of losing having had to abandon, in common with most of the B.E.F., so much equipment and stores during the fighting retreat from their positions in Belgium. They were still waiting to be resupplied.

When the order for withdrawal from the Escaut finally came, Robert knew it would be a dangerous manoeuvre to carry out as they would be in full view of the enemy. He went along each section of his company giving orders to thin out gradually and move back, placing the last three Bren guns behind the meagre shelter of a hedge to give covering fire.

The first men crawled out of their slit trenches and keeping low, ran the gauntlet of enemy gunfire to the relative safety of a nearby coppiced wood: their movement bringing down a fierce and unremitting barrage from the Germans onto both the trenches and the coppice. For a while, the rest of 'C' Company found themselves pinned down again, unable to move. They lost one of the Bren guns behind the hedge to a mortar attack, so Robert ordered the remaining two gunners to head for the trees and to keep changing their positions after firing on the enemy as the next men emerged.

He crawled back to the slit trenches, instructing the soldiers when to move, while their comrades in the trees gave additional covering fire with rifles.

Only when he was sure that everyone had gone, did Robert himself run, zigzag fashion, miraculously escaping injury, to arrive back safely with his company. Then, without further delay, they went deeper into the wood before melting away into the countryside behind to re-join the remainder of the battalion.

Robert's actions impressed his superior officers and later that day, much to his surprise, he learned that for his bravery and cool-headedness under fire and for saving the lives of his men, the R.W. F. colonel had recommended that he should receive the Victoria Cross.

Eventually, his thoughts expended, just as the lorries drew to a halt at their next destination, Robert finally slept.

In Brussels, the Reverend Mother looked up from the papers on her desk, reflecting on how quickly Claude, Hélène and little Aimée had adapted to life at the Convent even though they were not of the Catholic faith.

To her that did not matter. They were children in need of care and, on the strength of this, she was now looking after two other Jewish orphans. She had no doubt she would be called upon to shelter more.

It was a new direction both for her and the Sisters in her charge but one from which they would not shrink or be afraid.

She considered the two British soldiers who, in the middle of trying to defend her country, had regarded the safe welfare of three orphaned children above that of their own. She thought about them, particularly the kind and generous officer over whom the children had been so upset when the time had come for the two men to say goodbye. She sensed a deep attachment on both sides.

All at once, the Reverend Mother experienced a sense of destiny: a certainty that the Lord had led all of them to her for a reason. She resolved to wait patiently in faith until that purpose was revealed to her, in its entirety, at the appointed time.

CHAPTER 6

St Nicolas

Sophie had just finished the washing up after lunch when the postman put his head round the back door.

"Lots of mail today, Miss Sophie," he said cheerfully. "There's a couple of letters for Miss Edna and one for Miss Mae but you've got four! They said at the post office that you'd been waiting. Looks like they've all come at once."

Sophie's face lit up. "Thank you, Frank. Would you like a cup of tea?"

"No, thanks. I won't stay if you don't mind. You're my last stop today and I need to be getting home to help the wife. The little one's got colic again and Ethel's been up every night for the past week with her and is dead beat. Reggie's been a brick helping out in the house when he gets home from school, but it's not fair to ask him to tend the baby when she's screaming and kicking like she does."

"Poor little mite. What does Doctor Reynolds say?"

"He keeps trying to tell us that she'll grow out of it. But she hasn't yet. We've tried everything, as you know. Potions, powders, herbal thingamajigs. You name it, we've tried it, but none of it seems to make any difference. I mean she's nearly two now. It makes you wonder whether she'll ever grow out of it."

"She's had a cold as well, hasn't she?"

"Yes. One of these awful summer colds that seems to go on and on. The wife says she reckons that's why she's got the colic again."

"I am sorry."

"Well, I'd best be getting off now, Miss Sophie."

"Okay, Frank, and thank you. I hope Joan's better soon."

After the postman had left, Sophie decided that with her chores finished for the afternoon, with Aunt Edna asleep in the sitting room (having gone there ostensibly to read her book) and Aunt Mae resting upstairs on her bed, she would go for a walk, taking the letters with her to read outside in the fresh air.

She headed for one of her favourite places on the farm: a grassy summit overlooking *La Baie Mignonne*, a tiny cove with a tiny ribbon of golden sand at the base of the cliff. Here, hidden from view, was a grotto with a large, deep pool fed by a stream that cascaded down the high rocks behind, where sunlight cast dappled, golden radiance through primordial ferns, warming the water, creating a sheltered haven, a secluded world.

Sophie remembered the exquisite joy of discovery when, as a child exploring bravely on her own, she had first entered this enchanted world. From that moment on, it became her secret place, a refuge where she could bask in blissful solitude, immersing herself in favourite dreams and girlish fantasies to her heart's content.

The hill and the little cove belonged to the farm and could only be accessed via the farmyard, remaining undisturbed by casual visitors and prying neighbours. Only once had Sophie discovered anyone on the beach that she hadn't known or expected to be there – a boy, about fifteen years of age, lying naked on the sand

and reading the novel she had accidentally left behind and for which she had returned.

She smiled as she recalled their mutual shocked stillness and embarrassment when she appeared: how, on grabbing his clothes, the book had fallen from his hand, remaining open at the page he had reached; how they had stared at each other for an eternity before she scooped the novel from the sand and scuttled shyly away.

Looking back, Sophie realized the boy must have been able to read French fluently. At the time, she had just accepted this without question; after all, she and all her family could read French, why shouldn't he?

But how engrossed he had been in *La Chaleur de la Mer* – the novel that even now remained her favourite; how warm and kind his eyes became once he had recovered from the shock of being discovered. Even now, Sophie felt her cheeks become warm as she recalled the profound impression both he and the novel had had upon her own, thirteen-year-old sensibilities.

The book had been open at a particularly sensuous passage – beautifully written, its language understated, the sensitivity and passion of the lovers by the sea powerful and moving. The exquisite nature of their feelings for each other had touched her deeply, evoking nameless longings to be forever associated with that day.

Yet, unlike the mysterious boy on the beach and the couple in the novel, Sophie had never had the courage to take off her clothes outside. Perhaps one day, she thought, if ever she felt bold enough, she would throw caution to the wind and, like the boy on the beach, experience the daring sensuality of being naked in the open air.

However, the prospect seemed beyond her immediate grasp, for in this and other respects, despite her ability to be sociable, Sophie's was a reticent nature, intensely private; her innermost feelings protected assiduously from the outside world.

Notwithstanding this natural reserve or, perhaps, because of it, men found her captivating, yet Sophie had never fallen in love, nor had a serious romance. From time to time, her mother had produced potential suitors but like her aunts in that situation, Sophie had found none of them to be acceptable.

Even at Oxford, she had not met anyone she particularly liked. From the first, she had immersed herself in her studies (which she loved) as well as the dramatic society where she made brotherly friends with some of the male students who were allowed, under strict supervision, to participate. Also, Somerville undergraduates were only allowed out with a young man if accompanied by a chaperone, although many girls found ingenious ways of circumventing what they considered to be an outdated and outmoded attitude. Sophie had managed to get round this by simply not bothering as she had found no one she wished to go out with and therefore, inventing methods of deception wasn't worth the effort.

Because she had never experienced a serious relationship, Sophie hadn't had to deal with the emotional issues that some of her acquaintances seemed to enjoy discussing and disseminating with deliberate frankness, scandalizing their more innocent audience members with tales of audacity and sexual daring.

However, despite their best efforts, they had never succeeded in shocking Sophie, whose attitude towards the lives of others (paradoxically given her innate sense of modesty), was robust and tolerant.

Settling herself more comfortably, she opened her first letter.

Dear Sophie, wrote Edwin, *having a wonderful time and wish you were here.*

That was nice of him but Sophie didn't wish the same, wherever he was. Poor Edwin. He'd always meant well but he was definitely not for her. She read on:

Am surrounded by the most incredibly talented chaps and chapesses. Nearly everyone is friendly (well, there's always the odd one or two moody types wherever you go, aren't there?). It's just like being back at university but even better, if you get what I mean.

Sophie did – well, sort of, but she had no idea what he was doing or where.

I think you'd have to be here to understand fully. We work very hard and do very long hours but we let off steam with concerts and plays, cricket and rounders matches. My digs are fantastic.
Well, can't stop for more. Am taking a girl to the cinema.

Sophie's jaw dropped, momentarily caught off-guard.

Her name's Cicely and I met her on my first day. She sort of showed me round and we've become sort of very friendly. We've got lots in common. I think she likes me.
It's all right, don't worry, there's no romance…

The unwritten 'yet' leapt off the page at Sophie. *Did she mind?* she asked herself. *No.* Even a bit? *Still no.* She really did wish him the best of luck.

Well, toodle-pip, old thing. Thanks for your letter, by the way. Must dash!
Love, Edwin.

Sophie smiled. Did she mind about Edwin having a girlfriend? *No, not in the slightest.*

She laid Edwin's letter in her lap and looked down into the cove below, watching the waves lap seductively along the strip of sand, considering whether or not she should go down there.

She opened her mother's letter next.

Darling!
Received your tidings today. Glad you're settling in well. Mae says in her epistle that she and Edna are so grateful for your help and that you're being absolutely marvellous. I'm so pleased.

But how are you managing in yourself? You seem cheerful in your chatter – or was that just a 'keep Mum happy' type letter? You must let me know if you ever get desperate.

Sophie knew she wasn't desperate in the slightest. In fact, she could say in all honesty that, surprising as it might seem, she loved being at the farmhouse.

I would imagine it's very hard work but that won't do you any harm. Too much lazing about reading at home can't have been good for you.

Sophie felt indignant. She hadn't been lazing. She had always kept herself occupied.

How are you getting on with my two elderly siblings? There's such an age gap between us – they've always seemed more like my aunts than my sisters, especially when I was little!

Thinking about this, Sophie realized she hardly noticed any disparity in age between herself and her aunts. In fact, Edna and even Mae seemed younger in spirit than her mother, oddly enough.

Your father has become besotted with his Local Defence Volunteers. He keeps fussing about not yet having a proper uniform and proper army-issue guns. I told him he had to be patient. He said he'd been patient for weeks ever since the LDV was first formed!
Isn't the news stirring from Belgium? Apart from the Germans rushing about all over the place in their tanks, our boys seem to be doing well.

Not according to Aunt Edna, thought Sophie, *who obviously interprets what she hears on the BBC differently.*

If the Germans move further into France, you must come home asap.

The Germans are advancing all the time, Mother. Don't you read the newspapers or pay attention to the news on the wireless? Sophie sometimes felt exasperated by her parent who, on occasion, preferred to place her own perspective on what was going on in the world and proclaim this as being the truth of the situation, rather than listening to reality.

I'm too busy most of the time to do any reading for myself, so your father tells me what's in the newspapers. I don't believe what he says half the time. You know how journalists get things wrong.

Sophie didn't agree. They might not reveal things that would endanger the safety of the B.E.F. or lower morale at home, but in wartime, inaccuracy would be counterproductive.

44

Oh yes, and they're talking about bringing in conscription for women. If, as you say, you don't want to any part of this war, when you come home, you'd better find yourself a reserved occupation. Though I do think it's very unpatriotic of you, dear, not to join up. Especially when everyone here is working so hard for the war effort and our soldiers are fighting on the continent.

Sophie bristled at her mother's criticism but her conscience was relatively clear as she knew that since coming to St Nicolas, she had been giving considerable thought to what she might do once she returned to England.

Well, I've got some socks to knit for our boys in the B.E.F. so I won't stay for more. Do write again soon, dear.
Love,
M and D xx

With a sigh, Sophie put the flimsy paper covered in her mother's large but easily decipherable scrawl back in the envelope.

Without any shade on the hilltop, the afternoon sun blazed down relentlessly. She was feeling hot, sticky and uncomfortable and regretted not having brought any water with her to drink. The sheltered grotto invited her with the promise of verdant coolness.

Picking up her letters, Sophie made the precipitous journey down the stony path to the base of the cliff and within the shaded cavern, found a comfortable patch of sand upon which to sit, settling down to enjoy the letter from her very dear brother.

Dear Sis,
Many thanks for your lovely, welcome letter. It reached me just as I was at a bit of a low ebb and cheered me up no end. Have had some leave because of repairs to my mode of transport, which has been great. Wish you'd been at home so we could have had a bit of a gad-about together up country. There's so much I want to tell you but of course I can't write anything down as the dear old Censor would have a field day.

Let's just say, I've been here, there and everywhere, carrying out necessary 'errands'. Some have been fruitless, others successful. The successful ones have been quite exciting.

I'm doing my job well, so far, I think, and have no disasters to report (touch wood – your head will do).

Cheek! And Sophie touched the top of her head with a smile.

I've just done mine, too. So we're even Stevens. The powers that be seem pleased, anyway.

On my leave, Caroline and I managed to spend a few precious days together. She came up to see me but we could only have a little while as she's off gallivanting around with some entertainment outfit that she's joined.

Please try not to be shocked, Sophie, or think less of us, but we found a pleasant hotel and spent two incredible nights together. We neither of us could bear to wait any longer, you see. It was wonderful and amazing and I'm now more in love with her than ever

When the time came for Caroline to go, it was very hard for both of us to say goodbye but just before she left, I said that we ought to be married and as soon as poss, perhaps on my next leave. But, strangely, she seems to be dragging her heels a little. I thought she'd have wanted to be married quickly even more now.

Has she said anything to you? I hope it's nothing I've done.

Oh, Richard, thought Sophie. *I'm sure it's not.*

And she wasn't shocked either, not in the slightest. In fact, she admired them for their courage. After all, he and Caroline were already engaged. Any girl would be lucky to be loved by her brother. And he, for his part, was fortunate to have found someone whom *he* loved, while she, Sophie, had no one. There was no envy attached to this thought, only an acute sense of longing.

With a sigh, Sophie laid down the letter beside her.

She took off her sandals and wandered down to the seashore, dabbling her toes in the warm salty water. Once again, the passage that the boy had been reading from *La Chaleur de la Mer* drifted into her mind and she, lost in the pictures evoked by the novel and that day, turned back in the direction of the grotto and stopped about halfway, sitting down in exactly the same place where he had been. She ran her fingers through the sun-warmed grains of sand, watching each golden granule sparkle as it moved.

Had *he* done as she was doing now? Had he first of all sat down, thinking about trivial things – the events of his day, perhaps – before removing all his clothes because it was so hot?

Like today, she thought. She wondered if he had been for a swim first, or afterwards, for that matter. The sea, perhaps? No, inexplicably, she didn't think so. In the grotto's pool, then?

Yes, that would have been it. Perhaps she should do as *he* had done that day.

Sophie looked upwards and all around. There would be no one to see her.

Her heart pounding, she entered the grotto. Standing on the flat smooth stones at the edge of the pool, she slowly and deliberately, with shaking fingers, removed each item of her clothing; closing her eyes as she gave herself up to the wonder of the moment; savouring each new sensation as droplets of moisture from the waterfall caressed her front and the sun warmed her back.

She entered the water, gasping as its liquid-coolness embraced every part of her. She came up for air before treading water and swimming the length and breadth of the pool with languid, effortless strokes.

Afterwards, she lay on the soft sand, in the place where he had been, allowing the sun to dry her body, revelling in a newfound sense of freedom and release. She wondered if this was how the boy had felt that day so long ago.

With a jolt, she realized that he would have grown up, just as she had. What would she do if they ever met again? What would she do if he came to her now, at this very moment?

She looked down at her body and blushed at the direction of her thoughts.

For a long time, she lay on the warm sand, reluctant to move. Soon she would have to return to the farmhouse and her chores but before then, she had one more letter to read.

Caroline's.

Sophie considered leaving it until later, afraid lest her friend should express concerns about Richard; reluctant to cast any shadow, no matter how small, upon her own perfect afternoon.

However, the envelope would not let her wait. She dressed quickly and tore it open with trembling fingers.

It was full of intimate confidences of how much she, Caroline, loved Richard; how wonderful he was and how special their time together had been. How she loved him more than ever now. Caroline wrote that she knew he was the right man for her and that she was right for him. They had proved that during their few brief days together. And remarkably, she wrote, she felt only the slightest trace of guilt.

However, I've become involved with an entertainments' company. It means I'll always be very busy and that's going to make marriage difficult especially with the unpredictability of Richard's leaves.

I know he was concerned when I didn't jump at the chance of an immediate wedding. I do want to marry him, it's just that I can't see how or when at the moment.

Ironical, isn't it? Before he proposed, he was the one who wanted to wait because of the war and I was all keen to get married quickly. And now it's me who wants to wait. Funny how things change, isn't it?

I can't see any reason why we shouldn't just carry on as we are for the time being. It fits in better with our present lives.

I can't ask you not to say anything to him, although I'd like to, because I know that you and Richard have very few secrets from each other and deep down, I think he needs my reassurance via you that he has done nothing wrong. He hasn't. I really am the luckiest girl in the world.

I hope that one day you will find yourself someone as wonderful. You're too attractive not to. Try not to hide yourself away for too long.

Love from a very happy Caroline.

Sophie knew now that she would be able to reassure Richard and was glad that she could do so, that his deepest fears were unfounded. But she also knew that he would want to be married very soon to Caroline, whatever the circumstances of their present lives.

She wondered if she would ever meet a man with whom she would fall so deeply in love that she would be prepared to put aside everything in order to be with him; someone with whom she could share her innermost self; someone with whom she would find a relationship as magical, as overwhelmingly passionate and powerful as the one in *La Chaleur de la Mer*.

Sophie sighed. If only…

CHAPTER 7

Saint-Venant, France
1st Battalion, Royal Welch Fusiliers, 'C' Company

Robert had never before argued with a commanding officer but on this occasion he did, staying behind after the others had left H.Q.

"It's ludicrous, sir. You can't expect one exhausted battalion to take four bridges over a front of three miles with no antitank weapons and no covering artillery. It's suicidal!"

"Nevertheless, that's what has to be done. The Canal Line has to be held in order to delay the Germans so that most of the B.E.F. can reach Dunkirk for the evacuation. That's where all the remaining heavy guns have been taken in order to defend the perimeter." The brigadier drew in a sharp breath. "I don't like it any more than you do, Lieutenant, but nevertheless, we have our orders and they have to be carried out."

"And 6th Brigade have drawn the short straw."

"That's about it, I'm afraid. And I'll be honest with you, it'll take a bloody miracle for any of us to get to Dunkirk. The *Panzer* divisions are closing fast into this sector and the Royal Welch will have to wrest Saint-Venant from the German infantry, as they've already got there before us. It's imperative that we flush them out and then hold onto those bridges to delay the enemy's advance and allow our men to retreat."

"A hell of a task," observed Robert, understanding the magnitude of what was to come.

"Yes. Almost an impossible one." The brigadier smiled. "Well, you've done brilliantly since taking over 'C' Company, Lieutenant Anderson. Keep up the good work, there's a good chap."

"Yes, sir." Robert worked hard to suppress his urge for further protest. And his fear.

"Now, you'll have the Durhams on your left and the Berkshires on your right as you advance, so there'll be plenty of support."

"But no antitank guns or covering artillery."

"No." The brigadier was not unsympathetic, but there was nothing he could do. "Right then, Lieutenant."

Robert nodded in response, his lips drawn in a tight line.

"Good luck."

"Thank you, sir."

"Dismissed."

Robert saluted and left Brigade H.Q. feeling the tremendous weight of responsibility on his shoulders. Once again, the lives of his men would rest on the decisions he would make during the next twenty-four hours, all within an unachievable framework.

As he walked back to his unit, he reflected on the past few days. The R.W.F. had not stayed long in their positions on the border between Belgium and France. The rapidly changing military situation had demanded a further withdrawal and it had been another weary time of marching to reach the so-called Canal Line which, apart from the Dunkirk perimeter, was to be the final organized stand for British units in the French countryside. On arrival, the promised rest for his battalion as a reserve formation had lasted a mere two hours before they were once more recalled to frontline duty.

Meanwhile, the *Panzers*, for reasons known only to the German high command, had been halted in their advance. It was a tremendous piece of luck for the British but not so good for the Germans in the immediate vicinity as some infantry battalions found themselves ahead of their heavy-armour support. For the moment, that was to the advantage of the allies but Robert was well aware that it was only a matter of time before the tanks would be on the move again in support of their forward units.

His men were exhausted, as was he. Sleep deprivation and almost continuous marching on irregular and hurried meals were taking their toll. Yet, despite this, the battalion's morale remained high and Robert was determined to do his best for the men in his charge to ensure it stayed that way.

In the afternoon, he spent some time visiting his fellow R.W.F. commanders so that he was reassured they were prepared for what was to come and also because he felt that moral support, as much for himself as for them, was important. His final visit was to the immediate right-hand company of Durham Light Infantry and, in the absence of their C.O., he met up once again with Sergeant Smith.

"It's good to see you, sir," said the ever cheerful N.C.O., expressing genuine regard.

The feeling was mutual and for Robert, his relief at seeing the dependable Sergeant Smith again was such that, unexpectedly, in his state of complete and utter exhaustion, he was in danger of becoming emotional. He could only nod in reply.

Ron Smith was not slow to pick up on this. "They're a right b----r, these orders, aren't they, sir?" he said quietly.

"You're telling me."

"Good job my company's next to yours when we meet up later."

"Yes."

"So we'll be able to keep an eye on each other."

"Yes." There was gratitude in Robert's voice.

"You'll do fine, sir."

"I hope we all do."

"I'll let my C.O. know that you called." His lips twitched. "Did you bring any cards, sir?"

"Cards?"

"Calling cards…"

Robert smiled. "An oversight, Sergeant."

"A serious one, indeed, sir."

"Definite court martial material, I'd say."

"Of course."

"Thank you, Ron."

"That's the ticket, sir."

Robert returned to his unit, heartened by this encounter. However, all too soon, his worst fears were to be realized.

Things began well enough. That evening, three companies of the R.W.F. advanced westward, with the Canal de la Lys on their right. With very little loss of life on either side, 'A' and 'C' managed to capture the hamlet of Saint-Floris, even taking prisoners, but later, coming up against strong resistance, found themselves unable to advance any further.

Tragically, 'D' Company took a wrong turning and ran onto an ambush, suffering very heavy casualties. By the time the news reached Robert, there was nothing he could do to help and, concealing his despair, he gave the order for 'C' Company to withdraw from their positions once again as they would not now have the prearranged support.

The detached 'B' Company, having taken the village of Robecq, a few miles to the south of Saint-Venant, reached one of the bridges, but soon found themselves surrounded and besieged. At great cost, they held their objective for most of that day, but were forced to withdraw during the night after running out of ammunition. Thirty-five survivors broke out in small parties but tragically, only a handful reached safety.

Effectively, from that moment, both 'B' and 'D' Companies, together consisting of over two hundred men, ceased to exist. It took all Robert's self-discipline not to weep at the stupidity of war and for the number of lives lost – on both sides.

The next morning, a detachment of the Durham Light Infantry took over the defence of Saint-Floris while 'A' and 'C' Companies of the R.W.F. pressed on to Saint-Venant: a small, picturesque village in the middle of flat, open countryside that afforded little cover.

It was a fiercely contested battle with hand-to-hand fighting from house to house, garden to garden, narrow lane to narrow lane. Although both sides sustained casualties, the R.W.F. prevailed, eventually driving the Germans away and once again, taking prisoners.

With the supporting D.L.I. companies now arriving in the village, the R.W.F. pressed on, aiming for the more westerly bridge. A quarter of a mile from their objective they were pinned down in open ground by enemy fire. Once again, when he could see that their situation was untenable, Robert gave the order to withdraw. Even though he gave the order in good time, they only succeeded in regaining the relative safety of Saint-Venant with difficulty.

Exhausted and battle-weary, along with his comrades, Robert threw himself down onto the first patch of available ground he could find. The orderlies brought round hot, sweet, reviving tea to the men sprawled out in the houses, barns and gardens. After a while, Robert dragged himself onto his feet and went round to see his company, to congratulate them and offer further encouragement.

That night, with the enemy's camp fires visible all around them, they snatched what rest they could.

But Robert couldn't sleep. The hay upon which he was lying was prickly and uncomfortable and his mind overactive with the weight of his responsibility in an increasingly perilous situation as well as nightmarish images of the day's fighting.

Quietly, so as not to disturb the others, he went outside the barn and stood by the open doorway, contemplating the stars.

He began to question whether there was any point to all this.

Was anything they did today or tomorrow going to make any difference? Were the sacrifices being made here and now really going to affect the eventual outcome of the war? Did any of it matter if, as it seemed likely, they were going to lose this particular fight anyway?

With an ironic smile, he reflected that throughout history, the British were very good at making defeat sound like a heroic last stand, thus salvaging their pride and the nation's honour. However, and here his smile vanished, would the story of the B.E.F. in Belgium and France in 1940, which was inevitably nearing a disastrous conclusion, come to be regarded in this way? Or would their present valiant, last-ditch efforts be lost in the mists of time?

Unbidden, the final line of Wilfred Owen's famous poem came into his mind: *The old lie: Dulce et decorum est pro patria mori.*

The grim reality and his abhorrence of the brutality and ugliness of death in battle had prompted the poet, with bitter irony, to write these words and Robert, despite being a professional soldier, had always held them to be true within the context of the Great War. But now, in this new war, he wondered whether Owen was right in the broader intellectual sense. Was it really a lie, this belief that to die for one's country was a great and glorious thing, or was it, as Owen maintained, an empty ideal that had spurred on so many naïve and innocent men into becoming its victims?

Did the unnecessary tragedies of the last war have any similarity to or bearing on this one? Was there a greater purpose now or were their present efforts and the consequent loss of precious life – on both sides – just as futile?

The Great War was supposed to have been the 'war to end all wars' but it didn't.

Did that, therefore, render the sacrifices made back then worthless? Would the sacrifices made so far in this war be seen as pointless also? Would they even be remembered?

Did the Germans believe it was a great and glorious thing to die for their country? Some of them, probably. The Nazi fanatics, perhaps, who had an unquenchable thirst for power and glory, but not the ordinary man wrenched against his will from a peaceful, uncomplicated existence by external forces beyond his control. And definitely not the many friends he had made during his time in Germany as a student, most of whom abhorred what was happening in their country.

Knowing all this made what had to be done doubly difficult for Robert to bear.

He hadn't seen the men he had killed that day. He supposed he must have killed some. But it was as though he had been in some kind of dream totally detached from reality; where normal peacetime morality seemed to have no place. In the heat of the moment, without time to think or consciously register exactly what it was he was doing, it became a matter of his own or his friend's survival. It was either kill or be killed, that basest of animal instincts.

With a great effort of will, Robert knew he had to persuade himself to believe in what they were doing otherwise he might as well give up now. The purpose of his brigade's current situation was to carry on so that others might live to fight another day; so that as many of the B.E.F. as possible might reach Dunkirk and be able to go home to defend their country, and then, hopefully, return one day to the continent and defeat Nazism, the appalling regime that now held most of Europe in its thrall.

Robert was aware that he possessed true patriotism: loyalty to his country, to its freedoms, to its way of life combined with a natural, deeply held antipathy towards jingoism and xenophobia.

He knew that Owen's words were true, but this was a different war with different criteria and Robert knew that it had to be fought. Each man's contribution was a vital part in the eventual outcome and what he did today, tomorrow, next week, *mattered*.

He felt his eyes closing, and dragging his weary body back inside the barn to his patch of straw, he lay down. Even so, sleep still eluded him. Robert turned onto his back, his arms behind his head, channelling his thoughts into practical considerations.

In the situation in which they now found themselves, the preservation of as many men's lives as possible had become his own personal goal. He had an intellectual appreciation of military strategy but Robert knew that above all, intelligence gathered quickly and accurately and used to formulate planning was essential.

He found no beauty in battle; no purity in the outcome as some did. At that moment, with all his soul, he longed for *real* purity and beauty as an antidote to ugliness and death and the revulsion that threatened to engulf him.

He began to doze.

He was swimming. The water was deep and cold. He was in a pool where dappled sunlight played on the surface making it shimmer and dance. Icy rivulets ran over his body, embracing every part of him...

Robert woke up with a jolt, his mouth dry, his heart pounding, shivers going down his spine – the dream and reality as one.

He had been about fifteen and on holiday with his parents and sister on one of the Channel Islands. He'd wandered off on his own, discovering a rambling old farmhouse from which a steep little track wound its way downwards to a secluded beach. It had been a hot day and he had stripped off and swum in a freshwater pool hidden in some kind of grotto.

Robert smiled. It had been a glorious afternoon of self-discovery.

Returning to the beach, he'd found a book – *La Chaleur de la Mer* – a rather racy, but well-written French novel. He never managed to finish it, because a beautiful young girl had disturbed him. She must have been about thirteen, only a couple of years younger than he, and Robert recalled how she'd blushed a very deep shade of red when she saw him in all his glory.

Mightily embarrassed, he'd quickly covered the exposed part of his anatomy by grabbing his clothes, discarding the book where it remained open at the page he had been reading.

Once both of them had overcome their shock and surprise, they had stared at each other for what seemed like an eternity. He could still visualize the halo of bright sunshine behind her; could still remember the blue of her eyes and feel her gaze, steady and unblinking. But most of all, he remembered being enveloped in, what had seemed to him then, a golden aura of exquisite purity and beauty.

He couldn't utter a word, though he had wanted to. They had remained motionless, lost in that moment of perfection until, with one quick and graceful action, she had bent down to pick up the book and was gone.

He had wanted to run after her and ask her who she was. He had wanted to see her again, to be with her. But he wasn't dressed and by the time he was and had reached the summit of the cliff, she was nowhere to be seen.

The next morning, he and his family returned home, never to take another holiday on that particular island.

For a long time afterwards, he had thought about her. In that fleeting moment, she became for him a symbol of purity and loveliness.

Reaching out to that moment again and feeling comforted, Robert fell asleep.

The next day, the battalion endured heavy shelling but no further attacks were mounted by either side. Ordered to make a reconnaissance, Robert took note of the numbers of enemy tanks and infantry gathering in readiness for the next assault. He realized that the whole brigade needed to move back across to the north bank of the Lys Canal now before it was too late. The R.W.F. colonel agreed with him and sent their remaining transport back over the bridge in preparation for blowing it up once everyone was safely across.

However, to everyone's astonishment, the brigadier refused to give permission to withdraw, saying they had to maintain their present position. It was a strange decision as the German tanks would have been unable to cross this, the last remaining bridge, once it had been blown. The north bank would then have offered the British a much better and, relatively, safer defensive position.

In the light of these orders, they had no option but to dig in and try to defend their positions from the south bank. With only a few antitank rifles and one three-inch mortar between them, no heavy-gun support and no antitank barrier separating the battalion from the enemy, they stood no chance. Robert and his colonel once again questioned the decision but there was nothing they could do, the brigadier would not give way. In the end, they had to obey orders.

So, 'A' and 'C' companies of the R.W.F. were deployed in the forward positions with the D.L.I. dug in behind. They had no choice but to remain in their slit trenches for the night and await the inevitable attack.

Just before dawn, Sergeant Smith scrambled over to Robert.

"Hello, sir. Message from my C.O. He sends 'is best wishes and says if you can keep the tanks at bay, he'll buy you dinner at Claridge's."

"Tell him I appreciate the offer and if *he* can find a way to dispose of the tanks permanently, I'll buy him dinner at Claridge's every evening for a whole year."

Sergeant Smith chuckled. "Very good, sir." Then he said: "It's a bit of a bummer this, ain't it?"

"There have been lots of bummers these past couple of weeks."

"You're telling me, sir."

"But the B.E.F. have done valiantly, Sergeant."

"A heroic effort, you might say, sir."

"Absolutely." Robert hesitated. "You all right, Ron?"

"Yeah, nothing a cup of tea at home wouldn't fix."

"I'm with you there."

"Good. I'll hold you to that, Mr Anderson."

"I'll look forward to it."

"Well, I'd best be getting back, sir."

"Yes. See you later, Sergeant."

"See you, sir."

And then he was gone but not for long. At that moment, the artillery barrage began and Sergeant Smith scrambled back into Robert's trench.

"It's suicidal out there, sir."

"Best stay here then, Ron, and keep your head down."

"Seems wise, sir. I can be as much use here as back there."

For an hour, the heavy guns pounded their position, their range becoming increasingly accurate.

"We could do with one or two of those guns, ourselves," remarked Ron.

"Four arrived earlier, but as the forward observation officer had no map, he said he couldn't do his job. The battalion only has four maps altogether it would seem, none of which were any good for his purposes. So they all went away again."

"You're kidding me, sir."

"Nope."

"It's just one cockup after another, isn't it, sir?"

"Yes, unfortunately. But we have to make the best of it." Robert instinctively ducked his head as more shells came whistling overhead, landing about a hundred yards behind, sending earth and debris flying. "Hell's teeth! That was close."

Ron poked his head above the parapet.

"Oh, God, sir, that was my trench." He began to climb out.

"Stay here, Sergeant. That's an order. There's nothing you can do. Your medical people will see to the casualties."

"Yes, sir."

For what seemed like an eternity, they endured the intensive bombardment. Then, as suddenly as it had begun, the barrage lifted.

"Now we're for it," muttered Sergeant Smith darkly.

And, in the far distance, came the tanks – huge and menacing – rumbling slowly and inexorably towards them.

"Hold your fire until they're within range." Even as he gave the command, Robert knew it was senseless, hopeless. But they had to try.

'A' Company were the first to receive the onslaught. With their weapons ineffective against the *Panzers*, it was carnage and chaos as the tanks turned their machine guns onto the defenders.

Watching in horror, Robert knew he had to do something. He was not, *not* prepared to have his men suffer the same fate. Then he had a brainwave.

"Go and see how many Mills bombs we've got, Sergeant."

"Yes, sir."

He returned almost immediately. "Boxes of them, sir."

54

"What if we wait until the tanks are nearer and then get underneath them and throw the grenades into their tracks?"

"That might stop 'em, for a while, Mr Anderson. It might buy us some time to get back to the road and cross the bridge." He looked at Robert. "You and me then, is it, sir?"

"Yep. We'll choose a few other volunteers as well."

Robert sent a message to his colonel and the brigadier of his intentions and quickly selected some men to assist. He instructed the rest to be ready to head back to the road about a mile to the rear as soon as the order was given.

Patiently, Robert and his chosen men waited and as soon as the leading *Panzers* were within range, they climbed out of the trench and crawled along the ground, remaining hidden underneath the tanks' angle of fire. Quickly and accurately, they threw the grenades into the tracks and crawled back to the trench.

This delaying action didn't do the tanks much harm, but it must have frightened the drivers because, in a panic, they abandoned their vehicles and ran back to their lines under a continuous volley of small-arms fire from the British.

"It's a pity we don't know how to operate those tanks, sir," observed Ron. "We couldn't 'alf do some damage."

"I was just thinking that, Sergeant. Now, let's hope the brigadier does his stuff."

But the brigadier, having been given this unanticipated opportunity of escape, hesitated before giving the order for his battalion to fall back. While he was dithering, there came the whistling of shells as the tanks, albeit remaining motionless, resumed their attack.

'C' Company let fly with everything they had, but it was very clear that nothing could stop the enemy, who more or less had the measure of the trenches now, firing on anyone who raised their head above the parapet.

Defending bravely but with his company sustaining increasing numbers of casualties, Robert, using his initiative and without waiting for further orders, somehow succeeded in getting the remainder of his men out and back to the road. However, the tanks began to move again and the D.L.I., whom Ron had re-joined *en route*, found themselves more or less surrounded and had an even greater difficulty in extricating themselves.

Having at last caught up with the situation, the brigadier ordered Robert to send the survivors from 'C' Company, the remnants of 'A' Company and any D.L.I. that should appear, over the road and across the bridge, which was by now being plastered with fire from stationary tanks and rapidly arriving infantry further down the road.

So, like some grim P.T. instructor, Robert crouched beside the road launching each man on a suicidal journey from culvert to bridge. One after another, they went. One after another they were mown down. It was a terrible task with a terrible rate of attrition.

By the time the seventh man was ready to go, Robert could stand it no longer. He told the next soldier to stay put while, keeping low, he chose his moment and ran across the road to have a closer look at the bridge. There were girders up to the height of about a foot running along the middle and he realized that these could provide a modicum of protection if the men 'caterpillared' across next to them. In that way, he knew they might stand a chance.

He crawled back to the ditch and gave the word, waiting with bated breath as he sent the next man on his way. He saw him cross the road, slither along the bridge and reach the north bank of the canal successfully. So did the next man and the one after that until most of the surviving R.W.F. were now reaching safety.

Soon, some stragglers from the D.L.I. began to appear, about twenty-five in all. Finally, Ron arrived with a further half a dozen men.

"Is that it, Sergeant?" asked Robert appalled.

"'Fraid so, sir. Just me and the rest of my platoon. The others are either trapped or dead."

Robert let out a sigh. "Right then." He gave his friend instructions.

"Good luck, sir," said Ron, as the two men quickly shook hands. "See you in Dunkirk."

Robert nodded, alert and watchful, his attention on the road. "Now, Sergeant. Go!"

He saw him run to the bridge and caterpillar safely across to the other side.

Finally, it was his turn.

Robert waited for a burst of enemy fire and ran across the road once it had ceased, only to feel a searing pain as firing resumed. The impact of a bullet entering his lower leg caused him to fall back onto the bank beside the canal. He struggled to his feet and once more tried to gain the bridge. This time, he was hit in the hip and shoulder and collapsed onto the grass.

The R.W.F. colonel appeared, staggering under the weight of the wounded officer he was trying to save. Robert saw him attempt to cross the bridge, shouting the order to detonate the charges already in place. But he never made it. He was killed before he had reached the middle.

Sickened after seeing his colonel blown up before his eyes, his own body on fire with pain, Robert lay helplessly, waiting for whatever was going to happen next. He knew that given his proximity to the bridge, he wouldn't stand a chance once it was blown.

But to his amazement, nothing happened – the sappers had already left and there was no one to carry out the order.

The bridge remained intact.

Tanks began to rumble past him. He saw the first one hesitate, then move slowly across the bridge. Cautiously, others followed in a steady procession, shooting up any stragglers on the other side who offered resistance or tried to escape.

How ironic, thought Robert, as he drifted in and out of consciousness, that the bridge over which the enemy were now crossing had been constructed only a few days previously by British engineers after the main bridge, a mile or so upstream, had been destroyed by the Germans.

It was just one more piece of bad luck in a campaign that had become a complete and utter shambles.

As for what might happen to him? Robert closed his eyes.

Who could tell?

CHAPTER 8

St Nicolas

When Sophie and Edna returned from milking the cows, all was quiet in the kitchen. There was no sign of Mae. No breakfast being prepared; no cheerful music on the radio.

"I'll go and see where she is," said Sophie, and immediately went upstairs to her aunt's room.

Discreetly, she knocked at the door.

"Aunt Mae," she called softly.

When there was no response, she turned the door handle and put her head round the door.

Mae was fast asleep, but Sophie could hear her breathing, laboured and wheezy. Silently, she closed the door and went downstairs into the kitchen.

"I don't think Aunt Mae's very well."

Immediately, Edna was on the alert and the two women climbed the stairs and went into her room. Mae opened her eyes.

"I'm so sorry," she croaked. "I think my summer cold has turned into something else."

"You need the doctor, old thing," said Edna.

"No, no. I'll be fine. I'll take some echinacea and I'll be fine." Speaking made her cough, painfully.

Notwithstanding Mae's reluctance, Sophie was despatched to fetch Doctor Reynolds from Port le Bac. When she arrived in the little town, people were out and about despite the early hour, standing around in small groups chattering animatedly within an atmosphere of tension and concern.

"Oh, Sophie!" exclaimed Ethel, the postman's wife. "What do you think?"

"Of what?"

"Haven't you heard the news?"

"Not this morning."

"The Germans have crossed the Seine at Quillebeuf!"

"What?"

"That means they're only about two hours away from St Malo and four hours away from the Channel Islands. Frank says the Consell de Souverain are going to ask the British Government to evacuate the women and children in case the Germans come here."

Sophie took a deep breath. "Well, there's nothing we can do at the moment but wait and see what happens. Anyway, please excuse me, I must go and find the doctor. Aunt Mae's not well this morning. Her cold has taken a turn for the worse, I fear."

"Oh, the poor dear. And her with her weak chest and everything. Still, Edna's got you to help her, hasn't she?" Then a thought struck Ethel. "But I expect you'll be going back to England now, won't you, with this news and everything?"

Would she? Sophie couldn't answer. Her aunts still needed her; now, more than ever. The Germans weren't on the doorstep yet so there was no immediate need to panic and right now, she needed to see the doctor.

"Come in, my dear," he said, after Sophie had knocked at the door.

Doctor Reynolds was a widower in his late fifties, ruggedly handsome, looked after by his married housekeeper who came in each day to cook, clean and "generally interfere", according to the doctor. He was well liked by the islanders and there were several middle-aged widows in Port le Bac who had their beady eyes on him but whose clutches he had so far managed to avoid.

He was fond of Sophie, having seen her grow up and, being good friends with her aunts, was often to be found of an evening driving out to see them in his little Ford Prefect, a car that he had purchased in 1938 and of which he was particularly proud, for a game of whist or rummy or just a quiet evening of erudite conversation.

Andrew Reynolds felt at home with Edna and Mae and able to be himself in their company without fear of being pounced upon (figuratively speaking) or regaled with questions concerning someone's health matters. Nor would he ever forget the wonderful support they had given to both him and his now grownup son after his wife had passed away.

"Sophie, my dear! What can I do for you?" he said, looking up from his papers and smiling.

"It's Aunt Mae, Doctor. I do think you should come and see her. Aunt Edna is quite worried."

"Well, if Edna's worried, then that is what I shall do." He scanned his morning's schedule.

"How about eleven o'clock? The world and his wife want to see me this morning. If things continue like this, I really shall have to get that partner everyone keeps telling me I need."

Sophie smiled. "Thank you, Doctor. We'll see you later."

When he arrived, Dr Reynolds immediately went to see Aunt Mae, who was sitting up in bed, her shoulders covered by a shawl, looking pale and wan. He listened to her chest with his stethoscope and diagnosed bronchitis. He smiled.

"You'll be fine, as long as you keep warm and take it very easy."

She coughed. "But I have to get up and help. Edna, you know."

"Sophie's here. They'll manage fine. *You* must stay in bed. You've had bronchitis enough times to know the drill by now, Mae."

She sighed. "If only I was stronger…"

"I know."

A few days later, Sophie was in the yacht club near the harbour chatting to the Commodore, who was due to come that evening along with his wife, for a rubber of Bridge at the farmhouse, when a call came through from the Admiralty in London.

"Good God!" he exclaimed, replacing the receiver. "London wants us to mount an evacuation like Dunkirk. There are soldiers, apparently, that need lifting off from St Malo." He rubbed his chin, his thoughts racing. "I'm afraid our evening is off, my dear. Please give my apologies to your Aunt Edna. This is going to take a lot of organizing. We're going to need every available boat that we can lay our hands on and I must set to work immediately. Please forgive me." He turned to the telephone again.

"Of course. Would it help if I let Vera know?"

"It would indeed. Thank you, I'd appreciate that greatly," replied the Commodore, busy dialling the exchange. "Er, Jersey twelve, please," he said to the operator, and waved farewell to Sophie as she went out of the door.

Sophie mounted her bicycle and rode the short distance to the Commodore's house. It was a gracious, three-story white-painted building overlooking Port le Bac, with immaculate gardens, tended by an elderly gardener who came in each day to nurture his plants and manicure the lawn.

Bert was devoted to his work and justifiably proud of the results he achieved. When he wasn't ministering to the soil, he was to be found tending his lobster pots, selling the fruits of his labours in the fish market and the café on the seafront.

He called out with a cheery greeting, which Sophie returned, as she cycled up the drive, but she didn't stop to pass the time of day – she needed to deliver her message and return home as soon as she could.

Home. It was strange how quickly she had become attached to the farmhouse; how settled she was in her new life. She enjoyed the company of her aunts, particularly Edna who, despite her forceful personality, was turning out to be something of a kindred spirit.

However, Sophie knew that a greater burden of responsibility had fallen onto her own shoulders with Aunt Mae's illness. Her thoughts turned to Edna's staunch refusal to be evacuated should idle speculation of a German invasion become alarming reality.

"This is our land," she had declared robustly, after Sophie had first raised the subject. "And I'm blowed if I'm going to leave just because some government department says so. But you, my dear girl, you must go home."

That was before Aunt Mae's bronchitis; before her aunts had needed her help more than ever. What was Sophie to do now?

With a sigh, she rang the bell and the door was opened by the maid.

"Madam is in the garden. I shall tell her you are visiting."

"How lovely to see you," said Vera, waving a long-stemmed glass in Sophie's direction as she walked across the lawn after being announced. "Do have a pink gin."

"Er, no thank you very much," replied Sophie, taken aback by the slight slurring in the older woman's voice so early in the morning. "I'm afraid I can't stop. I just came to deliver a message from the Commodore." And Sophie explained what had transpired.

"Oh, how tedious," replied Vera listlessly. "It would have to happen today." She shrugged and took another large slurp from her glass. "I don't suppose Eric said what time he would be home?"

"I'm afraid not," said Sophie tersely, appalled at Vera's obvious lack of concern for the predicament of the soldiers stranded in France.

"Oh dear. I shall have no idea now what time to ask Cook to do supper." She sighed and studied her red-painted fingernails, each one polished to perfection, and patted her immaculate hair. "I suppose I shall manage." She drained her glass and poured herself another gin. "I presume Eric has to do this. I've told him to give up the yacht club, but he flatly refuses. I've said I'd really like to move back to London. Life for me here is so dreadfully *dull*." She picked up her magazine and half-heartedly flicked through it before letting it slide from her lap. She made no attempt to pick it up, leaving it crumpled on the grass. "Well, do give my apologies to your aunts. It was kind of them to invite us. We haven't been in an age. I suppose this'll give me more time to brush up on my Bridge skills. Not that it will do any good – the game is a complete mystery even though Eric has tried to explain it to me. He says I'll have to be a sleeping partner. I have no idea what that means."

Sophie had to work hard not to laugh at this. She had always liked the Commodore with his earthy sense of humour and well-meaning bluster, but found his wife, who was a good twenty years younger than he, to be both vapid and vain. She was secretly glad that the evening had been cancelled.

Hastily, she took her farewell.

The next afternoon, with all chores finished until teatime, instead of taking her usual walk, Sophie cycled down the hill to Port le Bac. She found the harbour to be full of craft of all shapes and sizes – fishing boats, private yachts and cargo vessels – all, that is, apart from a Royal Navy motor torpedo boat moored at the end of the pier, bobbing up and down in the water, awaiting their turn to tie up at the quayside and discharge their exhausted and bedraggled consignments of soldiers.

The Commodore, working in tandem with R.N. personnel, was in his element, directing the boats here, there and everywhere. This was what he knew best; what he excelled at. If he hadn't sustained such a serious wound at the Battle of Jutland and been invalided out of the Royal Navy and put on the retired list, then he would have been serving in this war. Even though his legs didn't trouble him too much these days, he couldn't stand for any length of time and found walking long distances painful and tiring.

The wounded were whisked away by two waiting ambulances to the little hospital, quickly returning for more, while the rest of the men sat on the harbour wall or lined the main street, their facial expressions a combination of exhaustion and relief.

The seafront café was providing a brisk service, with the townswomen rallying round to help prepare and distribute gallons of tea and mounds of sandwiches which the men ate and drank with relish and gratitude.

When at last the final soldiers had been landed and assessed, the uninjured were lined up on the quayside and marched off to Fort Noble where, it was assumed by the local population, they would remain to assist in the defence of the island.

However, this was not to be because within a few days, almost as quickly as they had arrived, they were shipped back to England on Government orders, along with the rest of the British Garrison and all their guns, munitions and equipment. The Lieutenant Governor of Jersey, a general in the British Army, also went away, as did all Royal Air Force and Royal Navy personnel from Guernsey, Jersey and St Nicolas, taking with them their fighter planes and fast motorboats.

60

The Channel Islands were now defenceless. Although nothing had been said officially, everyone deduced (correctly) that they were now living in a demilitarized zone. An uneasy atmosphere pervaded Port le Bac.

Soon, there was panic. There were queues outside the bank with people trying to withdraw their life savings. Extra money was sent from London to all the Channel Islands to keep up reserves. A few boatloads of disconsolate French refugees drifted across the sea to St Nicolas, bringing with them horrendous tales of bombing and strafing. Sounds of machine-gun fire and shelling could be heard from the mainland. Probing the Channel Island's defences, the *Luftwaffe* inflicted death and destruction upon the people of Jersey and Guernsey when tomato and potato-carrying lorries lined up on the quayside to unload their wares onto waiting cargo-carrying boats were mistaken for army vehicles.

At this news, there was dismay, disbelief, hysteria and widespread alarm. In response, the governing bodies of the islands called upon the British Government to provide the wherewithal for the immediate protection and evacuation of its citizens.

After some weeks, when the evacuation was finally announced, there was less of a rush to leave St Nicolas than expected. Alone among the Channel Islands, apart from Sark, the majority of residents for one reason or another resisted the call of England. The young men of military age went, of course, on their way to join the forces, together with many married women and children. But most of the population decided to remain on the island.

Including Sophie.

"How can I possibly leave you?" She had argued with Edna, strongly. "Aunt Mae is very poorly. You can't look after her and manage the farm as well. She's not well enough to travel to England and everyone else is so wrapped up with their own concerns that it would be impossible to find anyone to help you."

Edna, tired after all the anxiety and uncertainty, all protest spent, had regarded her closely, breathing deeply. "You do realize what you're doing, don't you? The risks you'll be taking?"

"Perhaps not. But I'll take my chances. How can I possibly leave the two of you in the lurch? I wouldn't be able to live with myself. And mother would never forgive me if I ran for home."

"Your mother may never forgive *me* for allowing you to stay," said Edna wryly. She heaved a big sigh. "All right then, my dear, I'll give in gracefully. If the Germans invade, which is quite likely, then I shall row you across to England myself."

Sophie looked at her. "With one arm?"

Edna chuckled before saying in all seriousness, "Well, whatever happens, we're in this together now, girl. You'd better write to your mother immediately and take it to the harbour today. Lord knows when the mail will get through next."

When she had written her letter, Sophie cycled quickly down to Port le Bac. She just caught Frank, the postman, as he was putting the final sack of letters on the last 'official' evacuation boat out of the harbour.

There would be others, perhaps, provided by the islanders themselves to take people across the English Channel, but Sophie knew with absolute certainty that none of them would be carrying her across the sea to home and safety. For better or worse, she was here now and here she would be staying.

Despite her stubborn resolve, the magnitude of her decision began to manifest itself within her consciousness as she stood disconsolately on the quayside watching the last cargo boat as it chugged its way out of the harbour.

Sophie thought of the letter, recently sent, from the King officially announcing the demilitarization of the islands, expressing his regret at the withdrawal of the British armed forces. She found comfort in his genuine belief that the link between himself and the islanders would remain unbroken, that their *'resolute fortitude'* in the face of current difficulties would ultimately *'reap the reward of victory'*.

It was unfortunate, though, thought Sophie, that the letter had been made public at a time when all Channel Islanders were still reeling from the effects of the *Luftwaffe*'s attack on Guernsey and Jersey. It had been greeted, therefore, with equanimity in most quarters rather than appreciation. However, as the official announcement that the Channel Islands had been declared a demilitarized zone was broadcast by the BBC on the nine o'clock news on the same day that the air raids had taken place, it was the British Government who had received the brunt of the islander's indignation and displeasure.

"Why didn't they do this as soon as the army left?" they asked.

"Why didn't the British Government tell the Germans?"

"Like shutting the stable door after the horse has bolted," they complained.

"It's insulting – don't they care for us anymore?"

"Why are we being abandoned?" were just a few of the heartfelt cries that went up, unfortunately never to be heard in the corridors of Whitehall.

As Sophie stood and pondered these things, she knew that her fate was now inextricably linked to that of her aunts.

As for what might happen to her? She mounted her bike and turned for home.

Who could tell?

CHAPTER 9

Saint-Venant, France

Roused from his injured state, Robert jumped involuntarily at the sound of voices.

"Ist er tot?"

He felt his body being prodded by the end of a rifle and someone pressed their fingers against the side of his neck.

"Nein."

"Sollen wir ihn erschießen?"

Robert's mind awoke from its stupor.

"Ich würde es vorziehen, wenn Sie nicht auf mich schießen würden," he managed to say.

Once he had overcome his initial surprise at this response, the German officer laughed.

"Ah, my English friend, as you speak such fine German and because you have requested so politely, we shall not shoot you."

"Thank you."

"But you are now our prisoner."

"I accept that I have no choice in the matter."

"Good. Then your wounds will be taken care of. Stretcher bearer!"

Robert felt himself being lifted gently onto a stretcher and until he came to again, this was the last thing he remembered.

When he did regain consciousness, he found himself in a large tent, wearing a hospital robe, his uniform having been removed. His wounds had been dressed with bandages and to his surprise, he was lying in a bed with clean, white sheets. A nurse, whom he assumed to be the matron, approached him.

"Gut! Sie sind wach. I shall fetch the doctor, now that you are awake."

After a short while, a white-coated doctor arrived and examined Robert's wounds. He did not say anything to him directly, but merely nodded and turned to the nurse.

"This one will be all right. The operation was successful and he has a strong constitution. Give him some food and water in an hour or so."

"Ja, Herr Doktor."

Once again, Robert slept and when he awoke next, it was dark. The ward was lit only by a dim oil lamp at the far end, but there was sufficient light for him to see that the bed next to him was now occupied.

"Hello," said the incumbent *sotto voce*. "I'm Harry Lawrence. Royal Berkshires."

"Robert Anderson. Royal Welch."

"So, we were together then, back there."

"Yes."

Both men were silent for a moment.

"Didn't go too well, did it?" ventured Harry.

"None of it did."

"We tried our best though."

"Yes."

Robert closed his eyes. But their best hadn't been good enough. From the beginning, the whole B.E.F. had needed better intelligence, more equipment, more supplies, more modern weapons and better lines of communication.

"What's your rank?" asked Harry. "It's difficult to tell who's who in this hospital get-up."

"Lieutenant."

"1st or 2nd?"

"1st."

"Same. Regular?"

"Yes."

"Me too. Doesn't really matter now though, does it?"

"Of course it does. It has to matter."

"Even though we'll be out of it?"

"I have no intention of 'being out of it'," and Robert winced as pain from his shoulder and leg radiated through his body.

"Where were you shot?"

"Shoulder, leg and hip."

Harry whistled. "You won't be going anywhere for a while until that lot's healed, then."

"No. But when it does…"

Despite his injuries, Robert could not disguise his determination to return to England.

He fell silent as the young nurse on night duty began her rounds, taking pulses and checking charts. When she reached him, he asked for a drink of water.

"Ich spreche kein Englisch," she replied, shaking her head apologetically.

"Ich möchte bitte ein Glas Wasser," said Robert.

"Ja."

After the nurse had gone, Harry asked quietly, "Where'd you learn to speak German then, old man? You're not some kind of spy are you, planted to get information out of us Brits?"

"Hardly, with these injuries."

"They could have been done deliberately."

Robert chuckled. "I'm no spy, I can assure you. I read German at university. And before the war, my family and I used to spend every summer in France, so I'm fluent in French as well. After I got my degree, I spent six months in Berlin on an exchange programme. When that finished and before I joined the army, I went south for the rest of the year, exploring Baden-Württemberg and most of Bavaria."

Harry whistled. "That must have been quite something."

"It was. In more ways than one."

When Robert didn't elaborate further, Harry asked, "Do you speak any other languages?"

"Welsh."

His companion regarded Robert with something akin to admiration. "Well I'm blowed. A ruddy linguist! You could be a useful person to know when we make our escape."

64

"So you've decided to tag along?"

"Maybe. We'll have to see. I'll be the ideas man. You know, behind the scenes."

The nurse brought Robert's water, temporarily stalling their conversation. She helped him to take some sips, and afterwards, when she had gone, Robert closed his eyes.

"You need to rest, my friend," said Harry. "We'll talk some more another time."

"As long as you're not a spy, planted to get information out of me," replied Robert, with a smile.

Harry chuckled. "My pater would love that! He's on the staff of the G.O.C. in Singapore."

"I'd keep that to yourself, if I were you," observed Robert, as he drifted off to sleep.

After a week, Robert was transferred to a hospital near Lille and remained there for a further month. He didn't see Harry again until they found themselves together in a battered old bus driving up through France and into Belgium in a convoy of similar vehicles, all carrying previously wounded men in varying stages of recovery.

With the weather being fine and sunny, with several stops for food and water and the accompanying German guards being vigilant but polite, a certain holiday spirit prevailed among most of the prisoners being transported.

There were some who stared morosely into space or remained on the bus when comfort breaks took place: too hot to move, too careless of what might befall them to make any effort. But many of the men exchanged stories if they found themselves out of earshot of the guards; their nervous laughter and forced banter echoing across the fields.

Some, like Robert, pondered their fate in quiet, discreet voices while looking out across at the countryside which, with its hedgerows and cultivated fields surrounded by gentle rolling hills, reminded them of England and home. They began to speculate on what might happen should the war be lost.

For Robert, after witnessing the sacrifices of his comrades to enable the return of others to England, this was unthinkable. He was unable to say where this inner conviction came from, only that he knew with absolute certainty that one day, the allies would prevail. They *had* to prevail.

Whatever the varying thought processes of the men were, these stops became relatively peaceful interludes amid a shared uncertainty for the future.

When they reached their destination – the *Gare du Nord* in Brussels – the accompanying *Wehrmacht* guards departed. They were replaced by soldiers wearing the distinctive uniforms of the *Waffen-SS*.

The prisoners were ordered off the coaches. Brutally.

Rifle butts and bayonets were employed to get the men moving out of the vehicles, where they were met with further denigration from additional *SS* guards at the station entrance. Up to this point, Robert had been well treated but the viciousness and arrogance of these men shocked and saddened him; his months of being cared for with humanity and compassion leaving him unprepared for this sudden onset of physical violence and verbal abuse.

Perhaps, he tried to tell himself, he should not look upon it as being totally unexpected. The Germans had made astonishing progress in their campaign and would now regard themselves as the masters of Europe. The British army had been pushed back across the Channel and from the Nazi perspective, had suffered an ignominious defeat.

How often he had heard the phrase, *'England in sechs Wochen'* while in hospital, so certain were his captors that England would be invaded in six weeks. Perhaps, as prospective conquerors, they felt they could act in any manner they chose. But this… this was sheer barbarism, unprovoked and extreme.

Robert wondered if it was a deliberate attempt to break the physical and mental resolve of their captives and render them more docile and easier to guard. If that was the case, they did not understand the mentality of their prisoners. Or was it just that these black-uniformed soldiers were acting in the traditionally perceived role of arrogant bully?

He hoped fervently that if the situation were reversed, the British would not deal with their prisoners in such a ruthless manner but according to the humanitarian guidelines laid down by the Geneva Convention: a document to which he knew the Germans were signatories. However, the *SS* soldiers were, at this moment, blatantly disregarding its mandate. Perhaps the *SS* didn't recognize the Geneva Convention and therefore ignored its protective clauses.

He wondered if it was a foretaste of things to come.

Bruised and battered, he and his compatriots were joined by hundreds of other prisoners who had been waiting in the forecourt of the station when they had first arrived. Together, they were herded along the platform like maltreated cattle to the boos and jeers of people lined up on the opposite platforms.

It was this that upset Robert the most. The other could be explained away, just about. This could not. He and his friends had come to the aid of the Belgian people. Surely there should be sympathy and gratitude rather than derision? True, the allies had lost the battle, but thousands of good men had died in the attempt.

Then his eye was caught by a woman who refused to call out. He saw her fall as a rifle butt was directed at her head from one of the soldiers standing behind. Although angry at her callous treatment and frustrated that he could do nothing, Robert now understood exactly what was going on.

To the victor, the spoils; to the losers, degradation and humiliation.

It was a brutal lesson to learn, but it fuelled his inner determination and resolve not to sit out the duration of war in some prison camp. He had to do *something*; he had to get back into the thick of it. But he also knew he had to bide his time and plan.

Very carefully.

They were pushed and shoved into the waiting cattle trucks, crammed closely together, sixty men or more to a wagon. There was little or no room to sit down and most had to stand. There were no sanitary arrangements, neither were the men allowed out of the trucks when the train stopped, so conditions were grim. No food was provided, apart from the odd loaf of stale bread thrown into the truck from a station platform, which only the men nearest the door could reach, together with the occasional bucket of water.

66

For three days, they endured this nightmare with the train stopping for long periods for no apparent reason or shunted from siding to siding to allow other trains to pass. One man died in Robert's truck and this was not discovered until they had reached their destination.

It took all his resolve not to succumb to the blind hatred that some of the men had developed towards their captors. He knew he had to maintain his integrity, his impartiality; his regard and respect for the German people as a whole; clinging onto his knowledge and belief that not everyone in that cultured and learned nation condoned or would behave in such a sadistic and brutal manner.

However, this resolve was tested to the limit when, after leaving the railway yards on reaching their destination, they were force-marched through the town to the taunts and derision of the waiting women lining the street. They were showered by stones and rocks or whatever the waiting civilians could lay their hands on, all directed with uncanny accuracy.

Robert, fortunately, found himself in the middle of the column and was protected to a large extent from the missiles and spittle directed at the soldiers. He shut his mind to its dehumanizing effect, struggling to keep up with the rest, his legs and shoulder on fire.

Further ignominy awaited the prisoners when they arrived at the Transit Camp just outside Mainz. After being lined up, the officers were separated from the other ranks and the recovering wounded directed to the hospital hut – where the same fate awaited them regardless of rank.

They were given a shower (blessed relief) then shaved of every bit of hair they possessed. When asked why by Robert, the barber replied, in very good English, that it was to make sure 'they did not have any lice'. The Germans seemed obsessed with lice, as they were also obliged to strip off and have their clothes put into an industrial dry-cleaning machine where poison killed any offending creatures.

Stoically, Robert submitted to these indignities, knowing that it was better to be clean than verminous, especially as lice carried typhus and typhoid fever. Many of the men who had joined them at the station spent most of the journey itching and scratching. Having spent three days and nights in such close proximity to them, Robert was grateful for his captors' Teutonic thoroughness. However, he was not alone in experiencing the humiliation of having all his hair compulsorily removed by someone else, especially when it came to his private parts.

Robert's wounds were checked and redressed and found to be healing well. He was told he would be left with scars, that he was "lucky to have been treated so expertly" and would be left "with a slight limp". Robert accepted this verdict with equanimity and resolved to work hard in ensuring that he was not.

It became yet another factor in maintaining his inner strength and identity, whatever unpleasant situations he may, in the future, be forced to endure.

After being given a rough set of clothing, he was shown into a room off the main ward and given a chair upon which to sit. Very shortly afterwards, a bespectacled man in a black coat entered and sat down opposite him. Robert refused the proffered cigarette.

"You are wise, my friend. It is a bad habit. Look, my fingers are stained yellow," he held out his hand, "but even so, I cannot stop." He smiled. "Tell me about

England. I like your country. I spent many months there and know it well. I have friends in London. Do you know London?"

Robert looked at him. "My name is Robert Llewellyn Anderson. Rank: Lieutenant. Service Number: 7346121. I am not obliged to tell you anything else."

"Of course not." The man's voice was silky-smooth. "But I am interested in your country. It is very beautiful. Such variety of scenery. There must be many things that are being done to protect England against invasion. Perhaps if you tell me, I can put your mind at rest as to their effectiveness and you will know your family and loved ones will be safe." He smiled again. "So, therefore, tell me about the defences your country is constructing. I shall keep this information to myself, of course. It will be our secret."

Did this man think he was stupid? In any case, Robert hadn't been home in eight months and even if he had and knew what was going on, he was hardly likely to say anything. Nevertheless, this man and what he might do next made him feel uneasy. He repeated his name, rank and number.

"Yes, yes," the man replied soothingly. "You must miss your family. Tell me where you were born."

"I am Lieutenant Robert Llewellyn Anderson. Service Number 7346121."

"Perhaps some beer? You like beer?"

Robert shook his head.

"No cigarettes! No beer! What do you like? Girls? I can arrange for you to visit a suitable establishment if you would just tell me what I need to know. What is your regiment and what number was your battalion? In which part of France were you fighting before you were taken prisoner?"

"Why don't you ask the fellow who picked me up? He could tell you."

"But I want you to tell me." His voice was insinuatingly nauseous.

Robert shook his head again.

Abruptly, the man changed tack. "What is the state of civilian morale in England?"

"I have no idea."

"Come, come. You must have."

"No. None." Robert was pleasant but noncommittal.

"What are the intentions of the Allied leaders?"

"I have no idea."

"Are you not interested in politics?"

Robert was, but he wasn't about to reveal that fact. He shook his head again.

"Will your country accept peace terms?"

"That's not for me to say."

"Is England turning communist?"

Robert laughed at him.

"What is the British people's opinion of Winston Churchill?"

"Who?"

"Stop playing games. You know very well who I mean."

Robert looked at him. Of course he did but again, he wasn't about to share anything with his interrogator.

Very unpleasantly, the man said, "You have not answered enough of my questions."

"As far as I'm aware, I haven't answered any of them," Robert replied, remaining outwardly calm while his mind speculated on what this was about and what might be the end result of this encounter.

"You are in no position to be impertinent."

"Well, look at it this way – if our roles were reversed, would *you* have given *me* any more information?"

Suddenly, the man burst out laughing. "Very clever, *Leutnant* Anderson. I admire cleverness and verbal dexterity." His manner became pleasant once more and he said, "As you will not answer my questions, you may go. The guard outside the door will take you back to the infirmary."

"Thank you," said Robert, slightly mystified by the man's lack of persistence, wondering what was going to happen next.

What happened next turned out to be nothing sinister. He was photographed, his fingerprints taken, his height measured, his weight recorded, his home address and next of kin documented. He was informed that these details would be passed onto the Red Cross who would notify his government. He was given a postcard supplied by the Red Cross which he could send directly to his family to let them know that he was safe.

He was then informed, officially and sombrely, that he was now a *Kriegsgefangener* – a prisoner-of-war.

So, having been shorn, deloused, registered, interrogated and his uniform returned (clean and smelling of chemicals) at the transit camp, Robert and his fellow P.O.W.s were now ready to be transported to their permanent camp. For him, this was to be Seeblick in Baden-Württemberg – an area of Germany he knew very well.

Robert couldn't believe his luck.

CHAPTER 10

St Nicolas

The invasion of the Channel Islands happened quietly. There was no bombardment, no rushing ashore of tanks or troops. There was no loss of life, no tragedies.

One German plane touched down at the deserted airport on Guernsey after making several reconnaissance flights. The pilot, acting entirely on his own initiative, took a quick look round the buildings to confirm that they were indeed empty and that the island was undefended from the air. After reporting these facts to his superiors, a transport plane with ground force troops was hastily despatched to the island, thus usurping the *Kriegsmarine* who had been charged with the responsibility of invasion but had been over-cautious and hesitant in executing their plans for an amphibious assault.

The only difficulty encountered by the *Luftwaffe* in landing were cows grazing at the end of the runway, but once these bovine obstacles had been scared away, they descended onto the grassy strip and immediately occupied the airport. Within a few hours, their superior officers were established in their chosen headquarters and in control.

It was nearly a week later that the first German troops arrived on St Nicolas. Silently, the people of Port le Bac lined the quayside and the sloping harbour road: expectant, afraid; looking on as the E-boat carrying a contingent of the German military moored alongside the pier. The senior officer on board, Major Albrecht von Witzenhausen, stepped onto the soil of St Nicolas to be greeted formally by the Meneur of the Consell de Souverain.

Major von Witzenhausen was a member of the German aristocracy: well-read, highly educated and a gentleman who spoke near-perfect English. He had entered the army as a cadet and served with distinction during the Great War before being invalided home near the end of the conflict after receiving a bullet to the chest. Once fully recovered, he moved into administration, taking an active interest in all organizational aspects of the military before choosing to retire in 1935. Much to his surprise, he was recalled once again to active service in 1938.

He was part of the old school, trained in the traditions of chivalry and decency, who lived and acted according to these principles and who took every opportunity to impress these values upon the younger soldiers in his charge. He was an excellent administrator as well as a clearheaded strategist; a strict disciplinarian who also believed in fairness and justice and was thoroughly professional in all that he did.

St Nicolas was very fortunate. Their new *Kommandant*, by virtue of his great experience, was well placed to oversee both the army of occupation and the military government (the *Feldkommandantur*) which, in accordance with military law, would take over the day-to-day running of the islands after the invasion troops had consolidated their position.

Alone among the Channel Islands, because of its strategic value in being so close to France, he would remain in charge on St Nicolas even after the arrival of the

Feldkommandantur. He was answerable only to the overall commander of the Channel Islands based in Jersey and the Military Government in Paris.

Major von Witzenhausen had no patience with Hitler's philosophy but was possessed of a deep patriotism for his country, the *real* Germany, which he saw as a separate entity from the totalitarian Nazi state. His views were well known amongst the intelligentsia and he was under no illusion that his superiors had given him this particular post to keep him out of the way. At the same time, however, he was very aware that they recognized in him the right person to handle the delicate job of achieving the *Führer*'s aim of total occupation of the islands.

Major von Witzenhausen clicked his heels and shook hands with Sir Anthony le Clerc, the Meneur, who then introduced the German officer and his senior staff to the other members of the Consell de Souverain. To the watching islanders the proceedings appeared to be more like the formal greetings given to visiting dignitaries than the arrival of an occupying force.

As he scanned the waiting faces above him, Major von Witzenhausen saw no fear or hostility, only a neutral curiosity. That was good. This was to be his kingdom; these were to be his subjects and he resolved to govern them fairly but within the strictures and guidelines laid down by the *Oberkommando der Wehrmacht* – the Armed Forces High Command.

He was looking forward to taking up his new post, which would probably be the last before he retired for good. Although still with the energy and vitality of a much younger man, having attained the age of sixty-five, he was looking forward to once more living in the country and tending his farm, surrounded by his children and grandchildren.

Major von Witzenhausen was escorted into a waiting car and, accompanied by the Meneur, whisked away to the Commodore's house, one of the finest on the island, which was to be his headquarters. The Commodore and his wife had been asked to move out by the Consell de Souverain, much to their resentment, to occupy the little lodge situated in the grounds.

Vera especially had protested vehemently but Sir Anthony had silenced her, explaining that if the occupying force was treated with courtesy, they might be more well disposed towards the people of St Nicolas.

Smiling flirtatiously at him, an expression of which he took absolutely no notice, being a happily married man occupying a very prominent position on the island, she had tried her best to make him change his mind.

In the end, she had had to accept his reasoning, privately deciding there and then to assuage her resentment of this inconvenience by bestowing upon the newcomers her own particular brand of welcome whenever the opportunity arose.

Vera was ambivalent about the war, not having any particular sense of patriotism, and had, as yet, found no one on the island to keep her amused. She had agreed to marry Eric three years previously in what she now knew to be the mistaken belief that his money alone would be enough to satisfy her needs and stave off potential isolation as she headed towards middle-age. Having relinquished her fun-loving, party-filled existence in London, Vera was disappointed to find St Nicolas society (and the male of the species in particular) so terribly *dull*.

After witnessing the arrival of their "new Lords and Masters", as Edna had so aptly phrased it, she and Sophie turned away from the quayside, untied Stargazer and trotted back home in the trap through the leafy lanes where red and pink campion now flowered in hedgerows bathed in warm sunlight. The summer was as beautiful as ever.

Nothing seemed to have changed. And yet everything had changed.

"They didn't seem too fierce," observed Sophie.

"No," admitted Edna.

"I've been wondering whether or not we should let on we speak German."

"Yes, I was wondering the same. We'll just have to see how things work out." Edna sighed. "Well, whatever happens, I think that Sir Anthony is correct in his attitude towards them. The new *Kommandant* certainly reciprocated in kind. He looked all right to me, rather agreeable, in fact. But from all the terrible stories we've been hearing, I suppose you never can tell."

"With bees."

It took Edna a moment to recognize Sophie's allusion but when she did, she chuckled. "I wonder what his character will turn out to be?" she mused, taking up the thread. "I imagine he sees himself as Owl."

"As long as he's not a Tigger bouncing around all over the place."

"Hm. That could become very tiresome. He's a little too long in the tooth for that, I think."

"Perhaps we should invite him to tea and give him honey just in case he's a Pooh Bear."

"He didn't look like a Pooh to me."

"No, much too stern. I hope he's not an Eeyore and down on everyone and everything."

"I don't think so. I'll wager there's a twinkle there somewhere. Perhaps we should tease it out of him."

"Depends how good his English is."

"If it's non-existent, then we would have to reveal that we speak German."

Sophie took a deep breath. "If only it might be that easy."

"I know," replied Edna, serious once more. "That's the problem. The test is yet to come, I think."

At first, life continued much as before, except that every time Sophie went into Port le Bac, she had to adjust to goose-stepping soldiers and German brass bands, who seemed to crop up everywhere playing over-jolly patriotic music in the High Street, in the park and along the harbour road. She didn't mind for herself, but there were plenty who took offence.

"Gets on my nerves," remarked Mabel, the taxi driver's wife who ran the café on the seafront, watching them from the window.

Sophie murmured noncommittally at this and continued to sip her lemonade, having entered the café in desperate need of liquid refreshment after doing her shopping in scorching summer weather.

"All day, every day they're at it. Don't they ever run out of puff?" continued Mabel.

"Beats me 'ow they don't melt with all this heat," added George, her husband, keeping a careful eye out for any potential customer approaching his taxi parked beside the harbour wall. "What d'you think Tommy, me lad?"

Tommy, a freckly boy of about ten years of age, put his head on one side to consider. "Me Mam says they're a bleedin' nuisance but I quite like them. They liven ev'ryfink up. We never 'ad nuffink like that in London before we left."

"No, I don't suppose you did," replied Mabel acerbically. "And *you* need to watch your language, young fella me lad," she added, privately resolving to have a quiet word with his mother on that score. This was St Nicolas, not the East End, even though she herself originally came from London and was not unknown to utter the odd swear word or two when provoked.

Mabel was proud of the fact that she had changed her ways considerably since coming to live on the island at the end of the Great War. She felt she had gone up in the world when an unexpected windfall from an unknown distant relative who died in the trenches had enabled her and George to leave the dreary streets of the capital and set up home and business here.

She thought that Gertie ought to make the effort to change as well. Still, it couldn't be easy for her with Cyril in the army and she left on her own with a lively, but goodhearted lad.

"Sorry, Mrs Hoskins," said Tommy, suitably chastised.

The victory parades continued unabated through the town centre for some weeks, attracting general curiosity at first but soon losing their novelty for the residents apart, that is, from small groups of boys who took great delight in running alongside the troops or copying their marching style.

The soldiers seemed unperturbed by this but the young lads were usually rounded up by the British policeman who always walked in front of the parades, and sent on their way or dragged home by worried parents afraid of what the enemy, should they take offence, might do to their offspring.

There were many people who resented seeing German sentries posted outside the Town Hall and disliked having to stand with grey-uniformed soldiers queuing to catch the bus or going into the little cinema, even turning their backs when greeted with a friendly smile or polite "Good morning."

They did observe, however, that the occupying soldiers seemed to have a particular passion for shopping – which was good for local businesses even though the retailers in the High Street quickly sold out of cigarettes, tobacco and other luxury items as, on arrival, their uninvited guests made a beeline for the still well-stocked shops.

Also, for some reason, the Germans loved anything that was British, especially Scottish cloth of which they bought rolls and rolls in order to have made up into smart tweed suits. Astutely, the only draper's in Port le Bac kept back his best fabric and only sold stock that had gone out of fashion and had been sitting in his store room and cupboards for years, thus making a tidy profit in the process and not depriving the islanders of the best quality fabric he had to offer.

It appeared to be every German serviceman's aim to have a photograph taken with a British 'Bobby' or outside a British shop, especially if the building had a famous brand name clearly displayed. Consequently, Woolworth's and Lloyd's

Bank became magnets for off-duty personnel keen to send to relatives back home this irrefutable evidence that part of Great Britain had been conquered.

The German troops were good-humoured, well-behaved and friendly towards the local population. They played football with the children in the park, picked them up and dusted them down if they fell over, even going so far as to organize a children's party, just to show how much they cared and how benevolent and kind they were.

The townspeople were surprised. Could these cheerful, courteous men really be the same Germans who were responsible for the atrocities they had heard so much about? Many shook their heads and said that it was only a matter of time before they showed their true colours, while others observed that perhaps stories of their cruelty had been grossly exaggerated.

"After all," remarked Ethel, the postman's wife, quietly to Sophie as they stood watching the marching soldiers, "they think they're winning the war, don't they, so they can afford to be generous, can't they?"

Sophie listened and politely acknowledged this observation.

Mae was making a good recovery. She was now sitting up in bed, or spending a little time downstairs on the settee, reading and resting.

Sophie had settled completely into her new routine as chief cook. Her culinary skills had improved beyond all recognition and whenever Mae felt strong enough, she would spend the occasional afternoon writing down recipes and methods to her aunt's dictation. There had been a few disasters at first but Edna had laughed them away, womanfully eaten them and wisely put it down to experience.

Sophie wished she could write about this to Richard, remembering his disparaging remarks about her cooking skills but, as all communication with the mainland was now forbidden, she decided to keep a diary so she could share her life with him when the war was over.

It seemed odd that she could contemplate this fact when they were just at the beginning of an enemy occupation and yet she could. Deep inside, she had an unwavering conviction that Britain would win the war. Where this came from she was unable to say, but it was there, nonetheless.

Yet Sophie did not resent or hate the Germans, as some people did. She just accepted that they were on St Nicolas. She did not find their language alien, as many people did, because she spoke it fluently herself. She was familiar with German literature and folklore and having lived in Germany itself, their ways were not strange to her, as they were to some. She was surprised at how quickly she became accustomed to the guns and marching.

Although Sophie never had been in the habit of going out in the evening on her own, she disliked on principle the imposition of the curfew but accepted it as part of their situation. She possessed no gun, neither did her aunts, so the edict demanding that all weapons should be surrendered, did not bother her. They didn't drink, so the forbidding of the sale of alcohol did not concern her, nor did the closing of all licensed premises. She and her aunts possessed no large boat, apart from a little sailing dinghy which hadn't been used for years and which they cunningly disguised and hid away in the barn.

"Just in case," remarked Edna to Sophie as they completed the deed. "But we won't tell Mae, will we? Otherwise she'll only worry. I'm sure she's forgotten that we still have it anyway."

Therefore, the hassle of obtaining a permit to leave the harbour at Port le Bac to go fishing did not affect Sophie either. Naturally, she was concerned for the people she knew and the three women sympathized with their friends who were affected

However, things began to change when the *Feldkommandantur*, the bureaucratic wing of the military, arrived. They gradually began to infiltrate every aspect of daily life and the restrictions on freedom became more pronounced as they set about implementing to the letter the edicts that came out of the Military Government in Paris, whether it was relevant to the Channel Islands or not.

Their first visit to the farm came about six weeks after the invasion. Sophie had gone out to check on Bluebell, one of the cows, who had seemed under the weather that morning and who had remained tethered in the barn rather than being taken out to pasture.

She came across two German officers with clipboards taking measurements and making notes on equipment and facilities. They did not see her, so she slipped quietly back to the house to fetch Edna and the two women made their presence known to the strangers.

"What are you doing here?" demanded Edna.

"No English," said the officer with the clipboard, who turned away from her and continued to make notes.

"Then perhaps you'd better get some."

Edna was terse and annoyed. Where had all the carefully cultivated courtesy and consideration gone? What right did these men have to walk around her farm as if they owned it?

She realized it was time to reveal her German. She repeated her question. *"Was machen Sie hier?"*

"We are here to survey your farm," he replied surprised.

"Warum wurde es mir nicht gesagt?"

"You were not told because there was no need for you to know."

"On the contrary, this is my farm."

"Nein. It is part of the German Reich now."

Edna bit her tongue. She was not going to argue for fear of reprisal. There had been a few tales of maltreatment filtering through from Port le Bac when orders had not been complied with. The honeymoon period was over it would seem.

The officer looked at Sophie and smiled.

"You are very pretty."

She ignored him. He shrugged his shoulders and returned to his clipboard.

Edna drew herself up to her full height and took a deep breath. *" Gehen Sie sofort weg, bitte. "* It was a command not a request. *"You may return and do your survey when you have gone through the proper channels."*

Taken aback, the officer said, *"We are finished here, anyway."*

His companion looked at him. Were they? He thought they'd only just begun. He admired the old lady for her stance, though.

"Really?" Edna was sceptical. *"I shall take this matter up with the Kommandant."*

"It will make no difference. You must present all grievances to the leader of your ruling council. The people of the island are not permitted to speak directly to Major von Witzenhausen."

"Why?"

"Because they are not."

"Hm."

Sophie recognized the inflection in her aunt's voice and knew that she would be determined to see both Sir Anthony *and* this Major von Witzenhausen, standing no nonsense from either of them.

However, Edna was obliged to do nothing, for the following morning, just as she and Sophie were returning from the dairy, a large car, which the two women recognized as belonging to Sir Anthony, drew up in the farmyard but instead of the Meneur, the driver opened the door to a tall, dapper-looking German officer who, when he emerged, clicked his heels and bowed.

"Please allow me to introduce myself," he said in perfect English. "I am Major von Witzenhausen. I wished to meet the *gewaltige* lady with her arm in a plaster cast, who made my officers return prematurely before they had completed their task and who, they tell me, speaks perfect German. To hear my language spoken properly is a rarity on St Nicolas and I am come to hear you speak it for myself."

"I am not a puppet to speak German at someone else's whim."

The major inclined his head, his eyes revealing a hint of amusement. "Of course. I was not suggesting that should be the case. I speak good English as you can hear. Perhaps we can talk in both languages." He smiled. "May I come inside?"

Edna relented, but only slightly. "If you must."

She showed him to the sitting room where Mae, her shoulders covered by a shawl and her feet resting on a pouf, was reading. She looked up from her book in surprise.

Edna introduced her. "This is my sister Mae. And this is Sophie, my niece."

Major von Witzenhausen clicked his heels and bowed once again.

"Please do sit down, *Herr Major*. I shall make us all some tea. I presume you like tea?" asked Edna.

"Yes."

Edna nodded at Sophie, indicating that she should stay. Sophie looked askance at her aunt. How would she manage in the kitchen with only one hand?

"Perhaps, my dear, you could join me in a moment?"

She nodded.

The three of them sat in strained silence for a while and when Sophie could see that Aunt Mae had recovered from her surprise, she went into the kitchen to help Edna. She closed the door quietly.

"What do you think? Good or bad? Trustworthy or not?" she said as she filled the teapot with hot water.

"Good, I think. He seems genuine. I suspect he's homesick."

"But he's only been on the island a couple of months."

"Yes, but he's no spring chicken and I would guess he likes his home comforts."

"How can you tell? We've only just met him."

"I don't know. Just something about him."

In the sitting room, Major von Witzenhausen scanned the room, then smiled charmingly at Mae.

"This is a very pleasant room. It reminds me of my home with all the trinkets and photographs."

"Indeed." Mae was polite but noncommittal.

"My town house is in Frankfurt but my heart is in Bavaria."

"Ah." She didn't probe further.

"This country home is a small *Schloss* situated high up in the mountains," continued the Major conversationally, "which has been in my family for many generations. It is a beautiful house in a beautiful situation overlooking a lake."

Mae nodded.

"I miss it very much," he added, but with a certain wistfulness.

"Ah."

After a few moments of silence he said, "Do you also speak German like your sister?"

Mae nodded again.

"And your niece?"

"Yes."

"All of you fluently?"

"Yes."

"I am curious. How is this possible?"

Mae took a breath. There could be no harm, surely, in telling him?

"My father was born in Germany, so when we were growing up, we spoke German as a matter of course. And French. My mother was born here on St Nicolas, but her grandparents came from France."

He smiled, his manner brightening. "And your niece?"

"My father taught her the language. She speaks French also."

Mae found herself in something of a dilemma. Had she revealed too much? After all, this man was supposedly the enemy. But he didn't seem like it.

She was saved from further quandary when Edna and Sophie returned. After her aunt had sat down, Sophie handed round the cups but Major von Witzenhausen declined the proffered biscuits.

"Thank you, no. I have not long eaten an excellent breakfast."

He took a sip of tea, appreciating the fine bone china and his comfortable surroundings.

"I wish to apologize for the intrusion of the two officers yesterday. Their work is necessary, I'm afraid, but they should have announced their intentions first."

Edna looked at him. "And what are their intentions?"

"Permit me to explain. The Channel Islands are now considered to be part of the *Département de la Manche*, a sub-district of the Military Government Area A, the headquarters of which are situated just outside Paris in Saint-Germain. The *Feldkommandantur* have been ordered to conduct a survey of the islands, the population and its distribution, housing stock and so on. But it is the farms that are of particular importance. We need information on the number of farmers and the size of their holdings, of their stock and storage facilities, the amount of land under cultivation, the variety of crops grown, the yield of normal harvests, the number of animals, milk production and so on. As you can imagine, it is a great undertaking.

"The question of food production will become increasingly important as time goes on. Formerly, as I understand it, and please correct me if I am wrong, the islanders relied on supplies from Great Britain to make up the shortfall of things which cannot be produced here – feeding-stuffs for dairy herds, fertilizers for the glasshouses and fields, crops that you are unable to grow or manufacture for yourselves. Obviously, that supply line is no longer available – until such time, of course, when Germany takes over England. So, not only is there the need to grow enough food for the inhabitants, but also for the soldiers stationed here.

"For them, we shall expect the farmers to supply us with milk, butter, vegetables and potatoes. Therefore, maximum production will be necessary." Major von Witzenhausen paused for breath and smiled at his audience. "So you see, we need to know what is the capacity of each farm. Then inspectors will be appointed to advise on the best use of land."

Edna looked at him. "I hardly think we need to be told how to best use our land. Farmers have been doing that here for generations."

"And very successfully, I have no doubt. But the situation now becomes quite different. I am sure you can appreciate that?" He smiled again.

"Could the French not supply us with seeds and anything else we might need?" asked Sophie.

"And they shall, but only to a certain extent. A stores assembly point is to be set up in France at Granville and each island is to appoint a representative who will procure the required items."

"You seem to have thought of everything," observed Edna drily.

"I hope so, *Fräulein Weissman*." He replaced his cup and saucer on the occasional table which had been placed in front of him and stood up. "Now, if you'll excuse me, I must take my leave."

"I'll show you out."

"Thank you." Major von Witzenhausen clicked his heels and bowed to Sophie. Then to Mae he said, "I hope I might be permitted to call again. *Auf Wiedersehen, Fräulein Weissman*."

"*Auf Wiedersehen, Herr Major.*"

At the door, he said to Edna, "My officers will call at ten o'clock tomorrow morning to conduct their survey. I trust that this is acceptable?"

"It would seem we have no choice."

"No, you do not. However, it is better that relations between us are cordial, do you not agree?"

Edna nodded, reluctantly, knowing it would be hard to relinquish her responsibility for the farm to strangers and in the process, diminish her independence.

She watched as Major von Witzenhausen climbed into his car and drove away.

So, the reality of occupation begins, she thought.

However, Edna had to admit that she found this man considerate and his outlook capable of reason.

Two weeks after the survey was carried out, a lorry full of German troops pulled into the farmyard. Two young soldiers climbed out of the back and the vehicle disappeared down the lane. Politely, they knocked at the back door.

When Sophie answered it, they announced, in careful English, that they were Helmut and Ulrich and that they had been chosen by Major von Witzenhausen personally to work on the farm. *Fräulein Weissman* was to instruct them in what they should do.

"You are required to provide us with lunch at midday and the Major himself will come to inspect our work to make sure it is good. As you can hear, we speak English, but we are told that you speak our language also."

Sophie smiled, amused by their upright and earnest desire to be of assistance.

"If you would like to wait a moment, I shall fetch my aunt," she said.

"Please be sure to tell her we speak good English."

"Of course. Where did you learn?"

"At military school. We were taught by our very fine teacher, *Hauptmann* Heinrich Hoffmeister, the best instructor of English in the whole of Germany," replied the soldier proudly. "He has prepared all of us who come now to the Channel Islands."

Involuntarily, Sophie gave a start of recognition. Had she been reading a book, Heinrich Hoffmeister's name would have leapt off the page at her. Yet there was no logical reason for this – the soldiers had to learn English from someone.

She shrugged her shoulders dismissively and went inside to find Edna.

PART TWO

MAY – OCTOBER, 1941

CHAPTER 11

H.M.S. *Benedict*
North Atlantic

Richard looked at his watch. He had been up on the bridge only for an hour. There were another three to go.

Time stretched before him like a suffocating fog.

He rubbed his hands together in an effort to keep warm while at the same time checking the compass. All was quiet. For the moment. The convoy was on course; the escorting destroyers and corvettes shepherding their charges successfully across difficult seas.

Their current position was to the south of Greenland where, even though the morning had dawned sunny and was as pleasant as could be hoped for in these latitudes, there was the heavy, ever-present Atlantic swell with which to contend.

Richard had long ago overcome his seasickness but since his ship had joined the Iceland-based Third Escort Group in the north-western approaches, the conditions had tested everyone's forbearance to the limit.

Especially his.

For Richard, loathe as he was to admit it, had had enough. He knew he was a reasonably good officer and good at his job but he had come to the conclusion that he was not a natural sailor.

True, he felt a sense of freedom on those rare occasions when the water was calm. He appreciated the early mornings on first watch when the weather was fine and the sun emerged over the horizon. He mostly enjoyed the camaraderie of his fellow officers, but that was about it.

Richard hated the ever-present stress induced by the constant threat of U-boat attack or mines; he hated the days when his dinner slid off the table onto the floor as the ship lurched and rolled from side to side. He hated the nights when he was unceremoniously ejected from his bunk onto the floor in rough conditions. He hated the boredom of staring out across interminable stretches of grey water merging into grey sky. But most of all, he resented the gradual atrophying of his intellectual abilities under the triple threat of sleeplessness, fear and tedium.

However, there was nothing he could do to change any of it. He had to grin and bear it and focus on the job in hand. He checked the compass again and called down to the wheelhouse for a slight adjustment in their course.

"Steer two degrees to port."

"Two degrees to port," echoed the helmsman. "Steady on course two-seven-oh, sir," he called up once the adjustment had been made.

Richard missed Caroline. Although she was more than happy for them to sleep together whenever he was on leave, she was still resisting his suggestion that they should tie the knot. His commitment to her was total and he desperately wanted to make their relationship official, to tell the world that they wanted to be together come what may.

True, they had been fortunate that his leaves had been quite frequent in the past year – those first wonderful few days at the end of May while the ship was under repair after being damaged while leaving harbour (with embarrassment all round); a whole fortnight between July and August when they managed to escape to Cornwall, and a further five blissful days in November. There had also been three consecutive weekends between January and February when H.M.S. *Benedict* was in port for a refit. How lucky he had been in comparison with some of the officers that Richard knew assigned to other ships.

It puzzled him how Caroline was usually able to meet him at the drop of a hat whenever he had leave. Especially at weekends. Surely it ought to be more difficult if she was as busy with this entertainment troupe of hers as she said she was? She was always evasive when he asked her about what she was doing, always changing the subject; never telling him about the events of her day, not talking about the myriad little details as she used to before the war.

If she hadn't been so loving when they were together and affectionate in her letters, he would have wondered whether or not she had someone else tucked away. He knew of several men who had received letters from home or who had come back from leave morose and despondent because their wife, fiancée or girlfriend had gone off with someone else.

He somehow knew this wasn't the case with Caroline but he also sensed that she was holding something back. Several times, vaguely annoyed that she wouldn't tell him anything, he had teased her, trying to prise whatever it was out of her, claiming that she was keeping some deep, dark secret from him. But each time, she had merely smiled, leading him up to their bedroom where she had, without preamble, taken off all his clothes thus putting a definite physical end to his verbal enquiries.

Alone with his thoughts, Richard's body ached with love and longing.

He heaved another deep sigh and checked the compass again. An additional course correction was needed. He duly gave the order and this was carried out.

His thoughts strayed to his sister. He'd actually had a letter from Sophie. She said she had been able to receive her first messages from the family via the Red Cross only in December – six months after the German invasion – and as a consequence of these erratic communications, Richard had received *his* first letter from her only in March.

Sophie didn't say a great deal. What was it, Richard wondered, about the war that turned normally talkative women into strange taciturn creatures or was it just that he was seeking more from them now? He supposed it must be very hard to put into a few words (all she was allowed) everything that had happened during the past ten months.

Sophie did mention that although Aunt Edna's arm was out of plaster, it was still very stiff, causing her an immense amount of frustration. She said Aunt Mae had fully recovered from some recent bouts of bronchitis and that she had an admirer who brought her flowers. Sophie added that it was all very prim and proper and they sat drinking tea while observing the social niceties. She said she found it rather sweet but stated that Aunt Edna did not approve, although she tolerated it. They also had two young German soldiers who had become an indispensable help on the farm.

Richard missed Sophie. He had been devastated when he heard that the Channel Islands had been invaded and she had not been evacuated; full of concern for his sister's safety; angry at his aunts and his mother for not insisting that Sophie return home as soon as the threat of real invasion reared its ugly head. If he'd been able, he would have gone to St Nicolas and dragged his sister home.

Well, he would *like* to have done that, but he was under no illusion that she would have probably resisted him. For all her apparent vulnerability, he was very aware that Sophie possessed a most determined side to her character; stubborn, even.

Just like their mother, thought Richard. No, not a bit like their mother. Margot was a very different kettle of fish.

He knew that she would be in her element with her war work at the Red Cross. She had written that there was so much to organize – parcels for the Channel Islands (now that the Germans had finally allowed the International Red Cross into the mix), food parcels for the enormous numbers of prisoners-of-war that the enemy had accumulated in France, not to mention socks to knit, blankets to crochet, emergency parcels to pack.

Richard appreciated that all this must be a tremendous feat of organization and he was proud that his mother was very much at the heart of things. She was now not only chairwoman of the local branch, but had been co-opted onto the Joint Committee of the British Red Cross and St John's Ambulance at their headquarters in London. The house in Maybury had become a collecting centre and completely taken over for the duration. His father, apparently, when he wasn't at his Club, spent all his time with the Home Guard.

Richard could imagine that and sympathized.

He checked the compass.

"Steer two degrees starboard," he ordered down to the wheelhouse.

"Two degrees starboard," said the helmsman, who, after a few moments called up, "Steady on course two-six-eight, sir."

Richard checked the compass again and spoke to the navigator down below, confirming with his colleague that their present course and speed were correct.

At eight o'clock, his relief came onto the bridge and Richard went down below for a bath and some breakfast before snatching a few moments' shut-eye. He was back on watch at midday as they were shorthanded, with two officers having gone sick. There had been insufficient time to replace them before H.M.S. *Benedict* had had to depart with the outward-bound convoy, leaving everyone who was able to take on extra Watches.

The captain was on the bridge when Richard went back topsides and they chatted for a while about the weather and the convoy. He was a friendly sort and the crew had enormous respect both for his capabilities and his approachability. If the aim of every captain was to create a happy and efficient ship then, within the confines of difficult wartime conditions, John Samuels had certainly succeeded.

Suddenly, a series of tremendous explosions rent the air to the right of the convoy as two merchant ships were engulfed by flame after torpedoes caught them amidships. With a sense of urgency but without panic, Captain Samuels ordered Action Stations and for a signal to be sent to all ships turning the convoy forty-five degrees away from the attack.

H.M.S. *Benedict* set off towards the likely position of the U-boat, scything through the water at maximum speed, her bow throwing up enormous waves either side of the ship which trembled and shook with the impact caused by such sudden velocity.

The corvette *Aster* gained ASDIC contact with the U-boat and began attacking with depth charges while everyone watched as the bulging surface of the sea erupted into a vast fountain, straining their eyes in the hope of seeing oil and debris.

Almost immediately, a U-boat surfaced not four hundred yards from H.M.S. *Benedict*. Captain Samuels immediately gave the order to open fire. The barrage, with every available gun manned by every available crewmember, was deafening and panicked the German submarine crew, who began to pour out of the conning tower onto the slippery surface of the deck.

The captain gave the order to ram and once more, *Benedict* increased her speed, but when he saw that the U-boat had not been scuttled as would normally have been expected, he rescinded the order and swung the ship round to starboard.

Twice the submarine crew tried to man their forward machine guns; twice they were driven back by accurate pom-pom and Tommy-gun bullets. A German sailor (they learned later that he had been the captain) tried to semaphore the bridge of the destroyer, but his signals were unintelligible in the spray thrown up by the heavy seas.

With bullets continuing to rain down upon them, the submarine crew began to jump overboard as fast as they could. By this time, the after deck was awash and the final two men clung to the conning tower amid a hail of murderous fire. Eventually, they too jumped into the sea to join their surviving comrades flailing about in the water.

Captain Samuels ordered his sailors to cease firing and when he saw the survivors being picked up by *Aster*, gave the order, "Away armed boarding party," choosing Richard, by virtue of the fact that he was the officer standing closest to him, to take charge and bring back from the U-boat whatever he could salvage.

"You speak German, don't you, Richard?" he asked.

"Yes, sir, a little."

"Can you read it?"

"Yes, sir, but only to a certain extent. It's been a while."

In that moment, Richard regretted that he hadn't been more diligent when he was younger. How he wished he had been more like Sophie and taken notice of his grandfather when he had been teaching his native language to them both.

However, feeling inferior that he didn't possess her talent for languages, Richard had lost interest early on. He'd enjoyed chess and crossword puzzles, though, and had spent many a companionable hour with the old man doing these as a sort of atonement for not being better at German.

"Well, do your best," said Captain Samuels. "It's not strictly necessary, but it might be helpful."

"Yes, sir. I'll see what I can do."

The gunner's mate issued Richard and his crew with revolvers and ammunition. Together with six seamen, a telegraphist and a stoker, in some trepidation, he was lowered into the ship's rowing boat, a traditional twenty-seven foot whaler, which was heaving about horribly in the turbulent seas.

Throughout the short perilous journey, they were pitched and tossed about on the water, needing all their strength to keep a forward motion. Richard knew he was no hero and he clung onto the tiller with one hand and the side of the boat with the other, outwardly calm as he was the officer in charge, but inwardly fearful and nauseous; his heart pounding so loudly he was afraid it could be heard, even above the waves continually crashing over the prow and dousing them in freezing cold water.

As time was of the essence, Richard steered the boat to the nearest side of the submarine which unfortunately, also happened to be the weather side – a place that received the full force of the wind and which would not have been his first choice in normal circumstances.

Rollers crashed wildly against the hull and with great difficulty, the whaler's crew secured the boat and clambered aboard the slippery spine of the submarine, their revolvers drawn.

Richard presumed the U-boat to be deserted, as they had encountered no hostile fire from the conning tower on their approach, but he knew he had to be the first to go inside as it was his duty not to risk the lives of his men until he could ascertain that all was safe.

He made his way precariously along the deck, his revolver drawn, his gasmask slung across his shoulders, slipping and sliding on the narrow, water-washed surface, holding on to whatever he could grab. He could see numerous holes in the conning tower casing, damage caused by *Benedict*'s three-inch and pom-pom guns and, approaching the conning tower on the starboard side, Richard was surprised to find the watertight hatch closed, especially given the precipitous haste with which the crew had left.

He unscrewed the spherical wheel, released the clip and immediately the hatch sprung open.

Cautiously, his revolver in his hand, he lowered himself through the eighteen-inch wide opening and climbed down the ladder to the lower conning tower where there was a similar closed hatch.

With some apprehension, he opened this also and, feeling rather vulnerable, descended the ladder backwards, gingerly stepping on each rung. If there was actually someone below, it was not a good position for him to be shot at, Richard thought ruefully. However, the control room below was deserted.

In the dim, ghostly interior, lit only by emergency blue lighting, there was an eerie silence, broken only by an ominous hissing sound. He stood motionless, sniffing the air for tell-tale signs of chlorine from leaking batteries. He detected none so, feeling somewhat reassured, he took a chance and discarded his gasmask.

So what was the hissing noise? A rupture in the hull?

With the Atlantic swell sending chilling echoes through the bulkheads and the roar of explosions from depth charges as the convoy's escort drove off further U-boat attacks, Richard experienced real panic – his mouth dry, his heart pounding, his legs weak, his stomach clenched into tight knots.

He held onto the table for support, fearful that the reverberations would detonate the destructive charges that must surely have been set inside their U-boat.

He had to do something to occupy himself; to take his mind away from the possibility of sudden oblivion.

Richard could see that the hatches fore and aft were open and reasonably well-lit so, with shaking legs, he set out to explore. To his great relief, he was able to ascertain that the submarine was abandoned.

With no enemy on board and no explosions ripping their way through the vessel, Richard made himself take deep, steadying breaths. After a few moments, feeling calmer and able to bring his sailors down below, he ordered the signalman to semaphore back to *Benedict* that the submarine was completely deserted.

"T'whaler's smashed to smithereens, I'm afraid, sir," reported the able seaman, apologetically, as he came down the ladder post-haste. "Against the sub. There was nowt we could do to save it."

"Well, get a message back to the ship to that effect. They'll have to send something else to bring us off," said Richard, trying to stem the bile rising in his throat.

Was it his fault for embarking his sailors on the windward side of the U-boat? Should he have gone to the leeward side where it was marginally more sheltered?

"There was nowt anyone could have done, sir."

"No. We had to make for the weather side. We needed to be as quick as possible."

"Yes, sir. Who knows when t'submarine might have gone down."

"Quite."

The seaman disappeared back up the ladder and after a while, the welcome thumps of another whaler arriving could be heard outside.

Reassured, Richard turned to explore the submarine as thoroughly as possible.

The haste with which the U-boat had been abandoned became very clear in the control room as books and gear were strewn everywhere. Richard organized a human chain to pass everything they could lay their hands on up onto the deck and into the waiting whaler for ferrying back to *Benedict*.

When the boat returned to collect the next consignment, the crew brought with them piles of sandwiches. Richard and his men were immensely grateful to whoever it was that had realized they would be on the submarine for some hours and thoughtfully provided them with this repast.

Fortified by their unexpected sustenance, they continued to work as quickly as possible, removing everything they could find. Richard ordered that all books, both in the control room and the wireless telegraphy office, with the exception of reading books, were to be sent up. He knew that speed was of the essence and that there wasn't time to sort through anything as there remained the possibility that the U-boat might sink.

Anything that looked remotely useful was seized and sent up on deck: code books, files, charts, the latter being neatly stored in the drawers under the chart table, together with some other equipment that Richard didn't have time to identify. Valuable metal sheet diagrams were unscrewed from the cabin roof and sent up as well.

It was all in perfect condition. No attempt had been made to destroy any books or apparatus.

Then the telegraphist called Richard into the W/T room.

"This is interesting, sir," he said. "It looks like some kind of typewriter but when I pressed a key, one of these here little bulbs lit up. When I pressed the same key again, a different bulb lit up. It's still plugged in, so it looks as though they were using it when the order came to abandon ship."

Richard took a closer look. There were metal wheels, plugs and lights and in the lid were instructions as to how it should be operated. He cast his eye over the German text, translating the words that he knew and piecing together the sense of the paragraphs.

"Looks like some kind of coding machine to me."

"Shall I unplug it and send it up, sir?"

"Yes, but make sure it's in a box of some kind and as watertight as you can make it. And tell them to take care with it. This could be quite important."

For some reason, Richard felt excited. He had always loved playing around with made-up codes when he was young, first introduced to it by his maths master at boarding school for whom it was a particular hobby. He had encouraged his pupils to follow suit, devoting whole lessons to its mysterious art, pursuing a theory that discovering coded patterns would help further the boys' maths skills.

As a result, finding sequences and structures had always been one of Richard's mathematical strengths. He wondered if Captain Samuels would allow him to experiment with this piece of equipment and the accompanying code books.

Richard looked round the room and ordered that all the signal logs, pay books and general correspondence should be removed as well. From the amount of paperwork it contained, it looked as though this had also doubled up as the submarine's general office.

Forward of the W/T room was the hydrophone office. Richard found that the set was still running and by turning a control knob, he could increase or decrease the sensitivity and alter the bearing on the gyro dial. This was unscrewed but unfortunately, after going to considerable effort in rigging a pulley system to try and bring it through the hatch, the attempt had to be abandoned as it was found to be too large to fit. Reluctantly, they had to admit defeat and leave it behind.

They searched the officers' gear, finding wallets, cameras and letters. These too were sent above and then Richard came across a cine camera. He took a few frames of the W/T and H/D offices but held little hope of having shot anything decent. It might be interesting to see what else the film contained, he thought, when they got back to the ship.

Once everything that could be moved had been removed, Richard took another cursory look around. He was all too aware of how long they had been and the danger still posed by their situation and the possible proximity of U-boats.

He signalled to *Benedict* that he thought the U-boat might be seaworthy and able to be towed and requested that an engineering officer be sent over to see if this was possible or that they could move the sub under her own power. After about half an hour, the officer duly arrived along with another couple of stokers.

Together, they looked at the engines. Despite fiddling with all the dials and switches, they found it impossible to get the starboard engine started. There were instructions (in German) and Richard was able to give a rough translation, but even so everyone could see these were not written in enough detail for the engineer to risk further damage to the submarine by continuing to try.

Meanwhile, *Benedict* had closed in on the U-boat and once Richard had come up on deck, they tried to secure a towing wire. Despite everyone's best efforts, the first one parted.

"Periscope, port bow, sir!" shouted the lookout on the destroyer.

The captain swung his binoculars round.

"So there is!"

He gave the order for an ASDIC sweep and with a shouted apology, *Benedict* set off to investigate, leaving Richard and his boarding party suddenly alone in the middle of the Atlantic Ocean with no ships in sight, clinging onto a submarine that was slowly sinking at the stern as her ballast tanks filled with water with all of them at the mercy of the elements in an increasingly tempestuous sea.

Immediately, Richard ordered his men below where, shivering with cold and fear, they battened down the watertight hatches.

Never before had he experienced such a complete sense of utter desolation.

CHAPTER 12

Seeblick POW Camp
Germany

The little town of Seeblick, from which the *Oflag* took its name, was set high up on a plateau, eighteen hundred feet above sea level and surrounded by rolling fields ploughed by oxen, with dense forest-clad hills beyond.

From the moment he walked towards the camp, Robert knew he was indeed fortunate to have been brought here – for several reasons, not least of which were the spirit-lifting, health-inducing surroundings but most importantly, because it was situated in an area that he had explored some years previously.

"Makes you think you never want to leave," remarked Harry that first night, as they bagged their bunks in the crowded wooden barrack huts that housed sixty inmates, twenty to each room.

"Makes you think it's an ideal place to escape from," replied Robert, already mentally calculating its nearness to the Swiss border.

"Not that you'd get far with a limp like that and a shoulder that won't let you lift anything much."

"I agree. But in this climate, things will improve, you'll see."

Robert's first letters home spoke of the beautiful scenery, bright sunshine and glorious air, reassuring his anxious parents and younger siblings that he was fine and in as good a situation as he could have hoped for given his circumstances. He wrote of the neat, orderly town with its timber-frame houses and castle bell tower that rose so high, it was visible for miles.

As time progressed, he wrote cheerfully of the friends he had made; how his health and fitness were gradually improving; how he kept himself occupied with reading, card games and crosswords. Some men were even creating gardens, he said.

He waxed lyrical about the wonderful Red Cross parcels that started to arrive after they had been in the camp for about seven months, just in time for Easter. He wrote that the parcels contained not only jumpers, scarves, gloves, socks, blankets, writing paper, envelopes, pens, pencils but, most importantly, they also provided lifesaving sustenance. Tinned food especially was a prized possession – corned beef, salmon, potatoes, carrots, beans, peas, peaches, pears, biscuits, jam (luxury!), cocoa, dried eggs and rolled oats were just some of the items supplied by the Red Cross and supplemented by next-of-kin parcels. He urged his parents to send him anything that was edible; as much as they could – he really didn't mind what!

Robert was full of praise for the Y.M.CA. who were providing them with a burgeoning library, musical instruments, props and costumes for the drama society that was rapidly gaining in popularity since its inception. He wrote of the plays and revues being created and how anyone could attend a class in just about anything.

When Robert reread some of his letters before sending them, he realized it sounded as though he was on some kind of camping holiday; that life seemed to be full of relaxation and entertainment. That was his intention, he supposed, to reassure and console his family. He presumed his father, especially, would read between the lines.

Of course, Robert failed to mention the disgusting *ersatz* coffee made from acorns and the watery soup served twice a day, with its pieces of uncooked swede floating in it, supplemented by potato skins gleaned from the German soldiers, who preferred to eat their potatoes peeled. The soup was served either with the occasional mouldy loaf or leaden black rye bread that under normal circumstances would be deemed inedible. Three times a week, the soup contained chunks of tough, gristly meat and cabbage leaves. Until the Red Cross parcels arrived, this had been the main source of nourishment.

In his letters, Robert deliberately omitted the continual gnawing hunger that plagued everyone; nor did he talk about the boredom, monotony and constrictions of camp life that, if allowed to take hold, had such a dispiriting effect on morale.

Although tolerance usually prevailed because the men were aware that friction was self-defeating, Robert accepted that some verbal conflict was inevitable. However, he neglected to mention the bickering and arguments, usually over something quite trivial, that could suddenly erupt as the men's frustration at being cooped up in a confined space with insufficient food boiled over.

Nor did he describe the shared feelings of guilt that they were sitting out the war in relative safety while their comrades were fighting the Nazis. He didn't tell his parents that this was one of the many reasons why most of them kept busy and occupied – not only to work through and dissipate their frustrations in order to keep their tempers under control, but also to give themselves an intellectual and physical outlet for their abilities, to acquire new skills and to give focus and meaning to their time and take their minds away from self-reproach or self-loathing.

Of course, Robert made absolutely no mention of the perimeter fence, consisting of two parallel ten-foot high, barbed-wire fences, six feet apart, with coils of razor-wire in between, that kept them imprisoned and enclosed. Nor did he give a description of the strategically placed observation towers, manned by guards equipped with machine guns and searchlights with clear fields of vision and the orders to shoot on sight any prisoner attempting to climb over or cut through the barbed wire. He totally forgot to remark upon the ferocious guard dogs that patrolled inside and outside the perimeter, ready to be released from their leads at the first sign of trouble.

No, he didn't tell them any of these things.

He also somehow managed to avoid telling them about the times they were left standing to attention for hours on end in the freezing conditions of a Bavarian winter – which had begun with the arrival of chilling winds and heavy snowfalls in mid-November – just to satisfy the whim of the *Gestapo* or *SS* officers paying one of their periodic visits to a *Wehrmacht*-run P.O.W. camp.

Nor did Robert say anything about the meagre fuel ration (briquettes made from coal dust or twigs gleaned from the woods nearby) for a stove that seemed designed to give out as little heat as possible and which was useless at keeping their hut warm. He ignored the fact that the men were unable to counteract the icy draughts that found their way inside, despite their best efforts at creating rudimentary double glazing by covering the gaps between the frames.

No, he would not worry his family with the privations he and his fellow officers endured, for there were many good things that compensated for the bad, including the fact that, on the whole, they were well treated by the guards and officers. There was the odd bully or two and a few others who were arrogant and impatient but for the most part, they behaved correctly and a wary truce existed between captives and captors.

He also knew that with all these omissions, he would give the camp censor the impression that he was settled and had accepted his situation; that he was here for the duration. Which, of course, was exactly the illusion he wanted to convey – for Robert was gradually formulating his escape plan.

The first part of that plan was to get fully fit again. Initially, the meagre diet and wintry conditions caused his wounds to heal slowly but as the weather improved, together with the arrival of the Red Cross parcels and those sent by his family, his progress became faster.

Unlike some camps, the *Kommandant* did not deprive his prisoners of tinned items for fear of the discarded cans being used as part of an escape attempt. Nor did he order them to be deliberately punctured, so that the contents became inedible, as a punishment for some minor misdemeanour or infringement of the rules. He allowed the prisoners free access to the stores where the parcels were kept, trusting that they would be distributed fairly under a system devised by the British officers. They were also allowed to prepare and cook the Red Cross meals themselves.

Robert developed a genuine respect for their *Kommandant*. Major Wilhelm Schmitt had been a P.O.W. in the last war and had been well treated by the British. Therefore, within the constrictions imposed upon him from Berlin, he reciprocated this attitude towards the prisoners in his charge. Robert even heard on the grapevine that, on no fewer than three occasions, by means of tact and guile, Major Schmitt had stood up for his prisoners' rights, thus tempering the more extreme suggestions of treatment towards the British by the visiting *Gestapo* or senior *SS* officers.

With the improvement in their diet, the legacy of Robert's wounds began to heal. He rejoiced on the day he no longer needed any dressings and although he accepted that he would be left with some scarring, he realized that because his wounds had been well treated from the first, with him now eating better food and taking gentle exercise, they had the potential to heal completely.

Having set himself attainable targets, Robert delighted in being able to walk a little further each day. Even in the late-melting snow, he gradually increased the number of turns around the outside of his barrack hut, muffled up with balaclava, mittens and scarf tucked firmly into one of the two large greatcoats shared by everyone in his room.

He began to do a little weightlifting, using chairs, the edge of a table, or whatever came to hand, trying to increase the strength in his injured shoulder. He participated in P.T. and games sessions but for obvious reasons, avoided football and rugby, contenting himself with the general exercise routines taken by a fitness-obsessed fellow officer.

Robert kept a deliberately low profile with the guards, so that when he did eventually leave, he would not be missed immediately.

However, he had yet to decide on the actual method of his escape.

As the weather improved, Robert began to map the layout of the camp – the position, size and function of the huts and the dimensions of the large, white, three storey building, with its terrace looking out across the compound, that housed the administration offices, officer's Mess and accommodation as well as the *Kommandant*'s quarters.

Robert assessed the towers, the searchlights and the routine of the guards. He began to study the personalities of the guards themselves: those that were diligent in their duties, those who were lax. He heard from his fellow officers which ones could be bribed, which ones were intransigent.

He inveigled himself onto tightly-controlled wood-gathering expeditions outside the camp, making surreptitious mental notes of his surroundings – roads, houses, farms, the paths leading to the forest but above all, signposts. When Robert returned to the camp, he would draw all that he had seen until he had built up a clear picture in his mind.

In May, as a morale-boosting exercise, the entertainments' committee decided to organize a stage show to be performed in one of the barrack huts which had a purpose-built concert hall with a proper stage, lighting and seating. When this had first been discovered, they couldn't believe their luck.

"The camp was originally built as a training establishment for the German army in 1939 before we took over," said Harry, who made it his business to know these things.

"Lucky them!" said Robert. "Still, it does mean we're able to live in conditions that are probably better than a lot of other P.O.W.s elsewhere."

"True. It goes completely against the grain to say it, but old Schmitty is probably as good a *Kommandant* as anyone could get. Apart from the food, or lack of it, we're sitting fairly pretty, I reckon." Harry stepped back to admire his handiwork on the scenery he was painting. "What d'you think, old man? More blue in the sky?"

"Possibly." Robert looked at the canvas and considered for a few moments. "How about a few clouds?"

"Don't know whether my artistic skills will stretch that far. But I'll give it a go." Harry began to create white, fluffy blobs. "You doing anything in the show apart from our Flanagan and Allen numbers?"

"Not this time. I'll do more in whatever the next production is going to be. I've got roped into doing the invites."

"So who's coming?"

"Schmitty and most of the German hierarchy. As well as our beloved Major-General Grant and the other senior British officers. As I'll be wearing that top hat and dinner jacket for my Chesney Allen impersonation, I've been nominated to show them all to their seats as well."

"Hard luck, old man." Harry contemplated his artwork again. "Howz about that then?"

"Very good! After the war, you should give up the army and take up painting fulltime."

"What and starve in some rat-infested garret because I can't sell my pictures? No, thank you. I've had enough of hunger to last me a lifetime. After we've won the war – see, your optimism is beginning to rub off on me – I'm going to open a restaurant where I can eat all the food I want, every day, all day. No more pitiful rations for me!"

Robert chuckled. "Perhaps we can go halves."

"No, old man, I can't see you in the catering business. You're an army man through and through." He regarded Robert for moment or two, his head on one side, and then pointed his paint brush at his friend. "Or are you? Nope, I've got it! A headmaster. You're a born leader."

"Really? I hadn't ever thought of myself as a headmaster. I suppose that's because my father's one."

"See, I told you. It's in your blood, old man. There'll be no escaping from it, you mark my words! Your French and German classes here are first rate. And besides, you spend enough time in the library for a whole score of teachers. Since we've started getting books, you've always got your head buried in one. Can't get any sense out of you." Harry dabbed a few more spots of paint onto the backcloth.

Robert smiled. "I enjoy reading. It's a good escape. If I hadn't taken German, I'd like to have done English at university. I love literature. You should give it a go sometime."

"What and spend hours reading other people's drivel or be incommunicado like you are when composing one of your wretched poems while chewing the end of a pencil? Not bloomin' likely!"

Harry grimaced at Robert, who laughed and stood up.

"Talking of books," he said, "two new boxes arrived today. I ought to sort them out before they get trampled underfoot."

"Rather you than me, old man. When I've completed this masterpiece, I'm going to find a quiet corner in the fresh air and have a ciggie. Though that's easier said than done in this place – the quiet corner, I mean. My family keep me well supplied with the pernicious weed, so I don't have any worries on that score. Ah, well, see you later. Rehearsal's at four, don't forget."

Robert smiled. "I'll try not to lose myself in a book or a poem and forget the time."

"You'd better not!"

"See you."

The library was situated across the compound from the concert hall in the same block as the Red Cross parcels store. Inside, it was not much more than the size of a garden shed but Robert had taken it upon himself to keep tabs on the books from the moment they arrived, devising a loan system that enabled them to be signed out, read and returned for further circulation. He had persuaded a couple of roommates to put up some shelving as well as a few others to fashion a small table and a couple of benches and chairs, thereby creating a pleasant reading area where a studious silence usually prevailed.

It did not matter that in Robert's hut several of the straw-filled palliasses had fewer wooden slats underneath them; there were still enough remaining to support even the heaviest of bodies. Of course, he had argued when he went to claim his wood, that because no one had expressed a desire to tunnel out of the camp, they would not be required for pit-props and, as the library was a resource used by nearly everyone, they would be supporting a 'good cause'. In the end, they were 'donated' with only good-natured objections and mild personal ragging thus enabling Robert to create a library of which he could feel justifiably proud.

The two latest boxes, courtesy of the Y.M.C.A., were sitting in the middle of the floor. This was Robert's favourite moment – the sense of anticipation before opening them up followed by the joy of discovery. True, there was always some dross: cast offs that no one else had wanted, but there had also been some absolute gems, real literary classics.

Robert opened the first box and picked up the first book.

Gone with the Wind. He smiled and wondered how many men in Seeblick would actually read that one. *The Grapes of Wrath, Of Mice and Men.* Someone obviously enjoyed John Steinbeck, he thought. On the other hand, perhaps they didn't and that was why the books were in the box. *Lost Horizon* (a good book to read in a prison camp). *Murder on the Orient Express, Death on the Nile, The ABC Murders* (everyone enjoyed a good Agatha Christie 'whodunit'). *Goodbye to Berlin* (someone had a sense of humour). *La Chaleur de la Mer...*

Robert did a double take. Carefully, he lifted the book out of the box. It was a brand new copy; unread, pristine.

The day of its original discovery leapt into his mind.

He could almost smell the sea. He could almost feel the sun's warmth. And he could see the girl, now grown up and beautiful, the way she had evolved in his mind: her eyes as blue as the sky, her features exquisitely perfect. He closed his eyes and immersed himself in the imagined beauty of her personality.

La Chaleur de la Mer remained his only tangible link with her existence. And he was now holding a copy of the novel in his hand.

Since the day of their original meeting, how many second-hand bookshops and libraries had Robert visited whenever he'd had the opportunity, looking for the novel that had, until now, eluded him? In England and Wales, even France, where he and his family stayed during the long summer holidays, had he scanned the shelves searching for this elusive book.

All to no avail.

In ten years, Robert had neither found nor finished *La Chaleur de la Mer*. And now, for it to turn up here, of all places – he could scarcely believe it. He turned the novel over and over in his hands; treasuring, savouring.

He reached for the signing out book. He would be the first to have this copy. For once in his life, he would be selfish. He wondered how many more men in the camp could read French fluently. Probably very few. Perhaps he would have the book out on permanent loan. Until he made his departure, that is.

The thought of leaving the novel behind filled him with alarm. Perhaps he might even take it with him. He could check beforehand that no one else wanted it.

Robert continued to sort through the box, carefully cataloguing each new find in a stock book that, after having taken on the role of librarian, he had discovered blank and unused in the drawer of an old desk hidden under piles of discarded rubbish left by the departing German army.

He had tidied and made the room usable and by doing so, the newly created library had become a bolthole, a small oasis of calm in the privacy-deprived existence that had been his and everyone else's lot for the past ten months.

Robert checked his watch and reluctantly put aside the rest of the books. He would finish putting them on the shelves another time. Placing *La Chaleur de la Mer* safely into the pocket of his battledress, he shut the door and made his way back across the compound to the theatre. It was time for the rehearsal.

A few weeks later, while standing in the wings during the actual performance of the revue waiting to go on stage and watching the act before his – having already waded through a violinist (who hadn't bothered to tune his violin... wait, he was supposed to be a comedian. *Ouch!* thought Robert, putting his hands over his ears); a group of chorus 'girls' complete with grass skirts and skimpy tops (Robert wondered what Major Schmitt and the other Germans would make of this particular manifestation of British humour); a magician (who was actually very good) – Robert had a sudden moment of sheer inspiration.

In that instant, as the ventriloquist came off and he and Harry took to the stage for their Flanagan and Allen impersonation, he knew *exactly* how he was going to make his escape from Seeblick.

CHAPTER 13

St Nicolas

Over time, Sophie discovered that no two islanders were affected in quite the same way by the occupation.

Some, like Mabel, who ran the café by the harbour, resented the German presence right from the start ("Who do they think they are, interfering with our lives and livelihoods?" she was heard to remark loudly on more than one occasion). Her husband, George, urged her to keep her mouth shut and try to be more careful, especially when their field-grey uniformed 'lords and masters' were around.

"They aren't my 'lords and masters', George. Neither are they yours, so don't you forget it," she'd retorted and he'd let the subject drop, deciding that to argue wasn't worth the hassle.

He knew there were plenty more folks who felt exactly the same as Mabel but they were very tight-lipped about it in public, keeping a polite distance from the occupying troops. Thinking about it, he knew he had a few gripes of his own.

Petrol was now in very short supply and he found himself banned from driving his taxicab, along with everyone else whose vehicle was over fourteen horsepower. As George was reluctant to experiment with the alternative – a dangerous-looking but cleverly designed gas-device – in case his precious cab blew up, it meant they had to rely on the café as their main source of income. What with food rationing as well, things were becoming pretty difficult and Mabel was forced to devise ingenious ways of creating meals that people would actually want to eat.

To help things along, George decided to take up gardening and converted the large patch of grass at the back of the café into a productive vegetable garden and Mabel became very proficient at making thick, nourishing soups from the produce he grew.

Fortunately, the soldiers seemed to like the café by the harbour and spent a considerable amount of time and money on the premises during the day. Hence the need, thought George, for Mabel to keep her trap shut, especially as their customers were impeccably well-behaved and tried hard to win round his reluctant wife.

In fact, she never seemed grateful for anything these days; always moaning about this or that and never appreciative of his efforts as she used to be in the old days. After all, he was trying his best to contribute towards the financial pot as well, supplementing their income by running errands and making himself generally useful to the wealthy, elderly ladies who might need the odd repair job or two done around their houses. It wasn't his fault that he could no longer drive his taxi.

George thought that his wife ought to show a little more gratitude at least. Still, he reasoned, they were all under a lot of strain these days, what with all the new rules and regulations that kept coming at you like lava from one of those volcanos he'd once seen on a travelogue at the cinema before the war.

Sometimes, you couldn't keep up with all the changes and he knew of several people, because they'd inadvertently broken some decree or other, who'd fallen foul of the recently arrived police attached to the *Feldkommandantur*, and who seemed intent on upsetting everyone.

No, one had to be careful, these days. Very careful.

Others on the island, like Ethel and her postman husband, Frank, were pleasantly surprised by the demeanour of the occupying forces, who totally belied the tales of atrocities purported by the newspapers when the press was free and British. Ethel and Frank allowed themselves to believe that the Germans were ordinary human beings after all. Apart from food rationing and other restrictive practices, the only thing that made life really difficult for them was that all bicycles had been confiscated. Frank's appeal for an exemption because of the nature of his work had fallen on deaf ears when he, along with everyone else in a similar position, had asked the Consell de Souverain to approach the *Feldkommandantur* with sound and practical reasons as to why they should be excluded from this very real inconvenience.

Frank found himself obliged to walk around the island now to deliver his post, which took forever. But, because of the island's isolation from Great Britain, he had fewer letters to deliver, so it wasn't that bad, he managed to persuade himself. Unlike many on St Nicolas, he was still paid the same wages for his job, an anomaly which he and Ethel took great pains to keep quiet about, especially from the German authorities. They could even afford to purchase a few items on the black market. After all they had the children to consider, didn't they?

Left to themselves, the children on St Nicolas found the German presence a great storehouse for imaginary games. They didn't play cowboys and Indians anymore but airmen and infantry with make-believe German guns and German tanks and planes. That was all they knew – after a year of occupation, the British garrison was a distant memory.

With his father being in the British Army, Tommy was a reluctant observer at first, but he soon joined in with as much enthusiasm as the others, much to his mother's concern, who fussed and worried a great deal lest he became confused and anti-British.

However, Tommy was a sensible lad. *He* didn't have any confusion at all. It was all very simple. His father was fighting the bad Germans and the ones on St Nicolas were the good Germans. They were two separate entities as far as he was concerned. Besides which, he had to join in with his mates, didn't he?

A few, very few, islanders thought they could have their cake and eat it – that collaboration was the only way forward, so that if the war ended with a German victory, they would be in the best position possible to reap the rewards of their efforts. If the Germans should lose, then in the relief and excitement of liberation, their unseemly labours might go unnoticed.

However, they did not bargain for the resentment and hatred that was quietly but effectively demonstrated when their actions were uncovered, particularly if it was to the detriment of someone else. Over time, many people on St Nicolas developed long memories.

There were also some young women who felt a natural desire for male company and found many of the occupying troops to be a willing source, especially as most of the local young men had left the island at the outbreak of war or during the evacuation.

The German soldiers were youthful, energetic, bored, far from home and had money to spend – able to give their St Nicolas dates a good night out at the cinema or the dance hall. Of course, for some, these dalliances developed into genuine love affairs but any girls who went out with the invaders, regardless of circumstance, received the derogatory label of 'Jerrybag' and were treated with contempt.

Despite knowing this, Vera kept to her resolve and lost no time in bestowing upon one particular German her own inimitable brand of welcome soon after he arrived. Being experienced in these matters, she demanded total discretion from the good-looking, high-ranking officer who fell for her charms and with whom she soon indulged in a torrid affair. As he seemed just as anxious for their relationship to remain a secret (his wife back home was known to another officer on St Nicolas) she knew she had no cause for concern and in complete secrecy, they enjoyed their liaison with total abandon. Frequently.

If the Commodore knew, he turned a blind eye, but it was doubtful that he suspected anything for his wife was worldly-wise and careful. Besides, he was only too delighted with Vera's renewed attentiveness towards him during the day – whenever she was at home, that was. He put to the back of his mind the slight niggle that she seemed to be out and about a great deal these days. He consoled himself with the thought that she was becoming more relaxed and settled now.

Eric also had to admit to a sense of relief that she had stopped being so demanding in bed. He wasn't getting any younger and had wondered many times since he had brought her to live in his house on the island whether it had been a mistake for a crusty old bachelor like himself to take on as "frisky a 'gel'" as Vera.

Sophie and her aunts viewed the occupation with equanimity. They lived on a farm, but they were as short of food as the next islander after the quotas had been complied with. So much was required by the German army or for export to France in payment for the coal, clothing, shoes, medicines, fertilizer and agricultural machinery supplied by the French, that many people felt deprived, and justifiably so.

For all their posturing and diktats, the *Feldkommandantur* had proved to be inefficient and not very successful at working out the best system for the island's agriculture and only succeeded in disrupting and disturbing a balance that had evolved over decades of careful land management and animal husbandry. Nor were their officials very good at anticipating the nutritional needs of not just the islanders, but their own troops as well. Very quickly, flour became scarce then potatoes, tomatoes and meat. To combat the latter, the military government ordered the slaughter of all chickens over two years of age, which resulted in an unnecessary egg shortage, and Edna bitterly resented having to plant wheat and barley in fields she knew were unsuitable for the task.

She often went without food in order that Mae should receive the nourishment that she needed, arguing that her physique could withstand fewer meals, whereas her sister's could not. Sophie's already slight frame took on a positively svelte appearance but she persuaded herself and her aunts that she was fine and that she felt like a film star. When the war was over and the Germans had gone home, she could put the weight on again, she said.

However, it was the confiscation of their radio because of some event or other that had taken place on Guernsey that really made Edna angry. She protested volubly in German to Major von Witzenhausen but, while he admired her fluency and rhetoric, he regretted he could do nothing to rescind the order for the time being.

"I could make separate arrangements for you to retain your wireless set but I know you would not want either of us to do anything that could be misconstrued as collaboration, *Fräulein Weissman*," he had replied smoothly, thinking that in his prime, he would have found Edna a highly desirable prospect. She was strong and capable and he had always admired that in a woman. His much-loved wife, regretfully, had not been like that, God rest her soul.

In fact, it was true to say that during the months that had passed since they first met, Albrecht von Witzenhausen had become very attached to Edna. His continuing gentlemanly attentions towards Mae were really a mask for his being able to be in the magnificent, older sister's presence. He knew she would have rejected out of hand any closer interest from him, even if by necessity, given the present situation, they remained outwardly formal and distant. So, he brought the younger sister flowers and chocolates, glad to see her smile as a result of his attentions and regain her rosy cheeks which were, sadly, so pale when they first had met.

Albrecht, genuinely, in a brotherly way, became fond of Mae during these visits, consoling himself with the sporadic presence of Edna, who came in and out of the room during his visits on the pretence of collecting this or that but in reality keeping watch, her lips pursed in disapproval, her eyes full of grudging interest.

This amused him, as did their sparring over various issues and the additional restrictions, about which, regretfully, he could do nothing. He relished their altercations, always conducted in German, delighting in hearing his home tongue spoken in the old way without any of the strident Prussian nonsense that sadly seemed so fashionable these days.

Secure and unthreatened in either position or personality, the Major happily withstood all of Edna's expressions of displeasure because he knew that ultimately, after her protest had been discharged, Edna had no choice but to acknowledge that this or that petty rule could not be changed.

He wondered whether she enjoyed these encounters as much as he did. He liked to think that she did.

On several occasions, under the genuine pretext of his wanting to see the progress made by his two *protégées*, Ulrich and Helmut, they had travelled together around the farm in the horse and trap expertly handled by her niece, the delightful young Sophie who reminded him of his daughter at the same age.

Outside in the sweet-smelling air, Albrecht enjoyed these afternoon jaunts immensely, finding in them a real escape from the constant drudgery of finding ways to keep the army occupied on an island where there was little to do militarily; of wasting his time mediating between the *Feldkommandantur* (military government), the *Feldgendarmerie* (field police), and the recently established secret police (*Geheime Feldpolizei*), whose methods and ideology he despised.

Each organization seemed to feel that their *modus operandi* was the only one that mattered.

There were many occasions when he felt like giving duelling pistols to the power-hungry despots who ran these organizations so that they could settle their petty differences the old fashioned way and leave him in peace.

Major von Witzenhausen knew, however, that he would have to keep a close watch upon and temper the activities of the secret police, though they would argue that he had no jurisdiction over them. He felt there was no place for them on a relatively small island like St Nicolas. Nevertheless, Hitler in his paranoia, had decreed that on the Channel Islands all anti-German sentiments should be eradicated and that the islanders should conform and obey the rules rigidly, especially after the abortive British commando raids on Guernsey and Jersey the previous year. The *Geheime Feldpolizei* had been allotted this task.

Then, to cap it all, Albrecht had had notification that the *Führer*, in his misguided wisdom once again, now wanted to increase the fortifications on the Channel Islands. This would mean the *Todt* organization and slave workers. How he abhorred that particular prospect.

It was all becoming too much for him. Although he was still in overall command on the island, he was beholden to the dictates of the Military Government in Paris and the whims of Hitler in Berlin, unable to change or alter the decrees that were being issued. On St Nicolas, Albrecht could take a certain satisfaction in making some of the edicts less intrusive and the punishment for any minor transgression less harsh but in reality, his hands were tied.

This had not turned into the posting Albrecht had hoped for when he had arrived here with such high expectations of doing good. He was beginning to feel increasingly weary.

His time spent in and around the rambling farmhouse helped restore his sanity and equilibrium and he looked forward to each visit. He always came alone, leaving his driver and uniform at headquarters, and felt as welcomed as could be expected from three staunchly British ladies to the *Kommandant* of an invading army.

Albrecht respected the women's unwillingness to fraternize publicly with either himself or his two *protégées*. He had placed Ulrich and Helmut on the farm not only to help but also as a safeguard, an insurance policy against the Weissman sisters or their niece being tempted to commit any transgression against the rules and regulations. He did not wish any misfortune to befall these ladies with whom he had spent so many pleasant hours.

Little did he realize that every time he came to visit, he was sitting upon a wireless set (cleverly concealed by Edna using the elaborate chintz covers and comfortable cushions) within the wooden frame of the easy chair that had become his preferred place to sit.

When the German police had arrived to take away their radio, Edna and Sophie only owned up to having one in their possession, innocently leading the officer to the offending set in the kitchen, which he duly confiscated.

Edna decided it was probably best not to tell Mae where the remaining wireless was hidden, as this would have made her anxious and worried each time the major came to call and unable to hide a guilty expression.

Sophie and Edna listened to the news every evening after Mae had gone to bed and Helmut and Ulrich had returned to their barracks in Port le Bac. They knew they were taking an extreme risk, but Edna was adamant that she wanted to know the truth of what was happening in the war from the BBC, rather than paying attention to the loudspeaker van (known as the 'quacking duck') that travelled the streets of Port le Bac dispensing propaganda and the latest set of regulations; or relying on the heavily biased German newsreels in the cinema; or the leaflets issued by the *Feldkommandantur* that wasted vast resources of precious paper as everyone immediately consigned their nonsense to the dustbin.

Edna and Mae continued to accept the assistance of Helmut and Ulrich on the farm, who were proving to be invaluable. The two aunts and Sophie found them to be polite young men yet knew them to be homesick, missing their families. The boys themselves, with their daily occupation of farm work, recognized that they were better off than some of their fellows who had no useful job to do during the day and who spent their evenings in the *Soldatenheim* drinking themselves into a comatose state. There would be a crackdown soon, they said to Sophie one day when she brought them their lunch.

"Is this behaviour normal in the German army?" she ventured to ask.

Before he replied, Helmut took a good look around him, as though the very tree under which they were sitting in the middle of the field might have ears.

"Yes. Quite often. The officers issue orders, but still the men drink when they are off duty. Many want to go back home now, you see, to their wives and families. They feel they have been here for too long."

"Some have made girlfriends," said Ulrich, "and they go out each evening. We are only eighteen and too embarrassed to ask any English girls to go out with us."

"We do not wish to be rejected."

Sophie smiled at their honesty. They were two likeable young men who, in normal circumstances, would have been snapped up by any decent girl who had any sense.

"One of our comrades took his own life yesterday," said Helmut unexpectedly.

Sophie was shocked. "Why?"

"He was not able to bear it anymore. He felt trapped here on St Nicolas. There is nowhere to go, nothing to do. He does not like the countryside or the people. He had been rejected by his fiancée at home who wrote to him."

"Two weeks ago, someone else did the same thing," added Ulrich.

"Does Major von Witzenhausen know?"

"Yes and he is very upset. He is taking steps to find ways of keeping the soldiers occupied and has ordered the officers to devise ways of keeping us entertained. They have no imagination, so we think they will not do this very well."

Sophie expressed surprise to hear them speak in such an open manner.

"You must not say anything of this to anyone," said Helmut, afraid lest they had revealed too much. "The *Geheime Feldpolizei* will come for all of us."

"I understand and I won't breathe a word," she promised. "Now," and Sophie cast around in her mind for a subject that might help lift their spirits, even though it meant that she would not be able to maintain her carefully cultivated reserve.

"Tell me about *Hauptmann* Hoffmeister. You mentioned his name the first day you arrived and we haven't spoken about him since."

Helmut's face broke into a grin. "*Ach, Fräulein* Langley, you would like him very much if ever you met him. He is an excellent teacher. His classes were the most popular in military school."

"He was not cruel like some of the other teachers," said Ulrich.

"No, he was very kind and we listened to him closely. He is that sort of person. He is someone…" and Helmut paused while he searched for the right words "…he is someone you take notice of."

"What does he look like?" asked Sophie.

"He used to look very tired sometimes," replied Helmut. "His skin sometimes had on it a grey colour."

"And his hair is grey also," added Ulrich.

"So he's very old?" suggested Sophie, picturing a venerable professor-like person.

"No, no!" Helmut laughed. "We asked him once what was his age and he said he was thirty-two years old. And that is exactly right for how he is. It is only his hair that is prematurely grey."

"And his skin when he is tired."

Sophie was amused and also intrigued. "How long ago was this?"

"Just before we came here. We had just finished our training," replied Ulrich.

"Do all soldiers have English lessons?"

"Yes."

"Why?"

"We are being prepared for the invasion of England."

"But I don't suppose that will happen, now." Helmut shook his head sadly. "And the English classes will stop."

"Why?" asked Sophie.

Ulrich looked round carefully. "Because Germany has lost the air battle for Britain."

"The *Führer* will turn his mind to Russia now," added Helmut.

"How do you know this?" asked Sophie surprised.

"We hear rumours." Helmut dropped his voice, confidentially. "In the *Soldatenheim*."

"Unlike some of our comrades, we don't wish to go home."

"We like it here."

"We do not wish to be sent to the East."

"You are safe here," said Sophie kindly.

"Yes," replied Helmut. "Thank you. But how long will we be able to stay?"

Unfortunately, much as she would like to have done so, Sophie could find no reassuring answer to give.

CHAPTER 14

H.M.S. *Benedict*
North Atlantic

The moment when H.M.S. *Benedict* turned to go was the most frightening of Richard's life. With ever increasing intensity, the wind and waves beat against the hull of the submarine which continued to list to port, unnerving the boarding party as they clung onto the deck watching the destroyer until her stern had disappeared over the horizon

With all possible material having been recovered, there was nothing more they could do other than wait down below. They battened down the watertight hatches and sat together in the confined space of the main control room surrounded by dials and levers, workstations and the periscope, which dominated the centre.

"All I can say is I'm glad I'm not in the submarine service, sir," muttered the telegraphist. "Couldn't stand being shut in here all the time with that racket going on out there. Must be terrible when they're submerged and we start depth charging them."

"Serves 'em right," said the able seamen. "They shouldn't have started the ruddy war in the first place."

Richard smiled. "I agree with both of you. Being down here for any length of time certainly wouldn't be my first choice."

"Give me the wide open spaces of the ocean any day," said the seaman.

"It's all right for you lot, out in the fresh air. Spare a thought for us stokers down below. Never see the light of day, we don't."

"So that's why you're always so pale and delicate-looking..."

"Watch it mate," replied the stoker good-naturedly, threatening to cuff the seaman round the ear.

"But at least you can come up on deck for a breather," said Richard.

"So can the submarine crew," responded the telegraphist.

"Not much of a deck though, is it?" observed the engineer. "I think I'd rather be stuck in the engine room of a ship than on the hull of a submarine or squeezed into the conning tower."

"Even though we always moan about it when we're down below?" said the stoker, enjoying the unaccustomed privilege of being able to talk freely with the officers. He'd have a rare old time telling his mates about this.

"Wouldn't be the ruddy navy without a good old moan now, would it, sir?" said the seaman.

Richard laughed. "Too right. But I still wouldn't like to do this for a living. The space seems so claustrophobic, you can hardly breathe. And the sailors have to sleep in close proximity to the torpedoes by the looks of things."

"Bit like sardines in a tin can, ain't it?" observed the seaman.

"I like mine in tomato sauce," said the telegraphist wistfully.

"I like mine without," came the rapid reply.

"Talking of sandwiches, are there any left?" asked the engineer.

"Here," and Richard threw the bag containing the last few sandwiches across to the engineer, who helped himself and then passed the remainder round.

"Cor, blimey," said the seaman, munching away. "Us eating with the officers, eh? It's a real privilege, sirs, I must say."

"Thank you, Adams," said Richard.

"But I can't say the same about being with the stokers," added the seaman, affecting condescension. "You lot 'ad better behave yourselves. We know your type," and he gave a knowing wink.

"Watch it mate," said the stoker. Then he smiled his lopsided grin. "This 'ere boarding party could set a new trend in service etiquette."

"Well, I wouldn't spread it around too much, otherwise everyone will want to join in and we'll have a mutiny on our hands when the request is denied," responded Richard amiably. "I'd hazard a guess and say that we'll be asked to keep quiet about what's happened today as well," he added.

"We can do that all right, sir," said the seaman. "We'll be as silent as the grave."

"That'll be the day," muttered the stoker.

"'Ere, what d'you mean by that?"

"Just joking, son."

"You'd better be."

"Some lucky find though, isn't it, sir, this sub?" observed the telegraphist. "I'd love to know what that machine does, you know, the one we found in the W/T office."

"So would I," said Richard with feeling. "*Benedict* ought to be coming back soon. Have a look topsides, will you, Adams?"

"Aye, aye, sir," replied the seaman. A few moments later he returned. "No sign yet, sir. Nothing. The whole ocean's as empty as when we came down 'ere first. I reckon we've been abandoned," he added, with a twinkle in his eye.

"Yeah. It's our punishment for sharing a mess with *un*able seamen," rejoined the stoker.

"Lord luv a duck. I never knew you blokes 'ad the brains to 'ave a sense of humour!"

"Now then, now then," said the stoker equably.

Richard and the engineer officer exchanged a smile.

"So, who's for I-Spy then?" suggested the seaman.

"Go on, then."

"Something beginning with 's'."

"Submarine."

"And I was trying it make it difficult for you."

"No chance," replied the stoker.

It was a further two hours before *Benedict* returned. They had been on board the submarine for nearly six hours when, having at last successfully secured the tow by means of extra hands and a large shackle, they returned to the ship feeling an enormous sense of relief.

After supper, the captain called Richard into his cabin.

"See what you can do with all these papers, will you? The ones that weren't in the canvas holdalls need to be spread out to dry. It's a miracle you got them here in as good a condition as you did. Use my cabin by all means. It's the largest on board and the most private. You know some German, so if you can put them into some sort of order, I'd appreciate it. Until we get to Iceland, that's your task. I'll get someone else to cover your watches for the time being. I know we're shorthanded, but I'll drag you topsides if things become desperate. I have a hunch you'll be happier down here anyway."

Richard grinned at the captain.

"Thought so. Now, it goes without saying that we must keep this as hush-hush as possible. The Admiralty are enormously excited about what's happened. You are not to breathe a word about anything you may discover to anyone. Understand?"

"Aye, aye, sir."

"I shall give the same order to the boarding party. And I shall take steps to ensure that the few prisoners we picked up are kept well away from the deck. They've been below the whole time, so I'm hoping they don't know we've got their submarine in tow, let alone recovered all this stuff." The captain smiled. "You did well, back there, Richard. And so did the boarding party." He chuckled, remembering something he'd seen. "I was watching through the binoculars and saw one of your sailors staggering along the deck towards the motorboat with an arm full of papers. He was engulfed by an enormous wave and I was convinced he would have disappeared once the wave had gone. But no, there he was, still tottering along the deck of the U-boat, still holding the papers. Amazing! So, well done to you all." Captain Samuels stood in the doorway with the doorknob in his hand. "Oh, by the way, I shall be in and out as I need to do various things. I'll turn in about ten o'clock. Try to keep the bed and desk clear, will you? There's a good chap. Enjoy your sorting."

"Oh, I shall. Thank you, sir."

Richard stood in the middle of the room and surveyed the muddle. The papers and books that needed drying out lay in soggy piles on the floor, in exactly the same way as they had been brought in. He knew his task was going to be a difficult one; he knew he would have to be careful so that the paper didn't disintegrate as soon as he began to separate the pages.

It would take him longer than the journey to Iceland and once there, he guessed that the ship would probably be detached from the convoy and sent post-haste back to Scapa Flow. He wondered what would happen after that.

Richard felt a personal involvement now with this find and, in a funny sort of way, he was grateful to Captain Samuels for recognizing this and entrusting him with what were probably very valuable documents.

He picked up the first book. The ink hadn't run, thank goodness. Now, the next thing he was going to need were clothes pegs. Lots of them...

When Lieutenant David Collins R.N. came on board H.M.S. *Benedict*, once more safe and secure on her mooring in Scapa Flow, Captain Samuels took him along to his own cabin.

"Looks a bit like a Chinese laundry, I'm afraid," he said apologetically. "But it's all in a very good cause, as you can imagine. This is Lieutenant Richard Langley. Richard, I'd like you to meet Lieutenant Collins, special liaison officer attached to the Admiralty." Samuels turned toward their guest. "Richard was the officer in charge of the boarding party and has been sorting and drying out our treasure trove since we brought the stuff on board. He's completely trustworthy, so knowing how suspicious and secretive you chaps are, you can feel at ease in his presence. I'd like him to stay while you examine the documents and he can answer any questions you may have."

"It's a pity you didn't manage to get the sub home as well, Captain Samuels," observed the newcomer.

"I agree. However, her stern was already low in the water when we started to tow her. We think that one of the ballast tanks had flooded as a result of damage caused by the depth charges from *Aster*. But in many ways, I think it was a blessing that she sank in the end. Saved a lot of questions all round and made it easier to keep the fact that we'd been on board and recovered all this stuff. Your superiors at the Admiralty agree with me. We'll get a German sub one day, and then you chaps'll be in clover." He smiled disarmingly at Lieutenant Collins. "Well, I'll leave you two to get on. Have fun!"

"He seems like a good sort," observed Lieutenant Collins, once Samuels had gone out of the room.

"He is – the best I know." Richard looked at the new arrival. "So, why are you here?"

"I've had orders to photograph every single document so that we still have all the info we might need if anything should happen to it while in transit."

"Is it that important?"

"Oh, yes."

"It's going to take a while."

"And I shall appreciate your help, Richard." He took off his cap and jacket and rolled up the sleeves of his shirt, looking around him. "Now where to begin…?"

Richard smiled. "With this," and he pointed to the typewriter-like machine.

David Collins stared at it open-mouthed.

"Do you know how long we've been hoping to come across one of the up-to-date models? My God, this really is some find." Then he gave Richard a penetrating look. "Do you have any idea what it is?" If he did, David hoped that the captain was correct that this officer was trustworthy.

"I think it's some sort of decoding machine. I've figured out how it works, as well. The instructions are in the lid…"

"You can read German?"

"Some. I learnt it as a child, but I wish now I'd paid more attention. Anyway, I knew enough to match the instructions up with these code-books. Look, I'll show you." Unable to contain his enthusiasm, Richard demonstrated. "It's quite simple, actually. When you press one of these typewriter keys, a bulb lights up a random letter on the circuit board behind. If you press it again, a different letter lights up. It's quite ingenious. In this way, you get a sequence of unrelated letters when you type in your message and there's your code. I used to play around with codes all the time when I was at school. The maths master was an aficionado."

"Which school?"

"Harrow." Richard paused. "Sorry to seem so keen, but I've enjoyed doing this."

"No, don't apologize. What did you do after Harrow?"

"Cambridge."

"Reading what?"

"Mathematics."

Reflectively, David said, "So, tell me more about the machine."

"There are four rotor wheels."

"Four!"

"You seem surprised."

Collins cleared his throat. "Er, yes. We've only had three up till now. Anyway, you were saying."

"The setting on each rotor wheel is set to a specific letter and each wheel has a different letter order. When you press the keys, each rotor wheel, which is connected to the light circuit-board, moves in turn thus increasing the number of permutations for each letter. There are spare rotors as well, each with a different sequence of letters so these can be exchanged according to prearranged instructions. It's a brilliantly simple and effective machine. To decode it, you just need an identical machine wherever your information is being sent, with the identical settings for the day and you can read your message." Richard smiled. "Well, that's it in a very basic nutshell. Oh yes, here are the settings for the whole of June and something called the *Offizier* code as well."

"The *Offizier* code! We've been after that for a long time as well."

"What's the significance?"

"All changes of code are first sent out in the officer's code."

"A double encryption, then?"

"Absolutely."

"Wow! And these codes over here are to do with the weather. Are they any use to you?" Richard asked the question even though he knew they would be.

David Collins rubbed his hands with glee and smiled. "Are you kidding? Well, my friend, we'd better get cracking. Are these papers and documents in some semblance of order?"

"Yes."

"Excellent."

Collins took out his camera and meticulously began to photograph each sheet of paper as Richard handed it to him; carefully documenting each one as he did so and putting it aside

"So, what's your connection to all of this?" Richard wanted to know. "Or shouldn't I ask?"

"Let's just say I'm a Royal Navy special liaison officer."

"So you deal with cloak and dagger stuff."

"Something like that. Why?"

"Idle curiosity."

David stopped what he was doing. "Interested?"

"What, for myself?"

"Yes."

"Goodness, I hadn't thought of it."

"You should."

"Why?"

"We can always make use of chaps like you. Maths degree, German-speaking, interested in figuring things out, naval experience. Do you do crosswords?"

"Occasionally."

"What sort?"

"Cryptic ones mostly."

"Quick at them?"

"Yes, on the whole."

"Play chess?"

"When I get the chance."

"You're exactly what we need."

"Who's 'we'?"

"Those in the know," David replied evasively. "Do you have a memory for detail?"

"I do, actually. But only if it's something I'm interested in."

"What are these, then?"

Richard went to pick up the book, but David stopped him.

"Tell me."

"Bigram tables."

"And this?"

"Enigma codes for the month of June."

Meticulously, David continued to photograph the documents. He picked up the next pile.

"How about those?" he asked.

"You sound like you're giving me some sort of test."

David smiled. "Perhaps I am, though it's not for me to decide the outcome."

"What do you mean?"

"You'll find out in due course. But it will have to be your choice. So, what are these?"

"They're charts giving the clear channels between the German minefields. And these are charts denoting the position of the submarines that are on fixed stations to refuel U-boats on patrol. While this – this is a sort of grid map dividing the Atlantic into squares with a list of U-boats assigned to certain areas."

"Do you have any idea just how important this haul is of yours?"

"I think I'm just beginning to realize."

The two men exchanged a glance.

"I'll tell you *exactly* how important it is," said David. "These documents, and any others we might find in the future, are absolutely invaluable to the war effort. Hauls like this could make the difference as to whether we win the war or not. Or perhaps how long it takes us to win the war. That's how important they are."

"You sound very certain of that."

"I am. Absolutely. You too could be part of that process."

"I thought I was already, serving aboard the *Benedict*."

"Of course you are, but in doing what I do, you would be part of something special, something extraordinary."

"What exactly do you mean? Helping to crack the codes as they come in?"

"Could be. There are other possibilities."

"Such as?"

"That's not for me to say but for you to find out, should you wish to do so."

Richard smiled. He was beginning to see through this man's evasiveness: giving out little snippets of information and then backtracking and revealing absolutely nothing.

He thought of Edwin and wondered whether the "something hush-hush" he had embarked upon at the beginning of the war had any connection with deciphering codes. Edwin's mathematical abilities had played a key part in his selection, Richard knew that much, and he was a dab hand at chess too. Better than he, Richard, had ever been.

They didn't speak again on the subject, but continued to photograph and log each item. It took several hours of backbreaking work. They paused occasionally for a welcome cup of tea and a sandwich or two.

"What was the sub like inside?" asked David, during one such tea break.

"Brand new, by the looks of things. A fine ship, as far as I could tell, with good quality fittings and instruments. Absolutely spotlessly clean, which I must admit surprised me, given the cramped conditions. The ward room had light, varnished woodwork and each cupboard was numbered and had a corresponding key to fit. There was only one cupboard without a key, which I broke into, and that turned out to be the medical cabinet. What else?" he thought for a moment. "Oh yes, there were bunks in both the officer's and crews' quarters and there was the usual artwork and reading material that you'd find in any vessel, above or below the water. There was plenty of tinned goods about and even a plate of abandoned mashed potato in the engine room."

"They must have called action stations very quickly then."

"Yes. I don't think they were expecting us."

David stood up and stretched his back. "I presume you've written your report?"

"It's with Captain Samuels."

"Good. Both yours and the captain's reports will make interesting reading. Now, arrangements are in hand to transport this lot back to, er, wherever."

Eventually, there was nothing left to photograph. Every book, every chart, every scrap of paper had been recorded and catalogued. The two men shook hands.

"Well, thanks for your help," said David, as he turned to leave. "And remember what I told you. You're just what we're looking for."

"If I should decide to fulfil this, er, suggestion of yours, how would I go about it?"

"Just apply for Special Duties, old man. They'll know about you when your name comes up."

Richard looked at him. "I see. Presumably, you're intending to tell *them* about me, whoever *they* are."

"That's about the size of it."

"Makes me sound like a marked man."

"You are, in a manner of speaking. But in a good way, I can assure you."

"I'd prefer to make the decision for myself, if that's all right."

"That's fine. But I do urge you to seriously consider it and don't take too long, either. Remember what I said, we need chaps with your abilities. I do hope we meet again."

"Thank you, and good luck with all this, wherever it's going."

As H.M.S. *Benedict* plodded through the water at eight knots with the start of yet another slow-moving outward convoy, Richard stood on the bridge, watching the radiance of the setting sun upon the water.

He thought of Caroline and Sophie, of his parents, of Edwin. He thought of his fellow officers and the tightknit community they had become. He thought of H.M.S. *Benedict* and that actually, when it came down to it, he had become very fond of the old girl.

Could he leave all this? Could he make such a leap into the unknown?

The answer came back to him as an unequivocal "yes".

However, Richard decided that he wouldn't make the change immediately. He would discuss it first with his captain. It was better not to rush into something like that.

Checking the compass, Richard called down a minor course correction to the navigator's station and once he had received confirmation of their course, he took in a deep breath of the evening air.

Yes, he thought. *I'll apply for special duties. Who knows where it might lead?*

CHAPTER 15

Seeblick POW Camp
Germany

"I need a dummy," said Robert, as he and Harry took their morning exercise round the compound, a couple of days after the camp's highly successful revue.

"Aw, diddums," responded Harry.

Robert laughed. "No, you chump. A life-sized dummy. One that can take my place at roll call."

"Even with our wondrous skills as prop-makers in the camp, I think someone might notice that a dummy doesn't talk or walk."

"No, but you could help it to do its limited best."

"Yes, I'm famous for my life-creating skills," responded Harry gaily.

Robert raised an eyebrow at him.

"Not in that sense, my friend. Well, not that I know of anyway." He grimaced at Robert, who laughed again. "You're determined to do this, aren't you? Escape, I mean. And you've come up with a plan, no doubt."

"Of course."

"Go on, then," said Harry, "tell me what's in that *über*-intelligent brain of yours."

"Well, the new shower-block is outside the main compound."

"A particularly clever place to build it."

"Especially from our perspective."

"Absolutely. Pray continue, Professor."

"One of the guards who escorts us there and back isn't particularly alert. He stands outside and smokes a cigarette while we're washing and doesn't usually bother to count us in on the return journey, only on the way out. So, my thinking is that we make this life-sized dummy, somehow conceal it in the washhouse, go for our evening shower, dress the dummy in my clothes and I change into some others and jump out of the window at the back."

"But all the windows are locked shut, aren't they?"

"Johnny is good at picking locks. Before becoming a ventriloquist, he was apprenticed to a locksmith. He says he's had a go already and apparently, it's an easy one to crack."

"I don't know – the talent we have in Seeblick. If that's replicated across all the other P.O.W. camps, then they must really be suffering at home! No tailors, prop makers, teachers, locksmiths. The list is endless. Go on," said Harry.

Robert smiled. "For some obscure reason, there are no patrols in the narrow area behind the shower-block until it's dark. The trees come almost right up to the fence, which I reckon I can easily climb, and then disappear into the wood behind. How does that sound?"

"Ingenious, certainly. Then what?"

"Then you and the others march back into the compound with the dummy supported between you, as if it were me. If old Fritz does decide to count you lot when you come out of the shower block, then hopefully he won't notice that I don't walk and talk for myself."

Harry considered this. "What about rollcall that evening?"

"Well, the dummy can stand in my place. Pull his hat down over his eyes, support him on either side and we'll get Johnny to answer my name. In fact, it was watching his ventriloquist act that gave me the idea for this."

Harry took a deep breath. "Well, you're a braver man than me. But I'll do all I can to help."

"Thanks, I was hoping you'd say that. I was also thinking…"

"No! Save us!" and Harry rolled his eyes to the heavens. "Sorry, Bob. Don't mean it. Carry on, Macduff."

"I was also thinking that if it works, other men could go out the same way."

"That might be interesting. I can just imagine it – a whole camp full of dummies and one man rushing around furiously at rollcall impersonating everyone who's gone. Even our lackadaisical guard might notice when the camp only has me and the ventriloquist left."

Robert laughed. "No, you idiot! This method could only support three attempts at the most." He looked at his friend. "You could be the next."

"Nah. Not me. I told you a long time ago, I'll be the ideas man. Or in this case, the supporter's club."

Harry fell silent, thinking that things wouldn't be the same without Robert. He'd really miss their friendship. It made being a P.O.W. bearable.

Sensing something of Harry's thoughts and sharing the sentiment, Robert said, "I'll send you a postcard. Let you know where I am."

"Yeah." Harry turned away for a moment, afraid of showing any emotion.

"We can always meet up again after the war's over."

"There you go, being all optimistic again." *It would never be the same.* Harry pulled himself together. "So, my friend, when do we start?"

"Now?"

"Well, there's no time like the present. So presumably we're going to ask Johnny, the ventriloquist, yes? He's a real whizz at prop-making as well."

"What, better than you?"

"No chance!"

"We'll need lots of *papier-mâché* for the dummy."

"Who I've just decided is to be called Oscar, by the way, as he's going to give the performance of a lifetime!"

Robert laughed.

"And clothes for you," continued his friend. "You'll need a disguise."

"Yes, I've been thinking about that. What about a local yokel, a woodsman or some such?"

Harry considered this. "You'd get further if you had a German uniform. Then we could get papers and things for you."

"I'd have to get a photograph and we don't have a camera in the camp."

"I could get one from one of the goons."

"No, too risky. They'd suspect something right away if we start bribing them for an object like a camera."

"Yeah, I suppose."

"You see, the Swiss border's only about fifty miles away…"

"That near, huh?"

"Yeah. So, if I dress as a woodsman, I can blend in better with the local scenery and be less likely to arouse suspicion. Greg's a dab hand with a needle and thread. He does a brilliant job at repairing uniforms and turning the stuff we get from the Red Cross into wearable clothes. I'm sure he'll be able to come up with a suitable outfit."

"True."

"I can travel at night and avoid the check points. I'll keep my P.O.W. tags and then if I'm caught, I won't be mistaken for a spy and shot. Perhaps I'll be able to lay my hands on some papers somewhere."

"If you're lucky. We'll have to work on that one." Harry stopped walking and put his hand on his friend's shoulder. "Well, you seem to have thought of everything."

Robert took a deep breath. "I certainly hope so."

"And there's nothing I can say to make you change your mind? It's a jungle out there…"

"I'll be fine. And careful, I promise. But this is something I have to do. I've felt the same ever since I was first picked up."

"I know." Turning towards their hut, they resumed their walk. "I know," reiterated Harry quietly, keeping his hand briefly on Robert's shoulder.

They sought out Johnny and Greg, who showed great enthusiasm for the idea, and the four of them went to see the Senior British Officer, who was also impressed and gave his consent for them to continue.

"There are no other sensible escape plans underway at the moment," said the S.B.O. "Some of the men have come to me with a hare-brained scheme for digging a tunnel under the wire and out through the hill behind hut six. I told them to go away and think up a sounder strategy," he added. "So, by all means go ahead with yours. I'll make sure it takes priority over any others that may come up in the meantime." He smiled at Robert. "I know you'll plan it carefully, Bob, and we'll do all we can to support you. I like the idea that this one can be used again if it proves to be successful. Come and talk to me when everything's finalized and we'll go through the details together."

"Yes, sir."

The four men set to work immediately. Harry watched in fascination as Johnny measured Robert's head carefully and methodically.

"Surely it doesn't matter that much?" suggested Harry.

"Oh but it does. This isn't just some old ventriloquist's dummy up on a stage. This has got to be lifelike and as convincing as we can make it as it could be scrutinized fairly closely. The longer we can keep Bob's absence concealed, the more chance he has."

"I thought dummy's heads were made of *papier-mâché*?" observed Harry.

"Not the best ones. They're carved from wood. Now, I need to measure your eye sockets, nose, mouth and the length of your chin. Oh, and ears, hands and feet." Johnny lifted up his tape measure again. "Keep still, Bob. Stop laughing."

"Sorry, I can't help it. But I do appreciate what you're doing."

"I know. If you get away from here, it'll give all of us a boost."

"Thanks. I'll try my best."

"Okay. That'll do for now."

"Where will you get the wood from?"

"Oh, I'll find it somewhere. Now, off you go, you two. I'll call you when I need you again."

Their next stop was the Red Cross parcel store with Greg. They searched through several bags of garments until they found something that seemed to match the clothes that the local people wore.

"I'll be able to adapt these, no problem. You'll need a change of clothes, so we'll nab one or two of the costumes from the revue as well. Now, we'd better tidy up in here before the goons think we're planning a mass breakout. And I'll need to measure you. I've brought a tape measure with me."

"Bet you never thought you'd have to endure all this measuring when you came up with your master plan," said Harry.

"No, but one has to be prepared to deal with all sorts of contingencies."

"Come on, stop yakking, you two. Let's get on." Greg picked up the tape measure. "Now, I want you to you to hold out your arms and stand up straight with your legs slightly apart. It won't hurt a bit."

"That's what they always say that when I'm out on a date," observed Harry with affectation.

"You should be so lucky," responded Robert.

"Huh?" said Greg, distracted. "Shut up, you two. I can't concentrate."

Harry smothered a guffaw of laughter and turned to the window. "I'll keep a lookout."

"Probably a good idea."

"Now I need your inside leg measurement." Greg handed one end of the tape measure to Robert. "Here, stick that in your groin and let it hang down to your feet."

"This I have to see," said Harry. "You might be the envy of every man in the camp."

Robert picked up a handful of clothes and threw them at him.

"Oh, do stop messing about," said Greg impatiently. "You two really are the limit."

"I could have told you my inside leg measurement and saved you the trouble and me the embarrassment," observed Robert good-naturedly, trying to control his laughter, not daring to look at Harry. "You only needed to ask."

"You might have shrunk."

"I probably have with our diet."

"I think we all have," observed Greg drily.

"Speak for yourselves," said Harry with a smirk. "I'm still the man I always was."

"As it is, one leg's slightly shorter than the other," said Greg.

"That could be interesting."

Robert was suddenly serious. "By how much?"

"A quarter of an inch. It can make a difference to the appearance of the clothes, you know."

114

"I shouldn't worry too much about it, Greg," said Harry. "He's not going out for a night on the town in white tie and tails. He's only a humble woodsman tramping across the Alps to Switzerland."

"You just let me get on with it. There, that's all." He scribbled some more numbers down on a piece of paper with a pencil stub and rolled up his tape measure. "Thanks, Bob. I'll find you when I need you again."

Harry and Robert walked back across the compound.

"I wonder if it was being shot that made the difference?"

"What to your leg, you mean?" Harry shrugged. "Possibly. But a quarter of an inch is hardly Mount Everest, is it? Besides, you might have been born like it."

"True. And I can walk and run quite well now. That's what's most important."

Robert had continued to be conscientious about his fitness regime. He felt good in himself and with the fine weather coming, it seemed the right time to go.

However, he realized it would be all too easy to stay here. Life was pretty good in this particular camp; that is, providing you were the sort of person who was content to let go of all personal responsibility and didn't mind being enclosed behind barbed wire.

Robert knew that he was not.

He needed to be a free man again; he needed to see his family and the countryside he loved so much. Once back with his regiment, he wanted to try and make sense out of the B.E.F.'s defeat but above all, he wanted to be involved in preventing such a catastrophe in the future.

For Robert, the key was to save lives while achieving military success. This could only be done with detailed intelligence, quickly and accurately disseminated. It was here he felt his future lay: to be involved in something that would make a *real* difference to the war effort. He knew that each branch of the services had their own intelligence units out in the field. But was this what he wanted?

There had to be something more, surely?

Beyond the perimeter fence lay a different world, a world that Robert had not been part of for almost a year and a world that had probably changed enormously in the meantime. But he knew he had to be out *there*, back in the centre of things.

Robert also realized he had two distinct advantages over most men attempting an escape from Seeblick, or indeed any P.O.W. camp. Firstly, he had travelled extensively in the area where he was imprisoned and secondly, he spoke both German and French fluently. Therefore, he was not going into this situation blind. He was certainly not going into it unprepared.

There just remained the thorny question of means of identification.

This was still unresolved when, a few weeks later, Robert began to assemble together the things that he would need. His clothes were sorted and made; someone had managed to procure a knapsack for him (from where, the scrounger had refused to reveal) and Oscar, the dummy, was near completion.

Robert had been amazed by the intricate detail that went into creating a dummy and the time and trouble that Johnny had taken over its construction. When Robert had thanked him, he replied:

"That's okay, old man. I've enjoyed doing it. It's kept me occupied and my mind off being confined in here. I was beginning to get a bit wire-happy. As Harry and Greg are not too keen on going anywhere, the S.B.O. has said I can be the next one after you, if you don't mind."

"Of course not! I think that's a fitting reward for all your hard work. So, show me how it operates."

Johnny separated the head from the body. "Well, this handle's connected to a rod which goes up inside the dummy's head and by means of springs and levers, you can move the eyes and mouth. It's quite simple, really."

"But clever. What about the hair?"

"When I went to see the S.B.O. and asked, he said he'd been thinking that some of the men's appearance was becoming slovenly now that our hair has finally grown back after transit camp, so he ordered short back and sides for everyone but particularly those men who have a similar colour to yours. From that I made a wig. Good, eh?"

"Brilliant and good for the S.B.O.!"

"As you can see, the hands are just a case of simple carving and the arms and legs are attached by straps onto the torso and easily removable."

"Where did you get the wood for all this?"

"Ah." Johnny made a wry expression. "I'm afraid that the hut next to ours lost some of its furniture. They were a bit peeved when they woke up in the morning to find it gone."

"And you kept quiet, naturally."

"Naturally."

"What about stuffing?"

"Some of the chaps in the hut opposite donated straw from their palliasses."

"Did they realize?"

"Not until they woke up with backache."

"I suppose you kept quiet about that, as well."

"Of course. No sense in making myself unpopular!"

Robert smiled. "Well, thanks, Johnny. I can't tell you how much I appreciate it."

"That's all right, old man. Just make sure you make a success of it."

"Oh, I shall."

The day he was due to go, arranged to coincide when the lazy guard was on duty, Robert nervously paced the compound, psyching himself up for what was to come; visualizing what he would do; going over and over in his mind every possible eventuality and corresponding contingency.

He'd been to see the S.B.O. the previous day, who had wished him luck and given the final go-ahead even though Robert still didn't have any identity papers.

"Just keep clear of those patrols, Bob," was his final piece of advice.

The dummy and his woodsman's clothes were already hidden in the washroom. All that remained to do was to sort through his personal belongings. Robert left his letters and Royal Welch Fusiliers cap badge with Harry to look after and bring back to England at the end of the war ("There goes your optimism again, Bob! Yeah, of course I'll bring them."). He decided to take with him his fountain pen and the one treasured photo of his family.

But what to do with *La Chaleur de la Mer*? He was reluctant to leave it with Harry, who would not understand his attachment. Letters were different. His friend could appreciate their importance. But a book? No.

Robert had read *La Chaleur* many, many times since it had first arrived in the camp, loving the fine use of language, the perfectly balanced narrative, the overwhelmingly passionate nature of the romance between the two main characters and their obvious devotion to each other. It had become both his solace and his refuge.

He'd asked around, of course, but no one else seemed interested or able to read it. So, he'd adopted it as his own, putting his initials inside the front cover as well as a poem that meant a great deal to him, one which, alongside the novel, evoked poignant memories of his lost girl on the beach.

La Chaleur de la Mer had become one of his most precious personal possessions and he couldn't bear to part with it. Yet Robert knew he had no choice but to leave it behind and this pained him greatly.

Then one day, while he was sitting quietly in the library finishing the novel for the last time, he knew exactly what it was he should do; what would be the *right* thing to do.

He would leave it behind as a gift for someone else. But he would not just put it anonymously and mundanely back on the shelf. It had to be found by accident, a discovery made all the more special by its unexpectedness. He composed a note to that effect, which he placed carefully between the middle pages of the book.

When the time came, Robert went into the little library, knowing that near the desk was a loose panel on the inner layer of the double wooden skin of the wall. He pulled this away and into the space behind, securely wrapped in a leather pouch for protection, he carefully placed *La Chaleur de la Mer*, as well as a stone and a feather – remnants of a wood-gathering expedition which had served as a small window for him into the outside world. As an afterthought, Robert tucked his lending-out book inside as well. Many pages still remained empty, but he knew that the next man assigned to take over from him was wanting to use his own system and would have no use for his venerable Germanic stock book.

He replaced the panel and with the contents of the leather pouch safely hidden away, Robert hoped that what he was leaving behind would have meaning and significance for the person who made the discovery. He gained comfort from this idea and it made leaving it easier.

Perhaps one day, somewhere, he would find another copy of *La Chaleur de la Mer*.

For the last time, Robert left the library, locking the door behind him and handing the key to his successor.

After supper that evening, they lined up as usual for their turn in the shower-block. Harry was unusually silent and thought that Robert looked exceptionally pale. They had made their farewells in the hut before leaving and there seemed nothing more that could be said.

The group were marched towards the side gate, which was opened for them, on through the perimeter wire, past the watchtower, where the attendant guard followed their every move with his machine gun.

Robert's mouth was dry and his heart pounding. Surely the guards would spot that something different was going on? Surely some kind of sixth sense would alert them that something was about to happen?

They reached the shower-block. The guard counted them all in and, true to form, stood carelessly outside smoking his cigarette.

The men undressed and began their showers, singing loudly, making their usual raucous noise. Nothing had to be different; nothing new that might arouse the suspicion of the guard and bring him in to investigate.

Robert brought Oscar out from his several ingeniously contrived hiding places while Johnny picked the lock on the window. Quickly, Robert undressed and put on his woodsman's clothes. Together, they assembled the dummy and dressed him in Robert's uniform, dampening his hair to make him look as though he had just had a shower. Finally, they put his cap on (minus the R.W.F. badge which Harry had tucked away among his possessions) and Oscar was ready.

Robert grabbed his knapsack, quickly shook hands with Johnny and Greg, briefly placed his hand on Harry's shoulder, and climbed out of the back window, which Johnny closed and locked again from the inside before quickly taking his shower.

When their allotted time was up, in the gathering gloom, the men were lined up once again, and marched back through the perimeter fence with Oscar in the middle of them, accompanied by the less than attentive guard.

However, another guard was at the gate doing a head count.

Harry, Greg and Johnny held their breath.

CHAPTER 16

St Nicolas

"Is the Major coming for tea today?" asked Mae, as she stood at the kitchen sink doing the washing up.

She looked forward to his weekly visits, although she kept this to herself, not wishing to antagonize her sister, who always seemed grumpy and out of sorts whenever he came.

"I think so, Aunt," replied Sophie, stacking the plates and cups from breakfast on the table after drying them, before putting them away in the cupboards. "He usually does on a Sunday."

Mae looked out of the window. It was a particularly beautiful autumn morning, with the trees at their resplendent golden-red best.

"I did wonder whether I might suggest a walk when he comes. However, I do feel a little jaded today."

"Then entertain the Major inside, Aunt. You're not under obligation to go anywhere."

"No, that's true. The poor man always seems so tired himself these days, I'm sure he'll appreciate the chance to sit down. I do think he uses his visits to escape from the pressures of command."

Secretly, she knew that he came to see her but would never dream of saying so. Whatever would Edna think if she realized? Mae didn't want Sophie to think that she was a fond and foolish old woman, either. Not that her niece would ever voice anything like that, she was far too polite and generous-hearted.

Major von Witzenhausen arrived promptly at three o'clock. He seemed subdued and solemn. He took his customary tea and biscuits with Mae in the sitting room and chatted for a while, before excusing himself and bidding her farewell.

He went out into the farmyard, seeking Edna.

"Major," she said, acknowledging his presence, when at last he found her in the barn putting new straw into the stalls.

"I wish to speak to you."

Something in the Major's manner made Edna stop what she was doing and look up.

"I'm listening."

"Not here. Will you permit me to accompany you on a small walk?"

Surely the old chap wasn't going to ask if he could propose to Mae?

She put down her pitchfork and they walked down the path to the wooden bridge over the stream that gurgled its way towards the cove.

"It is very beautiful and peaceful here. This has become one of my favourite places on the island. And being here with you… and, of course, your sister," he said, adding Mae's name out of propriety, "has come to mean a great deal to me."

Edna gave him a quick sideways glance.

"I shall be leaving St Nicolas very soon," said the Major, after a slight hesitation.

When Edna didn't respond but continued to lean on the parapet watching the fish swimming in the clear, sparkling water, he added, "I am being recalled to Germany. Other duties have been assigned to me."

They stood in contemplative silence.

"I'm sorry to hear that, Major von Witzenhausen," Edna said at length.

"Please, my name is Albrecht."

"I prefer *Major*," she responded not unkindly, using the German pronunciation. It was how she had come to think of him.

He inclined his head graciously. "As you wish."

"Mae has come to value your visits," she said.

"As I have mine with her."

How could he say that it was really Edna's company he valued most? Each rare occasion was special to him; a precious jewel in a golden crown.

"There are many changes coming, *Fräulein Weissman*, not all of them for the better. I shall not be here to temper the, shall we say, excesses of what is going to happen. The man who is taking my place is not as…"

"Wise," interjected Edna, unexpectedly.

Major von Witzenhausen inclined his head in acknowledgement, his heart beating quickly at this small nugget of praise.

"Thank you, dear *Fräulein*." He kept his eyes on the water lest he reveal too much. "Nor as tolerant. He is meticulous at carrying out his orders from above." He smiled briefly. "He and the *Feldkommandantur* will get on famously. Unfortunately. But life will become more difficult for you… for all the islanders."

"I understand."

"Keep your most favourite books and trinkets away from prying eyes – and they will be prying, of that you can be sure. Bury your most precious possessions in a place where they cannot be found." He looked at her then and smiled. "And please find a better hiding place for your spare wireless set. I have enjoyed sitting on it. I would feel… upset… if someone were to take my place."

Unable to help herself, Edna laughed. The sly old fox, so he'd known all along.

"Thank you for not acting upon your discovery," she said, meaning it.

He nodded. "I also wish to say that you and I have enjoyed some very stimulating, er…, discussions in the time we have known each other. But I ask you now to promise me something, *Fräulein Weissman*. You must be very, very careful when I have left and not do anything to antagonize the new *Kommandant* or his subordinates. They will come down hard on anyone who raises objections to their orders. It will be viewed as obstructing the legitimate work of the Military Government. You will promise me this one thing?"

Edna remained silent, her lips drawn in a tight line; a hint of unexpected tears in her eyes, a stab of pain in her heart.

This man cared. Genuinely.

At some cost to her pride and inner resolve to give nothing away, she replied, "I shall try, Albrecht. I promise you I shall try."

He gave a start at the use of his name and hope welled up inside him. "*Gut!* Then I shall not worry so much."

Risking all, he laid his hand over hers, and to his surprise, she didn't snatch hers away but responded by placing her other hand over the top if his, allowing them both to remain in this manner for a long time.

"Ich werde dich vermissen," he said quietly.

Edna nodded, not trusting herself to speak. She would miss him, too. The feeling surprised her.

"Vielen Dank für Ihre Güte und Freundschaft," she said, at last. And she meant it too. He had been kind and in different circumstances, they would have developed a real friendship. It was the least she could do to thank him. *"I shall never forget you."* The words slipped out before she could stop them.

"Ach, meine liebe Dame," and he took her hands in his before saying: *"You have gladdened my heart with your words! This being so, I feel able to give to you this,"* and, letting go of one of her hands, he took a small piece of paper from the pocket of his tunic which he handed to her.

Edna glanced at it, nodded and placed it safely in the pocket of her apron.

"I have its counterpart – your address – safely concealed within my luggage. One day, when this madness is over and there is peace again, it is my dearest wish that you and I might resume our friendship. I pray to Gott in heaven that this shall be so." This time, he lifted both her hands to his lips. *"I shall remember you always."*

Then he bowed, clicked his heels and was gone.

They went down to Port le Bac the day he departed – Edna, Mae and Sophie – and stood on the quayside amid the hustle and bustle of the harbour, watching as he boarded the powerful motorboat that would take him across to France before he travelled home to Germany.

Major von Witzenhausen stood on the landward side of the boat as it drew away from the jetty, his eyes never leaving the three women. Imperceptibly, he inclined his head towards one of them. Edna responded in kind.

He smiled and gave a brief nod before the boat gained speed and disappeared out of the harbour.

"Well," said Mae.

"Hm," said Edna.

"Cup of tea?" suggested Sophie, regarding both her aunts with equal interest.

They found a table at the back of the little café and ordered tea and cake.

"Cake? You must be kidding," said Mabel. "We haven't got any sugar or flour and I heard this morning that bread's going to be rationed. Goodness knows what I'm going to do for sandwiches. In the old days, I used to be able to go and ask a neighbour for a cup or two of flour or a loaf if we ran short. But not anymore. We can only buy rationed stuff from the shops and then only if we've got a permit. It's ridiculous."

"Ssh, Mabel," said Ethel. "Do keep your voice down otherwise you'll get us all in trouble and the *Gestapo*'ll pick you up and close the café."

Their friend Gert sniffed huffily. "Seems like we can't even express an opinion anywhere these days. We can't say a thing against the bleeders that's invaded us. I would've been better off staying in England and that's a fact. Cyril thought I'd be safer 'ere staying with his auntie than in our little house by the docks in London. Fat lot he knew."

"I think you'd better keep *your* voice down as well," observed George mildly.

"Now George Hoskins, give me one good reason why I should?"

"For Tommy's sake, if nothing else."

"It's good for 'im to 'ear the truth. He's getting far too pally with them there German soldiers if you ask me. He's even learning to speak their lingo."

"We've got to learn it at school, Mam, so I thought I'd get ahead and do some extra. They was pleased to 'elp."

"Yeah, I bet they was."

"They said I was doin' well, too. Although they reckoned my English weren't as good as theirs. They said I needed lessons from *Hauptmann* Hoffmeister."

"Who's 'e when 'e's at 'ome?"

"The man who taught them to speak English."

"Well, don't you take no notice. There's nuffink wrong wiv yer English. It's the way we talk. You should be proud of that."

Tommy looked downcast. "I am, but I would like to speak so's *everyone* can understand me."

"Never you mind about that."

Edna and Sophie exchanged a quick glance.

"Did you hear about those lads that got arrested by the *Gestapo* for daubing 'V' for Victory signs everywhere?" said Mabel, anxious to move the conversation on, despite George's attempts to tell her she'd already said enough.

"Yeah," replied Gert. "I really feel sorry for them lads. And did you know they've been put in jail now? The bleeding *Gestapo* are everywhere."

"They're not really the *Gestapo* though, are they, Mr Hoskins?" said Tommy, who had been sipping his small glass of orange squash very slowly to make it last.

"No, they're called the *Geheime Feldpolizei*."

"They're the same as the *Gestapo*, though. Always snooping around everywhere, making sure we're not doing anything we're not supposed to. Give me the British Bobby any day," said Mabel.

"Well, while we're 'aving a good old gripe about things, what about us 'aving to drive on the right hand side of the road now? Fancy us 'aving to do that?" Gert was on a roll, there seemed to be no stopping her. "And all these new signs in German everywhere. Nobody understands a word! Don't you find it an absolute pain, George?"

"I might if I still had my taxi."

"It's all right once you get the hang of it," remarked the doctor, who had just come into the café and caught the last line of the conversation. "I manage to get around just about, though it's difficult to get petrol most of the time."

"Well, at least they've let you keep your car," observed George.

"True. But it is rather necessary for my job, wouldn't you agree?"

"It *was* my job," muttered George sullenly.

Seeing Edna, Mae and Sophie seated at their table, Dr Reynolds came over to join them.

The general tone of the conversation changed when a small group of German soldiers, a few of whom were reeling from too many beers came in and ordered tea and cake.

"We're out of cake," said Mabel.

"Ah, we are sorry to hear that, *Frau* Hoskins. But we like your café, so just the tea will suffice."

They viewed the silent room with benevolent smiles.

"We are happy today," they announced to the assembled gathering. "We are going home! We shall see our families again. The *Führer* has ordered that a whole infantry division will be sent here to St Nicolas to replace us who came first. He is sending even more to Jersey and Guernsey. The *Führer* sees how important the islands are to Germany, but especially this one as it is closest to France. He wants the islands to become a fortress because he has decreed they will belong to Germany for ever and no one will ever capture them. So he sends whole divisions here. Do you know how many soldiers that is? A lot!" and he collapsed unsteadily onto a chair.

"Sei still!" said one of his comrades.

"Nein, I won't be quiet," said the soldier, brushing aside his comrade. "The new infantry division on St Nicolas will not be well-behaved like us because no one is better behaved than us. We are the best behaved unit in the *Wehrmacht*. We speak the best English also. Our teacher, he was *sehr gut, ja?*"

He paused and looked around expectantly for praise but even when none was forthcoming, he pressed on regardless.

"You understand us, yes? We have been friendly, yes? We know we have treated everyone with respect and courtesy. We have behaved correctly. We are the best unit in the *Wehrmacht*," he reiterated, thumping his chest with his fist. "Many English girls have fallen in love with us. We will be sad to leave them. I shall be sad to leave my English girl. We have done much loving."

He swayed unsteadily on his chair, suddenly becoming quiet. He stared morosely into his tea, which Mabel had placed in front of him, clattering the cup on the saucer.

"Three *pfennigs*, please," she said dispassionately.

Abruptly, he found his voice again. "You people are polite to us. We hear that in France they are openly hostile. We thank you for being polite; you, and all our friends on the Channel Islands…" and, after expansively throwing his arms wide, he suddenly felt the world spin and slid off the chair onto the floor where he promptly fell asleep.

The assembled company had both the grace and the good sense not to laugh, though Sophie didn't dare look at the doctor, whose lips were twitching.

However, Dr Reynolds went over to the young soldier to check that he was all right.

"I'd take him back to your barracks, if I were you," he said to one of his friends. "Let him sleep it off. He'll be all right in a couple of hours."

"Thank you, *Herr Doktor*."

His two companions lifted him to his feet and between them, marched him down the road and back to their quarters.

"Well, I never," said Mabel.

The next morning at the farmhouse, there was a knock on the back door which Sophie answered. Mae was in the dairy and Edna was out in Three Acre Field helping Jean le Rouge.

Ulrich and Helmut stood there.

"We have come to say goodbye," said Helmut.

"We are sorry to leave," added Ulrich.

"We have enjoyed working for you."

"You have been kind to us."

Sophie stood for a moment, not quite certain what to say. They didn't seem overjoyed at the prospect of going home.

"I expect you'll be glad to see your families again after all this time."

"Yes, we shall," said Helmut.

"We have missed them."

"But after our leave is finished, we do not know where we might be sent."

"It could be the Eastern Front."

"We ought to be proud if we were to be sent there to defend the honour of the Fatherland…"

"But the fighting in Russia is bad. The war there has been going on for six months and still Germany has not won. They said it would end after six weeks."

"We do not wish to be there for the winter."

"We would rather stay here, where it is warm and safe."

"Though there isn't much food," observed Helmut.

Ulrich turned to his friend. "I would rather be hungry than dead."

"Yes."

Sophie sighed. What could she say? She felt such sympathy for these pleasant, courteous, hardworking lads thrown into a conflict they had neither sought nor wished to continue with, and in which they would probably one day lose their lives. Yet they, like millions of soldiers all over the world, whatever their nationality, had no choice but to do their 'duty', whatever that 'duty' might entail, and the thought filled her with indescribable pain.

At that moment, she didn't care who was on which side, who was right and who was wrong; at that moment, Sophie saw all war as a hideous abomination.

Why couldn't the politicians fight it out among themselves? Why couldn't the leaders of the great nations stop megalomaniacs like Hitler from seizing power? Why were men so afraid to act before dictators like him became so greedy for power that their obsession gained momentum and caused untold suffering to millions?

"*Fräulein* Sophie, what is wrong?" asked Helmut full of concern, seeing her stare into the far distance with tears in her eyes.

"Are you sad at our going?" suggested Ulrich.

Hastily, she pulled herself together and brushed the tears away.

"My aunts and I will miss you very much," she said, very correctly. "You've been such a help on the farm and have worked so hard and so cheerfully. Thank you very much," she said, struggling a little to find words that would express how grateful they were but without going too far.

"We have enjoyed our time with you."

"We would like to present to you a gift from us both."

And they handed Sophie two little carved wooden figures – a bird and a horse.

"We know you like horses and we have listened to the birds out in the fields often while we are working and when you bring us our lunch," said Helmut.

"We carved these for you in our spare time."

Sophie was touched beyond measure by their thoughtfulness.

"I shall treasure these for always," she said unsteadily. "Thank you."

"And thank you also for the kind things you have said about us to Major von Witzenhausen. He has been very pleased with our work," said Ulrich, glad to see their honest efforts accepted with genuine gratitude.

"We must go now. Please permit me," and Helmut bowed and kissed her hand. So too did Ulrich.

"I wish I had something to give you," said Sophie.

Helmut smiled. "We shall keep your loveliness in our memories for always. Farewell."

And they waved as they walked down the lane and out of sight.

Giving way to her emotion, Sophie ran to find solace in her secret cove. But when she arrived at the cliff top, she found her way blocked by a burly sentry.

He raised his gun and stood firm.

"No civilians allowed. Military personnel only. Anyone breaking this rule will be shot or arrested. It is forbidden to come here."

Dismayed, Sophie turned away. Was nothing sacred?

CHAPTER 17

Location Classified

The light was bright, shining in his eyes. Robert could not see the person or persons on the other side of the table; could not see his tormentors.

They questioned him again and again. "Are you a spy?"

"No, I am not a spy! How many more times do I have to tell you?" He thumped the table in absolute and total frustration. "I am an escaped prisoner of war. And nothing else."

Exasperated, he put his hands over his face and exhaled.

"Sind Sie ein Spion?"

Robert lifted up his head. "Oh, very clever. *Nein! Ich bin kein Spion! Je ne suis pas un espion ! Nid wyf yn ysbïwr!* In how many more bloody languages do I have to tell you that I'm not a bloody spy?"

"You speak fluent German."

"Yes," snapped Robert. "I got a first in German at Oxford. You can check up. The records are at Trinity College. I have my cap and gown and a diploma to prove it. I also speak fluent French because I spent all my childhood holidays in Provence and I speak fluent Welsh because I was born in Wales and so were my parents. I have a gift for languages."

"You have travelled extensively in Germany."

"Look, we've been through this already. It was a *bona fide* exchange programme after Finals. Check with my College. Afterwards, I spent the rest of the year in the south of the country. I enjoy travelling. I like Germany."

"Enough to spy for the Nazis? You could have been recruited by them even back then."

"Oh, for goodness sake. I hate the bloody Nazis. That's why I risked my life to keep them out of Belgium and France in 1940."

"It's all right, Lieutenant Anderson. Please don't get upset," said a second voice.

"Upset? You've kept me here for I don't know how many days, firing the same stupid questions at me over and over again, taking no notice of the answers I am giving you. So before you ask *again*, I shall repeat them. *Again*. One at a time.

"I am not, nor have I ever been, a German spy.

"Yes, I worked for three months for the *Abwehr* but that was only because I happened to stumble across a suicidal German officer whose identity I acquired as a means to try and get out of the country.

"Yes, it led me to Brussels instead of Switzerland.

"Yes, I was given important information to bring back to England by a brave and honourable man whose identity I have already revealed to the head of British Intelligence to whom he is known personally.

"No, I was not furnished with that information as a sop to you lot so that you would be taken in, leaving me free to serve my so-called German masters in Berlin to my duplicitous heart's content."

"It's all right, Lieutenant Anderson."

126

"No, it's not all right."

Robert's assertions were passionate and forthright. "A lot of very brave people risked their lives to get me out of Belgium and back to England.

"Several very brave, high-ranking German officers and their associates are sailing close to the wind because they believe in the *country* of Germany and not the criminal Nazi state. They risk their lives every day to thwart the machinations of the *Gestapo* and the *SS* wherever they can.

"There are many in Germany who want peace; who want Hitler out of the way. They believe that without him in power, the whole corrupt Nazi system will crumble and millions of lives could be saved. But it is an almost impossible dream and they know that as well. He is surrounded by his bodyguard and protected by his henchmen. The Nazi system is deep rooted, its tentacles have spread far and wide into society. There will be no escape until the Nazis are defeated by the Allies.

"In the meantime, these brave people risk their lives by helping Jews to leave the country, and I can bear personal witness to this. They risk their lives by parrying the *Gestapo*; by giving the British Government by whatever means they can, including me, information that may be of some use, so that if it proves impossible to bring Hitler down by assassination or through the courts, at least they are doing something to try to weaken Nazism and hasten its demise. They are not spies, nor are they traitors. They love their country, the *real* Germany, and in what they are doing, they tread a very fine and dangerous line."

Robert looked earnestly across the table at whoever it was on the other side. "I am no turncoat or a German spy. Nor was I ever asked to be. I was never blackmailed or coerced in any way shape or form. Nothing was asked of me in return, I repeat, nothing, other than I bring back with me certain information and evidence that might just help shorten the war and ultimately bring those responsible to justice.

"And that is what *I* want to do, gentlemen, whoever you are, interrogating me now. I want to do something that will help shorten the war. To be allowed to use my abilities to further the war effort here. I want the Allies to win because I want morality, fairness, decency and justice – everything that we in this country hold dear – to prevail.

"I love my country, *this* country. I am a serving British officer and proud to be so. I want to make sure that the criminals who are running Germany are defeated. For all our sakes. Then the peoples whom they hold within their evil thrall, and that includes law-abiding, compassionate Germans, will be set free."

There was a profound silence in the room at the end of Robert's impassioned speech. No one moved, no one made a sound.

Eventually, someone spoke. "Thank you, Lieutenant Anderson. Thank you very much." The man's voice was quiet and calm.

"If we asked you to, would you agree to becoming an intelligence officer?" said the other man, unexpectedly. "British, of course."

Robert was so dumbfounded at this sudden about turn in attitude that he sat in stunned silence for several moments.

"After today, I could be awkward and say 'not bloody likely'," residual anger and tiredness making him petulant.

127

The man chuckled. "You could."

"But I won't, because you know that is exactly what I want to do."

"Good man."

"In what capacity?" asked Robert.

"We'll let you know in due course." He cleared his throat. "I'm sorry we had to put you through all this, Lieutenant. But we had to be sure. You know."

Robert took a deep breath. "I understand. I think."

"And, just to ease your mind, the children are safe and well. You need have no concern for them whatsoever. This is England, you know." The man smiled, although Robert could not see his face only sense it. "We know you've been worried about them."

"I have. And each time I've asked about them during the past three days, you've always given me some evasive answer." Robert took another deep breath. "They're children, not spies."

"We realize that. But you must understand, old chap, that we had to establish once and for all that *you* were not one." He smiled again. "And also that the children weren't being used by you as some kind of ruse to protect your, how shall we say… your surrogate identity."

Before his recent sojourn in Nazi Germany, Robert would have thought this man was crazy to even suggest such a thing, but now he could appreciate the logic. Just.

"You'll be able to see them again soon," said the other man.

"Thank you." Robert realized he would have to be content with that – for the moment.

"Now," said the first man pleasantly. "Outside the door is another new recruit who's been waiting rather a long time for us to finish. We've asked him to take you down to the canteen where you can both have a cup of tea and something to eat. I expect you'll be hungry by now. Be kind to him, it's his first assignment and from what I can gather, he's a bit nervous."

Robert sighed. He'd been back in the country for a week and during that time he'd been interviewed, debriefed, released, called back and interrogated. He was thoroughly fed up, exhausted, and worried about the children.

He'd been to hell and back before that and all he desired was to go home on leave and sleep in his own bed, peacefully and without fear. The last thing he wanted to do was nursemaid some timid, inexperienced greenhorn.

"Thanks," he said dispiritedly.

The man chuckled again. "He'll take you to the hotel where you'll be staying overnight. We'll see you both bright and early tomorrow morning. You'll be given a replacement uniform too, Lieutenant. That will be brought to you at the hotel. Oh, and if you want to swap stories with our new recruit, do by all means. Speak freely, get anything you like off your chest."

"Still checking up on me?" said Robert wearily.

"Actually, we're not. Though you have every justification for thinking that. You might find it useful to be able to share your adventures with each other freely and without fear. As long as it's in absolute private, of course."

"That goes without saying."

Were these people idiots? thought Robert. Hadn't they learned anything about his integrity during the past couple of days? And hadn't he just spent that time recounting 'his adventures'? Why on earth would he need to repeat them again to some stranger?

"We've told him the same thing, of course. From now on, it will only be with each other that you'll be able to share everything that's happened or will happen to you both, I'm afraid."

"And what is going to happen to us both?" asked Robert, curious despite his tiredness.

"All in good time, old chap. All in good time."

"Forgive me for asking, but I should like some leave first. I'm desperately tired and I haven't seen my family in over a year."

"All in good time; all in good time," he repeated.

Robert wanted to punch him.

"Now, we mustn't keep our friend waiting any longer. He's a lieutenant in the Royal Navy, by the way. His name's Richard Langley."

"Thank you for all your patience, Lieutenant Anderson," said the first man. "You will no doubt be pleased to hear that the interview is at an end. You may go. Sleep well," he added pleasantly.

"I'll try."

With relief, Robert left the room. The interrogation was over but it had left him with a nasty taste in his mouth.

When he closed the door behind him, he saw that the corridor was deserted apart from one solitary figure in naval uniform sitting on a solitary chair. He stood up when Robert approached. The two men shook hands.

"They must have given you quite a grilling in there," said Richard sympathetically.

Robert nodded. "Yep. They did."

"I'm glad they didn't put me through anything like that. Was it very gruesome?"

"It could have been worse."

"I expect you'll be glad of something to eat. I know I certainly am. Come on, it's this way. Let's go and grab a cup of tea. They do a passable scrambled powdered egg sandwich here as well. If we speak nicely to the serving lady, she might give us more than usual. They're worth their weight in gold and not as bad as one might think."

Too tired to do anything else, Robert allowed his guide, who certainly didn't give the impression of being nervous or timid, to lead the way.

"Well, you look exhausted, I must say, but I wouldn't have said you were the nervous or timid type," observed Richard, almost echoing Robert's thoughts.

"Is that what they said about me?"

"Yes."

"I'm neither. Thoughtful, maybe, but I'm certainly not timid."

"Nor me."

"They told me that you were! I thought I'd be nurse-maiding some feeble idiot. It was the last thing I wanted to do."

"Well, I'll be blowed! Why have they told us such utter rubbish? I mean, I might be new to this intelligence business, but I would like to think I haven't lost my social skills along the way." Richard paused for a moment. "What do you reckon's going on?"

"I've absolutely no idea. But right now, all I want is a cup of tea, preferably with lots of sugar in it and that scrambled egg sandwich, even if it does have its origins in powder. So, lead on, Richard."

The two men went down the steps into the basement canteen and ordered their food and drink.

"What is this place?" asked Robert. "It was dark when I arrived a few days ago."

"It's an old country manor house in the middle of nowhere which, as far as I can see, has probably been commandeered for the duration. Situated in a village called Chipping Banbury, so they tell me."

"Sounds like a name that someone's made up."

"That's what I thought when I first arrived – a combination of Banbury and Chipping Sodbury sprang to mind. From what I can gather, among other things, it's used to debrief returning officers who've escaped from P.O.W. camps as well as sussing out possible enemy agents. Only the ones in the former category who've been cleared are allowed the delightful egg sandwich – the others just get the powder." Richard paused and was pleased to see Robert's lips twitch. "I'd be interested to hear your story sometime, but probably not for a while. I imagine you've had enough for now. No doubt, you had to repeat everything over and over again. You must be sick of it."

"No. Too much happened to me and it's healthier to talk about it, I suppose. It will be a long time before I can let it go. But I would appreciate being able to switch off for a while, so thanks for that. What about you?"

"Me? Oh, I applied for 'Special Duties'. Simple as that and, hey presto, here I am! Sometime when you're rested and we're on our own, I'll tell you why and how. But fortunately, I didn't have to go through the trauma that you just have."

They ate their food in silence. Richard couldn't help noticing that Robert kept looking around discreetly and furtively, as though he thought he was being observed.

"You have had a rough time, haven't you?" he remarked. "And I don't just mean what happened today."

Robert shrugged. "Not particularly."

Richard looked at him. "You sound just like my sister Sophie."

"How so?"

"You've obviously been through the mill and yet you say, "not particularly" when I suggest it's been difficult. Sophie's like that. I remember one occasion when she fell off her horse, got dragged along the ground and ended up with badly bruised ribs and concussion. When the doctor asked her if it was painful, she shrugged and said, "not particularly," even though she was as pale as a ghost and black and blue all over. She has a gift for understatement. Rather like you, I imagine."

Robert smiled politely. He could feel his eyes closing.

Seeing this, Richard said, "Well, if you're finished, we'll get off to the hotel. You need your bed." The two men stood up. "I gather you've got nothing with you except what you're standing up in?"

"Yep."

"Well, we're more or less the same height, give or take an inch or two, so you can borrow a pair of my pyjamas and a dressing gown tonight. They tell me you've got a whole new wardrobe arriving tomorrow. I presume they've got your correct size?"

Despite his tiredness, Robert smiled. "Could be embarrassing if they haven't."

"Yeah! Oh, by the way, how are you off for shaving gear?"

"None."

"Well, I've a spare brush, soap and flannel. They provide towels at the hotel. It's not bad inside."

It was dark by the time the car arrived to take them to the hotel and Robert was grateful to Richard for taking over. They signed in and the two men went up to their rooms, which were opposite each other. Richard provided Robert with the items he needed and then turned to go.

"Thanks," said Robert. "I appreciate all this."

"Don't mention it. I hope you sleep well. See you in the morning. Breakfast is at eight."

"Goodnight, Richard."

"Goodnight."

Robert crawled into bed and fell asleep almost immediately but his slumber was disturbed by disjointed, incomplete images pervading his dreams, making him restless and agitated.

Erika, her eyes wild and filled with hatred; the children terrified and screaming; menacing night-filled streets.

He tried to run but his body was leaden, his legs unresponsive. A sinister figure with slicked-back hair leered up at him through the darkness...

Waking up disorientated and dislocated, shaking with fear and panic, his pyjamas sodden with sweat, Robert got out of bed and stumbled over to the chair, fumbling in the pocket of his jacket for cigarettes. With trembling hands, he lit one, inhaling deeply, feeling the drug percolate into his system, calming his nerves, allowing him to control his frantically beating heart.

Shivering, he put on his borrowed dressing gown and padded over to the window, drawing back both blackout and ordinary curtains, staring out at the fields lying silver in the moonlight.

England. He said the name over and over again. England. He was here. Safe. Home.

Needing to savour and imprint this reality upon his consciousness, Robert moved the easy chair across to the window and stayed there for the rest of the night, alternately catnapping and smoking until dawn.

The next morning, much to his surprise, Robert found his new uniform to be that of a captain.

"But that can't be right," he said to the issuing sergeant, who had knocked promptly and insistently on his bedroom door at seven o'clock.

"Oh, but it is. Reckon you've had a promotion, sir."

"So it would seem."

After he had gone, Robert stared for several moments at the battledress top with its four pips on the shoulder strap and the short line of medal ribbons above the breast pocket.

He looked at them closely. Yes, they were the correct ones. He picked up the cap and tried it on for size. It fitted, perfectly. He ran his fingers over the Royal Welch Fusilier's badge. Hopefully, he'd get back his original if Harry ever made it home. He must remember to send that postcard.

Taking his time, he bathed and dressed and, feeling only very slightly restored, went downstairs to the dining room.

"Well, you look smarter than yesterday," remarked Richard, who was already seated at their table.

"That wouldn't be difficult."

"Sleep well?"

"Not particularly. Too many nightmares."

"I expect they'll pass one day."

"I certainly hope so." Slowly, Robert sipped his tea, still acclimatizing himself to his surroundings, to being back in England.

"Well, we're off to see the chief wizard today back at his castle in Chipping whatever-it-is," observed Richard. "Perhaps our instructions will be to follow the yellow brick road."

"And find the Lion his nerve…"

"The Straw Man his brain…"

"A heart for the Tin Man."

"And Judy Garland?" added Richard hopefully.

"No chance," replied Robert. "With my dreams, it'll be the Wicked Witch of the West."

"Not the Sugar Plum Fairy?"

"Wrong story. She's from a ballet, the *Nutcracker*."

"So she is. Sophie used to love that when she was little."

"Sophie?"

"My sister."

"Ah, I believe you mentioned her last night. I must have been too tired to take anything in, I'm afraid," said Robert, not wishing to sound impolite.

"You really were on your last legs. You still look like death warmed up."

"At least I am warmed up."

"True."

"But all this repartee is too much for my poor addled early-morning brain to cope with," observed Robert, with half a smile.

"I thought you were doing a splendid job."

"Is this you being natural or are you under orders to cheer me up?"

"Just me, I'm afraid. The only instructions I had were to make sure you didn't keel over and that we could exchange our deepest, darkest military secrets in complete confidence."

"That's more or less what they said to me." Robert regarded his companion. "So, no reporting back to the powers that be? No descriptions of my state of mind or anything I might say or do?"

"Nope. None. I swear. Scout's honour." Richard gave a Boy Scout salute. "Just be yourself and I shall be myself, though the latter isn't probably such a pleasant prospect."

"I think you're doing a splendid job," retorted Robert, with a full smile this time.

A sudden thought occurred to Richard. "You haven't been told to report back on me have you?"

"What, with marks out of ten as this is your first assignment?" he teased. "No, I haven't. So I guess we can trust each other."

"Thank goodness for that." Richard smiled as well and placed his napkin on his empty plate. "Well, if we're all finished, we'll take that staff car back to the manor house. I gather we're not returning here afterwards, so you'll need to bring all your gear."

"Mostly your gear."

"True. Apparently, after we've received our orders, we're going on to somewhere else. It's all rather mysterious."

"That's the secret service for you, I suppose."

"Yeah. So secret that no one knows anything!" Richard made a face.

Robert laughed. "You're probably right."

It felt good to be able to laugh spontaneously again. For too long, he had had to watch his every word, his every expression.

The two men left the dining room, collected their belongings and travelled the short distance to Chipping Banbury to find out exactly what it was they would be required to do.

CHAPTER 18

St Nicolas

"Have you heard about Vera?" asked Ethel, the postman's wife, her manner confidential, as she sat at the kitchen table of the farmhouse drinking tea about a fortnight after the departure of Major von Witzenhausen and the original occupying force.

"No," replied Mae. "We're not often in town, so we don't really keep up to date with what's going on."

"A good thing too, if you ask me," observed Edna grumpily, who was not given to idle gossip, though she knew that Mae enjoyed the odd tittle-tattle.

"So, what's happened?" asked her sister.

"Nothing, except that she's been seen in quiet places weeping copiously. Rumour has it that one of the departing Germans was her lover. What do you think of that?"

Mae was shocked. "Goodness me!" she exclaimed, glancing at Edna, who remained stony-faced at this juicy nugget of information.

Thoughts of Albrecht von Witzenhausen flitted through Edna's mind. Her heart gave a lurch. She told herself not to be ridiculous.

Abruptly, she stood up and walked over to the sink where she began to peel potatoes.

Undeterred, Ethel continued. "According to Mabel, she went into the café wearing dark glasses, even though the weather was dull and overcast."

"What about the Commodore?"

"No one's seen him. He seems to have become a permanent fixture in their little house, not going out and about like he always did."

"Poor man, if the rumours are true, that is."

"Well, Mabel says that Vera," and she lowered her voice meaningfully, "is *that type*, you know. Mabel says she always knew she'd be a trouble to the Commodore from the moment she set foot on the island. She never could understand what he saw in her. Mabel thinks that it was probably his last chance, for a *fling*, you know. She's convinced that Vera only married him for his money."

"If that is the case, he's old enough to have known better."

But wisdom doesn't necessarily come with age, thought Edna, putting down her knife and staring out of the window.

Ethel began to gather her things together. "Well, I must be off! It'll take me a good while to walk back down to Port le Bac. I said I'd meet Frank at the crossroads so's he can help me carry these baskets. Thanks for still letting me collect the elderberries and mushrooms from your wood. Frank wouldn't know what to do without his elderberry jelly on his bread in the morning. Though this year's batch will be more sour because of the sugar rationing and all. The mushrooms will be a bit of luxury with our half-egg each at breakfast."

"You're welcome to come any time in the season, just as you've always done. There's more growing than we know what to do with. If we bottle and preserve it all, we'll be accused of hoarding; if we try and sell it, we'll be accused of operating on the black market and in either case, we'll end up going to prison. If we don't do anything at all, it'll just go to waste. Seems we can't win."

"It's ridiculous, isn't it?" Ethel stood up. "Well, goodbye, Edna."

Edna merely grunted in reply.

"I'll see you out," said Mae.

The two women left the kitchen and went into the farmyard.

"What's up with Edna?" enquired Ethel, once they were out of earshot. "She seems very out of sorts today."

"Oh, she's been like that for the past few weeks or so."

"She's not coming down with anything, is she? There's a lot of it about, you know."

"Oh dear, is there?" said Mae, suddenly becoming anxious.

"Don't you worry yourself, ducky. You'll be fine up here. All this fresh air and lots of farm food to eat. You're better off than we are in the town."

"No, we're not, I'm afraid. We have the same rationing as you, dear. We're subject to very strict controls, you know. And they check up on us. Woe betide us if we don't meet our quotas or try to hide away a little bit extra. The *Geheime Feldpolizei* search all the buildings when they make their inspections. It's a nightmare. The man on the next farm to ours went to prison for hiding a pig he'd slaughtered and not declared. No, one has to be very careful."

"That *Gestapo!* Everybody hates them. In Port le Bac, they're busy chasing after anyone who even hints at the Allies winning the war or says anything remotely controversial about the Germans. Since that new *Kommandant* arrived, it's been getting steadily worse. Even Gert's been quiet of late." Ethel stooped to pick up her laden baskets. "Well, it's a good job we can still talk freely up here, isn't it? Anyway, I really must go. Ta-ra!" and she gave Mae a quick peck on her cheek. "See you soon."

After lunch, Mae went for her customary rest upstairs in her bedroom and Edna allowed herself a few moments to sit down. She picked up a book and started to read it but could make no progress, despite several attempts at reading the first page.

She gave up and went over to the bureau and pressed one of the panels, which sprang open smoothly and cleanly. Inside the secret compartment were all her precious letters from Ralph together with her engagement and wedding rings, a dance card and a few photographs.

She extracted a small, faded sepia portrait of her former lover, looking handsome and proud in his uniform, and turned it over. On the back was written formally: *Captain Ralph Llewellyn, Royal Welsh Fusiliers, South Africa, 1902*, and then underneath, *To Dearest Edna, with all my love*. She turned the photo over again and touched his face.

Ralph. Her Ralph.

He belonged to another world now; a world she had left behind a very long time ago. And yet, her memories of him were as clear as though it were yesterday. She didn't grieve for him anymore although she often wondered how different things might have been had he lived.

Not that she was complaining. Before the invasion, she had been settled and content here on St Nicolas. Sophie's arrival and sojourn had added another dimension to her life, bringing the vibrancy of youth to cheer her twilight years.

Twilight years! What a load of old poppycock she was thinking today. She was no more in her twilight years than Mae was a... a female athlete.

Edna put the still-cherished relics back in their place. Then she went over to her handbag and took out a carefully folded piece of paper upon which was written a name and address in distinctive handwriting. She touched this also, and placed it in the secret compartment with her other treasures, assuming that Albrecht was now far away across the other side of Europe.

It might as well be the North Pole for all the good it will do, she thought.

With a sigh, Edna pushed the panel back securely, sealing away both the past and unlikely future, and shut the hinged flap of the bureau with a resolute clunk before locking it.

Sophie was out in the middle of Three-Acre field with Jean le Rouge. They were standing over the tractor's engine, which had stalled, trying to restart it. They had been trying for the past fifteen minutes but stubbornly, it refused to cooperate.

"Why can't manufacturers make mechanical things simpler?" said Sophie, running the back of her oily hand over her forehead in frustration. "We have to get this ploughing done while the weather's fine. And we've still got the tilling and sowing to do after that. We'll never get it all done at this rate before the next inspection."

"Well, I hate to admit it, but those two young German lads had this here old machine purring like a pussy cat. They just had the knack. Though I never thought I'd say it about a German." He suddenly looked worried. "You mustn't go tellin' nobody that I said that, mind. The wife'll have my guts for garters."

"No, of course not, I wouldn't dream of it."

Sophie gave the starting handle one last yank and the engine spluttered into life. They looked at each other in triumph. Jean adjusted the mixture while Sophie climbed up into the driving seat.

She was now doing much of the hard physical labour on the farm since the departure of Ulrich and Helmut. It was exhausting, but she found she was gradually building up the necessary stamina. Aunt Edna had taken over some of her chores as well as doing her own but even so, they were feeling the lack of hired labour acutely.

"Okay," called out Jean. "I'm ready for the off."

He steadied and steered the plough while Sophie drove the tractor. It wasn't easy, for either of them. Soon, Jean was puffing and panting and having to take frequent rests and Sophie became anxious lest he succumbed to a heart attack. There had to be an easier way than this.

After an hour, she stopped the tractor and switched off the engine. Jean mopped his forehead with his neckerchief and they sat down together under the oak tree and drank some tea out of a flask that Sophie had prepared that morning.

"I know you think they're lazy good-for-nothings," she said, "but what about asking for a couple of the unemployed flower-growers? We must have some help and the new *Kommandant* is demanding his quotas on time and to the nth degree without providing extra assistance. He says the troops are not here to work as farm labourers."

Jean grunted, "I suppose we'll have to. But you mark my words, them blokes'll be about as useful as a butterfly's fart."

Sophie was so surprised by this expression that she laughed out loud, causing Jean to chortle away too.

After the merriment had continued for some moments, once they had both finally recovered, she said, "I'll ask Aunt Edna to speak to the Controlling Committee at the Consell de Souverain. They can mediate on our behalf."

"They're useless too," grumbled Jean. "I mean, what have they done about all this thieving that's been going on? Nothing. Farm next door's lost half a dozen sheep in the past few weeks, and old Jim over the way had his henhouse broken into and his finest hens stolen, them that he's just reared after his others were slaughtered. Whatever's the island coming to? And our own police do nothing. They seem to have lost their sense of right and wrong since they've been taken over by the *Feldkommandantur*. No, I blame the new soldiers that's come onto the island, you know, them that's building the fortifications for those big guns on the east side, over by Falaise Head. They're a rowdy lot, Miss Sophie, not polite like the last ones. They can't speak English either like them others. They could do with that English teacher the boys were always going on about. What was his name?"

"Heinrich Hoffmeister."

So, thought Sophie, Helmut and Ulrich had spoken about him to Jean as well. Not for the first time did she wonder about this man. He must have made a profound impression on the lads for them to talk about him so often. There were other soldiers in Port le Bac who had mentioned him too.

"That's the one. I bet he knows a thing or two about manners, as well as English, because this new lot could do with a few lessons. They don't seem to take as much trouble to get on with us islanders. No, things is getting worse, and I don't know where it will all end."

· They sat in silence. There was nothing Sophie could say, other than listen sympathetically. Everything Jean said was true. Daily life was becoming a struggle; the enforcement of rules and regulations ridiculous.

Two weeks previously, the library in Port le Bac had been searched and all books containing anti-Nazi sentiments had been removed, along with anything written by Jews. Their own extensive library at the farmhouse had been examined on the same day and a few novels confiscated, even though the three women could see nothing wrong with any of them.

"It's a token gesture," Edna had stated defiantly after the *Geheime Feldpolizei* had gone. "They had to take something to justify their actions," she added, surveying the empty shelves and the books strewn in haphazard fashion everywhere around the room.

Then, yesterday, they had returned. Edna and Sophie had watched with a sense of concealed fury at their privacy being invaded yet again as the '*Gestapo*' inspected the house from top to bottom, this time looking for radios, weapons and any other books missed during the initial search that might be deemed remotely unsuitable.

It took Sophie and Edna an even longer time to clear up the mess that was left behind, but at least they had the satisfaction of knowing that their second wireless set was safe: now hidden in the inglenook fireplace behind some bricks which had first been removed and then replaced with the radio *in situ*. It was an ingenious hiding place and a strategically placed table lamp camouflaged the coiled-up electrical lead.

Apart from a few carefully concealed items within the house, their most treasured books, photographs and other possessions were safe and sound: meticulously wrapped in waxed cloths and placed inside empty milk churns, which were themselves buried deep in the overgrown garden behind the farmhouse.

Following his advice, Sophie and Edna had begun to dig a trench the day Major von Witzenhausen had left. It had taken them three days to make it sufficiently deep to hold everything before filling it in and adding camouflaging using leaves and small branches. But at least they had the satisfaction of knowing their possessions could not be tampered with.

More was to come, however.

Several weeks into these invasions of their privacy, in keeping with the other Channel Islands, it was decreed that all residents of St Nicolas born in the United Kingdom had to present themselves at the Town Hall for registration as British nationals.

First on the list to complete the long and tedious form were boys and men over the age of fifteen but younger than sixty-eight.

George and Frank stood next to each other in the queue.

"Any idea what this is all about?" asked George.

"None whatsoever," replied his friend, as they edged their way forward.

"Good job it's not raining," muttered George.

"*Quiet*," barked one of the accompanying guards.

The two men fell silent for a moment or two. They said, "Good morning" to the Commodore as he shuffled his way out and down the steps.

"He's aged a bit," observed Frank.

"Yeah. I bet it's because of what his missus was up to a while back," said George, with a wink. "But I have to admit I'd always taken him to be older than sixty-eight." They were now at the front of the queue. "Heigh ho, we're up next."

They sat down at one of the designated tables and began to complete the form. A while later, they emerged and after exchanging an exasperated look, went their separate ways.

A week or so after this, women and children were ordered to take part in the registration process.

"Bit of a bummer this, ain't it?" said Gert to Sophie. "'Ere Tommy, you stay wiv me," and she grabbed his hand, even though he was standing quietly, only a few feet away from her.

"I'd like to know what it's all about," said Ethel. "Frank said the form is very long."

"Your aunts were born here, weren't they?" asked Mabel.

"Yes, fortunately, but Aunt Mae's beside herself with worry about me because I wasn't," replied Sophie, picturing how Aunt Edna had had to pacify her sister and help her upstairs to her room with a cold compress for her aching forehead and to have a "little lie down" on her bed.

Sophie and Edna had regarded each other grimly when the time came for Sophie to begin the long walk down into Port le Bac. "Let me know what it's all about," were Edna's parting words as Sophie disappeared along the track.

"Good job we're not Jewish," whispered Gert.

"Ssh!" said Mabel. "Keep your mouth shut, otherwise we'll all be sent to Germany or wherever they're sending the Jews these days."

"Move along, move along, there," said the British policeman to the women.

Slowly and sullenly, the women went forward. The children were becoming fractious.

"Oh, do keep your lot under control," said Gert irritably to Mabel. "Why you 'ad to 'ave four of 'em is beyond me. One's enough of a bovver."

"Never you mind," responded Mabel sharply. "It's none of your business how many children George and I've got. It's what we wanted and it's what we got."

"I think it's nice to have as many children as you can," added Ethel cheerfully. "Frank and I are quite happy with our two, though I do still get broody every now and again."

"Well, don't 'ave any more for gawd's sake otherwise the 'ole bleedin' island'll be chock-a-block wiv kids."

Sophie wished that Gert would be quiet. She smiled at Tommy who smiled back. He was a nice lad, quiet and thoughtful, so very different from his mother. He seemed to cope with Gert's moods, never complaining, at least not publicly; absorbing himself in his nature books, collecting flowers, leaves, butterflies and bird's eggs, arranging them in his bedroom and cataloguing each one.

She supposed it was his escape. Tommy had once told her that he'd love to go somewhere that had forests and high mountains and gushing streams, like he'd seen once in a book he'd got out of the library, because he loved the outdoors and the fresh air. He wanted to live in a place where he could ramble to his heart's content and really get to know all about nature, but his mam said he was stupid for wanting something he could never have.

"But I shall, one day, you'll see," he'd said to Sophie, his freckled face alight with his dream.

At last, Sophie reached the head of the queue and entered the building.

Fifteen minutes later, she emerged from the Town Hall just as Vera was going in. She seemed very subdued these days.

"Do you think they might be sending us back to England?" she asked, displaying a momentary brightness of hope as their paths crossed by the doorway.

"I have no idea," replied Sophie.

She had to admit that was something she hadn't considered.

As she walked home, slowly and reflectively, she came to the conclusion that if she had any choice at all in the matter, she would prefer to stay on St Nicolas. Even with the invasion, she had no desire to go home.

How strange that she should feel this way despite the obvious dangers; despite the deprivations and petty bureaucracy; despite being under the 'German jackboot' as Mabel had once so eloquently phrased it.

Despite all this, she knew she wanted to stay. She felt settled and happy with her aunts. The farm had now become her home; she had no wish to return to her former life. Besides which, the war wouldn't last forever. One day the island would be free again.

One day.

CHAPTER 19

Maybury

When they arrived at Grange Manor, they were shown to a desk in the palatial entrance hall where Robert was handed identity cards, passes, tags and ration books – everything, in fact, that he would need for both within his regiment and the world at large.

He and Richard were then informed that they were to be given a month's leave, effective immediately. That was the first surprise. The second was each of them being given a buff-coloured envelope and told to wait.

"It's like being back at school and handed your progress report," observed Robert, after they had sat down across the other side of the hall.

"What were yours like?" asked Richard.

"Okay."

"I'd hazard a guess and say you're understating things again…"

Robert smiled enigmatically.

The two men sat down on a couple of easy chairs on the other side of the hall and opened their envelopes.

"Good God!" exclaimed Richard. "I've been given the D.S.M.!" He stared at Robert, amazed. "What's in yours?" Silently, Robert handed him the sheet of paper. "The V.C.!" Richard smiled and shook Robert's hand warmly. "Congratulations, old man!"

"And you!" said Robert.

Richard could hardly believe his eyes as he read the words on the paper. And Robert's heart was beating fast as he too read the citation: *For bravery under intense enemy fire in ensuring the men in his charge were brought to safety*, followed by a brief description of the events by the River Escaut and Robert's part in them.

How his life had changed since then; how many things he had seen and done. Somehow, it belonged to a different world; an age of innocence. Yet how could violence and suffering ever be described as innocent?

Robert jumped when a smartly dressed Wren addressed him. "Captain Anderson, please come this way," she said.

"I'll wait here with the luggage," said Richard, smiling expansively. "I'm not in any hurry."

The prospect of long-awaited leave stretched out before him like a holiday from school. Knowing from past experience he could never reach Caroline during the day, he resolved to telephone her that evening. He wondered how often she'd be able to get away during the next four weeks.

"Thanks," and Robert followed the Wren down a long corridor lined with noticeboards, and up some stairs, where family portraits hung in serried rows. She knocked firmly at one of the ornate doors before opening it.

Immediately, Robert was assailed by three children hurling themselves at him.

"Robert ! Robert ! Vous êtes ici !" shouted Claude excitedly, jumping up and down, grabbing his hand.

"Oui." Robert had to work hard to stop his eyes filling up with tears as he hugged all of them to him. *"Comment allez-vous ?"*

"Très bien, merci ! We have been given lots of food to eat..."

"...and kind people have given us toys. Look, Robert, I have a doll. I have called her Françoise!" and Aimée held out her doll to show Robert.

"C'est une belle poupée !" he said, solemnly shaking the doll's fabric hand.

"The English ladies are so kind, Robert. Thank you for bringing us here," and Hélène put her arms round his waist and laid her head against his chest. *"I know we shall be happy with you here in your country."*

"Even when they took us away from you, I did not worry," announced Claude. *"I knew we would be safe. I told that to the girls. They were worried. But we are fine. We even had jelly and ice-cream."*

Robert looked gratefully at the nurse who had been in charge of them. "Thank you, Sister," he said.

"They've been as good as gold," she said kindly. "They've slept well and I've never seen children eat so much."

"They were a long time without food." He had been, too.

"So I gather."

"Where are we going to go now?" asked Aimée.

Robert looked enquiringly at the nurse.

"Oh, they're to come with you, Captain Anderson. Once you've completed all the paperwork, they're to be released into your care until the authorities decide what to do with them." She saw Robert go pale. "You don't want the children?" she asked, suddenly concerned.

"No, no, it's not that," said Robert. "Of course I want them. They are my responsibility." He smiled. "I'm sorry to give the wrong impression. It was just the expression of the *authorities* deciding what to do with them that I found upsetting. In Nazi-occupied Europe, you see, the term *authorities* is used as a euphemism for the *Gestapo*. The children came close to being taken away by them in Brussels so for me, your phrase had a sinister ring to it."

"I meant nothing, I can assure you," she said.

"Forgive me, but I've been out of England for a while."

"Yes, the children have told me via our Wren interpreter. The man you need to speak to is Colonel Harris," she added more gently, beginning to understand. "He'll be able to give you more information than I can."

Richard nearly fell off his chair when Robert came back down the corridor with the three children all carrying their toys and a small suitcase each. He stood up quickly.

"Good grief! These aren't yours are they?"

"Sort of."

"What do you mean, 'sort of'?"

"I, er..." Robert was momentarily lost for words.

142

It was all becoming too much to have to cope with what he could see would be the first of many explanations. And until the children learned some English, he would be obliged to interpret all the time.

"Robert nous a sauvés des Allemands, Monsieur," said Claude, addressing Richard.

"Vraiment ?" replied Richard, much to Robert's surprise.

"Robert est un homme très courageux." Claude nodded.

"Mais oui. He is indeed a very brave man to rescue you from the Germans."

"You speak French?"

"Enough to get by. And German, but I read both better than I can speak them. You see, my grandfather was German and my grandmother was French. The whole family speaks both languages. Though Sophie's our champion linguist," he added. "Has a real gift for both languages. And then what does she go and do?"

Robert shook his head. "I've no idea, tell me."

"She goes and reads English at university."

Robert chuckled. "Which one?" he asked out of politeness.

"Oxford. Somerville."

His interest suddenly became genuine. "When?"

"Let me see, she was there '35 to '38. Why?"

"Just wondered."

Richard looked at him. "Were you at Oxford as well?"

"Yes. Trinity College."

"When?"

"1933 to 1936."

"So you were there more or less at the same time as Soph."

"More or less, although Somerville students were very much off limits to us males. Unless you went Scottish country dancing, of course, or met up in the town. I regret to say, however, I never met anyone called Sophie Langley."

"What did you read?"

"German."

"Good grief!"

"What about you?"

"What about me?"

"Did you go to Oxford as well?"

"No. The other place, I'm afraid. Cambridge."

"Well, nobody's perfect," Robert smiled. "Subject?"

"Maths."

"Clever clogs. When?"

"Same time as you."

"Well, I'm blowed."

The two men looked at each other again. The world was indeed small, thought Robert.

"So," said Richard, returning the conversation to the present. "What are you going to do with these children? I'm *really* curious now to hear your story. It's becoming more and more intriguing."

"Well, you'll have to be patient. In the meantime, I have absolutely no idea what I shall do with my instant family." He sighed. "I'd not thought further than getting them back safely to England. There's some colonel chap I need to go and have a word with apparently. Can you keep an eye on the children?"

"Yes, dear," said Richard, and Robert had to laugh.

Reminded very much of his own and Harry's banter and smiling at this most recent and promising possibility for friendship, he located the colonel, who turned out not to be particularly helpful.

"Strictly speaking, they're refugees, but as you brought them with you into the country, the authorities may be happy to leave them in your care for the time being. I suppose eventually they'll be put in an orphanage or billeted with some family. Though they'll probably have to be split up. Can't see anyone taking on three of 'em at the same time these days. Most places in the country are full to bursting with our own evacuees from the cities."

Robert knew that he was not prepared to have the children separated and billeted with strangers. Rashly, acting on the spur of the moment, he declared: "I'm prepared to take them on permanently, sir."

"Are you married, Captain Anderson?"

"Er, no, sir."

"What about your duties? You can't possibly care for three children as a single army officer."

"No, but my father," in at the deep end now, "is headmaster of a boarding school. They could go there. I'm confident that he and my mother will agree to look after them in my absence."

"Who'll pay for their education, school fees, uniforms and so on?"

Robert hesitated. "I shall."

"Well, I'll leave you to sort that out yourself. I'll inform the appropriate people of your intentions."

"Thank you, sir."

"No doubt they'll be in touch in due course."

"Yes, sir."

"Now if you'll just see my secretary and complete some forms..."

This done, Robert walked back to Richard, who was doing a sterling job entertaining the children.

"Well?" he said, looking up at Robert.

"I've just landed myself permanently with three children."

"What?"

"It was either that or have them billeted with strangers, separately,"

Robert sat down, exhausted. The world was going round. He just wanted to sleep. It was all too much.

"Look, old man," said Richard, seeing his pallor. "My car's parked outside. I don't live too far away from here. Why don't I take all of you back to my house for a bit? I'm sure that my mother won't mind. For all her fussy ways, she's a generous soul. Dad's probably at his club or out with the horses, so he won't mind either. Cookie will take them in hand, I'm sure. You need to rest."

"I need to see my own family."

"You need to sleep first. You can phone your family when we get to Maybury."

"This is incredibly kind."

"No, it's not." Richard smiled. "I have an ulterior motive. How else am I going to learn what happened to you?"

Weary, but grateful, Robert replied, "I wouldn't want to mess up your leave."

"You won't. Put it this way, the only person I really want to be with is my fiancée and I can't get in touch with her until this evening. Apart from being with her, I shall only laze around – something I'm only too good at, by the way. I might as well do something useful."

"If you're sure?"

"Absolutely." He stood up and gave a command to the children: *"Alors. Venez mes enfants. Suivez-moi à ma voiture !"*

"Oui, Monsieur Richard," said Claude, standing to attention and saluting.

After the final formalities had been completed at the reception desk, Richard led the way to where his car was parked and they set off for Maybury with the three children sitting on the back seat, waiting with remarkable equanimity for the next part of their adventure to unfold.

We are safe now, thought Claude. *Safe in England. Safe with Robert and his kind friend, Monsieur Richard. We do not need to be afraid ever again.*

For his part, Robert spent the journey trying not to fall asleep (why did he always want to sleep during the day when it was inconvenient but found it virtually impossible at night?) and wondering exactly what he was going to do with three young children.

"Richard! This is a lovely surprise!" exclaimed Margot, coming into the hall. "Why didn't you tell us you were coming? And who's your friend?"

"Mother, this is Captain Robert Anderson. We've, er, been working together. Bob, this is my revered mama, Lady Margot." The two of them shook hands. "We both have a spot of leave and I was wondering whether he could stay overnight and have a bit of a rest before going home," continued Richard. "He lives in Oswestry, so it's too far to travel today."

"Oh!" For a moment, Margot was taken aback, her mind's eye picturing the multifarious boxes piled up in the guest rooms and all of the downstairs reception rooms. However, she rallied almost immediately and said, "Of course. You're most welcome, Captain Anderson."

"Thank you," he replied. "The children?" he ventured.

"Ah," replied Richard, before turning to his mother. "He has three children," he said, a mischievous twinkle in his eye.

"Three children?" Richard chuckled at her surprised expression. Again, his mother quickly regained her composure. "What about your wife, Captain Anderson? Is she with you?"

"I'm not married, I'm afraid."

"Goodness! And you have three children?" Margot was shocked; things were becoming worse by the minute but, being a retired diplomat's wife, she swallowed her discomfiture and summoned up her best hospitable manner. "Well, they must come in, too. The air gets damp very quickly with these autumn mists."

Richard laughed. "They're Belgian, Mother. Refugees. Robert somehow managed to bring them back with him after he escaped from a P.O.W. camp in Germany."

"A P.O.W. camp? How brave!" Margot regarded Robert for a moment. This man could be just what she and her Red Cross ladies were looking for. But that could come later. For the moment she turned her attention to the children. "Do they speak French or Flemish?"

"French."

Margot opened the front door wider and beckoned to the children. *"Venez à l'intérieur, tout le monde. You have no need to be shy. We shall find something for your lunch."* Margot ushered them into one of the sitting rooms, piled high with Red Cross boxes. "I'm afraid there's not a great deal of room as I've turned the house into a storage facility. Did you have Red Cross parcels in your camp, Captain Anderson?"

"Yes, Lady Langley, we did. They were life savers. Literally."

Margot smiled broadly. "I'm so pleased. You see, I'm chairwoman of the local branch and sit on the Joint War Organization Committee for the British Red Cross and St John's Ambulance in London. I've never actually met anyone who has first-hand experience of our work. It's not the same when we read the reports from the Swiss officials who've visited the camps. It must be very different for someone who has actually lived there." She decided to go straight to the point. "I'm so glad you came here today, Captain Anderson. Would you be willing to give a talk to my ladies sometime?"

"Of course," replied Robert politely, not really taking in her words. He just wanted to sleep.

"We're having a fundraising auction next week," continued Margot. "That would be ideal. All about life in a prison camp. You can tell us whether or not we're doing the right thing. It would be so useful to know and would make my ladies feel that all their hard work is making a difference. I'd be so grateful."

"I'll do my best." The room started to spin again.

Margot regarded Robert. "Poor man. What on earth have you been doing to him, Richard? He looks just about done in. Are you hungry?" she said to Robert.

Despite his tiredness, breakfast seemed a long time ago. "Yes, I am, rather."

"Good. I'll tell Cookie to make us up an early lunch and then you must rest."

"Thank you."

"The children can sleep in the nursery. As all the guest bedrooms are stuffed to the ceiling, you'd best take your friend up to Sophie's room, Richard." A shadow passed over Margot's face but she quickly concealed it and went into the kitchen to organize lunch.

Left alone after lunch, Robert stood at the window of his bedroom for a moment, absorbing the view, watching the River Thames as it flowed gently along the bottom of the garden.

He liked Richard's family. He liked the warmth and generosity that Margot and her husband Edmund had shown at lunch towards the children and himself, all of whom were total strangers to them. However, it struck him as odd that no one had

146

said anything about Richard's mysteriously absent sister. What was her name? Sophie. He'd been too tired to ask about her during the meal. He'd only just managed to keep his eyes open.

Weary as he was, Robert took stock of his surroundings, feeling at home in the ambience of the room and wondering about the character of the elusive Sophie.

One portion of wall was adorned with pony club rosettes and later show-jumping trophies, while dressage cups stood on a tall chest of drawers. There were no photographs on display and he took this as an indication that she was not a vain person, although he did wonder what she looked like. There were no family photos downstairs, either. Perhaps Margot had removed them for safe keeping while the house was being used for storage.

Large bookshelves adorned the walls either side of the fireplace and Robert scanned the titles, seeing well-read history books, travel guides, poetry and classic literature, French novels (*La Chaleur de la Mer*? wondered Robert, hopefully. *No, unfortunately not*), German novels, English novels – wide ranging books that showed a broad intellectual curiosity and linguistic ability.

He continued to explore. He opened the door of her capacious clothes cupboard a little way and caught a glimpse of feminine, stylish dresses for evening and day-wear. It wasn't quite the thing for a gentleman to look inside a lady's wardrobe but intrigued, Robert opened the door further. Pretty blouses and skirts were contained within, along with practical trousers and jumpers, cardigans, warm shirts and riding gear.

He liked her taste in clothes. And the gentle aroma of her perfume that clung to them. Quietly, he closed the wardrobe doors.

He wondered if he would like the person who wore them and who read such diverse books. He wondered where she was. Why had no one spoken of her? Perhaps it just hadn't come up in general conversation. No doubt, Richard would tell him at some stage.

Suddenly, the bed looked very inviting. Leaving the curtains open as was his wont, Robert undressed and slipped between the sweet-smelling sheets. He felt warm and comforted. And safe. For the first time in a very long time.

Peacefully, he drifted off to sleep.

"Well," declared Richard, after Robert had been at Maybury for a week, having been persuaded by a concerned Margot to stay on until he was properly rested.

Much as he wanted to see his own family, Robert knew they would have worried unnecessarily if he had gone home in his earlier state of complete exhaustion. It was better to have regained some semblance of his usual energy before returning to Oswestry, particularly as he had the complexities of the children's future to discuss at home. He had spoken to his parents on the phone, able to reassure them that he was safe and well.

"Both my parents are out," continued Richard. "Dad's on some nocturnal Home Guard manoeuvre and won't be back till morning and Mother is spending the night at her club in town as she's got a late committee meeting. The children are fast asleep, according to Cookie, who's been having a whale of a time with them. So the evening's ours. And I want to hear the rest of this story of yours before you disappear into the wild Welsh border lands tomorrow and I disappear into the arms of my beloved for a few days, who I have to say has been very elusive this past week."

Robert stretched his legs out in front of him, warming his feet by the fire, and took a sip of brandy. "I can't refuse you really, can I?"

"Certainly not. Indeed, I pronounce you fit enough to stay up until the wee small hours, Captain Anderson, as I want to hear every last gory detail. You've had enough sleep during the past week to keep the whole county going, as well as plenty of restorative fresh air in between. Talking of which, Dad has really enjoyed having a fellow horseman around who can bash a ball as well as he can. Where did you learn to ride and wield a polo stick so expertly, by the way?"

"Riding has always been natural, I suppose. Like your sister, I did all the usual pony club stuff when I was younger. Then I lost touch for a while when I went to Oxford before taking up riding again at Sandhurst, where I was in the polo team."

"I see." Richard finished his drink. "Well, when this war's over you'll be able to resume your equine activities."

"Perhaps. Unfortunately, I asked my parents to sell my horse when I went across to France. There would have been no one to ride him, you see."

"That must have been hard. Sophie absolutely adores her precious Hestia."

"I can understand that completely. Her horse is very special."

"Well, Dad says she seems to have taken to you."

"As I have to her."

Robert wondered how Sophie would feel about a stranger riding her horse as he had been doing these past days. Edmund had assured him that she would have been delighted as Robert and the animal seemed to understand each other. Even so, Robert made sure he was very gentle with the mare, feeling the weight of his responsibility riding someone else's beloved animal.

"Now," said Richard, "enough idle chitchat. So, let's see. Over the past few days, we've chatted about the B.E.F. and rescuing the children as well as my little escapade with the U-boat that led me into the labyrinth of British military intelligence under the guise of Special Duties. And I've told you about Sophie. So, there's nothing left except Robert's Big Adventure. More brandy?"

"Yes, please."

"Cigarette?" Richard proffered his cigarette case.

"I've smoked far too many recently, so, no thanks."

"Sensible chap. Sophie hates my smoking. She thinks ciggies are nasty dirty, smelly things."

"And she's right about that." Robert smiled. "You're very fond of your sister, aren't you?"

"We're very close. I love her to bits and miss her very much. I can't bear the thought of her being trapped on St Nicolas."

"I have every sympathy for her. Having been a P.O.W., I know what it's like to feel trapped." He smiled nostalgically. "I went to the island on holiday once. It's a lovely place. I hate to think of it being under military law."

"So do I. And I worry about her and my two aunts."

148

Robert stared into the fire. He wondered if Sophie knew of his secret cove. Probably. And so too did a lot of other people, no doubt.

"Story time," said Richard, seeing the faraway look in his friend's eyes.

"Yes."

To his interrogators, Robert had told the official version. To his new found friend – and they had developed a genuine friendship during the past week – he would recount the human version.

He trusted Richard and knew that he would need to leave nothing out of the narrative.

CHAPTER 20

Maybury

After scaling the fence behind the shower block, Robert heard no sirens, saw no powerful searchlights, discerned no instructions being given to prowling dogs.

He knew then for certain that 'Oscar' and his companions were safely back in the compound. His absence had not yet been discovered and he breathed a temporary sigh of relief.

The first stage was over. Successfully.

The darkness of the wood was all enveloping and he knew he was free and clear.

Robert stood for a moment, focusing his mind on the next part of his plan: head for the hill road out of Seeblick, which was no more than a narrow track leading high into the mountains, and then take the long and winding path towards the Swiss border.

Fifty miles. He'd marched at least that far with the battalion after the River Escaut.

He knew he'd have to forage for food and water. He planned to seek out isolated farms and hamlets; remote villages where there would be fewer soldiers.

Anxious to press on, he walked through the night and on into the next morning.

Unfortunately, everywhere there seemed to be soldiers. Whole columns of them, forging across the fields, surging through the narrow tracks, taking up the entire width of the roads: an army on the move; laughing and joking, confident and carefree.

They smiled and waved as they passed by, sending out early morning greetings.

Jovially, they asked him where he was going on such a fine morning. Why wasn't he in uniform?

Robert subtly gained a limp and said he'd been injured in the Battle for France.

"Then you are a hero!" they'd called out before the last man disappeared beyond the trees.

His heart beating fast, Robert found a quiet place to rest, away from prying eyes; away from marching soldiers.

For all of that day and night he continued onwards, taking a more circuitous route; snatching sleep in barns or under hedges whenever he could; drinking water from clear, fast flowing streams; avoiding villages and hamlets, except for fleeting visits to purchase bread and meat with money acquired for him from a variety of German guards by a light-fingered fellow prisoner at Seeblick.

Five exhausting days later, he came within sight of the Swiss border. Cautiously, keeping well hidden, he surveyed the scene.

The border crossing itself looked quiet and relaxed. One sentry stood on duty, another was near the barrier, smoking a cigarette.

Suddenly, away to his right, there was a terrific commotion and shouts from some other border guards. Five men wearing British khaki uniforms were bundled out from their hiding place in the nearby forest, their hands held high above their heads, while being pushed and shoved by the German soldiers away from the border crossing. At gunpoint, they were forced to lie face down on the grass.

"That must have been an awful moment," said Richard.

"It was, especially as there was nothing I could do to help them. I was just too far away."

"It wrecked your chances, though."

"It did, but in many ways it was fortunate," replied Robert.

"Tell me," said his friend.

Quickly, Robert melted back into the dense forest, the way he had come, stumbling over fallen trees and jutting-out roots, losing his way in his anxiety to evade possible capture.

Breathing heavily, he paused and listened. No sound of pursuit, only that of a surging river somewhere deep in a ravine.

Robert sat on the grass towards the edge of the treeline, still concealed from view.

Then he saw him – a German officer, a *leutnant*, standing at the edge of the precipice, unmoving, lost in contemplation of the river below.

Robert froze in his hiding place.

But the officer neither turned to look behind him, nor removed his gaze from the water. It occurred to Robert that this man was possessed by it, that the gushing river held some kind of peculiar fascination for him.

The German officer began methodically to undress: removing first his Luger, his jacket, his shirt, trousers and finally, his underwear.

Unable to move, Robert was transfixed.

After a moment or two, the man moved to the very edge of the precipice. He gave out a strange, strangulated cry, lifted his arms out wide, leant forward and disappeared.

Robert realized that this was no ordinary dive. This was not a normal entry into the water. Something was very, very wrong.

Stunned by the unanticipated action, he waited for an hour, then two hours, then three.

But the man did not reappear.

Robert did not see him, as he would have expected, arriving back from further up the river bank, dripping wet but exultant after a daring escapade. Nor did he see him climbing exhausted and gasping for breath, up from the gully.

He saw none of these things. The *leutnant* had gone. For good.

Cautiously, Robert stepped away from his hiding place, gingerly stretching his aching, cramped muscles. He went over to the place where the man had stood and peered carefully over the edge.

There, sprawled out on bloodstained rocks below, was the German soldier, his body twisted and broken, his eyes wild and staring, his remains imprisoned by the branches of a spate-swept tree.

Sickened, Robert turned away. He had seen horrendous injuries occur on the battlefield, but this upset him more than he could say.

Guilt assailed him. Should he have stopped him? Could he have prevented this tragedy? Perhaps, deep down, he hadn't wanted to. No, Robert knew he wasn't like that. Enemy or not, this man was a human being. Besides, he had had no idea that the German was about to commit suicide until it was too late.

In any case, it always came back to a simple matter of survival.

Robert slumped wearily on the grass, his eyes resting on the pile of clothes. Beside them was a leather attaché case and a large suitcase. Looking around him, he dragged everything back into the shelter of the trees where he opened the attaché case.

Inside were various documents, a wallet containing a huge wodge of bank notes as well as a train ticket from Berlin and a letter, addressed merely to: *Die Liebe meines Lebens* (To the Love of my Life).

Carefully, Robert opened the envelope and removed the contents. There were two sheets of paper and a signet ring.

Liebchen,

How could you betray me? I thought we loved each other. Our time together was the happiest of my life but now I tear out my soul in grief and shame.

For you are nothing but a charlatan and a whore. Now, because of you, there will be hell to pay and I shall bear the brunt.

Knowing this, I cannot go on. I cannot take up my new post knowing that you will be there before me, plotting behind my back even before I have arrived.

In order to think about things, I have come here to the beautiful place where we spent our glorious leave last summer.

Do you remember? Does it mean nothing to you? How can you put that aside and do what you have done to me?

I could never betray you in the way you have betrayed me. Not in a million years. But right now, all I want to do is kill you. To tear your traitorous, conniving heart out of your body.

And because I feel like that about you and because of what you have done, I am going to kill myself instead.

> *Otto.*

"Goodness, that was all rather melodramatic," remarked Richard.

"It was. But so was his solution. He must have been out of his mind with anger and grief. Poor chap."

"How can you feel sorry for him? He was a German!"

"He was a man hurt by a woman's betrayal of him."

"True. But he was a Nazi. Serves him right."

"Not all Germans are Nazis," observed Robert.

"I thought they were?"

"A popular misconception."

"I'll have to take your word for that. But I'm listening. Go on."

Robert explored the attaché case further. There were letters of introduction from someone called Admiral Siranac to the head of the *Abwehrstelle* in Brussels...

Brussels? …stating that *Leutnant* Otto Stolze came from an upright and honourable family and was known personally to the admiral. *Rest assured, he will slot easily into our organization. You need have no worries about him*, was the concluding line.

There was another letter to Otto Stolze himself from the admiral, stating that his principal duties, '*in this most proud of Secret Services*', were to be in counterintelligence.

Counterintelligence. In the *Abwehr*. An idea began to form in Robert's mind.

What secrets might be learned if *he* became Otto Stolze? What information might he be able to collect and take home with him?

If he reached home.

It was a dangerous game to play. *If* he decided to play it.

He had no training, no knowledge of the setup in the German military, let alone the *Abwehr*.

His thoughts in turmoil, Robert turned his attention to the man's suitcase. There were ample clothes – casual attire, dress uniform, shoes, shaving things. And more money.

How much did this man have?

The suitcase contained everything, in fact, that would be needed for a foreign posting.

Robert searched through the pockets of the uniform. Identity cards, a mess bill and a travel warrant to Brussels.

Brussels.

The children were in Brussels. He would be able to check that they were safe.

Robert studied the man's identity papers. Fortunately, the photograph was not the best quality, being slightly grainy and blurred. From the written description, he saw they were of similar height with the same coloured hair and eyes. If this man had been short and fat with Aryan blond hair, then Robert would have abandoned the whole enterprise but, as things stood, he might just get away with it.

But what about the woman who betrayed Otto?

He read the letter again. '*I cannot take up my new post knowing that you will be there before me, plotting behind my back even before I have arrived.*'

Well, if she had betrayed him with another man, then she'd have a bit of a shock when he, Robert, turned up as Otto, wouldn't she? If there was more to it than that, then she wouldn't be able to say anything without compromising herself.

Balancing the danger to himself with the rewards of the vital information he might be able to glean, he decided it was a chance he had to take. It was his one absolute opportunity to do something that might make a difference.

Looking around him again, he took off his own clothes, packed them in the suitcase, and put on Otto Stolze's uniform.

"I bet that felt odd," observed Richard.

"It did."

"I can imagine. You must have felt like a traitor."

"Not really. I persuaded myself I was wearing a costume for a play. In any case, I knew it was the right thing to do; the only thing to do."

Checking that he had left nothing behind, he looked down at the river once again. The body had gone, the restraining branch swept away by the fast-flowing water.

Relieved and carrying both the suitcase and attaché case, Robert worked his way out of the forest. Once he had regained the road and found his bearings, he set off for the nearest railway station. The travel warrant was from Berlin to Brussels and dated two days hence. So first, he would have to get a train to Germany's capital city.

It seemed a roundabout way of reaching his destination, let alone England, but was necessitated by the documentation that he had in his possession.

Robert remembered a railway station in the small town he had walked through only the previous day.

He arrived to find it seething with German troops, presumably looking for further escaped P.O.W.s. At the station, two black-coated *Gestapo* men were watching the passengers closely as they went through the ticket barrier.

Robert purchased his ticket and made his way to the barrier. His ticket was checked and his identity card asked for. This he produced and was allowed through.

The *Gestapo* men seemed unmoved by his actions and did not board the train after him. So, remaining wary and alert, Robert found a seat and sat down, opening the newspaper he had purchased at the newsstand.

But he could not read a word. Surreptitiously, Robert looked around, but no one took any notice of him or spoke to him, even when he went to the dining car. It was as though he was invisible.

He reached Berlin without incident and stepped off the train at the *Anhalter Bahnhof* station, quickly gaining his bearings and finding a small hotel for the night. When asked why he was not staying at the barracks, he replied that he was taking up a very important post in Brussels and only stopping over for the night.

The manageress viewed him suspiciously (or was that just his imagination playing tricks?) but when other Germans officers came in, she was distracted and Robert was not questioned further.

"How did you know where to go?"

"Remember, I'd lived in Berlin for six months so I knew my way around. It was just a lucky coincidence that I'd chosen a hotel where other *Wehrmacht* officers happened to book in. With their girlfriends, I might add, for a raucous night. And it was, for I didn't get much sleep."

"You didn't join in?" Richard's expression was mischievous.

Robert looked at him. "No," he replied. "Definitely not my style."

"So, what's the city like these days? Sophie and I lived there as small children when my father was at the British Embassy so my memories are hazy to say the least."

"Take away all the Nazi flags and paraphernalia and it's still a wonderful city. It has some fantastic buildings. There's so much history, so many elegant and spacious streets. It has its seedy side, of course, but then what large city doesn't?"

"Any bomb damage?"

"Some, but not that you'd notice it. They haven't had many air raids."

"Not like London."

"Nothing like London. Yet."

"Was there an air raid while you were there?"

"No, fortunately."

"What did you do next?"

"After breakfast, I took the train, or rather trains, to Brussels."

After alighting at his final destination, Robert found his way to *Abwehrstelle* headquarters on the Rue du Roi, a moderately impressive, five-storey grey stone building with cornicing and a small central balcony.

With his heart pounding, Robert ascended the stairs and entered the building. He gave his name at the desk by the door and was immediately shown to a large office.

"*Ach*, come in, *Leutnant* Stolze. I am *Hauptmann* Brandt, head of the Brussels branch of the *Abwehr*."

There was no Nazi salute, no guttural exclamations of "*Heil Hitler*", merely a formal clicking of heels and a bow. This caught Robert by surprise.

"Do you have your letters of introduction, *Leutnant*?"

Robert handed these to the *Hauptmann*, who quickly scanned them.

"*Gut!* Everything is in order. You come most highly recommended from our Admiral himself." He smiled, briefly, and pressed a buzzer under the desk. "One of our secretaries will show you to your office."

Almost immediately, an attractive young woman dressed in the field-grey uniform of an army auxiliary, entered the room. Brandt smiled warmly at her, appraising her body briefly but openly.

"Erika, our new recruit needs to know where he is to work," said the *Hauptmann*. "And where he is to sleep. When you are settled, Erika will bring you back downstairs to me and we shall have coffee and a chat. How does that sound?"

It was as easy as that. Now all Robert had to do was to remain vigilant, making sure he didn't commit any errors. He needed to blend into the "*Abwehr* family," as *Hauptmann* Brandt had clearly expressed that that was how things were.

His work was to be in the Foreign Branch – the *Amtsgruppe Ausland* – specifically, the department dealing with the evaluation of captured documents and of foreign press and radio broadcasts. There was also liaison work with the O.K.W. – the *Oberkommando der Wehrmacht*, the high command of the German armed forces. The Foreign Branch was also the place to request *Abwehr* support on a particular mission abroad.

"Well!" exclaimed Richard. "What a gift of a job for a British spy!"

"I know," agreed Robert, with a smile. "But I didn't consider myself a spy."

He quietly began to familiarize himself with each department – the rooms where false documents, photos, inks and passports were created and passed onto *Abwehr* agents out in the field; the work done in the naval and air force sections. He familiarized himself with the workings in the office, although strictly speaking this wasn't his domain, where the Enigma machines were operated and from where messages were sent out and decoded as they arrived back.

Robert was on an impossibly steep learning curve, having to teach himself the whole complex setup as well as overseeing his own section. He said little at first to his colleagues, but observed everything, assimilating as much as was humanly possible.

He kept his head down and his work rate up. He taught himself to think only in German, even when he was on his own. He was often to be found working late into the night, partly as a means of avoiding the need to socialize, but mainly as a way of gathering as much material as he could to take home with him without arousing suspicion.

He was also preoccupied in determining the best way of subtly altering the meaning or emphasis of the intelligence information that he was charged with assessing and classifying so that he could reduce its effectiveness for the Germans.

It was a dangerous path littered with pitfalls.

He often saw Erika looking his way as she went about the department, filing the records of every report and observation. She would smile warmly at him whenever she passed by and he used to smile back.

One evening, she collected some papers from him for typing and told him that he had made several mistakes in interpreting that day's naval intelligence report. It had changed the meaning of the message completely.

Robert must have gone pale.

"Don't worry, *Leutnant* Stolze. It's easily corrected. But it's late now. Redo it first thing in the morning. I can easily type it up then. I won't say anything."

"Thank you."

She seemed reluctant to leave and stood in the doorway, never taking her eyes away from him.

"I think you work too hard and too late. And spend too many hours in your room. It is why you make so many mistakes."

"There have been others?" asked Robert innocently.

"Many. But no one else knows and I have corrected for you the ones that I have noticed. You are new to the job. It takes time to learn it well."

"Thank you." Robert didn't know whether to feel relieved or worried.

Again she seemed hesitant to leave.

"*Leutnant* Stolze?"

"Yes?"

"We, that is, the girls and I have noticed that you never go out, that you always keep to your room in the evenings." She looked at him, her eyes bright with interest. "You see, today, it is my birthday, and I had planned to go out. But my friend has a bad cold and cannot go. So I was wondering…" she paused, fiddling with the door handle, "…if you would like to take me out somewhere?"

How could he refuse?

"Where shall we go?"

"There is a lovely place in the *Grote Markt*. I have a table booked." She bit her lip.

Robert smiled. So, he was part of a conspiracy, albeit a potentially pleasant one.

He needed a break. He felt confident enough now to take an attractive young woman out for the evening. What harm could it do?

156

A warning bell rang in the recesses of his mind, but he ignored it.

It was late when they returned. She wasted no time in kissing him when they said goodnight and against his better judgement, Robert knew he had to see her again. The feeling seemed to be mutual and she readily accepted when he offered to take her to the cinema the next evening.

They began to see each other every day after work, spending time in cafés and bars. Very soon, Erika suggested that they go away for the weekend.

"Did you go?" asked Richard.

Robert drew in a deep breath. "Yes."

"But she was a German."

"At the time it made no difference to me."

Richard looked at him. "Don't tell me you'd fallen for her?"

"In a way, yes." He drew his lips into a tight line. "It was a stupid and foolish thing to do, but she was very attractive and very persistent. I was single and unattached, what man could resist?"

Richard considered this. "I suppose not," he replied. "Every man needs a woman at some time. Did she care for you?"

"Yes, at least I thought so then. But now…"

"Now you know better."

"Unfortunately, yes."

Richard looked at him. "It wasn't your…?"

"First time? No. That was a very accommodating French girl I met on holiday one year. Then I went out with a girl for two years while I was at Sandhurst and we got engaged. It all seemed very… suitable at the time. Both families were pleased."

"But she wasn't the love of your life."

"No. In the end, we parted just before I came across to France with the B.E.F. She decided she wanted to do other things with her life rather than get married to me. Although, looking back, I have to say it was the right decision."

Trying to understand and trying not to think of Caroline's consistent refusal to marry him, Richard observed, "You must have been very immersed in your new world for you to fall for a German girl."

"I was. I'd been in Brussels for nearly two months by this stage. I worked, ate and slept at the building in the Rue du Roi. Apart from going out with Erika, I hardly saw anything of the outside world. Therefore, I shut my mind to whatever might be going on. I had to remain single-minded to what was happening *inside* the building. In fact, I had acclimatized myself so well to that environment, that there were times when I felt I really was a member of the *Abwehr*."

Richard was silent for a moment, trying to put himself in Robert's place. He realized he could not possibly understand. He hadn't been there. So he asked, "What about the children? Did you visit them?"

"No. I felt nervous about doing so. I had immersed myself completely into my new identity, even at the expense of checking up on them. To let my guard down and be myself, even for a moment, could have been fatal. And even though we were on intimate terms, I certainly couldn't tell Erika who I really was."

"Of course not. What happened next?"

"Sometime after we came back from our weekend, things began to change."

"How?"

"One morning, I woke up to find Erika going through my things."

Robert fell silent, remembering their bitter argument when he had objected; how he had pulled her back into bed to try and win her round; how she had resisted at first before laughing and giving in and how tempestuous their lovemaking had been.

"Did she find anything?"

"No, because I'd made sure that nothing I had accumulated was left in my bedroom or office. I'd hidden it all in a left luggage locker at the station under another name."

"Simple but clever."

"Soon after this, the *Gestapo* began making frequent visits to the building, prying into each department; snooping around, appearing at inopportune moments. It made everyone nervous and uncomfortable. The relaxed working atmosphere disappeared. Everyone became suspicious of everyone else."

"A dose of Nazi reality."

"Yes. Then Admiral Siranac paid us a visit."

"The Head of the Secret Service?"

"Yes."

"The same admiral that knew Otto Stolze personally?"

"That's the one."

"I bet that was interesting."

"That, my friend, is an understatement."

Richard smiled. "So, tell me."

And Robert did.

CHAPTER 21

Maybury

There was frantic tidying and sorting before Admiral Siranac's visit. Everyone spoke of him in glowing terms – his perceptiveness, his kindness; how he wasn't like a military man at all, how he regularly visited all the *Abwehrstellen* "to keep the *Abwehr* spirit alive".

"Remember, he believes that the men who work for him in the Secret Service should behave like gentlemen when going about their duties, whatever you might be asked to do," stated *Hauptmann* Brandt, concluding his address to his staff on the morning of the admiral's arrival. "Please make sure that he finds that in you. That will be all."

As Admiral Siranac moved around the building, he said little other than making a comment or two here, giving praise and encouragement there, listening when someone wished to tell him of something, responding to questions, to queries; revealing to a casual onlooker that he took a close interest in everyone and everything.

Then he approached Robert who, out of the corner of his eye, saw Erika watching intently, standing in the corridor with papers in her hand, as though she had paused on her way to somewhere.

Robert saw only a momentary flicker in the admiral's eyes before the latter said to him, "Ah, my dear fellow! It's good to see you again. Perhaps when I have finished my rounds you will come and see me. I'm sure that *Hauptmann* Brandt will lend us his office."

"With pleasure, Admiral Siranac," said Brandt. "My room is entirely at your disposal."

The two men moved on and Erika's face was a picture of disbelief and what else? Something darker, more sinister: a hint of contempt and suspicion.

It was just before lunch when Robert was summoned to Brandt's office and he stood inside the door after closing it quietly. Admiral Siranac had his back to him, looking out of the window.

"Brussels has such character, don't you agree?"

"Er, yes, sir," stammered Robert.

Then he turned, his expression unfathomable. "Perhaps you will be good enough to tell me who you are. We are alone."

At that moment, although he knew the game was up and he would have to reveal his true identity and take the consequences, the only thing that Robert could think of was whether or not the room had been bugged.

"The *Gestapo* have been paying us many visits of late," he began cautiously.

"I see." Siranac considered for a moment, studying the man before him who had assumed Otto's identity, before coming to an instant decision. "Then perhaps we should have lunch together." He smiled. "I know, we shall take my car and travel out to a little *auberge* where they have the most marvellous wine and cheese. I discovered it quite by chance some months ago. I shall drive."

The powerful car sped out of the city. Robert glanced over his shoulder, anxious in case they were being followed.

"You seem most concerned as to whether we are being pursued?"

"Yes."

"I see."

Robert couldn't resist making the observation, "You are very trusting. I might be an assassin."

"You might." The admiral glanced at him and smiled. "But I think not. You are a gentleman. And English, I imagine."

"Welsh, actually."

Siranac laughed. "Either way you speak faultless German."

"Thank you."

They drove on a little way further.

"So, tell me, who are you?"

"I am Lieutenant Robert Llewellyn Anderson of the Royal Welch Fusiliers. I was with the B.E.F. in France and captured in May, 1940. I am an escaped prisoner-of-war from Seeblick Camp in Baden-Württemberg."

"And you killed Otto Stolze?"

"You said a moment ago that I was not an assassin."

"So I did."

"I am sorry to tell you that he committed suicide. I just happened to be in the wrong place at the wrong time."

The admiral seemed much saddened by the loss of this young man whose family he had known for many years. "Please tell me."

So Robert explained, concluding with the fact that he had retained the suicide letter which he had stored in a safe place.

"So you decided to assume his identity."

Robert nodded.

"A very brave and a very foolish thing to do. I presume your intention is to take back with you to England all that you have learned?"

"Yes."

"And what have you learned?"

"That the Admiralty's convoy cipher has been broken; how O.K.W. operates; how to prepare an *Abwehr* agent for a mission."

"The last one is an interesting one for you as a British officer, don't you agree?"

Robert smiled. "It's been very revealing."

"I also expect that your evaluation work has given you scope for quietly obstructing *Abwehr* efficiency."

Robert smiled, again.

"And have you secretly been feeding your discoveries to the British?"

"No, I'm not a spy. My only thought was to bring useful information back to England with me."

"Isn't that what spying is?" He glanced briefly at Robert. "No matter. Have you been in contact with any resistance movements in Belgium, and there are several, all of whom work independently?"

"No, it's been as much as I can do to keep my head above water inside the building, let alone become involved in anything outside."

"Good. Do you know anyone in Brussels apart, that is, from your work colleagues?"

Robert was silent for a moment before taking a deep breath. "Yes. I rescued three orphaned children from Louvain in May, 1940 and took them to a convent on the outskirts of Brussels so they would be safe."

"Have you been to see them?"

"No. It would have been difficult because I needed to keep my new persona intact."

"Would you like to see them now? And then I can be sure of your true identity absolutely."

"Of course."

Siranac smiled. "Please give me directions and perhaps they will provide us with lunch. The *auberge* has suddenly lost its charm."

The car swept into the driveway of the convent and the admiral brought it to a halt outside the main door. Robert got out and rang the bell.

The young nun's face was a picture of recognition and confusion.

"Please come in and wait. I shall fetch the Mother Superior."

When she came, she looked at Robert with a calm, yet masked expression.

"*Have you changed sides, Monsieur Robert?*" she asked in French, without preamble.

"*Non. It is a disguise. This is Admiral...*" Robert hesitated, "*...Freiburg. He knows who I really am.*"

"*You have brought a Nazi to see us?*"

"*Non, Reverend Mother,*" responded Siranac in perfect French. "*A German patriot.*"

"*I am a Belgian patriot, Monsieur, and I do not feel comfortable that my country has been overrun by yours.*"

Admiral Siranac inclined his head. "*Nonetheless, we are here, and for the time being, we shall stay. I personally wish you no harm.*"

"*No, but there are others who might.*" She took a deep breath. "*Please come into my office.*"

"I take in orphaned children, Admiral," she continued, still speaking in French. "Among whom there are many with Jewish parentage or ancestry. Including, I have to add, Claude, Hélène and Aimée." She saw Robert flinch. "The *Gestapo* wish me to register these children as Jewish so that the 'authorities' can decide what to do with them. So far, I have resisted every 'requirement' they have made and they have not troubled me for some days. But it will not be long before they return. I have been threatened several times, but still I will not do as I am bid. I am not prepared to give up any of them."

"It is a dangerous game you play," said the admiral. "The *Gestapo* will stop at nothing."

"Believe me, it is no game."

"I realize that is so."

She turned to Robert. "Would you like to see the children?"

He smiled. "Yes, I would, very much."

A few moments later, they appeared, looking well and happy until they saw Robert in a German uniform. Claude's expression changed to one of bitterness.

"You have betrayed us!" he declared. "You have become one of them," and he spat on the floor.

"Claude! Behave yourself. Monsieur Robert has not changed sides. He is doing brave work for the Allies."

Claude's manner changed instantaneously. "You have become a spy!" he said excitedly.

"You see," said Siranac, "even a boy so young has a grasp of your new occupation, even if you yourself deny it."

Robert smiled. "How are you all?" he said, as little Aimée came to sit on his lap.

"We are well," she replied. "But we are scared of the horrible men in shiny black coats who ask us questions and say that we will be taken away." She hugged him close. "Oh, Monsieur Robert, it is so good to see you again."

Admiral Siranac remained silent and thoughtful throughout this exchange and also during lunch, which they ate together in the Reverend Mother's office while Claude, Hélène and Aimée chatted animatedly to Robert.

After the children had said tearful farewells and been taken back to their classroom, Robert and the admiral took their own leave.

"I cannot thank you enough for everything that you are doing for the children, Reverend Mother. I wish I could do something to help," said Robert regretfully.

The Reverend Mother patted his arm. "I know, my dear, I know." She turned to her guest. "Admiral… Freiburg, I imagine that is not your real name?" The admiral smiled enigmatically. "I wish that we had met under different circumstances. I can see you are a good man."

"Thank you, Reverend Mother." He bowed politely. "You will be receiving very shortly a visit from my good and most trusted friend, Pastor Hans Bernhard." He repeated the name. "You will enjoy his company, I think. He is always most informative and knowledgeable and can advise you. Particularly concerning your Jewish guests."

"Thank you, Admiral," she replied, understanding the implication behind his words. "I am grateful to God for sending you to me in my hour of need."

"We both have much to be grateful for, Reverend Mother. Come, Robert, we must take our leave. There is much to discuss."

Once they were back in the car, the admiral turned to Robert and said, "I depart shortly for Berlin, but I shall return very soon here, to Brussels. In the meanwhile, I should like you to watch carefully over our little Belgian office. I have had suspicions for a while that there is a traitor in our midst, hence my visit today. I think there is someone to whom the *SD* and *Gestapo* mean more than the honour and gentlemanly conduct of the *Abwehr*. If you could do this small thing for me, I should be most grateful.

"If you find there is no one, then that is to the good. You see, the *Gestapo* arrested two of my *Abwehr* officers a few months ago and I have had to use much subtlety and sleight of hand to secure their release. Someone within our *Abwehr* family has been asked, no, coerced, into compiling false information. It is not the first time

162

this has happened when someone within the *SD* and *Gestapo* are set on their own agenda. Especially the *SD*, whose Deputy Chief of Security was once a friend of mine. I have quite a dossier on him and I have recently learned that he has one on me.

"We play this game of cat and mouse, you see. But I have to be very careful, lest if my position is compromised, then I shall be forced to resign and either he or one of his associates will take over the *Abwehr*. That I cannot allow, for then there will be no hope at all that Germany's honour will one day be restored.

"He is an evil man, though I have so far been successful in outmanoeuvring him using Hitler's regard and trust of me to my advantage.

"You see, Robert, I too am playing a dangerous game and one day, I shall pay for it with my life. Until then, I shall continue to do the things I do: to help where I can; to try and limit the excesses of the Nazi regime where possible and to allow the Allies to understand certain things that may help to shorten this disastrous war in which Germany finds herself embroiled."

"Good God!" exclaimed Richard. "You mean to tell me that the head of the German secret service is an anti-Nazi! That's unbelievable."

"But true. And he surrounds himself with like-minded people. He's a very brave, clever man."

Richard shook his head. "What sort of things does he do?"

"Well, he was an important factor in dissuading Hitler from invading Britain by presenting exaggerated reports from *Abwehr* agents in England that our defences were strong and well-organized. He told Hitler that it would be folly to invade unless Germany could win the air battle. Which of course, they didn't and still haven't, so Operation Sea Lion was abandoned."

"This is just… I don't know…"

"Another example, and this is the one that really upsets me, is that the Dutch were warned in advance, in a roundabout way admittedly, that the Germans were planning to invade in May, 1940, giving the exact date and time. This information was passed onto the French, who, because it couldn't be corroborated from another source, sat on it and did nothing."

"Oh, my word!"

"Also, the *Abwehr* were asked to obtain Dutch and Belgian civilian uniforms so that *SS* soldiers could infiltrate those countries ahead of the invasion. Siranac could do nothing to block this, but once the uniforms had been obtained and handed over, the Dutch and Belgian papers that week just happened to be full of conjecture about German troops dressed as train drivers and postmen. There was even a cartoon of Göring dressed as a tram conductor! Siranac also persuaded Hitler to abandon his plans to invade Switzerland, Spain and Gibraltar."

"He sounds like a remarkable man."

"He is."

"And Hitler suspects nothing?"

"No, he has absolute faith in him."

"Fortunately."

"Yes."

"What else did he talk about on the journey back from the Convent?"

"Ah. The painful bit…" and Robert drew in a deep breath.

"Anyway," continued Admiral Siranac, "in the hope that my Berlin office would be left alone, I had two members of staff, of whom I was suspicious, transferred, one of them being Otto Stolze. He had become besotted with a secretary called Erika Kleist and it was difficult to know which of the two was the guilty party. Have you come across her?"

"Yes."

Not Erika; it couldn't be *his* Erika.

The admiral threw Robert a quick look. "Even with you being Otto, the visits from the *Gestapo* have now started up in Brussels, just as they did in Berlin. In one way I am glad, as I was so hoping it was not Otto who was the guilty one." He looked at Robert again. "I asked *Hauptmann* Brandt to take Erika in hand as soon as she arrived. I gather he has been successful in ways that I had not anticipated."

The admiral frowned. This was one of the reasons he would not use women as spies, believing them to be both vulnerable and predatory at the same time. For him, it was not a satisfactory dichotomy.

Robert felt sick and rested his forehead on his hand.

"Ah, I see. You too have fallen victim to her seductive charms." Admiral Siranac was thoughtful. "I presume she has no idea of your true identity?"

"None. I cannot afford for anyone to know."

"Naturally. Except me."

"Except you."

"Ironical, isn't it? That it should be to the head of the German *Abwehr*, the organization from which you collect intelligence for the Allies, that you reveal this particular piece of information."

"For some reason, I trust you."

"The feeling is mutual." He paused, before saying, "I wonder…"

"You think Erika may be the 'mole'?"

"I'm afraid that *Hauptmann* Brandt is convinced of it. He was not taken in by her charms, as she would have expected, despite…" and he left the sentence unfinished. "So, Robert Anderson alias Otto Stolze, I think it is time for you to return home. Your heart may be in danger and your life also, as soon as it is realized that we have spoken at length. I should very much like to see that letter of Otto's. You say he mentions that Erika betrayed him? How? Sexually?"

"That's what I assumed."

"I think there may be more. Otto was not the suicidal kind. I also cannot understand it when you tell me he knew he would have to bear the brunt. The brunt of what?"

"I have no idea."

"In the meantime, I'd like you to see what you can find out."

"Yes, Admiral."

"And then arrangements will be made for you to return home."

"You can do that?" Robert was surprised. "Or more to the point, you are willing to do that, to let me go home, knowing all that I know?"

"I am head of the *Abwehr*. I can do exactly as I wish. Within reason."

And he smiled.

"Did he make the arrangements?"

"Oh yes."

"What about Erika? Did you ditch her?"

"Not straight away, otherwise she might have guessed something was going on. All I could do was deliberately wreck the relationship over time so that *she* would finish with me."

"You're a natural spy."

"No, believe me, it all sits very uneasily with me. I hate deception and distortion as much as Admiral Siranac hates violence. In all that he does, he seeks to limit the extent of the war. Sometimes he is successful, other times he is not. He couldn't persuade Hitler to halt the invasion of the Soviet Union, though he tried very hard. He believes it will be the ruination of Germany."

"He's probably correct."

"I know."

"Coffee?"

"Sounds good."

"Then you can tell me more about the traitorous *Fräulein* Kleist. Was she involved in some dastardly plot?"

"Unfortunately, yes."

"And was it you that uncovered the deed?"

"It was, I'm afraid." Robert's voice held regret and sadness.

Richard regarded his friend, carefully. "Do you still care for her?" he asked after a while.

Robert remained silent, staring into the fire.

Did he? Whatever the nature of his feelings, it would take a very long time for the scars to heal and the memories to fade.

"I'll get that coffee," said Richard considerately.

CHAPTER 22

Maybury

"So, what happened next?" asked Richard once he had returned, banking up the fire with a couple of logs and pouring out the coffee.

"Well…" said Robert, taking a deep breath.

"I cannot cover for you anymore, Otto," said Erika coldly, as she got dressed.

Still lying in bed, he looked up at her. "I never asked that you did so in the first place."

"I was trying to protect you."

"Were you? And does repeatedly going through my things here and at the office constitute protecting me as well?"

She hesitated. "It is necessary."

"Why is it necessary?"

Was he going too far, too fast, he wondered? He had had no training for this; all he had to rely upon was his intuition.

"Because I needed to know," she replied.

"What do you need to know? And why? So you can tell someone else of your supposed discoveries?"

She remained silent and looked down at the floor.

"Who, Erika? Who is it that you have to tell? *Hauptmann* Brandt? The *SD*? The *SS*? The *Gestapo*?" Robert bit his lip; he shouldn't have mentioned the *Gestapo*.

"This conversation is terminated." Abruptly, she gathered together her things and walked out of the room.

Thoughtfully, Robert set about his daily routine, checking the incoming messages, evaluating material gleaned from the Allies. None of it was earth-shattering, so he transmitted an accurate representation through the appropriate channels but bypassing Erika.

He didn't see her again for rest of the day, but spotted her as she was leaving the building, her coat open, revealing the low-cut dress she had worn on only one occasion during their time together, signing out at the desk and collecting an evening pass.

Making sure she had not seen him, Robert did the same and followed her.

In the darkness, she walked along the curfew-deserted streets; her high heels clicking on the rain-wet pavements, the sound magnified by the proximity of the buildings. She looked neither left nor right, nor over her shoulder.

Robert knew she felt confident that she was not being followed.

Eventually, she reached a rundown bar in the red-light district of the city and disappeared inside. Robert hesitated, standing half-concealed in the doorway of the building opposite, observing the situation; analysing possibilities.

He lit a cigarette – a recently acquired habit that enabled him to blend in more easily with his 'colleagues' and to which, much to his chagrin, he had now become addicted – as he observed the comings and goings of the *clientèle*.

166

It appeared to be a popular place with the *SS* and *Wehrmacht*. Some men went in alone and shortly afterwards, in the time it might take to down a few drinks, came out with a woman on their arm, strolling triumphantly along the street, one of them openly fondling his conquest – an action greeted with ribald comments from his companions – before they all entered the seedy hotel a few doors down.

What was this place that Erika had gone into? A pick-up bar? Why? Surely not for her the casual, paid encounter?

Robert waited until a new group of soldiers arrived, tagging along at the back of them as they entered the premises.

Inside, it appeared to be both a bar and a restaurant. A latticework screen siphoned the newcomers from the main body of the noisy, music-filled room and Robert remained concealed behind this for a moment or two while he took stock of his surroundings.

He spotted Erika immediately.

She was seated at a corner table in some sort of recess created by yet more latticework, deep in conversation with a man dressed in a dark suit with slicked back hair. They were eating a meal together and from their demeanour, it was obvious that their association was an intimate one.

"How did you feel about that?" asked Richard.

"Shock. Jealousy. Resentment. Anger. All of those things."

"Were you surprised to see her with another man?"

"Yes, despite the environment in which I found myself."

"And, presumably, despite the fact that you now knew she was the woman in Otto's letter and the one who had betrayed him?"

"Don't remind me."

"Sorry, old man."

"The thing is, after that first weekend we spent together, through some misplaced feeling of chivalry, I felt committed to our relationship."

"I can just about understand that," said Richard, thinking of Caroline.

Robert shrugged his shoulders. "And, given the intimate nature of our affair, perhaps I had hoped that Erika might begin to care for me. Despite my misgivings, I had come to care more about her than I dared admit to myself. Either way, I was caught out."

Silently, Robert once again chastised himself for his stupidity.

The booth next to Erika's was in the process of being vacated and, after ordering a drink and politely but firmly fending off the advances of a scantily dressed prostitute, he cautiously made his way round the edge of the room, always making sure Erika had her back to him, and sat down on the faded seat cushion, remaining unseen by his quarry but able to keep both of them in his line of sight.

Aware that the prostitute was maintaining an interest in him from across the room, he pretended to stare dejectedly into his beer.

The man's voice was discreet but clearly audible to Robert.

"Ah, darling Erika, I am relieved to hear that you have been doing good work for us here in Brussels. I was quite disturbed after the *débâcle* in Berlin."

"Were you? There was no need." She stroked his cheek. "I have missed you, Theodor."

His voice was silky with insincerity. "As I have you, my sweet. It has been very dull without you."

He kissed her neck and *décolletage*, moving one of his hands slowly down her body.

Robert bristled at this; both for himself and strangely enough, for the betrayed Otto.

Abruptly, the man called Theodor brought his hand back onto the table. He tossed back the remains of his schnapps and ordered a brandy.

"Now, we have other matters to discuss." He became business-like, cold. "Have you discovered who is impersonating that fool Otto Stolze?"

"No, not yet, Theodor. He plays a clever game of double cross. As I have said to you before, he leaves nothing incriminating for me to find. He is very careful, says nothing and covers his tracks well."

"But, Erika dear, my superior needs to have this information quickly, so that he can proceed with his plan unhindered."

"Who is your superior, Theodor?"

"Erika, darling! You should know better than to ask me a question like that! You know very well, I cannot answer it. I give you as much information as you need. We have been through this little charade many times. If you persist, I shall begin to think that you are duplicitous. And that…" and with one swift and skilful movement, he grabbed her hair and yanked her head back, exposing her throat. Seductively, he caressed it before applying pressure onto her neck, "…would never do now, would it?"

"No, Theodor," she said submissively, her face pale. "I shall not ask again."

"Good." His authority and dominance of her restored, he released his grip and took a sip of brandy. "I know you will not betray me. This plot of ours has to succeed. It comes from the highest authority."

Who? thought Robert. The *SD*? The *SS*? The *Gestapo*? Hitler?

"My superior wishes to take over the *Abwehr*. He does not feel it is being run along… satisfactory lines. In order to do that, as you well know, we have to discredit the esteemed Admiral Siranac."

Robert nearly choked on his beer.

"I understand your meaning well."

"I know you do, otherwise I would not have recruited you nor would I have included you in my deliciously decadent adventures." He raised a lascivious eyebrow, his mind contemplating the delights he had planned for later on. "You may also rest assured that your Jewish grandparents continue to be looked after."

So that was the hold 'they' had over her. At least it showed that Erika Kleist did care about someone in her life.

Hardly daring to breathe, Robert continued to listen to the conversation.

"I am grateful to you, Theodor," she said, her voice trembling.

After finishing his brandy and ordering another, Abetz continued speaking, his expression one of satisfaction. "I have now succeeded in placing an agent in every single *Abwehrstelle*, including Berlin, Prague and Paris. These have all been

168

successfully infiltrated. But there is still much work to do." He gave Erika a look that contained more than a hint of menace. "As my agent in Brussels, it is imperative that you make better progress with this new 'Otto'. Like the old Otto, he may be one of Siranac's men planted by him to spy on us. Or in this particular instance, on *you*. Our admiral's a wily old fox and has the knack of seeming to know everything, which is what makes him so difficult to discredit. Therefore, you will have to remain vigilant and very careful as to how you go about it. You have this one last chance to redeem yourself. When the real Otto in Berlin discovered what you were about, you came very close ruining everything, which was intensely stupid of you."

"Yes, Theodor. It will not happen again."

"Good. Unfortunately, after the release and exoneration of the *Abwehr* agents my superior ordered to be arrested in Prague, together with your bungled attempt at coercing the original Stolze in Berlin to work for us, my superior prefers to hold off for a while until Siranac is feeling secure again. When that happens, once we have sufficient evidence against this new Otto, we'll bring him in for questioning. And I shall take great pleasure in inflicting upon him my own particular methods of persuasion," he took a sip from his new glass of brandy and licked his lips, "to extract from him everything we need to know, just as I did with the real Otto, who sang like a bird," and he laughed maliciously.

Robert paled at this. His mouth went dry and he could feel his heart pounding.

"You hurt Otto?" Erika was not quick enough to hide her surprise. "You had him in for interrogation and then you let him *go*?"

Abetz shrugged. "He was being watched. Unfortunately, he disappeared."

With some trepidation she asked, "What did you find out, Theodor?"

"That you had told him everything about our little setup and how you tried to make him join us by blackmailing him. I was pleased with this. But he also said you had become lovers. Was he good in bed, Erika?"

The question was asked with apparent lightness, but Robert detected a hint of malice beneath the surface.

"Not as good as you, my darling," she replied quickly. "No one is, you know that. It meant nothing. I was trying to find things out and it was merely a means of doing so. You know that's what I do to get what we need."

Abetz continued as if she had not spoken. "He said that he was planning to tell Siranac everything you had told him. He said that he was in love with you. That he thought you were in love with him." He gripped her throat again, so tightly this time that she began to choke. "Were you, Erika?"

"No! No! I was careful, Theodor," she replied, putting up a shaking hand to soothe her throat as he released his vicelike grip with an arbitrary jerk of her neck.

"Not as careful as you should have been. Admiral Siranac was beginning to suspect there might be a breach of security in the Berlin office. In fact, my superior was so concerned that had Otto not disappeared when he did, we would have been forced to liquidate him if someone else had presumably not had the foresight to do it for us."

"Otto is dead?" Erika could not keep the shock out of her voice.

"You didn't know?"

She shook her head, her face pale. Abetz looked at her sharply.

"I hope for your sake that you had not come to care for him, Erika. He was nothing but a blind fool."

Anxiety crept into her voice. "He meant nothing to me. You know I'm in love with you and only you."

"Good. But remember this, Erika, there is no room in your life for any other man. Be very clear about that, Erika. You are mine to do with as I please and what we have could easily turn to dust if you make mistakes. You wouldn't want that to happen, would you?" He stroked her cheek with his fingernail. "So, if I were you, my sweet, I would assume that Otto is dead. No one has heard from him in a long time." He smiled at her maliciously and added, "Even his fiancée."

"His fiancée?"

Abetz laughed contemptuously. "So you didn't even know he had a fiancée? The infamous Erika Kleist must be slipping. You really will have to do better."

"I shall unmask this imposter, I promise you, Theodor. You have my word," she added hastily. "He makes mistakes in his work. That is his weakness. So too is his fondness for me."

"That's better. Now if we are all done here, we shall go back to my place and spend," he smiled, "a pleasant night of debauchery." He summoned a waitress. "Bring me the bill."

"It's on the house Herr Abetz. Compliments of the *maître d'*."

Theodor Abetz gave a nod in the direction of the *maître d'* and pulled Erika up out of her seat, pressing her body hard against his.

"Come, *liebchen*, let us get out of here, otherwise, I shall take you here and now in our little booth. In fact, that idea appeals to me greatly. Perhaps we might try it one time. But not tonight. Tonight I have other things planned," and he helped her into her coat. "I have invited a friend to join us. I owe him a favour."

"Good God!" exclaimed Richard, shocked. "What was her reaction to this suggestion?"

"I couldn't see as she had her back to me. But, irrationally, despite everything she'd done, I wanted to punch her brute of a boyfriend on the nose and save her from whatever she was going to be subjected to."

"You're far too gallant. I would've thought she was getting her just desserts. After all, she was nothing but a tramp"

"Don't rub it in."

"Sorry."

"Of course, I couldn't do anything without risking my own life. It wasn't the first time I found myself in a situation where I had to go against every instinct that I possess and be unable to help someone."

"As I said before, you're far too noble."

As Erika and Theodor left their booth and emerged into the main part of the restaurant, to make doubly sure that he was not spotted, Robert pretended to drop his cigarette packet, reaching under the table to retrieve it. Peering from under the cloth, he watched them until they had left.

He took his time in finishing his beer. He guessed it would arouse suspicion if he followed them out of the door straight away. No doubt, this place was suitably furnished with informants. He had no desire to be murdered on his way back to the Rue du Roi.

As he moved across the seat preparing to stand up, the prostitute approached him again.

"I am available for you, handsome stranger," she said, without preamble.

She sat down beside him, blocking his way out of the booth, and ruffled his hair with her fingers, nibbling at his ears, attempting to seduce him.

"Do you not find me desirable?"

Robert briefly stroked her cheek so as not to offend her, thinking quickly.

"I'm sure that you are very desirable… to men who like women." He stood up and smiled. "But I am not one of those men," and, pushing the table away, he walked casually around her, leaving her staring after him.

Quickly, she recovered her composure. "I can help there too."

He turned back towards her. "I'm sure you can. But not tonight. Not for me. I'm beyond help."

"Then why did you come here?"

"To wallow in the grief of my broken heart," called out Robert with a dramatic wave of his arm as he left the establishment, slamming the door behind him with an air of finality, anxious to be away.

Once outside, he stood still for a moment, breathing deeply, taking in huge gulps of clear, restorative night air before returning to the *Abwehrstelle* on the Rue du Roi and taking a long, hot shower to wash away the sordidness and pain of his evening.

"That was a stroke of genius," said Richard, "pretending you were, well, you know… of *that* persuasion." He uttered the words with difficulty and embarrassment.

"Was it? It was all I could think of to get me out of that situation. I was just intent on not arousing any suspicion on myself."

"I have to ask, but were you tempted by the prostitute?"

"Not for a moment."

"I'm glad. Were you followed on your way home?"

"No, I made sure of that."

"What about Erika?"

"She looked exhausted and very pale the next day, spoke to no one and moved around the office slowly and carefully."

"Ouch."

"That's what I thought. Her boyfriend was a nasty man."

"Why did she put up with him?"

Robert shrugged. "Who knows? The grandparents? Her belief in the 'cause'? Because she enjoyed it?"

"She was obviously seriously hung up on him. More than he was on her, I'll bet. He probably had a female in every one of the *Abwehrstellen* that he slept with whenever he visited." A sudden, disturbing thought occurred to Richard. "The consequences of that don't bear thinking about." He looked at Robert in consternation. "I'd get yourself checked out, if I were you, old man," he said concernedly.

"I did and I'm fine, thank God. But the whole episode opened my eyes to the sleazy side of human nature. It was not a pleasant experience, nor one I would wish to repeat."

They fell silent, each of them lost in their own thoughts, both staring into the fire's glowing embers.

"So, what was the plot?" said Richard, after a while.

"To find a way of discrediting Siranac and his management of the *Abwehr* so that someone else in the Nazi hierarchy could take over the running of it."

"And that's what Siranac had been afraid of, wasn't it?"

"Very much so. He hated the power-hungry attitude prevalent in the *SS*, the *SD*, and the *Gestapo*."

"What's the *SD*?"

"The *Sicherheitsdienst*, the intelligence agency of the *SS* responsible for internal security in Germany."

"So Abetz's 'superior' really did want the *Abwehr*?"

"Yes."

"Did Siranac have any idea who he was?"

"He thought that the most likely candidate was *SS-Oberst-Gruppenführer* Reinhard Ziegler, a very senior general in the *SD*. He'd been passed over when Siranac had been appointed head of the *Abwehr* and thought it should have been him, so he wanted to oust Siranac. There's so much empire-building and infighting going on that it's a wonder any of them have time for their real work. It's a viper's nest of intrigue."

"Except for the *Abwehr*, of course."

"Yes, but even they're not immune from following their own course, often at the expense of efficiency in intelligence gathering."

"And that course is bringing down Hitler, you mean?"

"Among other things and warding off the *SD*. But there's no infighting within the organization itself. It really is an '*Abwehr* family'. Unless you turn out to be a proven Nazi sympathizer, of course, and then you're out on your ear."

Richard poured himself another cup of coffee.

"So what did you do next? Did you warn Siranac about what was going on?"

"Well..." continued Robert.

Admiral Siranac paid another visit a few weeks after the first, staying for two days this time, and Robert told him all that he had discovered. The admiral seemed genuinely shocked.

"I had not realized the extent of their infiltration," he said, as they rode two of *Hauptmann* Brandt's horses around the *Parc de Bruxelles* on his second and final day. "You have done well and I can now thwart their little game."

"I was lucky."

"True. However, while luck plays a vital role in intelligence gathering, the ability to think quickly on one's feet and to be in the right place at the right time is also important, as well as knowing how to use the information received. But above all else, the ability to act a part is an indispensable aspect of our work. Acting is something I do every day, whether it is a matter of personal survival or to impress upon my chiefs of section the consequences and seriousness of the decisions they take." He smiled at Robert. "I have been told that my facial expressions reflect the words I speak when I recount conversations or describe an incident before my colleagues. It would seem I also walk around the room waving my arms and grimacing! I picture it all in my mind, you see, therefore it is very vivid to me."

Robert smiled. He had seen the range of the admiral's expressions, as well as his ability to mask them. "And yet you are a very private person."

"Indeed. I keep my innermost thoughts to myself and reveal little to the outside world, except in the way I have just described. There are very few men in whom I confide. You have become one of them." He touched Robert on the arm. "It is an irony for both of us – a German and an Englishman, sorry, Welshman – that in the middle of a world conflict such as this when our two great nations are at war, we have the capacity to trust each other. It is a pity there is not the opportunity for us to become friends. Perhaps we shall, one day." He sighed. "But not now, unfortunately. Now, it is time for you to leave us as your life may be in great danger. I am sorry that you have to go. In different circumstances, you would have made an excellent member of our *Abwehr* family."

"Thank you. I take that as a compliment."

"And so you should." He sighed. "We shall not meet again after today. Everything is arranged. You will receive your instructions via my trusted carrier. They are very clear and precise. They will be delivered tomorrow as part of the normal despatch from my office in Berlin. Look out for them."

They rode their horses back to the stable and changed their clothes in a private room.

"I tell you all this, Robert, because I want the British government to know my character. I abhor violence. I am not part of the conspiracies to assassinate Hitler. I wish to see him brought to trial in a criminal court and convicted under the rule of law.

"I do not pass military secrets onto the Allies, as some would like to suggest, as I am not a traitor. But I do seek to limit the war and mitigate its effects where possible. I try to help those who are persecuted where I can and I long to see the country that I love reinstated to her proper, rightful place on the world's peaceful stage.

"I ask nothing of you other than you take back to England a letter from me to the head of British Intelligence, who is known to me personally, outlining my desire for a secret meeting in a neutral country to arrange for a peace conference, as well as giving him the names of *Wehrmacht* generals who feel the same as I do. And one further thing, I wish you also to take certain documents that are evidence of the atrocities being committed under the Nazi regime. These are most important."

"I understand."

"Good."

When the time came for the admiral to go, the two men shook hands on the steps of the *Abwehr* building in the Rue du Roi.

"Keep up the good work, Otto. I wish you good fortune," he said, a hint of regret in his eyes.

"And you too, sir. Thank you for all your guidance in *Abwehr* matters. I shall be conscientious in carrying out your wishes."

Robert felt sadness too. He sensed he would never see this man again.

"Thank you."

And with a nod, Admiral Siranac left.

"He sounds a very brave man."

"He is. And an anxious one. He knows the knives are out for him."

"I can imagine. It seems incredible though that you could feel such support for him and want to help him. After all, he is part of the country we are at war with."

"He is one of those rare human beings who have the capacity, for all the right reasons, to inspire loyalty in anyone. He's a good man, Richard, working within an evil regime, treading a very fine line between listening to God and his own conscience while preventing his beloved *Abwehr* from being assimilated and his beloved country destroyed."

Thoughtfully, Richard nodded. "I think I'm beginning to understand." Then his features brightened, genuine curiosity taking over from philosophical analysis. "So, tell me, how did our friends at British Intelligence react to the documents you brought back with you? How did the Admiral deal with the infiltrators? How did you get back to England? What about the children?"

Robert was gratified by Richard's keenness to know. "Wait and see. I haven't told you about Erika yet."

"I'm not good at waiting."

"Patience is a virtue, my friend."

Robert smiled. It was good to talk, freely and without fear, as one man to another.

Perhaps his interrogators at Grange Manor knew what they were on about after all.

CHAPTER 23

Maybury

The coded instructions contained in the despatch from Berlin were brief but straightforward. They merely stated that Robert was to visit the convent children for the party that evening and that he should remember to take the birthday presents.

Robert understood the meaning immediately and knew exactly what he had to do.

During that day, whenever he had a few moments to spare, he sorted through his office, putting aside those things he would leave behind and placing in an attaché case the things he was planning to take. At the end of the working day, once back in his bedroom, he did the same.

He had just finished and was about to put on his greatcoat to leave when there was a knock at the door. Cautiously, he went to answer it, keeping the door knob firmly in his hand and himself on the threshold.

"Hello," said Erika, exuding false vulnerability.

"What do you want?" replied Robert with deliberate coldness.

"May I come in?"

She moved to enter the room but Robert barred her way.

"No," he said unequivocally.

"Oh, but dear, sweet, lovely Otto, I came to apologize. I was foolish and stupid to be so mean to you and storm off like that. You haven't spoken to me at all since then. I miss you so much."

Like hell, thought Robert.

"You are the most wonderful man I've ever met."

"Really?" He was openly cynical.

She wrapped her arms round his neck, attempting to run her fingers through his hair. He disentangled himself, holding firmly onto her wrists, keeping her hands away from him.

He certainly had to give her credit for her acting skills: at one time he would have believed her. But now, he saw through her absolutely and her close proximity left him with a feeling of disgust. He let her hands drop.

"Darling Otto. I need you. Please take me to bed. I want you to make love to me."

She reached for him, but Robert neatly sidestepped her hand and she missed.

Appalled at her blatant fumblings, he said, "Go away, Erika. I do not want to make love to you. In fact I do not want to see you ever again."

She stood uncertainly for a moment.

"But you have to." She became wheedling, childish and anxious.

"Why?"

"Because you must."

"Now you're being ridiculous."

"Am I?" Subtly, her manner changed, becoming anxiously persuasive. "I am in great danger, Otto. I need you to protect me."

"The only person you need protecting from is yourself, Erika." He was angry now. He had had enough of her; enough of this charade. "Go away."

He pushed her away from the door and slammed it in her face, locking it decisively.

"You'll pay for this, whatever your real name is. You'll pay for this," she shouted, hammering on the door. "I'll tell everyone that your name is not Otto Stolze and that you're a spy. Then you'll get what you deserve from the *Gestapo*."

Robert waited until he heard the lift descend then, taking a final look round his room to check that he had not left behind anything incriminating or that might be useful for his mission, he cautiously opened the door a tiny crack and peered out into the hallway.

After Erika's vocal gymnastics, he'd expected to see everyone crowding outside his room, waiting to pounce. However, the corridor was deserted. Perhaps they thought she was drunk and took no notice or, like good *Abwehr* employees, they kept their heads down and their noses clean.

He locked the door behind him and took the stairs rather than the lift. He signed out at the desk, collected his prearranged evening pass and went out into the Rue du Roi.

So far, so good, but as Robert began to walk down the street in the direction of the mainline railway station, he sensed that someone was following him. How he knew, he couldn't say, but he did.

Testing his theory, he stopped on the pavement to light a cigarette and paused to look in shop windows. Each time, he caught a fleeting movement in his peripheral vision of someone reacting to his every move. It was very subtle, but it was enough to confirm his suspicions.

He reached the railway station and went into the café-bar where he ordered a coffee. A few moments after he sat down, a man entered, carrying a neatly folded newspaper. He too ordered a coffee and sat down at a table on the other side of the room.

It was just like a spy thriller at the cinema. If the situation wasn't real and hadn't been so fraught with potential danger, Robert would have laughed and imagined himself to be in a film. It was, as ever, just as Admiral Siranac had said – the ability to act a part was paramount.

He finished his coffee and stood up, walking slowly out of the café looking at his watch and frowning. He went over to study the train times and saw the man leave the café and stand some way off, leaning against a pillar, pretending to read his paper.

Robert found a bench and sat down, maintaining an anxious expression and disposition, before leaping up and checking the train times again, intending to make his pursuer believe he was meeting someone who was either late or had not arrived at a prearranged time.

He went into the toilets and when he came out, the man was still there. Robert went into the café-bar again and ordered a beer this time. The man followed suit. Robert finished his own drink quickly and went to sit down on the bench again. His shadow resumed his watchful stance.

176

After a while, the man started fidgeting around and Robert could see he was desperate to relieve himself. As soon as he disappeared into the toilet, Robert seized his chance. He went quickly over to the left luggage lockers, opened his own, emptied its contents into his attaché case in one rapid movement and walked calmly out of the nearby station entrance where he jumped onto a waiting tram.

As it drove away, he glimpsed his pursuer frantically searching the station concourse. Robert sat back in his seat and smiled to himself.

He left the tram on the outskirts of the city, where he quickly walked the rest of the way to the convent.

He was not followed.

He was greeted politely and without surprise by the young nun at the door and ushered immediately into the office.

"All is well?"

"Yes, Reverend Mother. All is well," and Robert kissed her proffered hand.

"We'll make a good Catholic out of you yet," she said. "But we must not tarry. These are the instructions given to me by the very helpful Pastor that your friend the admiral sent to us. We must all leave first thing in the morning."

She handed Robert a thick, foolscap manila envelope, which he took.

"For the first part of the journey," continued the Reverend Mother, "you will be disguised as a priest, Father Jacques. I shall accompany you and the children as far as Rennes, where I shall visit my good friend, Bishop Leonardo du Jardin, at the *Cathédrale Saint-Pierre*, before returning to Brussels via Paris. At the cathedral, you are to meet a man called Georges, who works for the French Resistance. You will then travel with him to Concarneau on the southern coast of Brittany, where you will adopt the guise of a Breton fisherman. You will now be the children's 'uncle' who has been to collect them so that they can come to live with you after their parents were killed in an Allied bombing raid. Contained in that envelope are all the necessary permits and permissions for you, as an existing 'resident', and the children as 'new' residents, to enter the Coastal Military Zone, as well as our train tickets, travel permits and identity papers. Everything in fact that we shall need for our expedition and which is, Father Jacques, your bedtime reading."

Robert smiled. He could see Admiral Siranac's hand, or rather his imagination, behind this. The head of the *Abwehr* would have enjoyed concocting this little plan and arranging its execution.

"The Admiral, as ever, seems to have thought of everything."

"He is a very thorough man. He wishes to leave nothing to chance. Now, I have also been instructed to give you this file which contains identical versions – one in code which you will take back to England with you, and the other in plain language for you to read tonight – of the important information that the Admiral is most anxious that you take to England. Should the British Government wish to contact him, he has also provided the means for them to do so."

"I can't thank you enough, Reverend Mother. I hope you have not put yourself in any danger over this."

"My dear boy, in these troubled times, every day is dangerous. But it is important that God's work is done. Besides, it is best that I am not here for a few days. Apart from Sister Agatha, whom I trust implicitly, no one else knows that I am to accompany you. She has been instructed to say that I am visiting a particular convent in France."

"Won't the *Gestapo* wonder where the children have gone?"

"No. The *Gestapo* were here yesterday collecting details of the children in our care. I allowed them to believe I had given in to their demands and that they had won, may God forgive me," and she crossed herself. "Having got what they thought they wanted, my opinion is that they will not be back for a while. Fortunately, they appeared to be in a hurry and omitted to check the children themselves against the list I had provided them with. An unfortunate oversight on their part and a lucky escape for me as of course, I had omitted Aimée, Hélène and Claude and the other Jewish children." She smiled. "So you see, every eventuality has been thought of. I am looking forward to the challenge of our little adventure!" The Reverend Mother gave Robert the file. "Now, your clothes, German identification papers and the uncoded documents in this envelope are to be burned in our incinerator when you have finished with them. There must be no trace left of Otto Stolze or your mission." She smiled. "Your admiral was very precise about that."

"You've met him since the time we came together?" Robert was surprised.

"Yes, he has visited me discreetly on two other occasions. He finds peace with us, I think: a balm to his troubled inner conscience. Outwardly our religions are different but we have found much common ground in our spirituality.

"But now, we must prepare you for your new identity. I shall give you a brief insight into the ways of the Catholic Church, particularly from the perspective of a priest. Afterwards, you must take the time to read through the documents you are to take. Familiarize yourself with them in case they are lost or stolen and then you will be able to recount them to the British authorities. In the event of your being captured, you must dispose of them but even if they fall into undesirable hands, they have been presented in such a way that they cannot be traced back to Admiral Siranac without the greatest difficulty.

"I shall wake you very early in the morning. Our train leaves at seven o'clock. Leave your clothes outside the door and we shall deal with them. I personally will take from you the uncoded documents and anything that might identify Otto Stolze. Give them to no one else even if they demand them from you. You will find pyjamas and further reading material on your bed. But first, we must set to work."

They spent a few hours in deep conversation and Robert spent a sleepless night reading and trying to assimilate everything with which he had been presented.

"And what was in the file?" Richard was itching to know.

"Eyewitness accounts gathered by Siranac himself of the atrocities committed by the *SS*, who followed in the wake of the all-conquering *Wehrmacht*, against civilians and the military in Poland. Also in Poland, evidence of officially sanctioned, systematic wholesale 'elimination' of intellectuals, university professors, teachers, high-ranking officials, doctors, businessmen and landowners, as well as priests."

Richard was appalled. "Why?"

"So that the head of the *SD*, who had been placed in charge of the area, acting upon Hitler's orders, could satisfy his own fanaticism and impose the brutal, uncompromising authority of the Nazi conquerors on the Slav peoples of Poland."

Richard was shocked into silence.

"And not only that, but also, in their eyes at least, so that the less intelligent, the 'lower' classes, could be more easily 'Germanized'."

"A thoroughly evil enterprise," said Richard.

"Unspeakably evil. Siranac has a huge dossier that he never lets out of his sight and which he intends to take to Spain for safekeeping."

"Spain?"

"Yes, he has a long association with the country and Franco is a personal friend."

"Franco? War does indeed necessitate strange bedfellows." He saw Robert wince. "Sorry, old man, I didn't mean…"

"I know."

"What else was in the file?"

"Names of the German resistance leaders – high-ranking army officers and officials who would help the Allies depose Hitler and bring him to justice should the British government wish to take that route. And of course, the invitation to a clandestine meeting with our revered head of British Intelligence to try to set up a peace conference."

"Do you think they'll agree to all that?"

Robert shook his head. "No. I think they'll set up a meeting with British Intelligence but I think that Churchill will hold out for total defeat of Germany. It is probably the only way Nazism can be completely eradicated."

"Do you think he's right?"

"Yes, unfortunately. Deep down, I think Siranac knows that as well. However, he was most anxious that I should also convey that not all Germans are Nazis and that, like him, there are many who want peace before more lives are lost on both sides and their country is completely destroyed."

Not entirely convinced, Richard asked, "Was that all?"

"No. I also brought back evidence that Jews and other 'undesirables' are being systematically exterminated in concentration camps. And that there are many individuals risking their lives to bring Jewish people to safety, including Siranac. He's even disguised Jewish men and women as *Abwehr* agents in an effort to get them out of the country, providing false papers and travel documents and sending them on 'secret' missions to sympathetic neutral countries from which they never have to return and where they can live their lives in safety."

"I had no idea that all this stuff was actually happening," said Richard. "I thought it was all part of the government's propaganda; an exaggeration of the facts. But it isn't, is it?"

"No."

"So this really is a war we have to win."

"Absolutely."

"So, what happened in the morning?"

"We said our farewells and set off for the station." Robert chuckled. "Guess who we saw hovering around the concourse?"

"The man with the weak bladder?" suggested Richard.

"The man with the weak bladder," concurred Robert.

"What did you do?"

"Walked right by him and boarded our train."

"Ha! And he didn't recognize you? He wasn't a very good agent, was he?"

"No, thank goodness. He must have been trained at the Otto Stolze School for Spies."

"The real Otto trained spies?"

Robert smiled. "No, dummy. What I meant was that during my time at the *Abwehr*, I prepared many new recruits for spying in my own inimitable way."

"Really? I'd like to have seen that."

"Oh, I was very thorough."

"I'll bet," and Richard smiled.

"You see, my intention was that if they ever reached Britain, they'd be picked up straight away before they'd had the chance to do any harm. I presumed that because they would be so inept, the British Military would be unlikely to shoot them and they'd probably just be imprisoned for the rest of the war or persuaded to come over onto our side. Therefore, I tended to choose people with the worst English and sent them across with German-made equipment and a totally wrong idea about how they should behave when in England – instructing them to do anything in fact that would arouse people's suspicions!"

"Good for you! Siranac would have had a fit though, surely, if he'd known."

"I think he did know and found it all highly amusing."

"So…" Richard bent down and put some more coal on the fire, "…you managed to get on the train unmolested. What happened next?"

The journey from Brussels seemed to take forever. The children had obviously had it impressed upon them that their behaviour should be beyond reproach and it was. Aimée sat quietly, staying close to Robert, holding her favourite rag doll and observing the other passengers, while Hélène and Claude read or drew pictures on paper the Reverend Mother had thoughtfully provided. Everyone in their carriage seemed very taken with the three children and there were many smiles and nods in their direction.

The train stopped frequently and at Tournai, just before the border between Belgium and France, Robert spotted a group of German soldiers with *Kontrolle* shields around their necks standing on the platform waiting to board the train.

Robert and his little party had come successfully through the station checks in Brussels and he had great faith in both the validity and quality of the documents provided by the *Abwehr* but for some reason, he could not help but feel nervous. The Reverend Mother smiled at him.

"*Courage, mon brave,*" she said quietly, and patted his arm.

The guards came on board, spreading out into different carriages, methodically checking tickets and identity cards as the train once again started to move. For some unfathomable reason, their guard took an inordinate amount of time with the children's documents.

Seeing this Aimée, intelligent little girl that she was, smiled up at him and spoke.

180

Robert's heart was in his mouth.

"*We shall be meeting our aunt and uncle at the end of our journey,*" she said cheerfully, but carefully, to distract him.

"*Really?*" said the guard, who obviously spoke good French. "*And what will you do then?*"

"*Live with them. We are orphans.*"

The guard stopped looking at the children's papers. "*I was an orphan too,*" he said sadly. "*It is not very nice, is it? I lived all my young life in an orphanage. You are lucky to have a new family.*"

He gave the papers back to the Reverend Mother without completing his study of them and patted Aimée on the head.

"*Bonne chance,*" he said, as he continued down the carriage.

Robert gave Aimée a hug and she snuggled happily into the crook of his arm. He exchanged a glance with the Reverend Mother, his heart hammering in his chest.

He knew that it was one thing to be responsible for his own safety while escaping; it was a completely different thing when three children and the Reverend Mother were involved. Not for the first time was he assailed by doubts and anxieties as to the wisdom of their present course.

"God will protect us," said the Reverend Mother, as though she had been reading his thoughts.

Only slightly reassured, he nodded.

The guards alighted at Lille and so did Robert and his party where they changed trains, proceeding to their next destination slowly but without incident.

Tired and hungry, they alighted at Paris *Nord* Station, where they changed platforms and caught the train for Rennes. It was very crowded and seemed to be full of German soldiers. They were forced to share their compartment with three *Wehrmacht* officers who fortunately, because they were tired, slept for most of the journey and consequently, took no notice of Robert's little party.

"Ooh, look at the buildings," exclaimed Claude, as they walked through the medieval streets of Rennes, having left the station at the end of the first part of their journey. "It looks as though they're going to fall over."

"No," replied his older sister. "Look, they are being held up by the other buildings around them."

"I'm hungry," said Aimée, tugging at Robert's sleeve.

"It's not long now, little one," replied the Reverend Mother. "We walk beside the canal for a little way – see, here it is – and then we turn the corner, and voilà! There she is, *La Cathédrale Saint-Pierre de Rennes.*"

Overawed, the children fell silent as they entered the dark, cavernous interior of the church. Light filtered in from the windows high up in the wall and through the deeply coloured stained glass above the altar. Flickering candles created moving shadows.

"I don't like it in here," whispered Aimée, who had been so brave on the train but whose courage, because she was tired and hungry, now failed her. "It's dark and scary."

Robert lifted her up and she laid her head on his shoulder.

"I'm sure it will be fine," he said, his tone reassuring; his quiet voice echoing around the nave.

"I shall go and find Bishop Leonardo," declared the Reverend Mother. "I was expecting him to meet us and introduce us to Georges. The Bishop knew the time of our arrival," and she disappeared into the gloom, while Robert, also wondering about the mysterious Georges, and the children sat down on nearby chairs, awaiting her return.

She was gone for a very long time.

CHAPTER 24

Maybury

When the Reverend Mother did return, she was accompanied by a stocky, grey-haired lady with a nervous manner, who introduced herself as Bishop Leonardo's housekeeper.

"I am afraid His Excellency, Bishop du Jardin, has gone away," she began anxiously. "He left early this morning. He did not say when he would be back, but he told me to tell you that it is not safe for you to be here. He believes that the Cathedral is under observation – from whom he does not tell me." She looked around nervously at the dimly-lit, empty interior of the building before saying, "You must all leave here immediately. Let no one see where you go. I cannot help you further."

And with that, she disappeared into the gloomy recesses of the cathedral. Robert and the Reverend Mother looked at each other in consternation.

"What do we do now?" she said, her decisiveness and quiet confidence failing her for the first time.

Robert took a deep breath. "Well, we must find somewhere to stay for the night. Do you know anyone else in Rennes?"

"No, Bishop Leonardo was my only contact here." She frowned. "I do hope he's all right."

"So do I. However, I have a hunch that he's looking out for himself at the moment and therefore is probably quite safe. We dare not make any enquiries, I'm afraid. But how to make contact with Georges concerns me greatly." He considered for a moment. "If we are not here when he eventually arrives, he might assume that we have not come. Or, like Bishop Leonardo, he may not turn up at all. Again, we would not be able to ask. First of all, though, the children need somewhere to sleep and it must be a place nearby where I can keep the cathedral under observation."

"Can I help you do that, Robert?" asked Claude, who had been longing to make a contribution.

"Of course," replied Robert, "because I am bound to fall asleep. You shall sit at the window and wake me the moment a man arrives who is waiting and looking around him." He exchanged a brief smile with the Reverend Mother before saying to her, "Did anyone see you when you went to fetch the housekeeper?"

"No. Fortunately, I didn't have to leave the building as the Bishop's residence is attached to the cathedral and reached by an interior door."

"Good. So, children, we must go now and find a place to rest for the night."

Somewhere, a door creaked and footsteps echoed around the building. Robert put his fingers to his lips, indicating that the children should be quiet.

Two women made their way to a side altar and lit votive candles at the foot of a statue of the Virgin Mary, crossing themselves before mouthing silent prayers of devotion and intercession.

Robert shepherded his charges to the back of the church and out into the deserted square. Opposite the entrance to the cathedral was a café and inside, Robert enquired if they knew of anywhere in the vicinity with rooms where they could stay.

Seeing a Mother Superior, a Roman Catholic priest and three tired children before him, the proprietor quickly fetched his wife, who immediately went out of her way to accommodate them.

She apologized that she could only provide two rooms and apologized profusely that they were at the front of the building opposite the cathedral where the night-time chimes from the clock were at their loudest and would keep them awake.

"My husband wears earplugs, even at the back of the house," she confided.

Robert, smiling, replied that this was no problem; that they were most grateful to the proprietor and his wife in providing them with somewhere for the night before the curfew began.

The rooms turned out to be adequate and, after they had eaten a sparse meal of bread and cheese ("All that I can spare," their hostess told them), Robert and Claude took up their positions by the window, sitting in a couple of easy chairs, while the two girls shared the double bed. The Reverend Mother spent the night in the single room next door.

Claude fell asleep almost immediately and was most upset when he woke up to find that it was almost light and that Robert was awake.

"Have I missed anything?" asked Claude, anxious and sleepy at the same time.

"No. There has been no one." Robert stretched and instructed Claude to keep watch while he shaved. "You must tell me the moment anyone comes to the door of the cathedral."

Much to Claude's disappointment, he only saw two cleaning ladies with their mops and buckets and a cat.

They ate a meagre breakfast of rolls and bitter-tasting coffee in their rooms, with Robert keeping watch; thanked their host and hostess, offered to pay for their accommodation, were refused graciously, when just as they were leaving the café wondering what to do next, a lorry with a canvas hood drew up outside the cathedral. From it emerged a burly, suntanned man with a red and white spotted kerchief tied around his neck. He looked around him carefully.

Robert crossed over the square and quietly spoke the prearranged greeting: "You are Georges from Concarneau?"

"Ah, Father Jacques. Welcome," he responded correctly.

"Thank you. I am glad to be here."

Robert's hand was clasped in a vicelike grip and shaken vigorously.

"I was afraid…" Georges left the sentence unfinished.

"So were we…"

"However, all is well. But we must hurry. It is not safe. I shall explain more as we go. You have all the required permits and identity documents?"

"Yes."

"We shall need them. *Les Boches* are checking everything at the moment."

Georges helped the children up into the cab, and went round to the driver's side where he climbed in. Robert stood by the open passenger door and turned to the Reverend Mother, anxiety and sadness writ clearly in his expression.

184

"We must go," he said, because he could think of nothing else to say, and because he was aware of Georges' impatience to be on the move.

"Yes, you must," she said, with tears in her eyes. "I do not know when we shall meet again."

"We shall meet again when the war is over," replied Robert, with quiet determination, placing his hand on her shoulder, trying to keep his own emotions under control. "I shall come and find you."

"I should like that very much. I will pray for you all, for your safety and for your wellbeing."

"As we shall for you."

Robert took her hand in his and kissed it. She smiled in response and placed her hand upon his head in a gesture of blessing, before reaching into the cab and repeating the action with each of the children. Then she turned in the direction of the canal and was gone without a backwards glance.

"That must have been hard," observed Richard.

"It was." Robert stared into the fire. "Not only because I never imagined for a moment when I first left the children with her at the Convent in 1940, that our paths would be so closely associated later on, but also because I left feeling incredibly worried for her safety. I still am."

"I can imagine. And you have no way of knowing whether or not she reached Brussels in safety."

"No, and I probably never shall until the war's over. And who knows when that might be."

"She sounds like a remarkable person."

"She is."

"I suppose you'll become a convert to Catholicism now."

Robert ignored the hint of levity in Richard's words. "No, I don't need to. Faith is universal, isn't it, whatever religious path you choose to follow?"

"I hadn't thought of it like that before."

Once they were out of the town and on the open road, Georges said to Robert, "I am sorry that I was not here yesterday to meet you. Despite my protestations that the fish will quickly rot because the ice in the barrels will melt, the Germans would not let me leave the Military Zone to take my catch to the train station in Rennes, even though I do so regularly by order of the Military Government and have all the correct permits and papers to do so. The soldiers took ages to check everything and even inspected every barrel."

"Is that unusual?" asked Robert, thinking of the Bishop's unexplained disappearance and wondering if there was a connection.

"Sometimes. At the moment, there are rumours circulating that an escape line has been compromised. The *Gestapo* have been active in the Free Zone and it is said that they have infiltrated the 'Caribou' escape organization."

"You are not involved in that?"

"No. Mine is a different operation entirely, fortunately. But a discovery like that has a knock-on effect everywhere and for a while, security becomes draconian. It is quite shocking that the *Gestapo* were able to bypass the French Resistance security checks. Many people will be arrested now and suffer horribly." He spat out of the window. "That is what I think of the *Gestapo*."

"You are not alone."

"Will the Germans check up on us?" asked Claude anxiously.

"Yes, without doubt. I hope you have good documents."

"They've been all right so far, haven't they, Uncle Robert?" replied the boy, practising his use of Robert's new title that would carry them through the next part of their journey – the Reverend Mother having been insistent that the children address Robert firstly as 'Father Jacques' and from then on as 'Uncle' Robert, so that if spoken to by German guards, his titles would be second nature to them.

"Yes, Claude, they have. But the hardest part is yet to come, I think."

"I am sorry that you and the children will not be able to stay with us overnight as planned, but that cannot be helped. My wife is also most distraught that there will not even be time to rest or eat a meal. Because of the delay in my reaching you, we shall have to leave immediately we arrive back in Concarneau in order to catch the evening tide."

"We can manage," declared Claude bravely, "if it means we shall be free."

"Good boy," said Georges.

They had reached a secluded, remote area of the countryside, away from all signs of habitation. Georges stopped the lorry beside a wooded copse.

"I have brought clothes for you," he said, handing Robert a neatly folded pile of the distinctive, canvas smock and trousers worn by Breton fishermen. "With your colouring, you will blend in well."

"What should I do with my cassock and attaché case? I cannot risk either of these being discovered by the Germans as we enter the Military Zone."

"I'll show you."

Georges got out of the lorry, followed by Robert, who motioned to the children that they should remain inside the cab.

"Help me with these."

He lifted up the canvas flaps and began hauling the half-dozen or so empty fish barrels off the back of the lorry. When it was empty, Georges removed the sacking that covered the base and opened up a section of the wooden floor to reveal a hidden compartment that went deep into the base of the lorry.

"In here," he said.

"Clever," said Robert, depositing his priest's robes, which he had removed, and his attaché case containing the information garnered by his own efforts and the coded documents provided by Admiral Siranac. "You could hide a couple of men in here."

"And I have done. Many times and both ways, too. Usually, the Germans don't bother to lift off all the barrels and search them when they're full of fish because it is always assumed they have been passed before they leave the harbour. The barrels are rarely given a thorough examination when I'm on my way into Concarneau."

"Except at the moment."

"Except possibly at the moment. Now, you must get changed quickly, before anyone comes. The children can get out for a few moments to stretch their legs and relieve themselves."

Their tasks completed, they resumed their journey. Soon, the children fell asleep.

"As a Frenchman, what's your connection with the *Abwehr*?" asked Robert. "I assume there must be one, otherwise you would not have been involved in my little escapade."

"Yes, though I do not reveal it to a living soul, even to my wife. The consequences would be disastrous for me if it were to be discovered."

"I can imagine," replied Robert, knowing that while in France, he would not reveal the extent of *his* involvement, even to Georges, though he wondered if the latter knew there was a connection. "How did it come about?"

"When the Germans invaded in 1940, I found myself stranded in Antwerp. I won't go into details of how I came to be there or what took place but suffice to say I was offered safe passage back to Concarneau if I worked for the *Abwehr* as an agent. I completed all the necessary training and returned to my home town at about the time the Germans took control of France."

"I see." Robert suddenly experienced a moment of doubt as to this man's integrity.

Georges picked up on his tone and stated, defensively, "You worked for the *Abwehr*."

"True, but while I was there, I thwarted the Germans at every opportunity. I saw it only as a means of gathering information to take back home with me to England to help the Allied cause."

Georges nodded. "I understand, and it is the same for me," he said. "I am first and foremost a Frenchman, both by birth and inclination. That is where my greatest loyalty lies. Like you, I saw my recruitment as a heaven-sent opportunity to serve my country. So, I work for the *Abwehr* as well as the French Resistance and the British."

"I see."

"I am what is known in the trade as a double agent. Or in my case triple agent."

"Doesn't that produce a conflict of loyalties?"

"*Non!*" Again Georges was emphatic. "My great work is for the French Resistance in collaboration with the British and I assist the highest authority in the *Abwehr* when required. I do not peddle Allied secrets or impart information that might be helpful to the Germans nor am I asked to do so. On the contrary, to keep my cover intact, I deliberately feed them with misinformation that contains only a tinge of validity. This they accept without question because they need me for their own purposes and so, I maintain my credibility with everyone. I am plying my trade for the greater good. I answer to no one except my own conscience."

"Then you steer a narrow and dangerous path." Like Admiral Siranac.

"Yes."

His concerns about Georges momentarily satisfied, Robert asked, "How did you know that I once worked for the *Abwehr*?"

"It was necessary for me to have some intelligence about you and confirmation of your true identity. I had to be certain you were not a Nazi spy sent to infiltrate our activities. It goes without saying that I cannot reveal my sources."

"Naturally." Briefly, Robert wondered whether this man had a personal connection to Admiral Siranac or someone close to him.

"Now, enough conversation," said Georges somewhat abruptly. "We must discuss what is to happen when we arrive at the harbour in Concarneau."

"Provided we come through the checkpoints successfully."

"Of course. When this has been accomplished, I shall drive the lorry down into a deserted side street where we shall transfer the children into three of the empty barrels. Then I shall proceed to the unloading shed from where they will be taken on board my trawler."

"I presume there will be guards inspecting the barrels?" asked Robert.

"Yes. The German guards mark each barrel with white chalk and attach a docket to indicate that it has passed inspection before it leaves the shed. My colleagues will ensure that this has already been done with the barrels containing the children so that they will be successfully loaded onto the vessel."

To Robert, it all sounded very risky.

Georges was reassuring. "We are good at distracting them from their task."

Robert smiled. "I can imagine."

"After this, we will board. On each fishing trip, one vessel from the fleet is selected at random to be the German guard ship by the *Kriegsmarine* officers who will accompany us to the fishing grounds. If that is, unfortunately, the one also selected for use by the Resistance on that occasion, then this boat will mysteriously develop engine trouble and have to catch up with the fleet later and the guards will select another trawler."

"I see. What happens next?"

"We sail out to the fishing grounds, where we will spend two or three nights. We can only go out when the weather and the moon are right. You are lucky to have come at this time, the portents are good at the moment.

"Once out on the Banks, we shall quietly rendezvous with a Royal Navy boat: a converted Breton trawler painted in the bright colours of Concarneau and bearing the number of a vessel that has not gone out that trip. The Navy are dropping off two British agents tomorrow night, along with various items for the French Resistance. Unfortunately, they will not be expecting you."

"What happens if the Royal Navy refuse to accept us?"

Robert said the words 'Royal Navy' with a sense of relief, although the thought that they might be rejected by his fellow countrymen filled him with alarm.

"They will not refuse. They have taken several downed British airmen back to safety by this route. Sometimes they are warned in advance, sometimes they are not. But they always accept them and sort out who they are when they get back to England."

"Have you ever transferred *Abwehr* spies across to England this way?"

"No, never. The *Abwehr* does not make use of this scheme in that way. They use it in other ways to suit their own needs. Besides, I would not compromise the trust placed in me by the Resistance and the British."

188

"Of course not. I can see that you are a brave and honourable man."

Georges shrugged his shoulders. "I do what I have to do." He slowed the lorry. "We are coming to a checkpoint. Have yours and the children's papers ready. Do not react if they speak to you in German or English. They will try anything."

At the barrier, two German soldiers stood in the way of the lorry and one held up his hand, indicating that they should stop. He asked politely, in adequate French, that all the occupants should leave the cab, while his colleague watched them closely as they did so.

Cautiously, Robert helped the children down, who, fortunately, were still sleepy and stood next to him in a dazed fashion while the first guard checked the papers Robert had given him when requested. The young man scrutinized them thoroughly, taking his time. Occasionally, he looked up at Robert, who smiled and nodded, conveying the impression of being unconcerned.

Georges stood by and lit a cigarette, nonchalantly leaning against the bonnet, watching; waiting for his turn.

Eventually, the guard seemed satisfied and disappeared into the little hut, from where he emerged very shortly but without the documents. Robert looked at Georges, who shook his head imperceptibly. He took a deep breath, controlling his anxiety.

"Who is driving this vehicle?" asked the guard.

"Moi," replied Georges.

"Does it belong to you?"

"Mais oui!"

"Papers, please."

Meanwhile, the other guard meticulously searched the cab and then climbed up inside the back of the lorry. They could hear him moving the barrels around.

Robert's heart was pounding.

"Why did you not return by the entry point from which you left this morning?" asked the guard.

Georges shrugged. "Because I felt like a change."

"It gives variety to your day, *ja*?" He smiled with understanding and Georges nodded. "I too could do with variety to my day. Still, it is very quiet here and much better than the Eastern Front, *ja*?" He called out to his companion. *"Helmut, bist du fertig?"*

"Ja, Ulrich. Alles in Ordnung."

Robert knew that they had come through the checks safely, without discovery or mishap. Silently, he thanked Admiral Siranac for providing them with such authentic credentials.

"I will stamp your papers."

The guard called Ulrich disappeared into the little hut and re-emerged a few moments later, returning the officially approved documents to Robert and Georges. He patted Aimée on the head and, regarding both her and Robert closely, asked if she was looking forward to living with her uncle.

"Oh yes," she replied truthfully. "I love my Uncle Robert," and to prove the point, she gave Robert a hug. He smiled and held her close.

Satisfied, Helmut and Ulrich opened the barrier and waved the lorry on its way.

Once they were out of sight of the checkpoint, Robert sat back in the cab and breathed a sigh of relief. Georges offered him a cigarette, which he took.

"Those two seemed all right back there," he said, opening the window and taking deep draughts of the Gauloise. He spluttered and coughed.

Georges laughed. "Too strong for you, eh?"

"Yes. I've got used to German ones! Please don't be offended if I give this back to you!"

"Non, my friend," and Georges tucked the extinguished cigarette behind his ear. "This I shall keep until later. It is only on special occasions that I bring them out. They are becoming scarce now; unless, of course, you wish to pay a small fortune for them on the black market!"

And he slapped Robert on the back, relief making him expansive and jovial.

Once they reached Concarneau, having encountered a formidable German presence along the way conveying lorry loads of equipment and armament for what Georges said was to be known as the 'Atlantic Wall' – Hitler's plan to create an impenetrable fortress all the way from the north coast of Norway to the border with Spain – Georges drove the lorry into a deserted side street and the children quickly climbed out of the cab into the back of the lorry. Robert removed his attaché case and priest's robe from the hidden compartment and placed them in a fisherman's tote bag. The two men then helped each child into a barrel.

Only twelve-year old Hélène protested.

"You can't expect me to squeeze in there," she said. "I'll suffocate."

"There are several air holes, Mademoiselle. You will be able to breath. Men twice your size have hidden in there."

"But it stinks of fish!"

"Which would you rather do? Stink of fish and escape to England or stay here and be sent to a concentration camp because you have Jewish heritage?"

There was no answer to this, so Hélène acquiesced and allowed Georges to batten down the lid of her barrel. Then he and Robert climbed back into the cab and Georges drove the lorry down to the packing shed on the quayside. Here, the guards were already busy checking each barrel that was waiting to go on the trawlers.

Robert unloaded their cargo and placed it in the inspection line. Georges drove off and parked the lorry.

Suddenly, just as he returned, there was a great commotion as three large, disreputable-looking dogs ran into the shed, growling and fighting with each other. Soon they were joined by a fourth, all of them chasing round and round the shed, jumping up at the barrels, barking loudly, baring their teeth at the guards, some of whom backed off in fear, with everyone shouting furiously at the fishermen.

"Get those animals out of here," came the command, "or we will shoot them!"

A couple of fishermen half-heartedly attempted to corner the animals, all the while keeping an eye on their colleagues who, while the guards were distracted watching the unfolding pantomime, quickly placed white chalk crosses and attached dockets to the barrels containing the children. Eventually, the dogs were removed and the guards resumed their inspection – at the point where they thought they had left off.

Robert had to admire the nerve of the French fishermen.

190

Approved and documented, the barrels were then rolled up the gangplanks and loaded onto the fishing vessels with Georges and Robert carefully steering the children's barrels onto his boat. Soon, all was ready and with a huge sense of relief, they cast off.

It was to be a long journey to the fishing grounds, some twenty-five miles, and under cover of darkness, the children were released from their hiding places.

"You must stay down below in the hold. You must not be seen on deck. The guard boat will circle round, but they do not normally come on board while we are out here. But we cannot risk you being spotted."

"When will the Royal Navy meet up with us?" asked Claude.

"Soon, soon," replied Georges.

The fishing proceeded without incident and after a few hours, during a lull in the work, with the nets cast over the side, the guard boat out of sight, a fishing vessel of similar shape and design to the ones from Concarneau, came alongside.

"*Georges?*" a voice called out quietly and discreetly.

"*Oui, c'est moi.*"

"*All is well?*"

"*Oui. All is well.*"

"*Bon. We have some cargo for you.*"

"*Merci.*"

A rope was thrown which Georges caught and tied round a cleat, securing both boats together. One of the fishermen kept watch while three men stepped across onto the deck. The boxes of equipment that accompanied them were transferred quickly into the hold and while this was happening, Robert could see Georges involved in earnest conversation with the captain of the British vessel. Eventually, Robert was introduced. The captain regarded him closely.

"Please state your name and service number."

"I am Lieutenant Robert Llewellyn Anderson, 1st Battalion, Royal Welch Fusiliers, service number 7346121." He stumbled over his words; his accent containing more than a trace of German. He had not spoken English for months; had not thought in English for all that time.

The captain viewed him suspiciously.

"He is who he says he is," said Georges.

Finally, after some moments, the captain nodded. "Well, the secret service chaps can sort all this out when we reach England. There are three children as well, I gather?"

"Yes," said Robert. "They are with me. They are Jewish."

"Righty-ho. But you must be quick getting on board, we can't afford to hang about."

And they did just as they were asked, thanking Georges with a rapid, heartfelt, shake of his hand as they left his boat.

"So it was as simple as that," remarked Richard.

"As simple as that."

"No hair-raising, last minute escape from discovery by the German guard boat?"

Robert shook his head.

"No E-boat emerging unexpectedly from out of the darkness with all guns blazing? No *Luftwaffe* squadron dropping a hail of bombs? No torpedoes from a suddenly surfacing U-boat?"

Robert smiled. "Nope."

"No rough weather making the journey home hellish and frightening?" continued Richard hopefully.

"No, nothing. We motored our way back to Falmouth across kindly seas without incident. The children slept down below while I stayed on deck, impatient to see the coast of England again."

"What did you do when you stepped onto British soil?"

"Fell down on my knees and wept with absolute and total relief. It was the most wonderful feeling I have ever experienced."

"I'll bet! And then you were interviewed."

"Interviewed, skilfully debriefed, all my documents read and discussed and my time with the *Abwehr* dissected in the minutest detail."

"But sanitized by you with certain personal details omitted, of course."

"Of course! I was then congratulated, released and finally, interrogated all over again at Grange Manor. They really got their money's worth."

"And that was where I came in or rather, where I waited outside in the corridor," said Richard, smiling.

"Yes." Robert smiled back.

"Does it feel good to be back in England?"

"So good, I can't begin to describe it."

"I can imagine. Well, I think I can. I wonder what they've got lined up for us when we finish our leave?"

"I have no idea. But it looks as though we'll be working together."

"I'm glad about that."

"So am I. Thank you, Richard, for your hospitality. And for listening."

"Don't mention it, old man. Only too glad to be of assistance. Well, it's getting late, or rather, getting early. And we both need our shut-eye. I'll take you and the kiddies over to Shropshire in the car when you go home tomorrow, if you like. I'd like to meet your parents and see this boarding school of yours."

"I'd like that too." He stifled a yawn and stretched. "Well, goodnight, Richard."

"Goodnight, old man."

Once upstairs, Robert stood for a long time, breathing deeply; absorbing himself once more in the ambience of Sophie's bedroom.

After several moments, he undressed and moved the easy chair across to the window where he removed the blackout and drew back the curtains. He wrapped himself in Sophie's eiderdown, enlivened by its sweet fragrance, and absentmindedly fingered the trinkets she kept on her windowsill.

As his eyes began to close and sleep stole upon him, he climbed into her bed and drew the protective covers round him, feeling peaceful and once again, deeply thankful to be safely home.

PART THREE

SEPTEMBER, 1942 – MAY, 1943

CHAPTER 25

St Nicolas

"Oh, look at the poor things!" exclaimed Mae as she, Edna and Sophie, having just left the seafront café, stood by the harbour wall watching the ragged, emaciated slave workers disembark from the ships. "There's so many of them! Oh, Edna, can't we do something to help?"

"I'm afraid not, my dear." Her sister's expression was grim. "It would be far too dangerous. We'd be sent to prison, or worse."

She regarded the impassive, stony-faced *SS* soldiers accompanying the latest batch of Russian prisoners – sent to St Nicolas to fulfil Hitler's dream of the Channel Islands becoming an impregnable fortress – as other guards forcibly kept the onlookers away from the jetty.

"Surely we can give them some food? Some bread at least. They're so thin. I don't see how they'll manage to survive all that physical work. I wouldn't be able to. And they'll be so cold in those rags, especially as the nights are drawing in," continued Mae, her sympathy for their pitiful state thoroughly roused.

Understanding and sharing her aunt's concern, Sophie silently contemplated the dilemma with which they were faced. Like Mae, her instinct was to help; to ease the plight of these unfortunate people, but Edna was correct – it would be too dangerous.

Sophie felt anger and frustration at being unable to alleviate the obvious distress of the captives. She raged impotently at the cruelty and indifference to the human condition shown by the captors. And she berated herself for her lack of moral courage to risk everything and help them.

Silent and upset, the three women turned away from the harbour and made their way up towards the town where they met Ethel in a state of high agitation.

"Oh, Sophie, Sophie!" she called out, manoeuvring the pushchair and dragging a reluctant Reggie across the road to speak to them. "Isn't the news terrible?"

"What news?" asked Sophie, imagining some catastrophe on the war front.

"Haven't you seen the notice?" replied Ethel, her voice becoming increasingly high-pitched and shrill with anxiety.

"What notice?"

"The one that says we have to sell everything and pack up and leave. We're all going to be sent away to Germany!" and she promptly burst into tears.

"What do you mean, everyone?" asked Sophie, touching the hysterical woman on the arm in an attempt to soothe her so that she could make sense of her incoherent jumble of words.

"Haven't you heard? Haven't you read this morning's paper either? It's in there as well. We're all to be sent away! Our lives are ruined. Yours. Mine. We'll be left with nothing after this. Nothing, I tell you!"

"Calm down, Ethel," said Edna reasonably. "They can't possibly send the whole island away."

"No, I won't calm down and yes, they can. We're the conquered people. The Germans can do anything they like. They'll send us all away to those horrible concentration camps and we'll end up like the poor wretches who've been building the fortifications out at Falaise Head. And my family will end up dead. We'll all end up dead!"

Mae had gone pale with shock and Edna sat her down on a nearby bench.

"Where is this notice?"

"They've put one outside the Post Office in the place where they usually put all their latest rules and regulations, one outside the Council Offices and it's all over the Herald. Surely you must have seen it?"

Edna had not yet read that morning's paper.

"Mae, you sit here quietly while Sophie and I investigate. We'll be back as soon as we can and let you know what's happening. Ethel, you get yourself off home and have a cup of tea. There must be some mistake."

"There's no mistake," replied Ethel. "Go and look for yourselves. It's up there in black and white as clear as day – you'll see. I've got to find Frank."

By this time, Reggie had picked up on his mother's emotional state and had begun to cry. This set off little Joan in the pushchair and Edna and Sophie watched in consternation as Ethel, still agitated and incomprehensibly bemoaning the situation, walked off down the High Street with her two wailing children.

A crowd had gathered around the Post Office notice board. As Edna and Sophie approached, the townsfolk parted silently, making way for the two women to read the words that caused Edna to put a protective arm round Sophie's shoulder and hold onto her very tightly.

'By order of Higher Authorities the following British subjects will be evacuated and transferred to Germany (a) Persons who have their permanent residence not on the Channel Islands, for instance, those who have been caught here by the outbreak of war (b) All men not born on the Channel Islands and 16 to 70 years of age who belong to the English people, together with their families.'

"If you're one of that lot," said one of the men standing close by, indicating the noticeboard, "you get one of these," and he produced a blue sheet of paper which he gave to Sophie and Edna to read. "It's a deportation notice."

In bald terms, it stated that he and his family were to present themselves at the Harbour Packing Shed by two o'clock the following afternoon and to bring with them no more than one suitcase each. It contained instructions to *'outfit yourselves with warm clothes, strong boots and provisions for two days, meal dishes, drinking bowl and if possible with a blanket. Your luggage must not be heavier than you can carry and must bear a label with your full address.'* Each person should have *'a trunk packed with clothes to be sent afterwards, labelled with full address.'* It also stated the amount of *Reichsmarks* that could be taken and that all valuables were to be *'deposited as far as possible with the banks. Keys of houses to be handed over to the Constables.'* The document concluded with a warning that *'should you fail to obey the order sentence by Court Martial shall be effected.'*

"Haven't the Consell de Souverain done anything about this? Haven't they protested and tried to put a stop to this nonsense?" asked Edna, trying to use reason and possible action to suppress her rising sense of fear.

"I've been trying to see Sir Anthony all morning to find out what's going on," said the man, "but he's been inundated. I can't get near him without an appointment."

Other people in the crowd nodded in agreement.

"He'll see me," stated Edna, who was in no mood to brook any nonsense from someone she had known all his life and who was several years her junior. Chairman or no chairman of the ruling council, she would see him and have her say.

"Good luck!" said the man, moving away after seeing his wife and children approaching on their return from shopping for the two days' worth of provisions to take with them on their journey.

Leaving the Post Office, Edna and Sophie collected Stargazer and the trap and went back for Mae.

"Is it true?" she asked tremulously, seeing her worst fears realized in Sophie's pale face.

"I'm afraid it is," replied her sister, as she helped Mae into the buggy. "For Sophie."

As they left Port le Bac, cars could be seen travelling in all directions, stopping at houses, farms and businesses to deliver envelopes.

When the three women drew up outside the farmhouse, a German soldier accompanied by an unknown civilian in a black leather coat were just returning to their car. On seeing the horse and trap arrive, they approached the three women.

"Complete and return to us immediately the form that has just been delivered to this house. We shall wait in the car," said the man in the black coat. "There must be no argument. It is to be done now."

Her heart hammering, after handing Stargazer's reins to Edna, Sophie leapt from the buggy and ran indoors.

There, on the door mat, was an envelope containing the blue sheet of paper upon which were printed a set of instructions together with a form to be signed confirming that these instructions had been read and understood. There was a further section to be completed with name, exact address, date and place of birth, occupation and place of employment.

So, this was it. Her deportation order. Inescapable and official.

She was to be sent away and interned in Germany.

Feeling sick and knowing she had no choice in the matter, Sophie signed the form and returned outside to first show Edna and Mae before handing it to the occupants of the car, who thanked her politely before rapidly driving away.

Silently, they helped a weeping Mae into the house.

"Take her upstairs and put her to bed," said Edna. "I'm going back down into Port le Bac and speak to Anthony. Out of all the bizarre rules and regulations that they've come up with, this one has to rank among the most ridiculous." She took up the reins. "There must be something I can do and I shall not stay silent until I have found out what it is."

As Stargazer trotted down the lane once more, Edna reflected on Albrecht's warning that she should be careful. She knew she would keep her promise to him but oh, how she wished that he was still *Kommandant*; how she wished he was still here on the island and she could talk to him directly. Who were the 'Higher

Authorities' from whom the order had originated? And why should they make such an order now, two years after the start of the occupation? Had they forgotten the promise made to the islanders that, if the surrender following the invasion was peaceful, the lives, property and liberty of peaceful inhabitants would be solemnly guaranteed?

If Albrecht had still been here, Edna felt sure that he would have upheld that promise and dispensed with all this nonsense.

When she reached the Bureau de Consell, Edna was taken into an anteroom where she found Sir Anthony besieged by a crowd of people all clamouring for his attention. As soon as he spotted Edna, he asked a steward to show her into the council chamber itself and when he had finally managed to extricate himself, he entered and closed the door behind him with some relief.

"So, Anthony," began Edna without preamble, "what's this all about?"

"What you see."

"And have you made any protest to the *Kommandant*?"

"Yes, and in the strongest terms."

"And did that have any effect?"

"No, unfortunately. Apparently, according to the *Kommandant*, this order comes from Hitler himself. No one has the power to change it in any way, shape or form."

"No one has the courage to defy Hitler, you mean."

"Probably." Sir Anthony's expression was glum. "I'm very sorry, Edna, because I realize that the deportation order has caught Sophie in its net. Unfortunately, the *Kommandant* says the order has to be carried out to the letter."

"But why, Anthony? Why should they decide to do this now? It can't possibly be as some kind of reprisal. There's been no major rebellion on the part of the islanders; we've coexisted with the invader peaceably for over two years. As far as I'm aware, there have been no commando raids on any of the other Channel Islands recently. Therefore, there's no rhyme or reason for this ludicrous deportation order. As far as I can see, the English-born residents pose no greater security threat than the island-born people. In any case, in effect, we're already prisoners of the *Reich*; we none of us can go anywhere. Why would they waste money, time and resources in transporting and incarcering people in Germany? It defies all possible logic."

"I have no idea. I don't think the *Kommandant* has either. He's been ranting and raving about each of the Channel Islands having to fulfil its quota. He's running scared, Edna, that he may not find sufficient numbers to satisfy the 'Higher Authority'. Therefore, he's ordering the 'evacuation' to be carried out as swiftly as possible."

"I don't give a damn about his problems," said Edna, "but I do about Sophie's wellbeing. How do we know where she's likely be sent and under what conditions? For all we know she could be used as a hostage or forced labour or even billeted in a town that's likely to be bombed. Who'll look out for her safety? And what about the farm? We can't possibly manage without her. Surely there must be room for exemptions?

"At the moment, only on the grounds of ill-health." replied Sir Anthony, running his hand across his forehead.

It had been one hell of a morning, he told her. The deportation order had been read out by the *Kommandant* through an interpreter at the regular early morning council session. Then he, Sir Anthony, had had a private meeting with the *Kommandant* in order to find out more but discovered that the *Kommandant* didn't know anything other than that the order had come directly from the *Führer* himself and had to be implemented without delay.

"In the original deportation order," said Sir Anthony, "the selection process and deportation notices were to be made and served by our British policemen, but I wasn't going to stand for that. I insisted that the whole process had to be carried out by the occupying troops. It was the only concession I managed to extract from him," he added apologetically and regretfully.

Edna threw him a withering look.

"The *Kommandant* is so anxious to get things underway," he continued quickly, Edna's expression touching his own guilt at not being more forceful and insisting upon further clarification and concessions, "that in this first batch of deportees, he's just sending across to Germany as many people as he can find straight away who fit into categories a and b without stopping to think of the consequences for the island as a whole. What he might do tomorrow when he's had more time to consider the matter, is anyone's guess."

"Is there nothing I can do now, today, at this moment?"

"No, I'm sorry, Edna, but there isn't."

With a deep sigh, Edna thanked him begrudgingly and walked out of the Council Offices into the town square, her mind a confusion of anger and frustration.

Albrecht would have thought this through. He would have had to obey the order, of course, but he would have found some way of mitigating the pain and stupidity of forcing everyone to leave to whom the order applied regardless of circumstance.

How many people were they required to deport, for goodness' sake?

When she arrived home, grim-faced and exhausted, she and Sophie sat at the kitchen table in silence, their mugs of tea untouched. Eventually, Edna spoke.

"I'm sorry, my dear, but there was nothing I could do."

Sophie covered her aunt's hand with her own. "It's all right. I'd guessed as much, but thank you for trying anyway."

The two women looked at each other, both of them close to tears, knowing they must bow to the inevitable.

"I shall miss you," said Sophie.

"Oh, dear girl, I shall miss you, too."

"I feel so settled here with you and Aunt Mae and I've come to love working on the farm."

"It's been wonderful." Edna held onto Sophie's hand. "Whatever happens, you know you will always have a home here."

"Thank you and once all this nonsense is over, I should like to come back, that is, if you'll have me… I think that after years of not knowing what I wanted to do with my life, I may have found my vocation."

"Really?" Edna's face lit up briefly. "Of course Mae and I will have you!"

They didn't consider the possibility that Sophie might never come back; they didn't consider the possibility that the Allies might not win the war and that the island would never be free. They clung onto the certainty that Sophie wanted to come back and they would be able to resume the seasonal rhythms and patterns established so deeply during the past two years.

It was only then that Sophie wept, unable to contain her distress any longer. Edna went round the other side of the table and held her close.

"It will be all right," she said, consoling herself as much as her niece, kissing the top of Sophie's head.

Through her tears, Sophie nodded and tried to smile.

"Don't be afraid," said Edna.

"I'll try."

"Good girl." With a deep breath, Edna took control of herself again and said, "Before Mae comes downstairs, there's something I'd like you to take. It may or may not be helpful, but I shall feel considerably reassured if you were to have this."

Sophie dried her eyes and followed her aunt into the sitting room, where Edna went across to the bureau which she unlocked before pressing the secret panel.

"I never knew about this," said Sophie.

"Ah, it's my hidey-hole. Not even Mae knows about it. So you mustn't breathe a word."

She showed Sophie the photograph of Ralph Llewellyn.

"He looks very dashing."

"He was. And he was also a lovely man."

"What about his family?"

"I never knew them. His parents had passed away before he and I met. I believe he had a sister but they weren't close. I wrote to her after he died, but she never wrote back."

Sophie gave the photograph back to Edna.

"What was it you wanted me to take?"

"A copy of this," and Edna handed Sophie a piece of paper upon which was written Major von Witzenhausen's address.

Sophie looked up in surprise and smiled, despite her grief.

"Aunt Edna! You're a dark horse! And all the time the Major was here, there's me thinking he was quietly courting Mae but in reality, he was courting you!"

Edna blushed. "Hardly, my dear! There was nothing. Even if there had been, I wouldn't have done that to Mae for anything. However, the day Albrecht came to say goodbye, without uttering a word, we sort of expressed what we both felt. Nothing will come of it, of course, but we exchanged addresses. And I'd like you to take a copy of his home address. Write to him if you find yourself in difficulties. He will help you if he can, I'm sure. He was very fond of you. Apparently, you reminded him of his daughter when she was young."

"Really? I never knew."

"No, we both of us are good at hiding our true feelings."

Sophie smiled and copied out the address.

"I'll keep this safe," she said, carefully folding up the piece of paper before adding, quite matter-of-factly as though she was going on a holiday: "Well, I suppose I'd better go and pack."

"I'll come and help. Not that you need any help…"

"But I'd appreciate your company."

"Yes."

"It'll be interesting to see how much I can stuff into one suitcase."

"You ought to wear as much as you can. You never know what you might need, wherever it is you're going. Some parts of Germany can be very cold."

"Yes, Aunt."

And the two women reluctantly climbed the stairs to Sophie's room.

The next morning, Sophie and Edna lifted her suitcase, trunk, food and everything else she was required to take onto the trap. Jean le Rouge and Old Fred came to help and to say goodbye.

Stargazer's harness was bedecked with red, white and blue ribbons.

"I thought we ought to show a bit of cheerful defiance," said Jean, "so I put these here ribbons on. There's going to be a lot more of that today, you'll see," he added, nodding his head sagely, before climbing up into the buggy. "I'll tag along and help with this here trunk. Old Fred'll keep an eye on things here, won't you, old boy?"

"Arr," came the reply.

Sophie smiled and waved. "Bye, Fred, and thank you."

"Arr."

The scene that greeted them when they reached the harbour was both uplifting and heart-warming and they could see that Jean was absolutely correct in his assumption (or had he gleaned some inside knowledge?).

Horses, traps, prams and suitcase-carrying wheelbarrows were all decorated as though it was the day of the St Nicolas Fête. Crowds of people, brightly dressed in red, white and blue, singing patriotic songs, shouting "God Save the King!" and waving tiny, homemade Union flags, lined the roads leading to the harbour, ignoring the half-hearted attempts by the German soldiers to keep them away from the immediate vicinity.

The atmosphere was more akin to a celebration than to the spectre of loved ones being sent away into the unknown.

The deportees walked along the road to the Packing Shed like visiting royalty, shaking proffered hands from the people that lined the route, stopping to speak to the well-wishers, accepting little farewell gifts. Whatever had been their private distress and grief the previous day, the islanders were determined to put on a show of solidarity and cheerfulness so that everyone would know they could not be suppressed or defeated.

The occupying *Wehrmacht* troops who, like the islanders, hadn't understood why the deportations had to take place, stood around looking sullen and confused. They had been told to expect trouble and disorder, even rioting, and had arrived at the harbour heavily armed with fixed bayonets and machine guns. Now they looked away, embarrassed and shamefaced at this unmistakable demonstration of peaceful defiance.

There were a few well-directed jeers and taunts at the soldiers but these were drowned out by cheers and shouts of support as each new group of deportees left the Packing Shed and made their way towards Victoria Pier.

When her turn came to be registered, given a health check and then receive a medical certificate pronouncing her fit to travel, Sophie hugged Edna and consoled Mae, who was crying silently into a sodden handkerchief.

"I don't know how we'll manage without you," she sobbed.

"You'll find a way," said Sophie reassuringly, holding tightly onto Edna's hand while she spoke to Mae. "I'll write as soon as I can."

"Yes, my dear," said Edna, "just as we will to you." She released her own grip on Sophie's hand. "Now you must go."

"I'll keep an eye out for her," came a man's voice close by.

"Doctor Reynolds!" exclaimed Sophie, "But surely you can't be going?"

"I'm afraid so, my dear. By some quirk of fate, my parents were on holiday in England when I was born. So even though I've lived here from when I was about two weeks old, it would seem I'm still classed as an undesirable alien. But we'll be all right, won't we?" he said, putting an avuncular arm round Sophie's shoulder.

"I bleedin' well 'ope so," muttered Gert. "Mabel, can't you keep those kids of yours under control? They're all over the place."

"Oh do shut up, Gert," replied George. "We've got enough to contend with without you wittering on all over the place."

"I think I've just discovered another reason why I don't want to go," remarked Dr Reynolds under his breath, before saying his own regretful farewells to Edna and a doubly-distressed Mae and moving away to allow Sophie to say goodbye to her aunts.

"Look after yourself," said Mae.

"Oh, I shall. And you do the same."

"I feel considerably reassured that Dr Reynolds is going too and can keep a watchful eye over you, though I shall miss his ministrations. Where will we get another doctor from? Oh dear, oh dear."

Sophie exchanged an expression of affectionate exasperation with Edna.

There being nothing more that could be said, after one last hug, and not wishing to prolong the agony, Sophie picked up her suitcase, turned and joined the others making their way into the Packing Shed.

Eventually, all business completed, she emerged once again and walked down to Victoria Pier where she stepped onto one of the crowded German transport ships that was to take her across the short stretch of water to France and the next chapter of her life.

As the boats drew away from the quayside, someone in the crowd started singing *There'll always be an England* and voices on board ship and along the harbour took up the song, sending the deportees away with rousing patriotism and a soul-strengthening exuberance that was to sustain them through the journey to whatever might lay ahead, as well as sending out a defiant message that the British spirit was indefatigable.

CHAPTER 26

France/Germany

Sophie stood on deck, leaning against the railings, watching the outline of St Nicolas disappear into the gathering gloom of evening. A buoyant spirit continued to prevail as all around her, people began to find a space and settle down for the journey, reclaiming their luggage, laying their blankets on the deck; some trying to snatch what rest they could, while others continued to chat excitedly.

For a brief while, they felt the illusion of freedom within the exhilaration of a sea voyage, even though that voyage was to an unknown destination and their fate uncertain.

There were some, like herself, who found it impossible to sleep and for her part, Sophie had no desire to join in with the general chatter. She quietly observed Dr Reynolds as he went round the deck checking that everyone was comfortable and in good health, paying particular attention to the elderly and the very young.

Finding that all was well, he came to join her. "How are you doing, Sophie?" he asked.

"Oh, I'm fine, thank you," she replied. "How about you?"

He seemed surprised by the question. "Me? Oh, not so bad. Worrying about my practice and my patients."

"What's going to happen to them?"

"Apparently, the German military doctor will be looking after them. There's no other qualified physician on the island, so I hope to goodness they'll be well treated."

Sophie thought of Aunt Mae. She hoped so too.

"This doctor paid me a visit at the surgery yesterday. We had a lengthy conversation and I showed him where I keep everything. He seemed well qualified and efficient but he'll have his work cut out to cope with the patient load. Even I was considering training someone up to help me."

"Perhaps the *Kommandant* will draft in another doctor from Germany to help."

"He'll certainly need it. Thank goodness Sheila will still be around."

"The patients prefer you though, rather than seeing a nurse."

"Perhaps, but she'll be able to deal with minor ailments and a lot of people will refuse to see a German doctor." He sighed. "Unfortunately, it's out of my hands and there's nothing I can do."

Someone called out to Dr Reynolds and he excused himself and went away to deal with whatever the problem was.

"Hello."

Sophie sighed. It would seem she was not going to be allowed to have her own thoughts and the solitude she craved.

"Vera."

"Sorry, but am I disturbing you?"

"No, not at all." *Why does one have to be so polite all the time?* thought Sophie. *Wouldn't it be good if I could say exactly what I thought for once and tell Vera to get lost?*

"I need to talk to someone."

Sophie was surprised. Why her? Why now? They were not close, nor had they ever been. "Oh?" she said.

Vera hesitated. "I'm not all bad, you know."

"Forgive me, but why are you saying this to me, now, at this moment? We haven't spoken to each other in over a year." *And before that, even on the very rare occasions when we did speak,* thought Sophie, *you made it plain I wasn't worth the effort.*

"I have to get things off my chest. Who knows what might happen to us." When Sophie failed to respond, Vera pressed on, her words tumbling out: "Ever since that, *débâcle*, you know, my little indiscretion last year, no one seems to want to have anything to do with me."

Taken aback at this frankness, Sophie remained silent.

"Eric has forgiven me but some people in Port le Bac are still calling me a Jerry-Bag. I wish they wouldn't do that. It makes things very difficult especially as I wasn't the only one who had an affair with a German soldier." She stopped for a moment, her thoughts far away. "I did love him, you know."

"Who, Eric?"

"No, Günther."

Sophie was feeling embarrassed now. She had no wish to become Vera's confidante, nor could she do so without passing judgement, so she said nothing and continued to stare out to sea, watching the moonlight as it shimmered on the water. It was quite, quite beautiful and she wished that Vera would go away.

"I thought it would be all right at first. He was married, I was married," she hesitated for a moment. "It was just going to be a casual fling, you know, nothing serious."

Sophie didn't know. *What about the Commodore?* she thought. *He was your husband – didn't his feelings matter?*

"Unfortunately, I fell in love. We both fell in love and suddenly it became very serious."

Still Sophie said nothing.

"Then he had to go away. Poor Eric, he was heartbroken."

Sophie felt confused. "Why?" *Why should the Commodore be upset at the departure of his wife's lover?*

"Because I was so upset."

"Really?" said Sophie, experiencing a surge of indignation on Eric's behalf. "I would have thought he was upset because you had had an affair."

Vera looked down at her immaculately painted nails.

"He seemed quite happy all the time Günther was on St Nicolas."

Sophie found that very hard to believe.

"He must have known, surely?" she asked, unable to comprehend he was not aware that something was amiss. Not that she was any kind of expert in these matters, of course. "Everybody else seemed to." She didn't mean to be unkind.

Vera hesitated.

"No, Sophie, I didn't know," remarked the Commodore, unexpectedly emerging from the shadows and making both women jump. "At least, not until it had been going on for some time. You see, my wife found it impossible to keep the change in her feelings to herself and I knew something was afoot. And besides, as you are well aware, in a small society like that of Port le Bac, something of such a scandalous nature cannot stay hidden for very long, especially in the situation in which we found ourselves."

"Oh, Eric!" exclaimed Vera, feigning brightness. "What a shock you gave me! How long have you been there?"

"Long enough." The Commodore cleared his throat. "I apologize for my wife burdening you with her misdemeanours, Sophie. I am sure that you find it most distasteful. Come, Vera, I have found us both a seat. I suggest we take advantage of our good fortune and occupy them." Taking his wife by the arm, he led her away. He touched his yachtsman's cap and said to Sophie, "I apologize once again and I appreciate your discretion in this matter."

"Of course, Commodore."

Sophie exhaled, relieved that Vera had gone. Suddenly feeling hungry, she took out one of her sandwiches which she ate slowly and followed this with an apple.

"Lovely, ain't it?" said a boy's voice at her elbow.

Couldn't anyone leave her alone?

"Being on the water, I mean. Me Mam's having one of 'er moaning sessions, so I thought I'd come up on deck for a while. I'll get into trouble, but what the 'eck? Besides, what's she gonna do? Beat me? 'ardly! There's too many people around. Do you like being on the water, Miss Sophie?"

"Not particularly, Tommy. I don't mind when it's calm like this, then it's quite pleasant, but as a rule, I don't like it."

"Now me, I love the water. When we lived by the docks, before the war, I used to go down to the Thames when there was this big stretch of mud at low tide and I used to go larkin' about on it wiv me mates. Me Mam hated it when I came home all filthy dirty and she used to scold me something terrible, she did. But I didn't mind. There was lots of creatures that lived in that there mud, worms and such. I once saw a dead crab. He was huge! He 'ad long pincers, he did. They was fearsome big! I took 'im 'ome with me but me Mam went spare and told me to throw it away. She said it was disgustin'. Me Dad laughed and told me to bring it to 'im. I sat on 'is knee and we made a right good study of it. He told me all about the different kinds of crab and where they lived and how they caught their food." Tommy fell silent for a moment. "I miss me Dad," he said wistfully.

"I expect you do," said Sophie.

She liked Tommy. He was a good boy, dealing with a difficult, abrasive mother and an absent father with a maturity and stoical good-natured temperament that extended way beyond his ten years.

They stood together in silence for several moments, looking out over the water, listening to the steady throb of the engines.

"What's goin' to 'appen to us when we reach France, Miss Sophie?"

"I imagine that we'll be put on a train that will take us through into Germany."

"'Ave you ever been to Germany?"

"I lived there when I was about your age. My father was the British Ambassador in Berlin for many years."

"Cor, that must 'ave been sommat. Was it an important job?"

"I suppose it was, though my brother and I just accepted that this was what my father did for a living."

"Can you speak German?"

"Yes, Tommy, I can."

"I can too, but only a bit. I like speaking it, it feels good in me mouth, though me Mam won't let me say a word and flies into a rage if I take out me German word book the teacher gave me. She says I'm being a traitor. But I'm not, am I, Miss Sophie? *You* can speak it and you're not a traitor."

"That's right. Perhaps when we're settled into wherever it is we're going, I can help you a bit."

"We won't be able to tell me Mam, though. She'll 'ave me guts fer garters – and yours," he added.

Sophie smiled. "It'll be our secret, I promise," and she crossed her heart.

"Cor, thanks, Miss Sophie."

Suddenly, Gert's shrill voice penetrated their companionable conversation.

"Tommy! Tommy! Come 'ere, you little toe-rag!"

"I'd better go. Ta-ra fer now then," and Tommy smiled, his excitement shining in his eyes. "And thanks, Miss Sophie." Taking a deep breath, he called out: "Comin', Mam!" before picking his way along the crowded deck.

It was into the early hours of the morning when the little convoy of two civilian and three troop ships docked at St Malo. The islanders remained on their boats for what seemed to be an eternity until finally, they were allowed to leave.

They collected their luggage from the quayside and walked the short distance to a railway station. Here, they were directed onto a train, sitting in second-class passenger carriages in unexpected comfort. Everyone was given a bowl of soup, a fourteen-inch German sausage and a loaf of bread. They were informed that this ration was to last them for three days. Sophie was grateful to Aunt Edna for providing her with enough food to supplement.

For five hours they sat in a siding and when at last the train began to move, everyone was thoroughly fed up and tired. Gert, Mabel and Ethel wasted no time in expressing their displeasure. In no uncertain terms, Dr Reynolds told them to be quiet, much to Sophie's relief.

For Sophie, like the boat journey, it was as though she was going on a holiday; a diversion from the confines of life on St Nicolas under the Occupation. Ironically, she once again experienced a sense of freedom and spent much of the journey staring out of the window, lost in her own thoughts, watching the countryside as it unfolded – the miles and miles of apple orchards; the vista of gently rolling hills.

Resolutely, she closed her mind to what might await them at their eventual destination.

Their route took them from St Malo down through Brittany to Rennes, before travelling to the south of Paris and into Germany via Belgium and Luxembourg. They were obliged to change trains frequently – at Rennes, Le Mans, in Paris, where they sat for yet another five hours in a siding, before following the course of the Moselle valley across to Stuttgart (another change; another unexplained delay) and Ulm.

Eventually, after three weary days of travelling, they alighted at their destination – Seeblick, a picturesque village surrounded by forests and pasture land, with a tree-hung river that rippled and meandered through the little town.

It was the most beautiful place that anyone had ever seen and Sophie rejoiced that this was to be the setting for their internment.

"If we had to be anywhere," she remarked to Dr Reynolds, "then this is the sort of place I would have wished for."

"I'm inclined to agree," replied the good doctor. "The air up here is fantastic. Should do everyone's health a power of good."

"Cor, Miss Sophie," said Tommy, coming to join them, "ain't it wonderful? I can't believe it what I'm seeing! It's the sort of place I always dreamt of!" and he scampered off happily to collect his luggage.

As they progressed through the village, women came out from neat, timber-frame houses, curious to see the latest inmates heading for the camp, which had witnessed a variety of *clientèle* since it was first built. However, they were genuinely upset to see women and children among their number and immediately brought out lemonade and small, homemade biscuits for as many of the weary and footsore travellers as they could manage to provide with sustenance.

The accompanying *Wehrmacht* soldiers slowed the pace, content to wait and allow the refreshments to be consumed – much to the relief of the Channel Islanders who were sweltering in the blazing September sun with all the clothes they were wearing, as well as having to lug their suitcases and other bags along the hot, dusty roads.

There were many smiles on both sides and much appreciation from the islanders for this small act of kindness by the villagers. It laid the foundation for what became a lifelong friendship between the local people and the internees.

However, when they had walked up the last steep hill and arrived at the prison camp, they were presented with a bleak picture of grim reality. The holiday spirit evaporated instantly and everyone fell silent as they passed through the tall, forbidding inner and outer gates, the double row of barbed wire fences and the high, threatening watchtowers manned by heavily armed soldiers.

Many islanders felt cowed and ashamed even though they had done nothing wrong to deserve such incarceration; others experienced defiance and anger. The majority, Sophie included, reacted passively, merely waiting with rapidly beating hearts to see what would happen; resigned to their fate.

Once everyone was inside, both inner and outer gates were locked with an ominous clunk of finality that reverberated around the camp and the islanders were ordered to line up in rows in an enormous compound surrounded by large, barrack-like huts.

On arrival, the men were body-searched, a few at a time, leaving the women and children standing in the heat. One woman fainted but the guards remained unmoved and refused to allow the doctor to tend to her, ignoring the angry looks and resentful stares.

Eventually, once the frisking had been completed, the women and children were led away to a large, white, three-storey building where they each had to complete a form giving their name, address, date of birth, place of birth and next of kin ("Ain't we already done this at 'ome?" muttered Gert to Mabel, who nudged her and told her to be quiet) and given a prisoner number. Any money they had brought with them was confiscated and in small groups, they were taken away for a medical examination, after which, they were inoculated against typhus. Finally, they were given a blanket, allocated a barrack hut and directed to their specified room – the men and women being segregated on opposite sides of the compound.

Each hut had three rooms holding around twenty people in each, some sleeping in bunk beds ranged along one wall, others in closely packed single iron-framed beds, situated along the other two sides.

Sophie, fortunately, found herself the first woman to enter her particular room so, being an ex-public schoolgirl, she wasted no time in choosing a prime position – an upper bed in a bunk with an unobstructed view of the enormous clock tower that dominated the village below the camp, and the Alps rising magnificently beyond.

There was a noticeable lack of slats to support her straw-filled mattress so before anyone else arrived, Sophie quickly purloined a couple from the lower bed that seemed to have more than hers and rearranged these to make her bunk safe.

She adopted the nearest wardrobe and little bookshelf that was fixed to the wall next to and on a level with her bed, viewing its grimy state with some distaste, and settled herself as the others began to arrive and choose their beds.

With a sinking heart, she realized she would be sharing a room with Ethel and her two children, Mabel with her four as well as Gert, Tommy and Vera. There were several other women whom she knew only slightly and a few she had never met before.

The room was in a terribly squalid state. There was rubbish strewn over the floor, which, along with the tables, was filthy. Layers of dust and grime covered the furniture and fittings. There was a nasty black mould on the walls and worst of all, the unmistakable odour of vermin, whose tell-tale droppings were everywhere.

A woman called Marian, whom Sophie didn't know and who she later found out came from Jersey, rather than standing around bemoaning the situation as Gert and Mabel were doing, rolled up her sleeves and, obviously having come prepared, produced a dustpan and brush, a bottle of Jeyes Fluid, some floor soap, a scrubbing brush and a small bucket. She filled this with water from the washroom and set to work on the table tops, persuading other women to sweep the floor at the same time. Once that was done, she went down on her hands and knees and scrubbed the floor vigorously. Someone else produced some floor cloths and by the time the women and children were called for the evening meal (watery soup with bits of swede floating in it) with most of the women pitching in to help, the room smelt fresher and was in much more of a habitable condition.

Marian stood in the middle of the floor with her hands on her hips, surveying their handiwork.

"Well," she said, "that's a good job done. We'll get that grime off the windows tomorrow and I suggest we have a cleaning rota, ladies, to make it fair. I'd like to think we'll have the cleanest room in the whole camp. It'll be something to keep us busy and occupied and give us a bit of a challenge."

"That's what she thinks," muttered Gert, under her breath. "I'm not bleedin' well spending my time on me 'ands and knees. I 'ad enough of charring when I lived in London."

If Marian heard her, she chose to ignore the remark and instead, thanked those women, including Sophie, who had helped her.

"I don't like dirt," she announced. "Never have. I like a nice, clean, tidy house and we're going to keep this room exactly the way it should be. All right, girls?"

Meekly, gratefully, unable to resist, all the women nodded. All, that is, except Gert, who folded her arms and sniffed the air.

After supper, there was a roll call, which seemed to take forever, as the German soldiers seemed incapable of counting correctly and had to keep starting again. Eventually, their bodies aching with exhaustion from travelling, the physical exertion of the walk from the station to the camp up a steep hill carrying their luggage and standing around in the heat, the internees returned to their huts.

"It's a bit like a holiday camp, isn't it?" observed Ethel, as they undressed.

"If this was a holiday camp," retorted Gert, getting into bed after having first checked it for mice and fleas, "I'd ask fer a refund. Food's flippin' terrible, so's the accommodation."

"It might get better," said Tommy.

"No chance," replied Gert. "We oughta be able to cook fer ourselves. We'd make a far better job."

"I know I would!" exclaimed Mabel.

"Maybe," said Ethel, sounding sleepy.

"Okay to put out the light, everyone?" asked Marian who, without waiting for an answer, climbed out of bed and turned off the switch.

Gradually the room fell silent; apart, that is, from the sounds of people in varying stages of slumber.

Still wakeful, Sophie lay in bed on her stomach, her head facing the window. She could see the moon and the stars, finding consolation in their constancy; seeing in them a freedom from the constraints and uncertainties of this new situation thrust upon her by the vagaries of war.

She turned over onto her side by holding onto the narrow headboard in order to find a more comfortable position.

As she did so, she felt something carved into the wood. The engraving was deep and clear and after investigating further, she was able to trace the distinct letters 'RLA'.

Drawn to her discovery, she minutely followed the line of the initials over and over again with her fingertips until she had memorized and could visualize in her mind every indentation, every groove, every slight imperfection in the carving.

She wondered who RLA might be and when he had come here. Where was he now?

Perhaps she would never know but his initials seemed to speak to her, giving both hope and comfort on this, her first night in the strange new world of captivity in which she found herself.

Eventually, with her fingers touching RLA, Sophie fell asleep.

CHAPTER 27

Seeblick POW Camp
Germany

Seeblick Camp, in common with the majority of P.O.W. and internment camps in Germany, was run by the *Oberkommando der Wehrmacht* who, when the original order was issued for the internment of the Channel Islanders, was reluctant to fulfil its obligation as they did not wish to be responsible for women and children.

As time progressed, with a few harsh exceptions, the individual guards at Seeblick were not unkind in their treatment of the internees, but it was run very much along the lines of the male P.O.W. camps with which the *O.K.W.* were used to dealing.

There were three roll calls a day – at seven in the morning, at midday and at seven in the evening. These took place outside in the large compound in front of the main barracks and always took an inordinate amount of time to complete. When the weather was fine, it was difficult enough; when it was wet and windy, it was unbearable. When the first snows arrived towards the middle of November, it became untenable. Even so, the *Kommandant* insisted that they took place, despite many children catching severe colds and two elderly people contracting pneumonia.

Generally, the food was poor – for breakfast, *ersatz* coffee made from acorns which was also available during the day and which, when the weather became colder, the women used to save for hot-water bottles for the children at night; at lunchtime, there was a thin watery soup with bits of cabbage or uncooked swede floating in it and one loaf of mouldy bread with a little margarine shared between four people. Supper consisted of more soup with bits of meat or fish, supplemented with peelings which the internees managed to scrounge from the German soldiers, who preferred their potatoes peeled. Sometimes the internees received a whole jacket potato each – a food item that for the first few months came to be regarded as something of a luxury.

The men and women were segregated into separate huts, although visiting during the day was permitted between the hours of two in the afternoon and seven in the evening. Access and contact in the compound was unrestricted until lights out at ten o'clock.

Although the windows in some of the huts were double-glazed, the heating stoves proved inadequate to the task, providing hardly any warmth for the size of the rooms. Each hut had its own internal toilet and washing facilities but these areas had no heating at all. Some people preferred not to wash and were ostracized by their fellow inmates until they did.

Two barrack huts were used for the infirmary, with one each for men and women. A smaller hut, containing four individual rooms was used as an isolation ward. A further barrack hut had been used at one time as a theatre but was now in a dilapidated state, with broken scenery, torn curtains, overturned furniture and a general air of neglect and careless vandalism. The designated kitchen area for use by the internees was in a terrible condition, dirty and disorganized with cooking facilities in a very poor state and few usable utensils.

There were no recreational facilities of any kind and exercise could only be taken in the main compound.

Apart from the wonderful, uplifting scenery and the readily available hot showers in the communal shower-block (which unfortunately was situated outside the main compound, necessitating the endurance of freezing conditions there and back) it was generally a depressing and disheartening setup.

No written communication with the outside world or contact with family and friends back home was allowed and this, together with the poor conditions, fuelled much anger and resentment. Gert and Mabel earned themselves the nickname of the Moaning Minnies. However, despite being irritating and loud, they unashamedly voiced what everyone was feeling.

Sophie just wished she wasn't sharing a room with them.

The *Kommandant* spoke very little English and Sophie was asked by the St Nicolas internees to act as their official interpreter. The Commodore was voted in as camp leader, fulfilling the role that the senior British officer would have done in a military P.O.W. camp and, because of the presence of women, Marian was elected as Women's Leader, much to her delight. She knew she could put her organizational skills to good use and have the camp looking spick and span in no time.

The three of them began to formulate plans for the things that they, on behalf of the internees, wanted to see happen within the camp, together with a list of requirements. However, they found themselves stymied at every turn by the intransigent, narrow-minded *Kommandant*, who threatened to have all three of them thrown into solitary confinement if they persisted in their "*lächerlichen Ideen*".

"I don't think our ideas are ridiculous at all," remarked Sophie, as they walked slowly back from the daily meeting with the *Kommandant* at the Big House as it was known: the enormous three storey building that took up one side of the compound and housed both the German administration offices and Mess for the officers and guards.

"I think they're eminently practical and sensible ideas," said Marian reasonably. "This man won't listen. He has no understanding and shows no willingness to make our lives better."

"I'd like to punch him on the nose," observed the Commodore, a remark that was so unexpected, it made Sophie and Marian laugh.

"He must address the issue of overcrowding," said Marian. "Since the Jersey and Guernsey folk have arrived from their transit camp, it's a nightmare. The showers are cracking under the strain and with no increase in the rations, there's less to go round. Lots of mothers are going without food at some meals so that their children don't go hungry."

"At least we have freedom of movement within the camp during the day," said Sophie, trying to find something positive. "Ethel thinks the men ought to have the children at night sometimes so that the women can get a decent night's sleep."

"Ethel would," replied Marian, with feeling.

"She has a point though," said Sophie. "The children on the whole are coping remarkably well, but you and I both know they're so hungry, that they often lie awake at night and cry."

"True," replied Marian. "A few of the mothers could do more though. They seem to be a particularly lazy bunch in our room."

The Commodore had been listening quietly to this conversation and after Marian had gone on her way, he quietly asked Sophie how Vera was coping.

"Not so well," she replied honestly. "She seems very subdued and quiet. A bit down, I'd say. A few of the other women have made one or two nasty, snide remarks which upset her."

The Commodore was silent for a moment before saying, "She won't talk to me. I've forgiven her, of course, but she won't communicate. I don't quite know what to do." He sighed. "Ah, well, I promised the doctor that I'd look again at the hospital huts. Not that it'll make any difference. Whatever changes we want to make or any requests that we have, the *Kommandant* takes no notice."

And so it continued until the beginning of December, when two things happened.

Firstly, many Jersey families were moved to another camp, as were all the single men from sixteen years of age upwards (with the notable exceptions of Dr Reynolds and the Roman Catholic priest) thus temporarily bringing some relief from the extreme overcrowding and more breathing space for those who remained.

The second occurrence was the departure of the *Wehrmacht*. All internment camps now came under the control of the *SS-Reichsführer* (the highest rank of the *SS* although fortunately, no *SS* troops were ever deployed in the Channel Islander's camps) and the Head of the German Police, together with the Ministry of the Interior in Berlin. The German Foreign Ministry, the Ministry of the Interior in Baden-Württemberg, the Prisoner of War Department of the *O.K.W.* and the Foreign Interest Section of the Swiss Legation in Berlin were also all involved.

The internment camps became the epitome of the National Socialist polycratic system at work, where different authorities pursuing differing interests all had a hand in the decision-making process and the supervision of the camps. It seemed to work – after a fashion – but communication was often laboured and changes happened slowly.

On the day the *Wehrmacht* left, the *Schutzpolizei* moved in. The new *Kommandant* had not yet appeared and his place was taken temporarily by his second-in-command, a man called *Leutnant* Schauerlich. He spoke little English and from their first encounter and for the first time in her life, Sophie mistrusted and felt uneasy being around another human being.

She hated the way he stared at her throughout the daily meetings where instructions were given out by the Germans and requests made by the internees. She disliked the way he always asked her to remain behind at the end of every session, offering her cigarettes and chocolate, which of course she refused, becoming more persistent and physical in his attentions towards her as the weeks went by.

He would stand ever closer to her, touching her shoulder or holding her arm in a vicelike grip as he talked, eventually offering her specific privileges and his protection if she consented to bestow upon him certain favours in return.

Throughout these unpleasant encounters, Sophie stood rigid and unresponsive, leaving as quickly as she dared without seeming to be impolite. She sensed that he would be ruthless if she was blatant in her refusal to succumb to his advances.

She began to dread the daily meetings and the way that after early morning roll call, he would make a point of talking to her, standing so close that she could feel the heat of his breath on her cheek. He would watch her from the window of his office as she made her way to the showers and was still there waiting for her return. He would appear at inopportune moments – while she was walking round the compound taking exercise or helping Dr Reynolds in the infirmary.

Unwisely, Sophie kept her fears to herself, unwilling to share her concerns with anyone; convincing herself that there was nothing she was unable to deal with; arguing that there was nothing anyone could do and that if they did try, it might lead to reprisals.

One morning, about a month after his arrival, Sophie was summoned to his office to act as interpreter. She knew she dare not refuse and there was no time or opportunity to find someone to tell where she had gone or for someone to come with her. So, with trepidation and a strong sense of misgiving, she went across to the Big House.

Outside *Leutnant* Schauerlich's office, the secretary was not in his customary place at his desk so she knocked on the office door and was ushered inside by the *leutnant*. With her back turned, he quickly and quietly turned the key in the well-oiled lock.

There was a large fire burning in the grate and he suggested she take off her coat. Against her better judgement, Sophie did so and without saying a word, he took it from her with one hand, allowing the other to slide down her arm until her hand was clasped tightly in his own. With three rapid movements, he discarded the coat, pinned her arm up behind her back and pulled her towards him, holding her so tightly that she could hardly breathe.

"No!" she said, gasping with pain and fear, her struggles rendered futile by his grip. "Let go of me!"

"You see," he whispered into her ear, "I have made the room warm for us. We shall not be disturbed."

He attempted to kiss her and Sophie used this as her opportunity to break free. She kicked him hard on the shins and squirmed out of his arms before making for the door. But he was too quick for her.

Swiftly and decisively, he grabbed her and pushed her across the room, forcing her down backwards onto the desk, clawing violently at the buttons of her blouse. She screamed as loudly as she could before he struck her across the cheek and covered her mouth with his, pulling at her undergarments while his other hand pushed up inside her skirt. She struggled furiously and tried to kick him away but he hit her again and pinned her down with even greater force, renewing his efforts.

Suddenly, she heard an almighty crash and felt someone dragging him away from her before seeing the new arrival land a heavy punch on her assailant's face. *Leutnant* Schauerlich staggered backwards but recovered quickly, striking the man with such force that it sent him reeling to the ground.

Thoroughly roused and not wanting to be denied his conquest, he moved back towards Sophie, who rolled out of the way before he could touch her again. The newcomer staggered to his feet, grabbed *Leutnant* Schauerlich from behind, spun him round and punched him again, this time knocking him out cold with a well-judged uppercut. Then, stooping to pick up his glasses which had been flung across the room, the officer stumbled towards the lock-shattered door and closed it.

Ashen-faced and with his breath coming in uneven gasps, he slid down to the floor, unintentionally blocking Sophie's potential escape route. He fumbled in the pocket of his tunic for a small bottle of pills, one of which he swallowed, while Sophie, in a state of total shock, trying in vain to hold the shredded remains of her clothes across her chest, also sat down on the floor with her back leaning against the desk and stared at him.

With his breathing gradually returning to normal, the officer looked across at her for a moment and, unable to conceal a flicker of interest for her in his eyes, removed his tunic belt and Luger and began to unbutton his jacket.

"Nein! Nein!" she managed to cry out, though it emerged as nothing more than a croak. *"Fass mich nicht an!"* Had he knocked out *Leutnant* Schauerlich so that *he* could take over?

"I am not going to touch you," he said, in perfect English. "I am not like *him*," and he nodded his head in the direction of the unconscious man, his tone full of disgust. "But soon, other people will come and you need to cover yourself. Here," and he removed the patterned knitted jumper he was wearing underneath his uniform jacket and threw it across to Sophie, "put this on. It will keep you from being cold and save you from embarrassment."

He watched her quietly as she hastily pulled it over her head.

The jumper felt warm and somewhere within her subconscious, she was grateful to him.

"The colour suits you," he said simply, as he buttoned up his tunic and replaced his belt and gun.

Still in a state of shock, Sophie continued to stare at him, though she no longer felt afraid.

"Permit me to introduce myself. I am *Hauptmann* Heinrich Hoffmeister," he said quietly, "and I am the new *Kommandant* of Seeblick."

Buried within the recesses of her mind, his name seemed familiar but at that moment, she could neither think nor speak.

Having recovered his own equilibrium, Hoffmeister stood up and came over to Sophie, where he gently helped her to her feet and led her over to one of the easy chairs positioned in front of the fire.

"I will find someone to fetch the doctor," he said.

Other words seemed to be forming on his lips, but he appeared reluctant to utter them.

"He didn't succeed," said Sophie, guessing the reason behind his hesitation and finding her voice at last.

Relieved, Heinrich looked at her and smiled.

"Thank you," he said. "That was the question I was struggling to ask tactfully. But he will be punished, I can assure you. Severely. The *Wehrmacht* and police authority take a misdemeanour such as this very seriously. There will be nothing he can say in his defence. I am witness to his transgression against you. He also struck me, his superior officer, which is in itself a court martial offence. It was fortunate that I arrived to take up my post when I did."

For a brief moment, he left the room and then returned, handcuffed the still unconscious man to one of the substantial desk legs and sat down in the easy chair opposite Sophie. He smiled.

"I have called for the English doctor. I hope that is acceptable to you?"

Sophie nodded.

"He will have to treat both of us, yes?"

Amazingly, she managed a smile, grimacing with the pain of her split lip, which steadily dripped blood onto the *Hauptmann*'s jumper. She could hardly see out of one of her eyes and she wanted to cry but no tears would come.

"Thank you for saving me," she managed to say.

And it did feel like that. She looked at his bruised face.

"You are hurt," she said.

"It is of no consequence."

But it wasn't insignificant.

"I expect I look a sight," she said.

Hoffmeister shook his head but said nothing.

Sophie noticed that his eyes behind his clear-framed glasses were very blue.

She wanted to lie down in her bunk next to the comfort of her RLA and sleep away the nightmare of what had just happened. But she couldn't cope with the inevitable questions that would follow her return, and the noise and confines of her room would be unbearable.

"Once the doctor has examined you and treated your injuries, would you like a room where you can sleep on your own?"

Sophie nodded, tears of gratitude welling up in her eyes and spilling over down her cheeks. Heinrich Hoffmeister produced a handkerchief from one of his trouser pockets which he gave to her.

"It is clean enough to wipe away tears, I promise you, but perhaps not to place upon a bleeding lip."

"Thank you."

A moment later, Doctor Reynolds was shown into the room by the secretary and with a glance, he took in the overturned chairs and contents of the desktop scattered across the floor and the prone figure of *Leutnant* Schauerlich handcuffed to one of the desk legs. Immediately, he knelt down beside Sophie, shocked by the state of her face.

"My God! What's been going on here?" He looked accusingly at the injured *Hauptmann*. "What have you done to her?"

"He's done nothing to me. He rescued me," and Sophie immediately began to sob violently, unable to control her distress.

"I will explain later," said Heinrich, his expression full of consternation. "Please could you treat her. Her lip is bleeding. She needs a cold compress for her eye. I could find nothing suitable. She must go to the infirmary straight away."

The doctor refrained from saying that he did not need to be told his job, recognizing in his words the officer's genuine concern.

"We can take her there once she has stopped crying."

"Crying is the best thing for her. It is a good release."

"Yes."

After a while, once Sophie had recovered a little of her composure, Heinrich Hoffmeister and Dr Reynolds helped her along to the infirmary. At the *Hauptmann*'s insistence, Sophie was put into one of the side rooms in the isolation ward and after a cold compress had been applied to her eye and her lip seen to, she lay down on the bed and immediately fell asleep.

Dr Reynolds then treated the new *Kommandant* who, after introducing himself, seemed most willing to submit to his ministrations.

Briefly, he recounted what had taken place.

The doctor was horrified. "The bastard didn't...?"

"No. It is most fortunate. But he will be severely punished. Even as we speak, the police guards will have taken him into custody where he will remain imprisoned in solitary confinement. The appropriate authorities will be notified and he then will be sent away and tried by court martial. I shall myself be a witness."

"Good." Then Dr Reynolds, anxious that Sophie's character should in no way be besmirched by what had taken place, said, "She is a lovely, innocent young woman and wouldn't have done anything to provoke this."

"I am glad to hear this, although to think otherwise had not occurred to me."

And it really hadn't. Heinrich had heard Sophie's screams just as he reached his new office and after shouldering the door open and entering the room, had seen her struggle before he had leapt into action. He hadn't hesitated and had immediately surmised that the fault was Schauerlich's.

"Thank you," replied the doctor, relieved.

Sophie soon began to recover physically from her ordeal, but the psychological effect was to take much longer. She stayed within the hospital until her injuries had healed sufficiently for her to be seen in public again without arousing too much curiosity and too many intrusive questions.

The new *Kommandant* came each day to check on her progress and just before she left the infirmary, he said, "I have proposed a tour of the camp with Commodore Ellington and Mrs Maundell. I would be most appreciative if you would accompany us on this tour. I wish to take stock of things. A cursory inspection has revealed to me that many things are not right and I wish to rectify the situations."

"But before, I was only acting as interpreter and you speak perfect English. Surely, I won't be needed?"

"The Commodore and Mrs Maundell speak highly of your ideas and wish you to accompany us. I may need help with difficult words..."

Heinrich smiled, aware that he wanted her to be there because he liked her, very much; that he wanted to know her better and this seemed to be the most satisfactory way. As an honourable man, he also knew he would have to be cautious. For a long time until she had recovered. Fully.

Sophie looked up at him. "Really?"

"Yes." He smiled again.

Suddenly, she was assailed by doubts. Was it too soon? Would she be able to cope?

As though he was reading her mind, Heinrich said: "I think it will not be too much for you. The occupations will be good for you and keep your mind away from things that are better not dwelt upon. You must say if you become tired or overexerted."

"Thank you. That is very kind. But I should like to be involved. There's so much that needs to be done." He was quite right. It would be better for her to have some semblance of a routine; to take her mind away from unpleasant thoughts. And she felt safe with him. "Therefore, I accept."

"Good. It is settled."

He smiled yet again. Sophie began to like his smile.

"I am glad to see you are healing well," he said, before pointing to his own cheek and his bandaged hand. "Please notice that I too have fading bruises. We shall both of us be able to return into public life without worry, I think."

After he had gone, Sophie suddenly remembered where she had heard his name before. A *Hauptmann* Heinrich Hoffmeister had taught English to Ulrich and Helmut, the two young German soldiers who had been ordered to help on the farm.

Could this be the same man? If it was, how could it be that an instructor of English to the German army now found himself *Kommandant* of a civilian internment camp?

CHAPTER 28

Seeblick

It was a bitterly cold January day when the four of them, well wrapped up against the snowy chill, began their tour of inspection. Two days before this, at morning roll call, the *Kommandant* had urged the internees to voice their concerns to Commodore Ellington and Mrs Maundell freely and openly. He reminded them that their words should be directed at improving conditions within the camp and not the general situation in which they found themselves. It was an opportunity for them to decide upon their future wellbeing, he said, and not the occasion to berate or insult the *Third Reich* or the German people, nor criticize the previous administration at the camp.

Given those parameters, the majority of internees responded positively and the *Kommandant* listened carefully when told of people's genuine complaints, making copious notes on the inadequate heating in the huts, the state of the theatre, the lack of recreational facilities, the deplorable conditions of the internee's designated kitchen and the poor diet.

"It seems ridiculous to me as well," observed Marian, as they began their walk around the compound, "that we have to go outside the perimeter fence for our showers. They're well heated and kept very clean and there's plenty of hot water but then, you catch your death on the walk back into the camp. Can something be done about that?"

They considered suitable alternatives. There was a smaller-sized barrack hut in a very sorry state situated at the back of the compound. It had been divided up into three rooms with a door from each leading directly outside into the compound. A cursory glance revealed that most of them had been used for storage at some time.

"It might be possible," said the *Kommandant* thoughtfully, "to knock down these buildings and construct a new shower block in their place. We could keep the existing facilities in order to allow more people to shower more often. The existing block would therefore only be used by those hardy souls who are willing to brave the freezing conditions," he added.

Sophie smiled up at him. He smiled back, his eyes kind and very blue.

"We need books," she said quickly, turning her attention to the interior of the room outside which they had stopped, where the remnants of some shelving were still attached to the walls and a few bits of furniture, a couple of chairs, a table and a three-legged stool, were upended across the floor.

"Books are very important," agreed the *Kommandant*, allowing his eyes to rest upon her. "I shall contact the War Prisoners' Aid of the Y.M.C.A. and Y.W.C.A. to see what can be done. I believe they have also been known to provide musical instruments." He wrote this down. "What else? What provision has been made for the children's education?"

"None," replied the Commodore. "There hasn't been anywhere to set up a school. All the barrack huts apart from the theatre one, are fully occupied."

"There are large, good-sized rooms available in the… what is the name you give to our administration and guard building?"

"Das große Haus," replied Sophie.

"Ach, so. Das große Haus – the Big House. We shall go there now and seek out suitable accommodation. What about schoolteachers?"

"Unbelievably, we have only one teacher remaining with us. The rest have either gone to Laufen or Wurzach when the men and boys were transferred away from here."

"I was a schoolteacher before the war," said *Hauptmann* Hoffmeister. "Perhaps I may be permitted to take some classes until someone else has been trained. I promise not to indoctrinate the children with National Socialist principles," he added.

"I'm very glad to hear it," declared the Commodore. "Though I should still prefer to have your word on that."

"I give you my word, unequivocally," replied Heinrich, surprised by the Commodore's additional request, yet not taking offence.

In that moment, Sophie warmed to him. She liked his gentlemanly, courteous manner and in this, there was a similarity both to her grandfather and to Major von Witzenhausen.

With the Commodore and Marian walking on in front, Heinrich saw her contemplating him and smiled, causing Sophie to blush and look away.

"What were you thinking?" he asked with a directness that took Sophie completely by surprise.

Quickly, she cast around in her mind and recalled the question she had wanted to ask ever since he had first introduced himself.

"Where did you teach before the war?" she asked.

"At a school in Berlin. I was the English master."

Her heart beating a little faster, she asked, "And once war was declared?"

"Before the war began, I had been… unwell… and was not deemed fit for army service, so I was conscripted into the er… military as a civilian to teach English to the new army recruits."

"In preparation for the invasion of England."

Heinrich looked at her in surprise. "How do you know this?"

"I have met some of your former students. There were many in the first wave of soldiers that came across to the Channel Islands with the invasion."

For a moment, he hesitated. "Really?" he remarked cautiously.

"Two were sent to work on our farm – Helmut Gerber and Ulrich Schmitt."

"Ach, die schrecklichen Zwillinge. Yes! I remember them. The terrible twins!" He laughed softly. "They were good boys and inseparable friends, I seem to recall."

Sophie smiled. "And they are a credit to you as they speak excellent English. In fact, all the soldiers who spoke of you were very complimentary about your teaching. Helmut and Ulrich mentioned you frequently."

This time a hint of colour crept into the *Kommandant*'s pale cheeks.

"Really?" he said with confidence. "I am most gratified that you should tell me this. But it is something of a coincidence is it not, that I should be here, now, in charge of a camp full of people from the Channel Islands and that you already know about me?"

"Yes." She blushed again. "But life is like that, perhaps?"

They had reached the Big House and their conversation came to an end.

The four of them entered the building and the *Kommandant* led them to two eminently suitable rooms, dirty and neglected certainly, but nothing "a good dust and a sturdy broom won't fix," declared Marian, anxious to get on with the task. "There are already chairs and tables in here and space for a blackboard. Perhaps we should make establishing a school one of our first priorities."

"I agree. We can use this room for the little ones and the other for the older children. The young people need to be occupied. I have noticed an element of bad behaviour around the camp since I have been here," said the *Hauptmann.* "Idleness is not good for young people."

The Commodore agreed and next, they made their way back across the compound to the internees' kitchen.

"These are in an appalling condition," said the *Kommandant*, "and unusable in their present state. Perhaps Mrs Maundell can add this to her cleaning list..." he added, glancing astutely at Marian who was busily writing notes, even as he spoke. "The Red Cross should have been providing you with additional food and clothing. Switzerland is the Protecting Power for the camps and the Protecting Power is responsible for notifying the Red Cross of the camp's needs. How many inspections have there been since you arrived here? I could find no paperwork on the subject."

"None, as far as I'm aware," replied the Commodore.

"None?!" exclaimed *Hauptmann* Hoffmeister, horrified, "but that is all wrong! There must have been at least one when you first arrived. I shall find out. What about Red Cross Parcels?"

"We don't know anything about them," said Marian.

"This then I shall make *my* priority. The Red Cross will be notified immediately. The diet you have is poor and unfortunately, I can do nothing about the rations provided by the prison authorities. Therefore, you must have your foodstuffs supplemented. Because you have received nothing, it would appear that Seeblick has not been given official camp status as yet." Annoyance crept into his voice. "It is not right that this has not been done after so many months." He breathed deeply to calm himself. "What about milk for the babies?" he asked.

"Very watery. Some of the little ones are not thriving as they should," replied Marian.

"*Ach*, this is very bad. I shall rectify this situation immediately when we have finished our inspection."

They went into the theatre hut and decided that it wasn't beyond redemption, but there were too many other things that needed to take precedence for the time being.

"What about roll calls?" said Sophie. "Is it necessary to have three each day? We stand outside in the freezing cold for ages, and everyone gets thoroughly chilled. Many people have become ill because of it."

"That is a good point. I shall arrange that there is only one per day. The women and children can stay in the rooms, but the men must come outside."

"No man is going to escape while his wife and family are here, surely," observed Sophie.

"Nonetheless, I am duty bound to insist that they should still do so. For the women and children, I shall appoint a guard for each barrack hut and at roll call, it will become his responsibility for seeing that everyone is present and accounted for." He wrote this down. "Anything else?"

"Exercise and recreation," said the Commodore. "We need things to occupy us. There's far too much malicious gossip and inaccurate speculation going round the camp. Idleness only breeds this kind of thing. Everyone needs to be kept busy."

"I agree. However, I leave you to organize this. I have overall authority but the day-to-day running of the camp must be your collective responsibility. May I suggest that you appoint a leader for each hut who can ascertain trades and professions as well as the thinking up of ideas? In this way, you can collate these informations and begin to look at the best way to occupy people's minds and bodies. I will help where I can." He smiled. "Now, if you will excuse me, I must return to my duties. We shall all meet again first thing in the morning, yes?"

And with a bow, the *Kommandant* made his way across the compound to the Big House.

"He might be a German," said Marian, once he was out of earshot, "but he does seem like a gentleman. Well, I'm going to organize a cleaning party, and we'll set to work on those kitchens."

Marian strode purposefully away. The Commodore spotted Vera and excused himself, heading off in her direction, leaving Sophie standing nervous and uncertain in the middle of the compound, checking that no one could creep up behind her and catch her unawares. Whereas before she had always been relaxed and tactile, any sudden movement now made her flinch, triggering anxiety and uneasiness making her wary of any physical contact.

To those who knew what had happened, in public at least, it would seem that she had made rapid progress in recovering from her trauma, but only she and the doctor knew of the inner apprehensions that caught her unawares, reducing her to bouts of unstoppable tears and anxiety.

At these moments, she would flee to the sanctuary of wherever she could find solitude – something that was usually impossible in the crowded conditions of Seeblick – and try to work her way quietly through her anguish.

During the day, Sophie was relatively successful in controlling her innermost fears, providing she kept herself busy, but it was at night when she had no mastery over the terrors that pervaded her dreams and caused her to wake up sweating and shaking.

So, still standing in the compound and wishing to allay the current direction of her thoughts Sophie returned to her room and lay down on her bed, staring at the ceiling.

She had nothing in particular to do; no book to read, nothing to occupy her mind.

She closed her eyes and tried to sleep. Almost immediately, Schauerlich's face reared up in her imagination. She felt the hotness of his breath on her cheeks; felt his hands pawing at her body.

Seeking comfort, she traced the initials on her bunk: something she often did at night when she was unable to sleep: the simple carving offering her a sense of wellbeing. Resolutely, she tried to think of other things – of her bedroom at home in Maybury; Hestia, her horse; the farm on St Nicolas; the little cove at the bottom of the gully.

The boy on the beach.

But the boy had become a man. He had grown up, just as she had.

This was the daydream she latched onto.

She pictured him lying on the sand reading *La Chaleur de la Mer*. She imagined herself lying next to him, both of them bathed in glorious, warming sunlight. She felt him take her into his arms and put his lips to hers before they stood up and ran hand-in-hand to swim in the pool: free and unfettered, laughing and joyous.

And all through this daydream, Sophie felt unthreatened and happy, safe and secure.

"You stupid bleedin' boy!"

Gert's shrill voice penetrated and shattered Sophie's dream.

"What the hell d'you think you were doing?"

"Aw, Mam, it were all right. I wasn't doing nuffin' that nobody else weren't doin'."

"Don't you answer me back, you little toe-rag. Go on, get out of my sight before I take the strap to you."

"Mam!"

"You 'eard. Now scarper."

Sophie opened her eyes and saw Tommy walk dejectedly out of the room, his head hung low; his shoulders hunched over.

That wasn't all.

Mabel began shouting at her eldest for being led astray by Tommy and Ethel was fussing over little Joan, who at that moment chose to begin her incessant wailing again, suffering from the hacking cough that had kept everyone awake for the previous three nights.

Sophie sat up in her bunk, unsettled and irritated. The room felt claustrophobic and the atmosphere unpleasant. Living in such close proximity to other random human beings could take on nightmarish proportions. There was frequently no escape from its all-pervasive, all-encompassing, perpetual, relentless invasion of her soul.

She wanted to be back with her aunts at the farmhouse. She missed her work on the farm; she missed her precious moments of solitude. She worried constantly about Edna and Mae's wellbeing and missed them terribly. At that moment, she wished she was back on St Nicolas.

Or did she?

Sophie was aware that despite what had recently happened to her, despite the shortcomings of the physical situation here in Seeblick, since the arrival of the new *Kommandant*, the whole atmosphere of the camp had changed.

Incredibly, it seemed less oppressive than that of the island.

Here at Seeblick, there was no collective fear lurking at the back of people's minds that they might be arrested at any moment for some petty misdemeanour and interrogated by the much feared *Geheime Feldpolizei*.

Here at Seeblick, it was a relief to be away from the ridiculous rules and regulations regarding quotas and supplies that dominated farming life under the island's occupation, no one ever knowing what would be demanded from one day to the next.

The police guards who had recently taken over from the *Schutzpolizei* at the camp were friendly, especially the latest batch, most of whom lived locally, whereas many of the soldiers who had arrived on the island after the departure of the original invading force, had been officious and harsh.

Apart from missing her aunts and the farm, Sophie began to wonder if she preferred being here at Seeblick to being on St Nicolas, even though she was a prisoner behind barbed wire: a captive in a foreign land. Somehow, she felt safer, an incongruous and ironical thought given the behaviour of *Leutnant* Schauerlich towards her. But he had gone, she told herself. Forever. And the new *Kommandant* was a good man.

However, a distant nagging concern that the German authorities might have some objectionable future fate stored up for the internees came into her mind, threatening to reduce her perceived security of life here at the camp to that of a temporary illusion.

Feeling apprehensive again, Sophie got up from her bunk and, after putting on her coat, hat and scarf, left the room and went outside into the compound. Hearing snow-crunching footsteps nearby, she turned and saw Tommy wandering aimlessly around.

"Are you all right, Tommy?"

He shook his head and kicked at the snow in a desultory fashion.

"Want to talk about it?" she asked, presently.

Tommy shook his head. "Nah, not really," he replied morosely. "I just wish me Mam would leave me be. Seems I can't do nuffin right."

"I don't quite know what to suggest," replied Sophie, feeling helpless.

He shrugged his shoulders and dug his hands more deeply into his pocket.

"There's nuffin you can do. But thanks for the thought, Miss Sophie. At least you allus treats me like I'm a person and not some nuisance to be bashed around." He sighed. "Don't get me wrong, me Mam's not that bad, she just can't 'elp moaning about every little fing and it really gets me down sometimes."

"Sounds like we both need something to occupy ourselves. Why don't we go for a brisk walk round the compound and see how many doors and windows there are?"

"Okay."

They began with their own hut and by the time they had reached number twelve, they had garnered a whole crowd of children, joining in the counting with them, seeing who could call out the numbers loudest.

Sophie wasn't sure what to do with all these excitable youngsters so eventually, after she had managed to quieten them and gain their attention, she came up with the idea that they count the huts again but this time in French. This was greeted with enthusiasm and the group, now consisting of at least a dozen or so children of varying ages, set off with Sophie in the lead. She took her time, making sure that everyone could say each number and retain it. Once they were back where they started, they repeated them for good measure.

The children seemed reluctant to disperse, so Sophie suggested they went round again, this time counting in German. Surprisingly, none of the idly watching parents objected and when they were back at their starting point, Sophie taught them other words in both French and German, pointing to the sky, their shoes, coats and hats.

Eventually, having had enough and much to Sophie's relief, the children gradually dispersed, laughing and chatting.

Drained and exhausted and wondering what to do next, she stood in the middle of the compound – back where she had been a couple of hours previously.

"Ihre Aussprache ist sehr gut," said the *Kommandant*, making Sophie jump as he came up behind her. Seeing her reaction, he added hastily. "I apologize, I did not mean to startle you. I had thought that you were aware of my presence."

"No." Sophie took a deep breath.

"I apologize again. To approach you unexpectedly was not tactful on my part."

She shook her head. "It's all right."

"Forgive me, but I could not help overhearing, what you were doing with the children. Your accent is very good. Perhaps once the school is set up, you would like to give language classes?"

"Perhaps, although I had never thought of myself as a teacher, more as a friend, keeping the children amused."

"The right kind of friendship is an important part of teaching. To gain a pupil's trust and respect, means he or she will work hard and do well. Not all teachers know or understand this. It is an important skill to learn." He smiled at her, his eyes gently penetrating. "Now, you will once again have to excuse me, *Fräulein* Langley. I have only just this moment returned from the town and this has necessitated my being away from my desk for too long. We shall talk another time, yes?"

He bowed and Sophie watched him as he turned and walked in the direction of the Big House.

Almost immediately, breathless and excited, Marian came across the compound to Sophie.

"Have you seen the Commodore?"

"I'm afraid not. Why?"

"You'll never guess!" she declared.

"What?"

"Our new *Kommandant* has been into Seeblick and he's come back with a delivery of milk for the babies! He must have paid for it himself. Otherwise, how else would he have got it? I shall organize the mothers to bring their babies so we can share it out at teatime!" and Marian rushed off to find the Commodore.

Open-mouthed, Sophie looked towards the Big House. Facing her and standing on the steps, was the *Kommandant*. She smiled and nodded in his direction, knowing he must have overheard Marion's remarks.

"Danke schön," she mouthed.

"Bitte schön," he replied.

224

Despite the distractions provided by Sophie, and still feeling upset, Tommy was unwilling to return to his hut. He couldn't face the thought of his mother going on at him and giving him the fourth degree as to what he had been doing every time he went out of her sight. And he hadn't done anything wrong earlier in the day – it was just harmless mischievous fun. The guards hadn't minded having paper aeroplanes thrown at them. In fact, Fritz had made quite a game of it.

Instead, Tommy made his way to the dilapidated building that would become the new shower block. Perhaps here he could be on his own and think his own thoughts.

He could see that the first of the three partitioned rooms in the hut had been used as a store room at one time. The windows had been painted over, obscuring the light, and old cardboard boxes and broken wooden crates were strewn around the floor. Floorboards had been torn up and there was a strong musty smell emanating from the room. Tommy decided not to venture inside.

The second one yielded a pleasanter result. The windows were intact and bedecked with the shredded remains of brightly-coloured curtains. Dust and dirt lay everywhere, but this room had escaped the worst ravages of whatever had befallen Seeblick before the internees from the Channel Islands arrived.

He righted the three-legged stool as well as the chairs, table and bench, all of which were roughly hewn but serviceable. They might be useful in the new schoolroom that Miss Sophie had been talking about. He would tell her when he went back to his room.

Tommy noticed that the walls were wooden and seemed to be of a double skin construction. In some areas, the inner panels had been ripped away and in one place, he could just make out something stuffed into the gap.

Curious, he placed his hand cautiously into the opening. His fingers touched something that felt like a bag and using all his strength, he yanked at it. The inner wall seam in front of it disintegrated, revealing some kind of leather pouch.

Tommy sat down on the three-legged stool and pulled open the drawstring. Inside was a feather, a stone, a couple of German exercise books and a reading book that looked foreign. He liked the feather and the stone and put them back in the bag for safekeeping; he'd look at them later when his mam wasn't around. He opened the novel but as it was in French (?), he didn't understand a word of it. If it was French, Miss Sophie would, he thought excitedly. He'd take it to her and ask her to read it to him. He put it back into the pouch.

"There you are you little toe-rag!"

Tommy nearly jumped out of his skin, so absorbed had he been.

"I've been looking everywhere for you! Why are you never around when you're needed? It's time for roll call." Gert grabbed him by the wrist and pulled him off the stool, which clattered sideways onto the floor, and hauled him out of the hut. "We're going to be late and it'll be all your fault!"

Dragged along by his mother, embarrassed at the sniggers from the other children making their way to the huts, Tommy held onto the leather pouch tightly, wishing he'd had time to find a safe place before his mother realized he had it and confiscated it, which she inevitably would.

They arrived at the hut just as their appointed guard was doing roll call. Tommy stood by his bed keeping the leather pouch concealed behind his back, hoping to find somewhere in which to secrete it away from his mother's prying eyes.

Suddenly, he had a brainwave. When he thought her attention was on the guard who had completed his task and was leaving the room, he quickly dropped the pouch and shuffled it underneath his bed with his foot.

His mother was onto him in an instant.

"What's that you got?" she demanded to know.

"Nuffin."

"You stole summat?"

"No! I ain't no thief."

"You stole summat, didn't you?"

"No, I never. 'onest I didn't."

"Give it 'ere or else."

Aware that all eyes in the room were on him, Tommy had no choice but to hand over his possession. Downcast, he extracted the pouch and handed it over to his mother.

Gert pulled open the drawstring and tipped the contents onto the bed. "Where d'you get this?" she said.

"Found it, in one of the old 'uts where they're gonna build them new showers."

"Stole it, more like."

"No, Mam, I never did."

Gert investigated the contents. She picked up *La Chaleur de la Mer* and flicked through the pages. Mabel peered over her shoulder at the book.

"A filthy novel, I don't wonder," she said. "Looks like it's in some foreign language."

"Well, you ain't keeping *that*, that's for sure," said Gert to her son, cuffing Tommy round the ear. "If it's not stolen, then this lot is going where it belongs – in the fire."

She shoved everything back inside the pouch and moved purposely across the room towards the stove but Mabel intercepted her.

"Hang on a minute, Gert. That bag looks useful," and she took it from her.

"'Ere, you get yer 'ands off it. If anyone's going to 'ave the bag, it's going to be me," and she yanked the bag out of Mabel's hands.

"My idea."

"My son found it."

"Well, I need it." And Mabel grabbed the bag back.

"You ain't 'aving it," and the two women tussled over the bag, pulling it back and forth while Tommy squirmed with embarrassment and Sophie looked on in fascinated horror.

"Ladies, ladies," said Marian, unwilling to allow the argument to continue before it escalated into a physical fight. "Such uncivilized behaviour."

The two women looked at each other sullenly.

"Well," said Gert, coming to a decision. "In that case, neither of us is 'avin' it." And she went over to the stove where she opened the door and flung it inside before wiping her hands in front of Mabel's face in a gesture of triumph, an action that caused her erstwhile friend to stalk out of the room in high dudgeon. "C'mon you," she said to her son, "yer filthy you are. I don't know 'ow you do it. I'm goin' ter give you a good scrub." She looked behind his ears. "Lord, luv a duck! There's enough dirt there fer a whole field of cabbages."

"But Mam," protested Tommy. "I 'ad a wash yesterday."

"Yeah, and yer 'avin' another one today." And with that unequivocal statement, Gert grabbed the towel from the back of her chair and pushed Tommy out of the room.

Gradually, the inmates dispersed to their various tasks or interests and as soon as everyone was occupied or out of the room, Sophie leapt off her bed and ran over to the stove where she opened the door and, coughing from the acrid smoke that was now being produced by the thick leather pouch as it heated up, she grabbed a pair of tongs and lifted it out of the flames.

She'd tell Tommy in the morning that she had rescued it and that she would look after it for him. If he still wanted it, of course.

That night before lights out, under the cover of her bedclothes, Sophie investigated the contents of the bag for herself. Fortunately, there was not too much damage as the stove was being its usual ineffective self and had only singed the outer layer of the leather.

Inside she found a feather, a stone, a couple of German exercise books and the "foreign language" novel, which had aroused her curiosity and prompted her spur-of-the-moment rescue attempt. It might be something she could read to keep her mind occupied.

Lifting up the covers higher to allow more light, and turning the book over, Sophie almost called out with excitement as she read the title: *La Chaleur de la Mer*.

For several moments, she cradled the book in her hands, unable to believe her eyes. Her favourite novel. But *here* of all places?

It had obviously been read many, many times, yet it was still in remarkably good condition.

Almost reverently, she opened the front cover and then she saw them – 'RLA' – the same initials that were carved into her bunk.

It must be the same person. It *had* to be the same person.

There was also a poem written on the flyleaf in a clear, distinctive hand. Settling herself, Sophie began to read:

There swims within my life a fish
Which is the deep and glittering wish
Evoking all the hills and waters
Of sensual memories.
Your image and those days of glass
Being lost become no loss
But change into that image
At the centre of my thought,
Itself no less precious

Than the original happiness.
(From Three Days *by Stephen Spender)*

For several moments, she sat very still, rereading the words, wondering who this man was and what had prompted him to write this particular verse on the flyleaf of *La Chaleur*. Whatever the reason, she knew he must possess an understanding of poetry.

In the middle of the book, he had tucked a note, written in his characteristic hand.

Dear Discoverer, it ran.

I leave this book to you as a gift; a novel that I hope will give you as much pleasure and enjoyment as it has me.

I had previously spent many years searching for a copy of La Chaleur de la Mer *and was amazed when this one turned up here, of all places.*

It is hard to leave it behind but I cannot take it with me. Hopefully, by the time you read this, I shall be safe and sound back in England.

The feather and the stone are souvenirs of a wood-gathering expedition I once went on in the forest near the camp. I brought them back with me as symbols of the world outside the wire. The exercise books reflect my feeble attempt at being Seeblick's librarian.

I send you this message from captivity in the hope that one day we shall all of us attain true freedom of mind and spirit wherever we might be.

I wish you well.
RLA
June, 1941

Motionless, Sophie held the letter in her hand for a long time, feeling an unaccountable affinity with its author. The simple phrasing spoke to her soul, as though he had written directly to her. Suddenly, she wanted to meet him; to know what he looked like; to see what kind of person he was.

She hoped he had reached England safely but most of all, she hoped that he was still alive.

As she reread the poem and the letter, a shiver travelled down her spine and, assuming it to be from the encroaching cold, once the lights were out in the room, apart from the book, she carefully replaced the items in the leather pouch which she pushed down the bed under the covers.

Later that night as Sophie lay awake in her bunk, she pondered the events of the day – the kindness and consideration of Heinrich Hoffmeister; the incredible blue of his eyes; her responsiveness to the unknown RLA, whose distinctive handwriting rested safely inside her beloved *La Chaleur* which she now held close to her breast.

For the first time in a long time, untroubled by nightmares or unmentionable fears, undisturbed by extraneous sounds, Sophie fell into a deep, peaceful sleep.

CHAPTER 29

Somewhere in England

It was a bright cold January morning with a thin layer of snow dusting the ground when Robert and Richard, joining hordes of other people all heading in the same direction, showed their passes to the sergeant at the gate of a long driveway leading towards a redbrick country manor.

The N.C.O. scrutinized the documents carefully and looked the two men up and down, tutting with disapproval at their red-eyed and dishevelled state, before waving them on.

"Well, that's another mission successfully accomplished with another about to begin and no leave in between," remarked Richard, as they walked through the gates of Bletchley Park. "Though they might have given us time to smarten ourselves up a bit before reporting here. I wonder what they have in store for us this time? Collecting samples of sand and soil from foreign climes was not my idea of fun."

"But essential to the war effort," replied Robert. "Just be grateful you didn't actually have to go ashore in a canoe and then spend several hours crawling about on your hands and knees in the shadow of German bunkers with machine guns."

"Just be grateful you didn't have to spend several hours cooped up in a midget submarine being tossed around in a rough sea waiting for you chaps to come back."

"At least you were warm and dry."

"At least you had fresh air and could enjoy yourself on the beach without feeling seasick."

"Of course. Freezing conditions in the middle of winter is always the best time to have fun at the seaside."

The two men grinned at each other.

"It beats some of the other things we've been asked to do, especially when we first began," remarked Robert quietly and discreetly, as both men moved away from the crowd. "After all those weeks of initial training, so much valuable time was wasted because we were sent from pillar to post by a British Intelligence service who, apparently not knowing what to do with us, tried to use us to score points off the other clandestine organizations rather than focusing on the job in hand."

"Well, my friend, if you hadn't kicked up such a fuss once you'd twigged what was going on, they'd still be trying that on with us now. It beats me why some of the different intelligence services in this country can't just stop being suspicious of each other. They waste too much time and energy behind the scenes promoting their own vested interests if you ask me."

"I agree," replied Robert. "And what's more, by being insular, they consign cooperation for the greater good to the dustbin. There were times when I actually wondered if they realized who the real enemy was."

"Perhaps all secret service organizations in every country are bitter rivals."

"Perhaps. That's certainly been my experience with the two organizations I've had dealings with – here and in Germany. Anyway, look on the bright side, our missions since being involved with the I.S.T.D. have been a Godsend. At last we've been able to get on with things that really can make a difference."

"Even if it is only collecting and evaluating holiday snaps or collecting sand samples…"

Robert smiled. "Or, more to the point, compiling detailed topography of the areas about to be used in military operations."

"Not to mention enemy communications and port layouts."

"Absolutely. Operation Torch last November was very satisfying. I felt proud of our contribution towards that."

"So did I." Without batting an eyelid, Richard added, feigning disappointment, "But I'm still upset we weren't asked to collect sand from North Africa before the Allied landings took place."

"I know, it was such a shame. But your midget submarine only likes going to France and that sandy beach was just too big for me to manage on my own."

"What was it called? The name escapes me…"

"The Sahara, I believe."

"Ah yes, so it was."

They grinned at each other again.

On reaching the main house, they were told to report straight away to one of the operational department heads at Bletchley Park.

After the initial greetings had been exchanged, Sir Humphrey Travis said, "Sorry to drag you here after you've hardly set foot back in England but we needed you both pretty pronto. You come highly recommended as being quite the experts in your particular field of intelligence gathering and a reputation for not being pushed around or hoodwinked."

Robert and Richard exchanged a glance.

"News travels fast, dear boys," he added.

"Thank you, sir," replied Richard. "We'll take that as a compliment."

"So, how have you both found working at the Inter-Services Topographical Department in Oxford under the watchful eye of Admiral Godfrey from the Admiralty's Operational Intelligence Centre?" Sir Humphrey chuckled to himself. "I love all these longwinded names, don't you? Confuses the socks off most people, especially when one starts talking about the I.S.T.D. and the O.I.C. Great fun, though, eh, what? Anyway, old Godfrey's very proud of the significance of his little creation and guards its reputation assiduously," he concluded with a smile.

"Our work has certainly been interesting," replied Robert pleasantly, raising a discreet eyebrow at Richard. "We've spent some of our time in Oxford at I.S.T.D. headquarters with the map-room boys and the photography department and we've been out and about on fact-finding missions for them. All in all, it's been very worthwhile."

Travis looked down at the open file on his desk, "So it would seem. You've just got back from France, I believe?"

"Yes, sir."

"And before that, you were the I.S.T.D. liaison officers on topographical intelligence with the Royal Navy and the British Army in the build-up to Operation Torch?"

230

"Yes, sir."

"Well, you're about to add another string to your topographical bow. When you two chaps have had a chance to smarten yourselves up a bit, I'll get someone to show you around. You won't be allowed to see everything, of course, only what will concern you." He smiled. "Even *I* don't know everything that goes on here. It's very hush-hush, you know, and absolutely vital to the war effort. Can't afford to give anything away, you see. What we do here will shorten the war by years, so absolute secrecy is vital. When you've settled in, report back here and I'll give you your next assignment. Rather a plumb job, I believe. Not that I know anything about it, of course." He cleared his throat. "Now, what codename have you two been operating under?"

Robert and Richard glanced at each other once again.

"Perhaps we'll keep that to ourselves for the time being," replied Robert.

"It's very hush-hush, you know," added Richard.

"Quite so, quite so." Sir Humphrey smiled. "Well, off you go then and spruce yourselves up. My secretary will show you to the facilities and tell you where your billet will be."

He pressed a buzzer on his desk and in walked an attractive young woman who, when she saw Richard, went pale with shock. It was nothing to the expression on Richard's face.

"Caroline, please show these two gentlemen to the facilities where they can get changed. Then bring them back here and later, you can show them around. Hut Four for Lieutenant Langley and Hut Sixteen for Captain Anderson." He looked at her, concerned. "Are you all right, my dear? You seem to have gone very pale suddenly."

"I'm fine, thank you, sir," replied Caroline hastily, glancing at Richard, who was staring at her in amazement.

"Good. Well, I'll see you later, chaps."

After acknowledging his remark, the three of them walked out of the room and closed the door behind them.

"What on earth are you doing here?" exclaimed Richard, taking both Caroline's hands in his, suppressing the urge in such a public situation to take her in his arms and greet her thoroughly and properly.

"I work here," replied Caroline, swallowing hard and removing her hands from inside his.

"Since when?"

"The beginning of the war."

Richard smiled broadly, relieved. "I knew it! I always thought there was something bogus about that entertainment troupe of yours. I'd even begun to wonder if you'd, you know, found someone else."

He found even saying the words difficult.

"I knew you were worried, but I couldn't say anything."

"Of course not." He took her hands again. "Never mind all that now. I just can't believe this!"

"I know," she replied, allowing a small amount of the longing she also felt to creep into her voice.

Robert smiled and gently cleared his throat.

"Oh, I'm so sorry," said Richard. "Darling, I'd like you meet my friend and colleague Captain Robert Anderson of the Royal Welch Fusiliers. Bob, this is Caroline – my fiancée."

"I'm very pleased to meet you at last," said Robert, shaking her hand. "Richard has told me a great deal about you."

"Really? Good or bad?"

"All of it good."

"How long have you and Richard been working together?"

"A long time."

"In that case, I'm surprised we haven't met before," said Caroline.

"We are silent partners in crime," replied Robert. "However, on our rare moments of leave, we have tended go our separate ways. We're in each other's company too much as it is while we're on duty!"

"Careful, me old mate," and Richard narrowed his eyes at Robert, who chuckled.

"Only joking – we really are the best of friends. But I have other commitments which take up a great deal of my free time, you see."

"He has three children," said Richard, a mischievous twinkle in his eyes.

"Goodness! I expect your wife is glad to see you when you do get home. Are your children away at school?" she asked conversationally.

"I'm not married."

"Goodness!" Caroline looked at Robert askance then said diplomatically, "Look, why don't we all meet up at the end of the day? After you've settled in at the cottage where you're to be billeted, we could go out somewhere for a meal. Then we can talk and catch up – well, as much as we can, given our…"

"…secret endeavours," finished Richard.

"Exactly."

"That's very kind," said Robert courteously. "However, I'm sure that you two won't want me hanging around playing gooseberry."

"It's fine, honestly," said Caroline who, catching Richard's pained expression, added hastily, "Now, I must show you both where to wash and change and when you've done that, if you come back to the entrance hall, I'll give you that tour." She hesitated before saying to Richard, "Edwin is here too."

"Edwin! Where does he work?"

"In Hut Six."

"Which does what?"

"Can't tell you that, I'm afraid." She hesitated again and then said, "He's engaged."

"Engaged?"

"To Cicely. She works in his Section. Will Sophie be upset, do you think?"

"Sophie? No. She was never interested in Edwin in that way. She tolerated him rather than anything else because he's been part of the family setup for yonks."

"But I always felt she was fond of him."

"She is, but not in the same way that Edwin is of her. He asked her marry him several times. She always refused. Didn't she tell you?"

"Yes, but I suppose I've always been so anxious that she should find someone of her own, that I tried to make her change her mind. I mean, I had you and didn't want her to feel left out. She's far too attractive to stay single and I wouldn't want her to be wasted on someone who didn't deserve her. She needs a boy like Edwin who's intelligent and attentive."

"But Edwin's not the person for her," observed Richard.

"No, I suppose you're right." They had reached the washroom. "Anyway, here we are. I'll meet you downstairs in, say, half an hour. You can leave your kit and caboodle at the desk and collect it later."

"I presume from that conversation that Caroline and Sophie are close," observed Robert, as they washed, shaved and changed into clean uniforms.

"They're best friends. They were at school together and have been close ever since. Caroline always used to come and stay with us in the holidays. We've known her for years.

"And Edwin is your friend?"

"His father and mine were in the diplomatic service together so the families have known each other forever. Edwin went to Eton and Cambridge and I followed on in his wake. He has a brilliant mathematical mind. Got a doctorate while I just about managed to scrape my degree. It's funny, isn't it?"

"What is? You only just managing to scrape your degree?"

"No, dummy. How we've all ended up here."

"All of you except Sophie."

"Yes. All of us, except Sophie, who of course is holed up in some internment camp in Baden-Württemberg. Seeblick. Where you were."

"So you keep telling me," reminded Robert gently.

"I do, don't I? I must be losing my grip."

"You're not, but I'll be the first to tell you if you do. Actually, come to think of it..." and Robert neatly sidestepped his friend's well-aimed swipe. "No, it's just that you're worried about your sister and like to talk about her. Frequently."

"Do you mind?"

"Not in the least. Because of that, I almost feel as though I know her."

"Have you heard from Sophie recently?" asked Caroline of Richard, later that evening as they, Edwin (who had been equally shocked when told that Richard would be working at Bletchley Park), Cicely and Robert sat around the cosy fire in a local hostelry after eating supper there.

Robert stared into the flames, cradling his beer, in danger of falling asleep; only half paying attention to the conversation, his thoughts turning to the events of that day.

When he had been shown into Hut Sixteen, Robert was amazed and gratified to find cryptanalysis of *Abwehr* codes taking place.

"We cracked most of these a while ago now, thanks to some British officer who escaped from a P.O.W. camp and worked for the *Abwehr* for four months, would you believe. He came back with all sorts of useful info. It's made a hell of a difference in deciphering the Army Enigma as well. We can now decrypt most of the codes sent by the *Abwehr* to their operatives in the field, wherever they are, and vice versa. It's helped us to identify any agents coming over here too before they've had the chance to do any damage. Mind you, they're so badly equipped and so badly trained, that it's not hard for the M.P.s to pick 'em up. We've turned most of them, under threat of firing squad, onto our side as double agents and they now feed the info we want them to feed back to their masters in Berlin, or wherever."

Although delighted, Robert remained silent about his identity. He didn't want a fuss; it was enough that what he had done, despite the pain and the agony it had cost him, had made a *difference*: a real and tangible difference.

However, inwardly, he did question why he wasn't sent here to work immediately after his secret service training. He spoke fluent German; he'd had all that experience of the *Abwehr* and how both it and the German army worked. Surely, his expertise would have been invaluable when analysing the significance of the decrypts?

But no, frustratingly, after a couple of months of shilly-shallying about, along with Richard, he was sent to a secret department that dealt with subjects (geography and geology) of which he had only a passing knowledge. On the other hand, his extensive travelling in France and Germany had been invaluable when looking at locations and sifting through the masses of information that was brought into the I.S.T.D. headquarters at Oxford's Manchester College.

And his contributions *had* made a difference there as well. Without accurate topography, no clandestine military operation could be carried out without an enormous, unnecessary risk. It would be like going in blind and reduce the chances of a successful outcome to virtually nil.

The Allies needed up-to-date maps of roads, railways and ports, of the countryside, of the distribution of buildings – any information that would give a clear picture of the areas targeted. All incoming documents from whatever source then had to be collated and disseminated.

Robert supposed he would just have to accept that his superiors really did know what they were doing, that there was some overall plan for him and they weren't just shuffling him around like a pack of cards. Perhaps they were waiting until he had proved his worth and they knew he could be trusted.

Robert knew that Richard, when they discreetly compared notes later, on his tour around Bletchley Park, had been curious as to why he had not been asked to work as a translator on the decrypts in Hut 4 from the Naval Enigma or given the chance to shine on actually decoding it, wherever that was carried out. Both things would have been right up his street.

Richard couldn't conceal from his friend his pride in the fact that he had recovered the most up-to-date naval Enigma machine and brought it, together with all the associated documents, safely back to the ship and thence England but, like Robert, he too had kept publicly quiet about his contribution when the R.N. lieutenant showing him round spoke about the breakthrough that had come way back in 1941 with the discovery of this particular Enigma machine.

"We owe the crew of H.M.S. *Benedict* a real debt of gratitude," he had said, as he guided Richard back to the main building where he and Robert joined forces again. "Without that, we wouldn't have been able to achieve our breakthrough in keeping the convoys away from the U-boats."

He had left them with a cheery, "Toodle-pip then," as they reached Sir Humphrey Travis's office and went on his way.

Robert and Richard then received the news from Sir Humphrey that their main role two months hence would be to act as liaison officers between Bletchley Park and a certain Colonel Ashton-Hill, "who, from March, will be assisting the Chief of Staff to the Supreme Allied Commander working on possibilities for the Second Front."

He had looked at their enquiring expressions.

"Why, the Allied landings in Europe, of course!"

"Really?" said Richard.

"Yes, old chap."

"What exactly will this entail?" Robert had asked, wanting specifics.

"Your new role will utilize the knowledge you will acquire while working here at Bletchley over the next couple of months, advising the colonel on vital information you might uncover and feel he should know about, while at the same time employing the skills you have so admirably demonstrated with the I.S.T.D." He regarded them astutely. "And when all this comes to fruition, you'll be making as vital a contribution towards winning the war as anyone."

Perhaps, thought Robert, drinking the last remaining drops of beer in his glass, *perhaps the powers-that-be are finally giving us the role they had intended for us right from the beginning. Perhaps they do know what they're on about after all, just as they did when they gave me permission to confide in Richard when I first got back from Brussels."*

"Yes, I actually received a letter from her the other day," replied Richard to Caroline's question, the mention of Sophie rousing Robert from his reflections. "She seems very cheerful and settled, oddly enough."

"I thought that too when I read my last letter from her," said Caroline.

"Sophie hasn't written to me," declared Edwin morosely.

Cicely looked at him sharply, then asked of Richard, "What's she like, this sister of yours?"

She had always wondered about Sophie ever since she had known Edwin but had never asked, afraid that despite their engagement and fondness for each other, her fiancé had not quite left his first love behind.

"Captivating," responded Edwin immediately.

Cicely looked at him severely this time.

"Despite her being my sister," said Richard expansively, "she is adorable. Most of the time."

"You're just biased," observed Caroline good-naturedly. "But I do agree. She has something special about her…" she considered for a moment "…an exquisite purity, a delicateness – something that's very difficult to define."

"But there's nothing frail about her," said Edwin.

"Certainly not," replied Caroline. "She has a very determined side to her character."

"Stubborn, more like," added Richard. "She'd be a match for any mule."

Robert, who after discovering Sophie was at Seeblick, now paid close attention to any conversation whenever her name was mentioned, laughed at this.

"She sounds perfect," he said.

"You mean to say you like pig-headedness in a woman?" teased Richard.

Robert chuckled. "I admire determination. It shows character. Providing that whoever it is, is also open to reason."

"Oh she's that, as well," said Caroline, looking at Robert afresh as a picture of Sophie sitting next to him embedded itself in her mind. "It would be perfect in fact if she was here, now," she mused, unable to shake off the image.

"I only wish she was," added Edwin wistfully.

"Oh do shut up Edwin," said Cicely, having had as much of this particular conversation as she could stand. "It's getting late and time we were off. We have an early shift tomorrow." She turned to Robert. "It was nice to meet you. I've no doubt our paths will cross again. Come on, Edwin, do get a move on," and she pulled him up out of his seat.

"Yes, dear."

As the two of them went towards the exit, Edwin was heard to say, "It is you, and only you, I love, Cicely, you know that."

"Of course I do, but you must stop mooning about Richard's sister. I know you asked her to marry you years ago, but from what Richard said when I first asked him about it, she wasn't a bit interested in you. You're engaged to me now, and I'm *very* interested in you, so buck up, there's a good fellow, and forget that you ever had any feelings for her."

"Yes, dear," replied Edwin, his spirits and usual bounce restored by this vote of womanly confidence.

He gave Cicely an enthusiastic peck on the cheek and put his arm around her, leading her out of the inn in a slightly awkward fashion but with a spring in his step and joy in his heart.

"Sophie once said that he always reminded her of a highly intelligent puppy," remarked Richard not unkindly, as he, Robert and Caroline watched them disappear through the door.

Robert laughed. "I think that seems a fair observation. He means well and even though I've only just met them, Cicely seems to be right for him." He looked at his two companions. "Well, I think that you two need to be alone, so Richard, I'll take myself off back to our little cottage. I'll see you both in the morning. Bright and early, mind."

"Unfortunately," said Richard. "However, don't take it personally."

"Wouldn't dream of it!" and with a knowing wink at both of them, he went out of the door.

That night, feeling lonely as he lay awake unable to sleep, Robert thought of Sophie, feeling as he had done so many times before, an ever-deepening affinity with her.

He had read her books, ridden her horse, slept in her bed and now, she was where he had been.

At Seeblick.

He wondered if she might be the one to discover *La Chaleur de la Mer* and read its inscription and the note. He wondered if she might, by some remarkable quirk of fate, be sleeping in his bunk where he had carved his initials.

Turning onto his side, he told himself not to be so ridiculously fanciful.

Robert's last thought, before he fell asleep was that, despite the length of time he had known Richard and the number of times he had stayed at his house, he still had no idea what Sophie looked like. He was intensely curious and yet somehow, he didn't want to know.

He was afraid that if he did, it might spoil his illusion of Sophie who, from the moment that he had first heard about her, had become for him a comforting mercurial presence in his mind, and not some static image in a photograph.

CHAPTER 30

Seeblick

Dearest Aunt Edna and Aunt Mae,

It was so good to have your letter. I'm sorry to hear that you've been unwell again, Aunt Mae. Perhaps the warm spring weather on St Nicolas will help you improve. We are still up to our eyes in snow here.

The theatre is being refurbished at the moment and is nearly complete. I am also now the librarian as the Y.M.C.A. are supplying us with so many books that it's been impossible to keep track of them. The Kommandant has allocated a large room for us to use in the Big House as a library.

He is incredibly kind and helpful and we are really very lucky. I do hope that he's allowed to stay. He makes being here more than bearable. We often talk to each other.

Well, I think that's my apportioned number of words. I haven't counted them, but I've got used to the amount of space my handwriting covers. I wish I could write more often.

Hope to hear from you soon,
Love from Sophie xxxx

Heinrich Hoffmeister, after finishing Sophie's letter and placing a 'Passed' stamp upon the envelope, got up from his desk and stretched his back before going to the window where he stared absentmindedly down into the compound.

As camp censor (a role he had been obliged to undertake personally as a replacement for *Leutnant* Schauerlich still had not been forthcoming despite repeated requests) he read an awful lot of letters, but once a month when it was her allotted turn, he looked forward to Sophie's, brief as they were obliged to be.

He knew about her aunts on the farm; that her brother was very dear to her; that her friend Caroline still refused to set a wedding date. He knew that Sophie's mother worked for the Red Cross and that Sophie hoped that her father was exercising the horses properly.

Heinrich also knew that she had mentioned him in every letter.

He gave a start as he saw her walk across the compound and, stepping back so that he could continue to observe her without being discovered, he saw her disappear beneath the balcony. A few moments later, there was a knock at the door and she was shown into his room.

Quickly, he covered the letters on his desk. He did not wish her to know that he was the camp censor. He liked to see her thoughts on paper as they came naturally.

"Hello," he said.

"Hello," she replied.

"What can I do for you?" he asked gently.

"Marian, that is, Mrs Maundell…"

She always begins like this, he thought, feeling his heart beat a little faster. *Always making it seem as though it was someone else's request. Never 'I was wondering' or 'I was thinking'.* "Yes?"

"Erm... Mrs Maundell was wondering whether we could have an area in which to grow our own vegetables. It would help supplement the Red Cross parcels with fresh produce. We get plenty of tinned stuff but fresh veg during the spring and summer would be lovely. The Red Cross sent several packets of seeds with their last consignment and..."

"It would seem a pity to waste them," he concluded for her.

He took great pleasure in finishing her sentences. She rarely did the same for him but when she did, it was not without embarrassment and always with a tell-tale blush, which he found most attractive.

"Yes," she said. Then: "You have a new jumper on underneath your uniform jacket."

Thrown for a moment by her unexpected directness, he said, "Yes, my sister sent it to me for my birthday."

"Oh." She seemed surprised by this simple revelation. "It looks very warm and the colours are lovely."

"It is and they are. My sister has good taste."

"Does she knit all the jumpers that you wear? You have several different ones." Realizing she was going beyond her accustomed reserve, Sophie bit her lip.

So she notices my jumpers, thought Heinrich. "Yes. She is always concerned that I should be warm enough."

Despite herself, she was curious. "Are you allowed to wear knitted jumpers under your uniform? Surely the German army with all its rules and regulations wouldn't permit it?"

It was an obvious question and it made Heinrich smile. "They do not. However, I am *Kommandant* of Seeblick. Who is going to report me? I am in charge and it is very cold here in the winter. Besides, I am a civilian drafted into the military to act in an administrative capacity."

"Which means what, exactly?"

"That I can wear a jumper underneath my uniform in order to keep warm."

Even Sophie couldn't help smiling at this. After a moment or two, she ventured, "When was your birthday?"

"Yesterday."

"Happy birthday for yesterday," she said, trying to remember how old Ulrich and Helmut had said he was.

"I have reached the grand old age of thirty-five," he replied, seeing the question in her eyes.

"I wasn't going to pry."

"I know."

"But you knew what I was thinking."

"Yes." His heart began to do somersaults. He felt dizzy and sat down.

Seeing him go pale, Sophie said, "Are you all right?"

He nodded and reached for a small bottle of tablets that he always kept in his pocket. "I shall be recovered in a moment."

"Perhaps you're coming down with something. There are some nasty illnesses going round the camp at the moment."

"So the doctor tells me. No, I can assure you it is not that, *Fräulein* Langley." He smiled, the colour returning to his cheeks. "See, the moment has passed and I am all right again."

"Well I must go."

You don't have to go, he thought. "As you wish," he said.

Sophie hesitated, half turning away from him. "We're thinking of putting on some kind of show to celebrate the opening of the theatre. I… that is, we, were wondering if you would like to come to one of the performances."

"And will you be in this show?"

"Yes."

"Then I shall take great pleasure in attending." He wanted to kiss her.

Sophie blushed a very deep shade of red.

"Perhaps you will let me know when all is ready."

"Yes." Resolutely, she turned to leave. "Now I really must go."

"Of course."

Her own heart beating, she walked quickly to the sanctuary of the library and busied herself sorting the latest boxes of books that had been delivered that morning, hiding her burning cheeks within the safe comfort of stories and cardboard.

A few weeks later, Heinrich, along with the police guards, sat in the front row of the newly refurbished theatre and enjoyed an evening of entertainment that showed just how much real talent there was within the camp: the whole proceedings stage-managed by the man and his wife who had run the little theatre-cum-cinema in Port le Bac.

There were choruses and solo songs, dancers, a juggler, a magician, a very funny ventriloquist, a string trio (musical instruments courtesy of the Y.M.C.A.) and a soliloquy from *Hamlet* recited by Sophie as Ophelia.

With Sophie dressed in white and a cleverly fashioned garland made from scraps of paper in her hair, Heinrich thought her to be the most beautiful woman he had ever seen.

It gladdened his soul that for once, he was able to look at her to his heart's content without fear of discovery; allowing his emotions free rein, his admiration and desire concealed by the darkness of the auditorium.

As the applause rang round the theatre and the lights came on, he became aware that letting go mentally was not a wise or sensible thing to have done.

For all he could think about now was Sophie in this context and his thoughts filled him with both hope and despair, for he could not deny any longer that he was in love with her. However, there were too many obstacles preventing them from being together. Even if she returned his feelings, he knew that it was hopeless.

Heinrich did not wish to embarrass Sophie by asking her to be his mistress, the only option available to them until after the war. He knew that to do so would cause her immense difficulty with her fellow islanders and could cost him his own good standing among the internees.

It wasn't that he cared about that more than he did about Sophie; it was just that he cared so *much* about her and didn't want her character to be besmirched or her reputation damaged, nor her life made uncomfortable in any way.

Heinrich took a deep breath. No, there was no choice. They would have to continue as they were and perhaps in time he might be able to find a way for them to be together in secret.

He knew he would find waiting very hard; even harder than he had before because he had now allowed himself to dwell on possibilities. He also knew that now, above all else, he wanted to claim her for himself.

At the end of the evening, he left without speaking to anyone and Sophie, who had changed quickly hoping to see the *Kommandant* afterwards, stood alone in the rapidly emptying auditorium, filled with disappointment that he had gone without saying a word about the show or her part within it.

Over the next few days whenever they met, Sophie was polite but distant and Heinrich was upset by this. Indeed, even more than that, he had to admit that he felt wounded by the change from her usual careful responsiveness to him.

Heinrich resisted approaching her overtly until one morning, he received a letter in the day's post that filled him with alarm. Unable to hold back anymore, he succumbed and sought her out in the library.

"Do you have a moment?" he asked.

"Perhaps," she replied noncommittally, keeping her eyes averted from his.

"I wish to explain something to you."

Sophie continued to log in and tick the returned books in her well-used ledger. From the inflection in his voice she sensed they were moving into uncharted territory. Feeling nervous, she flicked back to the beginning of the book and glanced at R.L.A.'s handwriting, finding security in its nonthreatening familiarity.

"You do?" she managed to enquire.

Heinrich took this as an encouraging sign. "Yes. I wish to apologize."

"What for?" Sophie was genuinely puzzled.

"I regret that I went away after the performance without speaking to you."

She paused in her marking; the pen poised above the page on which she had been writing. "Why did you?" she asked quietly.

"Because I could not stay." At the last moment his courage failed him.

"Oh." Despite her caution, Sophie experienced disappointment and resumed her task.

"You were wonderful," he said.

"I've always enjoyed amateur dramatics."

"Ah, it is a peculiarly British thing, this amateur society business?" he ventured.

"Yes." She began to open up a little. "It is, I suppose. It's a way of being involved in something that you would not otherwise do."

"But there is no financial recompense for the performances. I have much difficulty in understanding this."

Sophie smiled. "Most of the time, the members of a dramatic society pay for the privilege of belonging."

"I believe we do not have such an equivalent in Germany."

"You don't, as far as I'm aware."

"How do you know this?"

"I lived in this country when I was a child."

"You did?"

"My father was the British Ambassador to Berlin for several years."

"He was? You must be proud of him."

"I am."

"I know the city well." He sighed. "It is much changed."

"I would imagine that it is."

She stacked the pile of returned books neatly.

He wanted to touch her hand but he dared not.

Heinrich took a deep breath. "I have had a letter this morning ordering me to send all single women to Liebenau internment camp. It is recently converted and has very good facilities. It is better than here and not so overcrowded as there are to be fewer internees. It is not public knowledge yet. I wished to speak to you before I make the official announcement here and take whatever action is needed."

Sophie, having gone very pale, stopped what she was doing. She looked at him in consternation.

Seeing this, Heinrich said very quietly, "I do not desire that you should go."

"You don't?" Sophie's heart was beating very fast. Momentarily out of her depth, she refrained from asking why.

"No, I most certainly do not wish you to go," he repeated emphatically. "But what about you, *Fräulein* Langley, would you want to leave here and go to Liebenau?"

"No, of course not!" she exclaimed.

How could she say that she was happy here; that she didn't want to go away? It would sound too ridiculous for words.

"Then I shall arrange that you are not transferred."

"How?"

"I have friends in the Ministry of the Interior from where this order comes."

"Mrs Maundell must stay as well," said Sophie hastily.

Heinrich looked at her with an expression of bewilderment. "Why?"

How could she say that the presence of Marian would act as a stabilizing influence; someone whom she could trust; a voice of reason to whom Sophie could turn as a safety net should the situation with the *Kommandant* become more than she could manage?

"She… she keeps everything running smoothly. Without her, the Commodore and the doctor would be unable to cope. And if they can't cope with everything, you'll have to sort out the chaos," she said, her words tumbling out with nervousness and confusion.

The *Kommandant*, amused by this, smiled. "Therefore, I shall do this thing also. I do not wish to make my life disrupted by having to deal with chaos."

With his words of confirmation, a momentary chill of fear touched her heart. "And will you, because you are going to allow both Marian and me to stay, require certain favours from me in return?"

"Nein! Absolut nicht!" he said emphatically, knowing that he hadn't even considered such a possibility. Until now, that is; until Sophie had put the idea into his mind. But even so, Heinrich knew that within this particular context, he would not act upon it.

So relieved was she by the conviction and immediacy of his response that Sophie smiled at him, her eyes open and alive.

For Heinrich, her smile was like the sun coming out from behind a dark cloud. Suddenly, his world was filled with light.

"Danke," she said.

"Bitte," he replied circumspectly, when all he wanted to do was take her into his arms. However, he could not. For the moment.

For what seemed like an eternity, they each held the other's gaze before Sophie broke the spell and picked up her pile of books.

"I must return these to the shelves," she said.

"And I must return to my duties." He smiled gently. "We shall meet again?"

"Of course. Tomorrow morning as usual. The doctor would like to discuss the new supplies of medicines which have been sent."

Heinrich hesitated before saying, "I understand," aware that this regular daily meeting was not what he had intended.

But perhaps it is better this way, he told himself. *For the moment I shall hold back. Until she is ready and comes to me of her own free will.*

CHAPTER 31

St Nicolas

"Come in, dear boys, come on in!" boomed a gruff but friendly voice as Robert and Richard entered Colonel Freddie Ashton's room in Norfolk House in London. "Sit yourselves down once you've locked the door. There's much to talk about today."

Robert and Richard took their usual seats in front of his desk.

"What news have you from B.P.? Turned up anything in those *Abwehr* decodes? Learned anything new about Hitler's Atlantic Wall from the naval decrypts?"

For a while they talked about the latest progress in the war and when everything that could be discussed had been considered and deliberated, the colonel said, "Well, now that's all out of the way, I've a proposition to run by both of you. As you're both aware, here at Norfolk House, we're exploring suitable locations for the future Allied invasion of France – we think Normandy will prove to be the best place in the end – but I've been asked to consider other options which may or may not prove to be suitable. I'd like us to take a close look at one particular scenario, if only to rule it out. What d'you think?" He smiled amiably and enquiringly at both of them.

"Well, yes," began Richard cautiously, "that sounds reasonable."

"It would help if we knew exactly what it is you're proposing," observed Robert pointedly, having sensed that Freddie Ashton was withholding some vital piece of information in addition to the immediately obvious. He hadn't worked with this man for these past few months not to be aware of his devious methods.

The colonel chuckled. "Well," and he unfolded a large map and spread it out across a table next to his desk.

The three men leant over it.

"Here you see the Channel Islands," he said, tapping his forefinger on their location, "situated not *too* far away from the Contentin Peninsula, the northern shore of which is the preferred area for the Second Front. The island of St Nicolas," and he pointed to a tiny dot on the map, "is only twelve miles from the coast of France and tucked into an ideal position under the peninsula itself. I've been asked to find out if there's any mileage in launching an amphibious assault on the island, overrunning the German garrison and thereafter using St Nicolas as a base from which to launch a simultaneous invasion on the southern shore of the peninsula at the same time as the main assault on the northern beaches."

"What about the Germans on the other islands?" asked Robert, thinking the whole thing sounded farfetched and impractical. "As soon as they're aware something's going on over at St Nicolas, they'll immediately send reinforcements across."

"Ah! That's where the R.A.F. will come in. They'll launch continuous bombing strikes on the other islands so the Germans have to keep their heads down. The plan is also to have a sub in the area to sink any ships if they try to counter attack from the sea. Cunning, eh?" Fred gave a broad smile.

"Sounds risky to me," said Richard. "What if the weather's unsuitable for flying?"

"The whole thing's ridiculous," interjected Robert, not wasting any breath on speculation, "not to mention downright dangerous. And it would be especially harmful to the civilian population."

The colonel laughed. "I agree entirely. That's exactly what I told Combined Ops when they came up with this, yet another of their hare-brained schemes. However, I'm afraid we're lumbered with investigating the possibility. Unfortunately, the Prime Minister is rather taken with this idea and has ordered me to see whether or not it's feasible." Freddie Ashton sighed. "The sooner Combined Ops are sent to meddle somewhere else, the better. I hear that Burma is on the cards. Send 'em there quick, I say, then I can get on with my job unmolested."

Robert and Richard exchanged a knowing glance. During their time at the I.S.T.D. they had personal experience of how doggedly determined Combined Ops could be. But then, so was everyone for whom the organization in Oxford was required to produce evidence.

"The problem is," continued the colonel, "we have no idea of the exact strength of the defences on the island. No one has gone to St Nicolas since the Channel Islands were invaded in 1940. There've been a couple of forays onto the other islands – all of them complete disasters both for the locals and the poor devils that were sent across. They ended up either dead or as P.O.W.'s with nothing to show for their efforts and, I suspect, created an atmosphere of mistrust between the Germans and the civilian population. So what's being suggested here really is a tricky proposition."

"Can't the R.A.F. photography chaps at the I.S.T.D. do a run over the coast of St Nicolas to assess the strength of the defences?" asked Robert.

"They've already tried and can't get in close enough; too much flak. It's not worth taking the risk. We'll need every single plane and pilot we can muster for the invasion, whenever that's going to be. So, we have no choice but to send someone across to St Nicolas."

He looked at the two of them for a moment.

"Hang on a minute…" said Richard, as realization dawned.

"You can't possibly send us, sir," interposed Robert. "We work at Bletchley Park. Once anyone's done that, they're not allowed to go out of the country. Besides which, we know the embryonic Allied invasion plans. We're an absolute security nightmare."

"True, but consider this. We need a Royal Navy man who's highly skilled in navigation and can give an assessment of the coast for a possible large-scale amphibious landing. We need an army man to look at the German garrison and shore batteries in order to assess their precise strength and numbers. We then need to know whether it would be possible to take them by surprise and overrun them quickly."

"There must be any number of servicemen better qualified to do all that than we are," observed Robert. "I'm not exactly *au fait* with the capability of German armaments."

"And I've not been on board a ship in yonks," added Richard.

"Gentlemen, gentlemen. All of that is immaterial. You're forgetting exactly who you are and what you've already achieved."

"But that was before we worked at Bletchley Park." Having raised the subject, Robert was not going to let go of it.

"Of course, and I've always considered that to be a complete waste of your combined talents," said Freddie.

"I haven't," muttered Robert. "I regard it as being nothing less than a privilege."

"Except, of course," continued Ashton hastily, "for that recent thing you uncovered, Robert, which we'll go into in a moment."

Richard looked at his friend quizzically. "What recent thing? You never told me about that, whatever it is." He seemed slightly huffy.

"All in good time, all in good time." Freddie Ashton regarded Richard for a moment before continuing. "Anyway, you've worked together successfully in all sorts of unlikely scenarios. You both speak German – especially you, Bob. And you're fluent in French as well, which is an added advantage on the Channel Islands. You also have first-hand knowledge of how the German army operates. While you, Richard, know St Nicolas like the back of your hand – and have relatives there, aunts, I believe, who could come to your aid if necessary. Therefore, this gives you a greater sway over any previous or future compatriots."

"I wouldn't want to involve Edna and Mae."

"Hopefully not." Freddie smiled again. "But you may have to. And you've been to St Nicolas as well, Bob, I gather. On holiday."

"How did you manage to unearth that little nugget of information?"

Freddie Ashton merely smiled enigmatically before saying, "Now, I'm sure you can see, gentlemen, that all this is to our advantage."

"Whose advantage?" said Robert. When no answer was forthcoming, he asked quietly, "Do we have a choice?"

"Of course."

"Like hell," he muttered.

"As Bob has already pointed out," said Richard, thinking up whatever means he could to dissuade the colonel from sending them on such an impossible mission, "what about our connection to Bletchley Park, sir? That really troubles me. And it ought to trouble the authorities as well."

"Believe me, it does, enormously. But you see there is no choice."

"I thought you said we had a choice." Robert gave Ashton a penetrating look.

The colonel remained silent again and looked down at the map.

"And if we're caught?" asked Robert. "As spies we'll be handed straight over to the *Gestapo*."

Freddie Ashton regarded both of them seriously. "Then you must make damn sure you are not caught, gentlemen. If you should have that misfortune, then this mission becomes a one-way ticket. As you know, MI6 do a nice line in cyanide pills."

Richard was roused to rare anger. "Do you mean to tell me that you're asking us to risk our lives and if caught, run the additional risk of giving away Ultra – our nation's greatest contribution to winning the war – as well as the possible location of the Allied invasion in order to *disprove* some hare-brained scheme that no one thinks will work anyway?"

"Ah, on the surface, perhaps," Colonel Ashton smiled enigmatically. "But there is more to it than that. Bob will know some of what I'm about to say already because it was he who translated and made sense of the original *Abwehr* decrypts and, after he'd spoken to me, was under orders not to tell anyone, even you, Richard. However, things have moved on to such an extent that we now need to take urgent action to counteract some very dangerous developments. So, gentlemen, listen carefully to what I am about to tell you…" and he took a thick folder out from a locked drawer at the bottom of his desk and began to speak.

An hour later, Robert and Richard emerged from his office into the courtyard and looked at each other.

"Bloody hell!" exclaimed Richard.

Robert exhaled sharply. "You're telling me," he said.

The night was dark with a just a glimmer of moonlight. Silently, their oars muffled, the canoes cut through the water.

Rocks loomed out at them: strange shapes, alien in the darkness. A strong current took them shore-wards, their uniforms bulky in their backpacks; their weapons resting against their legs, concealed in the front section of each canoe.

Behind them, the submarine disappeared beneath the waves in a sucking swirl of water, leaving them alone in the all-enveloping opacity.

They paddled on through the night, checking the compass, straining to see through the inky blackness as the moon disappeared behind a cloud; making sure in the diminished visibility that they were not about to encounter unexpected and unwanted visitors.

Eventually, there came the welcome hiss of surf, the sound of waves breaking gently on the shore.

This was it.

They headed for the right hand-side of a little cove, beaching their canvas boats and dragging them along the sand to a type of grotto created by an overhanging cliff. Without hesitating, they shrugged off their backpacks and stripped off their wet clothes, rubbing themselves dry before changing into uniforms and strapping on Lugers.

Together, they bundled up their sodden garments and put them into bags, packing these in the front of their canoes. They tied long ropes around both prows, concealing and securing them tightly in the lush vegetation that abounded in and around the grotto. Together, they lowered the canoes over the edge of the wave-smoothed stones, allowing time for them to fill with water, before paying out the ropes as the boats gradually sank into the deep recesses of the pool.

Satisfied that all was as it should be, Robert and Richard left the security of the hidden cavern and covered their tracks.

Everywhere was quiet, save only for the sound of waves upon the sand.

For a moment, Robert allowed his mind to dwell on exactly where it was they had come to and his heart beat faster with something greater than fear and adrenalin.

She might be here – his lost, unknown girl from the past.

Cautiously and warily, they climbed the steep track. Occasional flurries of shale skittered downwards.

Each time this happened they stopped, hearts pounding, ears alert to the possible sound of patrols and fatal discovery.

But nothing happened.

As they reached the top of the incline, they came across a somnolent German sentry; his snores reverberating around the rocks, his corpulent frame blocking the narrow path; a lit cigarette smouldering in his hand, a rifle propped up by his side.

He was too large to step across and the sides of the gully were too steep to go round him.

Robert and Richard exchanged a brief glance.

The soldier was having a wonderful dream. He was reliving the previous night where, off duty, he'd spent the night with a local girl. His first conquest since coming to the island.

He was about to kiss her when she kicked his foot. Then she kicked it again. Hard. Dozily, he realized this was not part of his dream. He could feel pain.

In sudden panic, he woke up and felt for his gun but his hand grasped thin air. It had gone.

He heard the unmistakable sound of a rifle bolt being drawn back.

In total panic, he called out, *"Nicht schießen! Nicht schießen!"*

Robert laughed harshly. *"Nein, I will not shoot you. But you neglect your duty, soldier. You are lucky we are not British commandos."*

The soldier struggled to attention.

"I am very sorry, Herr Kapitän. It will not happen again." He was surely going to be court-martialled now. And then shot. Inwardly, he cursed the girl who'd kept him awake all night.

"Gut. Then make sure it doesn't. I will say nothing on this occasion. But if I should hear ever again that you have fallen asleep on sentry duty..."

"Ja, Herr Kapitän. It will not happen again."

"Then we shall let the matter drop." He gave the sentry his rifle back.

"Danke schön, Herr Kapitän." The soldier was so busy thanking the captain and his lucky escape that he completely failed to question how Robert and Richard could possibly have emerged from the seaward side of him.

Glancing back, they saw him standing rigidly to attention, his eyes scanning the horizon; his rifle poised to repel a whole army of invaders.

Once they were out of earshot, Richard whispered, "God, I'm glad it's you I'm with on clandestine missions. That was jolly quick thinking."

"Nein," replied Robert self-effacingly, "I learned the hard way, my friend. However, although it's nearly morning, we do need to hole up somewhere until it's fully light. To wander around on our own in the semidarkness is not a good idea."

"We could try my aunts' farm. It's not too far away."

"I thought you said you didn't want to involve them."

"I don't, but they might offer us breakfast and we'll work better on a full stomach. I'm starving!"

248

"It would be better to just hide in a barn and find food later."

"Maybe, but I think we ought to make contact, if only as an insurance policy."

When they arrived at the farmhouse, a light was on in the kitchen. From the way the shadows flickered as the occupants moved around, Robert deduced it was an oil lamp. Was there no blackout on the island?

Richard took a deep breath and knocked at the door. "I hope she doesn't come at us with a shotgun."

"This is German-occupied territory, not the Wild West, you numbskull," said Robert.

The two men exchanged a wry smile.

However, Edna was not smiling as she opened the door to find two German officers standing on the threshold knowing that inside the kitchen, she had an escaped Russian slave worker eating breakfast at the kitchen table, an illegal chicken waiting to be cooked for dinner in a pot in the oven and out of the corner of her eye, Mae about to collapse in a heap on the floor.

For a split second no one moved.

"Hello, Aunt Edna," said her nephew brightly. "Aren't you going to let us in?"

"Good grief! Richard!" she exclaimed. "Come inside. Quickly, quickly!"

Whereupon Edna stood back to allow the two men inside before closing the door and locking it. Immediately, Robert went to Mae's aid.

"Do you have any smelling salts?" he asked.

"Oh... er... yes," Edna stammered. "On the dresser, there."

"Sorry to shock you, Auntie," said Richard, as they watched Robert kneel down on the floor raising Mae's head to administer the reviving substance. "This is my friend Bob Anderson."

"Ah," was all Edna could manage. She was lost for words, oscillating between shock, relief and joy, experiencing each emotion without recovering from the existing one.

Coughing and spluttering, Mae came round and almost fainted again when she saw she was being supported by a German officer.

"He was starving," she muttered imploringly. "Edna told me not to take him in, but he looked so pathetic and so thin standing there on the doorstep. He was in rags, begging for food, so I invited him into the kitchen. I hadn't the heart to send him away. We'll be sent to a concentration camp now won't we?" And she promptly burst into tears.

Kindly and reassuringly, Robert said, "It's all right, we're not German. In fact, we're very British. And if you look across the room there, you'll see someone whom I have no doubt you'll recognize." He helped her up into a sitting position and Mae did as she was asked.

"Richard!" she exclaimed, relief flooding through her. "Dearest boy! What on earth are you doing here? You shouldn't be here. It's much too dangerous!"

"Don't worry, Auntie Mae," he said, coming across the room to help Robert lift his aunt onto a chair. "We'll be all right. We can't tell you why we're here though, nor must you tell anyone that you've seen us." He introduced Robert again, this time to Mae.

"Thank you for rescuing my sister," Edna said to Robert. "She is quite delicate."

"That's all right. But we must be on our way. We don't want to risk putting you in any danger…"

All at once, into the farmyard came the sound of lorries arriving and the slamming of doors combined with loud guttural instructions to search the house and outbuildings to be followed almost immediately by an impatient hammering at the door.

"Open up immediately or we shall be forced to break it down."

"Goodness me! Goodness me!" quavered Mae.

With rapid, dexterous movements, Robert pushed the astounded, trembling Russian under the table, ensuring he was completely hidden by the generous folds of the chenille tablecloth, threw off his cap, undid the top buttons of his jacket, put his booted foot up on the spare chair and made it seem as though he was in the middle of eating the meal at the table.

Following Robert's lead, Richard grabbed a cup and poured himself some tea.

The hammering resumed. "Open up! Now! *Schnell, schnell!*"

Edna looked across at Robert, who nodded.

"I am coming!" she said. "Be patient, be patient. I am but an old woman."

Robert had to admire her nerve and knew that he could rely on her in a crisis. He hoped her sister would be just as coolheaded if put to the test.

As Edna unlocked and opened the door, a leather-coated man, accompanied by two armed soldiers pushed his way past her: the man's slicked-back hair garnering in Robert both the shock of recognition and of having unexpectedly hit the jackpot so soon after their arrival.

Seeing Robert and Richard seated at the kitchen table, the man said, hiding his annoyance, "*Ach, I see the Wehrmacht are here before me. Even so, this house is to be searched. I have reason to believe you are harbouring an escaped Russian prisoner.*"

"*The house has been searched already*," said Robert, with a shrug of his shoulders, adopting the polite insolence and scarcely-concealed dislike with which the *Wehrmacht* and *Waffen-SS* officers treated each other, "*as well as the barns and the outhouses. There is nothing.*"

"*Nevertheless, I wish to see for myself.*" The man directed the soldiers upstairs.

He studied Robert and Richard closely. He had not seen these two before in Port le Bac and since his arrival on the island, had made it his business to identify every single occupying soldier by sight. It was possible he could have missed a few, of course. There were so many, a couple of thousand of them at least and by his reckoning, there were about three German soldiers for every local person. And that didn't include his own department, which was expanding rapidly.

However, the man's well-honed instinct told him that this might turn out to be better than anything he could have hoped for. An escaped Russian *and* a couple of spies. His credibility rating would go up again if that proved to be the case.

"The weather is nice for the time of year, yes?" he said pleasantly in English, all the while watching Robert closely.

"*What did you say?*" came the reply.

"*Do you not speak English?*"

250

"Englisch? Nein, nein!" and Robert turned his attention to mopping up egg yolk with the remains of his bread.

"There is stormy weather on the way, I hear," said Edna evenly. "It could become very rough."

The man stared at her contemptuously.

After some time, the soldiers came back downstairs at the same time as the others arrived from the yard.

"There is no one," they said.

"You are sure?"

"Yes, absolutely."

"Verdammt!"

The leather-coated man had been so sure that, following a tipoff by his most trusted snitch – a useful and accommodating native Channel islander with a grudge against just about everyone – that the escapee was holed up here.

He glanced at Mae, looking pale and wan.

Sensing weakness, he smiled. *She will crumble easily*, he thought.

He thrust his face up close to hers and prodded her chest with his finger.

"Do you know the penalty for hiding an escaped slave? You will be tortured then sent to a concentration camp where you will surely die. If you cooperate and tell me where he is," and he allowed his voice to soften, "I will make sure that nothing bad happens to you and you are not sent to a concentration camp."

"I have no idea what you're talking about," said Mae quietly. "There is no one here."

He stood up straight. "Next time, old woman, I will take you with me and we can spend time together at *Geheime Feldpolizei* headquarters in Port le Bac. You'll be begging to tell me everything I need to know by the time I've finished with you."

"I will not," replied Mae, a hint of defiance in her eyes, her bottom lip trembling.

Angered by her response, the leather-coated man slapped her across the face with the back of his hand using all the force he could muster.

Immediately, Edna went to her aid but Mae stoically remained upright and resolute, despite her mouth and nose being covered in blood.

While he admired her courage, inwardly, Robert was worried for her. He knew that in many ways, her kind of bravery was the most foolish.

"That's how to get what you want," the man in the black coat said to Robert, who continued to sit impassively, giving nothing away; concealing his own bitter dislike for this man and for what he had just done.

"Work on her after I am gone. Do what you like. See what you can find out."

When Robert failed to respond, the man stared at him and realized that this officer was not easily cowed but neither was he openly hostile as so many members of the *Wehrmacht* were these days. He perceived an inner strength that would take a long time to break.

He liked this attitude in a man. It was most attractive. He sensed a challenge, a game.

He addressed Robert again. *"What is my name?"*

"Do you not remember?" came the reply, delivered with a raised eyebrow that held a touch of finely judged insolence.

"*Ja. But I wish you to tell me who I am. Do you not know?*" he said, hoping to catch out this officer with his opening gambit. If these two had just arrived – and he was certain they had – then would not know who he was.

"*Of course I know,*" replied Robert. "*How could I not? You are Herr Abetz. Theodor Abetz.*"

Stymied at the first hurdle, Abetz's face reflected a moment of anger before he reluctantly took his leave.

The game was only just beginning.

"*When you have finished with her, search the premises again,*" he said to Robert. "*Report anything you find to me.*"

"*Ja,*" responded Robert laconically. "*But there is nothing. It would seem your sources were inaccurate on this occasion.*"

"*Perhaps.*" Abetz stood framed in the doorway, his slicked back hair and shiny black coat sinister against the half-light. "*But I don't think so.*" He addressed Edna and Mae. "*Be warned. You have both been lucky today but rest assured, I shall be back and I do not intend to go away empty-handed next time.*"

He slammed the door behind him as he left.

Richard went to say something but Robert stopped him, moving over to the window and discreetly watching Theodor Abetz get into his car.

He stayed there for a long time, making sure that Abetz had driven away with the two lorries and the full complement of soldiers inside them.

Robert had to be certain that they had all gone; he had to make sure no one had remained behind to disturb them. They could not risk a surprise interruption while they decided on the best course of action to fulfil both their mission and ensure the safety of Richard's aunts.

Standing there at the window, he remembered Theodore Abetz in the seedy bar in Brussels with Erika.

He remembered the claustrophobic life he had led as part of the *Abwehr*.

He felt once more the haunting nightmare of possible detection and of being hunted down and Robert wondered if he had the strength to do it all again.

But this time it was different. This time, as long as he and Richard managed to stay free and clear, *he* was the hunter. However, he would have to keep reminding himself of that fact otherwise he might find himself unable to cope.

CHAPTER 32

Seeblick

At last, the warm, spring weather was beginning to reach the mountains and a slow thaw began to set in around Seeblick and the surrounding area until the compound was no longer covered by snow. The gardeners were able to dig over the soil and plant their vegetable seeds and Heinrich suggested a patch of ground that might be suitable for growing flowers. One or two budding horticulturists took up this idea and set about its creation.

People began to take an interest in outdoor pursuits. Games became very popular with football, handball and P.T. sessions being the preferred options. The ladies' 'Keep-Fit' classes were a particular favourite – especially among the onlooking men who proved themselves to be a regular, appreciative and very enthusiastic audience.

Indoors, the drama society was by now well established, aiming to produce a play or a review at least once a month. Here, Sophie was in her element, becoming deeply involved with the performances both on the stage and behind the scenes. Also, she continued to discharge her duties as librarian and overseeing camp life alongside the Commodore, Marian and lately, Dr Reynolds. And, she found plenty of time to read.

It was ironical that she was able to find happiness and such a measure of contentment here, of all places, in a prison camp. She was never bored as some protested they were. She was never one to bemoan their situation, as many did – and frequently – nor did she complain or refuse to join in as some did.

Philosophically, she made the best of everything on offer and behind all of this she was always aware of the benign presence of the *Kommandant*, whose blue eyes she often saw directed at her and whose kind manner and sense of humour always made her smile. His behaviour towards her was exemplary and she was grateful for this. She didn't want things to be complicated; she preferred them just as they were.

However, a tiny part of her acknowledged that she found him attractive but, she told herself, it was wrong to have that kind of feeling for him. Very wrong.

One warm and sunny day she went to the Big House to deliver some returned library books where, through the open door of his office, she saw the *Kommandant* agitatedly pacing the floor. Unusually, he seemed irritated by something. He looked up and saw her observing him.

"Are you all right?" she ventured.

"No. I am most displeased and upset."

"Oh?"

He stood still. "Do you have a moment that you could spare me?"

"Of course."

She went inside his room, where he closed the door behind her and indicated that Sophie should sit in one of the easy chairs by the fireplace, where a small fire burned in the grate. He did not sit down himself but stood leaning against the mantelpiece, agitatedly changing his position every few moments.

"I have just now discovered from the Commodore that there are certain members of the internees who seem intent on disrupting the smooth running of our camp. He has stumbled across letters these people wish to send home and also to the Red Cross insinuating that conditions and facilities here are very poor and that they are not being well-looked after or catered for. I find that insulting! What more can they expect? Why would they want to do such a thing? I fail to understand."

"So do I." Sophie wondered who this could be and concluded that Gert and Mabel were the obvious suspects.

"There are many new improvements that have been undertaken. The school is flourishing. Two new teachers have been trained and therefore my temporary services in the classroom are no longer required, yet they bemoan the fact that I instruct their children as though I was some kind of monster."

"That's so unfair. The children were and still are very fond of you. Everyone I know has said what a fine teacher you are."

"That is kind. For my part, I am sorry not to have continued but I was no longer needed and thought it best that the children were taught by islanders. Besides, the administrative tasks imposed on me from higher authorities place a considerable burden upon my time and stamina. In many ways, it is therefore a relief to have given it up, but I have no doubt whatsoever that I would much prefer to teach class than do tedious paperwork."

"What else did the Commodore say?"

"He said that they think I am a cruel and unfeeling person."

Sophie was shocked. "But nothing could be further from the truth! You're regarded by the vast majority as a trusted person in their lives. They think of you as a friend and as a gentleman."

Heinrich sat down in the chair opposite her and with her words, seemed to relax a little.

"Thank you," he said, wondering how she regarded him. After a moment, he said, "I tour the camp and talk to people…"

"I know and it's very much appreciated."

"I enjoy it."

"So do they."

"Do you?"

Sidestepping his question, Sophie said, "I mean, what is there to moan about? The kitchen is fully operational, the meals prepared and cooked now by a rota of very capable islanders. Therefore, even the quality of the food provided by the prison authorities has improved. The Red Cross parcels are regular and plentiful and they supplement and enhance our diet. We are very lucky." *To have you allowing us to do this*, she thought.

He saw the blush in her cheeks and drew closer towards the edge of his chair.

"There are any number of trades and skills here among the islanders. The artists especially deserve great credit, they are most talented and do much fine work. They have produced some beautiful cards," he said.

"I know. Then there are shoemakers and repairers…"

"Who are most ingenious with their use of Red Cross boxes. I have never seen such fine footwear made from so very little."

"And there are classes in just about anything – dressmaking, English Literature…"

"Architecture, drawing, painting…"

"German, French, Italian…"

"Crafts and toy-making…"

"Even boatbuilding and design."

Immersed in their conversation, Sophie smiled at him and Heinrich felt his spirit soar.

"You realize that I do know all about the courses in electronics and radio construction," he said, giving her a knowing wink, his good humour restored.

Sophie opened her eyes wide in fear and embarrassment. "You do? We thought we'd managed to keep that quiet."

"Oh ho, you did, did you?" Heinrich laughed and said, "It is all right, I will not tell the authorities, but I *shall* warn you in advance when the *SS* come to call. We must make sure that your radio construction efforts are well hidden otherwise I shall be in deep trouble as well."

Sophie smiled at him appreciatively. "Thank you," she said. "With everything that's going on in the camp, I don't see how anyone can possibly be bored or discontented or think that you're some kind of monster."

"And how about you," he asked softly. "Are you contented?"

For a moment she held his gaze and his heart began to beat a little faster. He inched closer to her.

"Yes," she said honestly. "I am." She hesitated. "You see I'm doing all the things I enjoy the most."

"But behind barbed wire?"

"A minor inconvenience," she quipped lightly.

Heinrich smiled. "So, you are doing everything you enjoy most. Except there is one thing missing."

"Oh?" Sophie was puzzled.

"Your work on the farm and your horses." The words slipped out before he could stop them.

She looked at him in amazement. "How do you know I like to ride? I've never told you that."

"Ach! Das ist peinlich. Ich habe schon zu viel gesagt," he said, forgetting that Sophie could speak German.

"Why is it awkward that you've said too much?" she asked.

Heinrich's pale cheeks flushed a dull red. He decided to be open with her. "Because I am camp censor."

"Oh." It was Sophie's turn to blush as the truth dawned. "And you read everyone's letters?"

"Yes."

"Including mine?"

"Yes."

Then he must know how often she mentioned him. Sophie sat still for a moment uncertain as to what to do or say. All she could feel was the steady and penetrating blueness of his eyes as they regarded her.

He moved towards her, intending to take her hand.

Sophie almost leapt out of her chair and said abruptly, "I must go and put these books away."

"Of course," he said softly.

Quickly, she left the *Kommandant*'s office, her heart beating wildly, not with fear but with a sensation that she found both pleasant and disturbing. Hastily, she sought the sanctuary of the library where she sat staring out of the window, half wishing that he might follow her.

In the event, it only took a few days to root out the troublemakers. The main culprit was, as Sophie had surmised, Gert, aided and abetted by Mabel.

"Have you actually sent any letters?" asked Sophie, when the two women were interviewed by the Commodore, Marian and herself.

Both women flushed a guilty red.

"Yeah," muttered Gert sullenly. "We smuggled 'em out of the camp with the men in the lorry taking the internal mail to Würzach. We'd found out the Red Cross was visiting so we asked them that's at Würzach to give 'em our letters."

"But why would you do such a thing? Why would you make up all these lies?" asked the Commodore, deeply upset.

"'Cos we're bleedin' well fed up wiv being 'ere, ain't we, Mabel? We've 'ad enough. We want to go 'ome."

"Well, we can't, so there's no point in making life any more difficult for everyone than it is. The *Kommandant*'s a good man and we're very fortunate. What on earth were you thinking of?" The Commodore was genuinely upset.

Marian was not so restrained. "How dare you do this! We're well treated here and now that things are becoming more organized, our lives are improving. We don't need stupid women like you messing things up for us. The *Kommandant* would be quite within his rights to take away our privileges and make life harder for us again."

"As it is," said the Commodore gravely, "we can't let this matter go unpunished." He thought for a moment. "You two are on toilet cleaning duty for a fortnight. It's about time you did something to earn your keep."

"You can't do that."

"I can and I am."

Gert folded her arms defiantly. "Just try and make us."

"If you don't do as you're told, you can spend the time in Bow Street and the whole camp will know exactly what it is you have tried to do. In that situation, I'll make damn sure that your lives *are* made an absolute misery."

"You wouldn't dare!" said Mabel.

"Believe me, I would. There are many people who've had about as much of your moaning and groaning and general nastiness as they can stand. A bit of time to reflect on your behaviour won't go amiss. Neither of you have done anything to contribute to the general good or made any effort to try and make things happier and more bearable here."

"It's not a bleedin' 'oliday camp," muttered Gert sullenly.

256

"I think we're all very well aware of that. We're *all* very well aware of the barbed wire and the armed policemen and the fact that we're stuck here for the duration, however long that might be. We all have times when we're fed up and feel hemmed in and we'd all like to go home because we miss our homes, our friends and our families. But we can't so we have to face up to our situation and make the best of things."

"Well I ain't," and she folded her arms defiantly.

"Why not?" said Marian.

"I ain't gonna go round 'elping any bleeding Krauts, am I? There's lots that feels the same as wot I do."

"How is helping your fellow islanders helping the Germans?" Sophie was mystified.

"Well, if you don't know, I can't say." Gert was on the defensive now.

Mabel had had enough. "C'mon, Gert," she said. "We've done wrong and let's accept our punishment and get out of here."

"I'm not a child."

"Well, you're certainly not behaving like an adult," observed Marian.

"So when does our punishment take effect?" asked Mabel.

"As of now," replied the Commodore.

"What about the kids?" asked Mabel. "My youngest has got an 'orrible sore throat."

"And Tommy's been complaining of an 'eadache and sore throat as well."

"They're not the only two. A lot of children and some of the adults have developed the same symptoms just recently. But don't worry, they'll be taken care of," said Marian, thinking that this pair of women really were the limit.

"They'd better be," said Gert. If she thought about it, she didn't feel too good herself.

She and Mabel disappeared out of the door into the compound, heading towards their hut, with Gert still muttering rebelliously.

"So," said the Commodore, "which of us is going to inform the *Kommandant*? I've got to go and sort out a simmering problem between two of the men that developed into a fistfight yesterday. After that, I shall write a mitigating letter to the Red Cross to rectify this unfortunate situation."

"And I promised Doctor Reynolds that I would do a stint in the infirmary this afternoon. He's rushed off his feet at the moment. He thinks it might be some kind of epidemic brewing as so many people are going down with similar symptoms."

Although she was worried by the possibility of an epidemic, Sophie smiled. It had not gone unnoticed that Marian and the doctor were spending a great deal of time in each other's company.

"It's because," added the older woman hastily, in order to hide her own embarrassment, "neither the German doctor nor the nurse from the village are able to come. She's very unwell herself and the doctor has his work cut out dealing with an outbreak of scarlet fever in the town."

"Oh?" The Commodore was concerned. "I hope it doesn't spread to here."

"So do I. Fortunately, we're quite remote so Dr Reynolds is hoping we'll be all right. But he is anxious because the symptoms here are identical to the onset of scarlet fever. Anyway, I must dash. Sophie, dear, it looks like you'll have to go and tell our *Kommandant* that we've sorted things out."

"It does, rather, doesn't it?"

With some trepidation, having nothing else to prevent her from carrying out this task, Sophie made her way to the Big House. On her arrival, she was told by the duty guard that the *Kommandant* had a visitor and that she should wait or come back later.

Sophie decided to go to the library and read for a while before trying again. Unusually, the room was deserted and in her ledger, she began to tick off the returned books that had been left on the table and put them back in their place on the shelves.

It felt very hot in the room and she took off her jumper. She sat down and began to catalogue some new books. She heard the door latch click and looked up to see the *Kommandant* appear in the doorway. He shut the door behind him and came to sit beside her.

"Hello," he said.

How lovely she looked.

"Hello," she replied, confusion welling up inside her.

"You wished to see me?" he said hopefully.

"Yes. To let you know that the two women who were responsible for those letters have been put on cleaning duties for a fortnight and that the Commodore is going to contact the Red Cross to make everything right again."

"Oh." Hiding his disappointment that her visit was not of a more personal nature, he said, "*Ach*, but this is good it has been dealt with and resolved so quickly. They will not try anything like that again I imagine."

"No, I think not." She moved to stand up but felt dizzy. It was so hot.

"Don't go," he said softly, holding onto her hand and keeping her beside him.

"I must," she said, trying to remove her hand from his without success as she seemed to have lost all her energy.

"Why?"

"Because..."

All manner of excuses went through her mind: it was too dangerous, it wasn't appropriate; she couldn't deal with his attentions or her own emotions.

Of course, she said none of those things and they just stared at each other for what seemed like an eternity before Heinrich took her other hand.

"You cannot deny this attraction between us any longer."

"I can and I will," she replied defiantly.

Tenderly, he placed his hand on her cheek and smiled as he felt its warmth. He leant forward and kissed her lips.

It was a gentle kiss, lingering and sweet, one that made no demands on her but contained enough strength to hold Sophie and Heinrich in its spell until, a little later, they heard the thump of approaching footsteps.

Quickly, they drew apart and Heinrich stood up.

"*We shall meet again soon, meine Liebe?*" he asked softly in German.

Her eyes cast down, Sophie nodded imperceptibly.

He touched her cheek again and left the room before they were discovered.

258

That night, tossing and turning, unable to sleep, feeling alternately hot and cold, Sophie traced RLA's initials on her bunk; reliving every moment of the *Kommandant*'s kiss in her mind, moments that led her on innocent flights of fantasy; silently communing to RLA everything that she felt.

For RLA had become her solace: a silent consoling presence to whom, in the absence of a truly close friend, she inwardly confided her deepest fears and deepest wishes.

Tonight these were profound indeed and nothing could calm her confusion of mind and spirit.

There was no future in any relationship with Heinrich Hoffmeister. It was all wrong. It shouldn't be happening; it was an impossible situation. Even if they kept everything secret, it was still impossible.

She liked her world to be ordered and safe. Her contact with Heinrich had become neither ordered nor safe. Once again, she felt as though she was being swept along by events over which she had no control.

She touched the initials again in the hope that she might rediscover her former simplicity of mind. But to do that, she needed to talk to the real RLA, whoever he was, and not just the fragment of him, a remnant left behind.

It never occurred to her that he might be very different from the person she imagined him to be. He had become such a positive certainty in her mind that, together with the grownup boy on the beach, he had taken on the mantle of everything she had ever desired in a man.

Once again, she thought of Heinrich's kiss and the gentleness of his touch. It was undeniably pleasurable but lacked the passionate immediacy of the first kiss between the lovers in *La Chaleur de la Mer*: a first kiss Sophie had always dreamt of experiencing.

She chastised herself. Novels were rarely like real life were they?

But, she told herself firmly, whatever her feelings might or might not be, this had to stop before it went any further.

Better to do that now before it becomes really dangerous, she thought. *Better to do that now before the whole thing spirals out of control.*

CHAPTER 33

St Nicolas

The sea was sparkling in the bright sunlight, its reflection dancing off the waves. Robert pulled his German officer's cap lower down over his forehead, shielding his eyes from the piercing diamond glints, as he walked along the cliff edge studying the monstrous concrete ramparts and gun turrets already in place and those being constructed, notating his observations on a clipboard.

As he approached, the *SS Todt* organization guards supervising the workers regarded him with passive indifference before returning their attention towards their group of emaciated slaves hacking deep trenches out of the rocky terrain, kicking them if they slacked for a moment in their task, beating them as they struggled to put great concrete slabs in place.

The *SS* soldiers wore their black uniforms and distinctive insignia with glacial arrogance; their immutable attitude reflected in the harsh lines of their faces. They had been especially chosen for this task and carried out their brutality with no thought of the pain they were inflicting.

Robert turned away, sickened by what he saw, needing every sinew of self-control not to protest and prevent the monstrous ill-treatment of these men, women and children by pushing every single one of the guards off the edge of the cliff.

"*I hope you're not considering making a fuss,*" said a voice behind him, making him jump. "*Like one of your fellow Wehrmacht officers did last week. He objected to the treatment of these sub-humans as our beloved Führer has categorized the East European Slavic race. I had the officer in question court-martialled for his intervention. He will not do such a thing again.*"

A shiver of fear traversed Robert's spine; not just for the picture of absolute cold-heartedness this incident presented but also for the realization that Theodor Abetz must have been observing him.

How long had he been there, wondered Robert? How much of his own physical revulsion had Abetz witnessed?

Robert chastised himself for being careless and allowing himself to become so absorbed in his surroundings that he had not noticed Abetz's arrival. He berated himself for his lapse of concentration. Somehow, he had to recapture and maintain the mindset he had had while working at the *Abwehr*.

But Robert knew he was finding this increasingly elusive. He wondered whether it was because of Richard, Edna and Mae or being surrounded by English people all day every day that made it more difficult to maintain his new persona. Or whether, after so long at home and because of his intense experiences while in Germany, he had reached the limit of his endurance in this particular situation.

It was all of those things, he concluded. More than ever, therefore, he had to be on the alert at all times, knowing he could not let down his guard, even for a moment. It was not just his own safety that was at stake this time, but the people he was responsible for and to – Richard, Edna, Mae, his country, even Admiral Siranac.

He looked round and saw the black Citroën and the driver. How could he not have been aware of Abetz's arrival? And why was he here? Had Abetz followed him or was his presence mere coincidence?

"What brings you up here?" asked Robert with an outward calm that masked his inner tension.

Abetz appeared to find the question insolent. *"That is not your concern. However, it is my concern to ask the question of you."*

"Why? I am entitled to go where I am sent on duty."

"By whose authority?"

Robert gave the name of a high-ranking *Wehrmacht* officer.

"You have papers giving the necessary orders?"

Robert produced the required documents.

"You will find that all is correct."

During the week they had been on St Nicolas, he and Richard had made rapid strides insinuating themselves into the occupying force. By night they slept in the cellar or the barn at the farmhouse; by day they mingled with the off-duty soldiers in Port le Bac or at the *Soldatenheim*, sometimes together, sometimes separately; drinking beer and gleaning titbits of useful information but never staying long enough for anyone to ask just *exactly* who they were.

It was a situation fraught with potential jeopardy.

Robert spent time in the harbour café drinking endless cups of tea or coffee with the officers, listening to and joining in conversations while Richard searched the disused silver mines and underground caverns that abounded on the western seaboard of the island; both of them taking calculated risks – such as Robert's fortuitous and *bona fide* official study of the progress of the defences on the island.

He hoped that the officer from whom he had acquired this particular duty and, temporarily, his identity (having rescued him in a parlous, drunken state the previous evening in the *Soldatenheim* and discovered his intense desire to be elsewhere the following day rather than carry out his orders) was having a fruitful time with his new lady friend.

He and Richard had also ascertained that Theodor Abetz generated a great deal of resentment and intense dislike among the decent German officers who felt that since his arrival, he had wielded power above and beyond that of his appointment. These officers avoided his company whenever possible, expressing open disapproval for his brutal methods of interrogation at the *Geheime Feldpolizei* headquarters, feeling there was no place for it on an island where the vast majority of the general population were law-abiding and docile.

These officers did not share Abetz's fanatical view that subversiveness was rife on St Nicolas and therefore needed to be rooted out; they did not agree that the occupation should be carried out under a regime of constant fear and harassment.

Many were disgusted by his vociferous support for his fellow *SS* in their inhumane treatment and near starvation of the slaves as the latter constructed Hitler's dream of making the Channel Islands an impregnable fortress.

Most of the *Wehrmacht* soldiers were just glad to be where they were and not on the Eastern Front; happy with their lot in this warm and pleasant paradise, despite the boredom, despite the frequent food shortages and physical restrictions of living on a crowded island.

Robert had also discovered that in secret, one or two high-ranking *Wehrmacht* officers were even considering assassination.

"*So, what is your reason for being up here?*" asked Abetz, shifting his attaché case into his other hand and standing so close to Robert that the stench of his breath made the latter's stomach churn.

"*My superior officers need a report on progress. Just as it states in the document you have just read.*"

Theodor Abetz regarded Robert with the disappointed look of someone who has just lost his favourite toy. He had been so sure there was something suspicious about this man and his friend whom he had first encountered last week in that broken-down old farmhouse and whom he had more recently observed in and around the town.

The document was genuine as well, even if the officer's name to whom it referred was indecipherable. No matter. He would find out who had issued these orders and to whom.

However, he still found it odd that until now, no one had seemed to know exactly who these two men were. And Abetz had been irritated by the *Kommandant*'s apparent lack of concern and cooperation with his probing and requests for assistance. He had been angered by the refusal to provide him with the soldiers he had demanded to carry out round-the-clock surveillance of the two men.

Neither had his superiors in Paris acceded to his repeated requests for cooperation, stating that in the past, every time he had asked for some supposed spy or miscreant to be rooted out, his suspicions were proved to be totally unfounded.

They told him to go away and to stop wasting their time.

Abetz, highly insulted by their attitude towards him, had retorted by calling them *Dummköpfe* who wanted to believe that nothing was amiss by burying their heads in the sand. Afterwards, he realized that by doing this, he had not done himself any favours.

But – how dare they call his ideas *lächerlich*! How dare they say such a thing to Theodor Abetz, holder of the Iron Cross for services rendered to the beloved Fatherland! There was nothing ridiculous about his ideas, nothing at all. How dare they not listen to his well-founded assertions that St Nicolas was crawling with British spies and subversive residents!

He'd show them. He'd show the hierarchy in Berlin as well as the *Wehrmacht* on St Nicolas that he was still a good officer in the *SS*. He'd show them that he wasn't a failure because he'd been unable to bring down Admiral Siranac. He'd show them that he hadn't been careless or negligent in failing to protect his idol Reinhard Ziegler from assassination in Karodice in Czechoslovakia the previous year. He'd even fought off the assassins and wounded one of them in the gun battle, hadn't he?

Despite this, he'd been court-martialled, only narrowly avoiding the firing squad because of his previously impeccable record and by literally begging on his knees to be allowed to assist in tracking down the perpetrators.

He'd done that successfully, hadn't he? And been given the responsibility of punishing of those who had shielded them, letting his superiors know of its success but at the same time, covering his tracks in case there were any repercussions in the future; realizing that in the heat of his zealousness, he had gone too far, even venturing beyond his orders, by obliterating the little village and its inhabitants off the face of the earth.

As a precaution, therefore, he knew he must keep with him at all times the documents that exonerated himself from blame and cleverly laid the onus on someone else, keeping them under lock and key in his attaché case; never letting the latter out of his sight, never letting anyone see the contents.

Yet, despite this, despite the brilliance of his actions in redeeming himself, he'd been sent to this stupid little island from where he was supposed to plan and execute The Great Idea – an audacious suggestion he supposed Admiral Siranac had concocted to keep him out of the way, knowing it would never succeed or that logistically, he would never be able to carry it out from a hellhole such as this.

But he'd show them. He would make it succeed and if he did, he would become great again in the eyes of the Nazi hierarchy. He'd do it for the glory of the Third Reich and in the process, what glory he would reap upon his own head!

Therefore, until the opportunity arose to put The Great Idea (devised by him since coming to the island and the only copy of which – written in his own hand and not yet shared with anyone as it was *his* scheme and his alone – also resided safe and sound in his attaché case) into action, he'd continue with his assigned duties and investigate these two elusive officers, even if he had to work alone, and prove that his suspicions had been correct. He'd begin by taking this one in for questioning now.

Yet even as he made this resolution, Theodor Abetz hesitated, surprising himself by an unaccustomed reluctance. There was something different about this particular officer who stood before him; something that intrigued and yes, attracted him – something he hadn't felt since Reinhard's untimely demise.

Abetz decided to cultivate him.

"*The defences are coming on, are they not?*" he observed casually, lighting a cigarette and blowing the smoke languidly into Robert's face. "*The Allies will dare not invade and the Channel Islands, like France and the rest of mainland Europe, will be part of the glorious Third Reich for a thousand years.*"

What a load of drivel, thought Robert, coughing pointedly.

"*What brings an important man like you to St Nicolas?*" he asked conversationally after a while, not expecting to be told anything revealing but surmising that flattery might reveal a chink in this man's egotistical armour.

With habitual disdain, Abetz was about to insult Robert for asking such a stupidly insignificant question but changed his mind on hearing the word 'important'.

"*I was ordered here by the Führer himself.*"

He regarded Robert for a moment and, gratified by what he took to be an expression of personal admiration towards himself, decided to toy with him and then pursue him to satisfy his own needs; something to brighten his dull, insipid existence on this dull, insipid island where sexual encounters (wherever and whenever he could find them) and extracting information from prisoners, were his only diversions of any consequence.

Besides, who knew what nuggets of information such a pursuit of this man might reveal?

"What brings you here?" he asked, allowing his manner to soften.

"My duties."

For an absurd moment, Robert wanted to ask him about Erika, about Admiral Siranac; to persuade him to reveal the true reason for his coming to St Nicolas – a place that Abetz must regard as something of a comedown after the dizzy heights of Brussels, Paris and Berlin.

Robert wondered whether Abetz had blotted his copybook in some way.

He thought of the coded messages uncovered at Bletchley Park – warning messages that seemed to emanate exclusively from *Abwehr* headquarters with enough evidence to place Abetz at the centre of a conspiracy to carry out a daring incursion onto the British mainland.

The revelations that Robert had interpreted in the decrypts were deemed dangerous enough for the British secret service to risk all by sending him to St Nicolas: firstly, because of his ability to identify Abetz; secondly, his first-hand knowledge of his character and thirdly, because it was assumed that Robert would not fall prey to Abetz's renowned chicanery.

"How have you found the women here?" asked Abetz, lowering his voice to a confidential level, hoping to engage Robert's interest in his own favourite pastime.

"Not to my taste," replied Robert, thinking quickly.

"When I can get away, I go across to the brothel set up by our brothers-in-arms on Guernsey," said Abetz. *"It's full of delicious French whores and handpicked local girls who, after a bit of persuasion, are most accommodating to my, shall we say, decadent little proclivities. Perhaps we should go together sometime?"*

No chance, thought Robert. He smiled. *"Perhaps."*

"You like women?"

Robert shrugged.

A lascivious smile curled the corners of Abetz's lips. *"Or maybe you prefer men?"* He placed his hand on Robert's shoulder. When Robert neither drew away nor replied to his question, Abetz accepted this as acquiescence and said, *"I use both. It makes no difference to me."* He shrugged his shoulders. *"They each serve their purpose."*

"Really?" said Robert, shocked by such an admission; keeping his voice neutral, offering neither censure nor encouragement; hiding his inner revulsion of this man. He thought of Erika and her maltreatment, and sensed a dangerous turn to the conversation.

Drawing closer to his prey, Abetz whispered in Robert's ear; his manner tinged with calculated seductiveness. *"I know of somewhere suitable, somewhere we can be alone and undisturbed."*

"I have my duties to perform," said Robert, his bearing rigid, his mouth dry with fear. *"If you'll excuse me, I must continue with my survey."*

"Of course." Abetz squeezed Robert's shoulder and reluctantly removed his hand. *"I shall leave you to proceed. But if you should ever..."*

"Thank you."

Abetz's hooded eyes followed Robert as he continued along the cliff edge, a growing desire playing around the edges of his mind; a desire that began to take serious hold.

Yes. He'd focus on snaring this man to satisfy his own needs. He would allow it to develop into a tantalizing game for them both, during which, he would ultimately sweep away any reluctance with his guile and seductive powers.

There was no doubt whatsoever in his mind as to the eventual outcome.

And afterwards, when he had grown tired of this particular quarry, he would have the officer tortured and shot as the spy his intuition told him that he was.

Abetz smiled maliciously. Yes, it would be fun.

"I was nearly sick on the spot," remarked Robert that night, as he and Richard lay on their mattresses in the cellar at the farmhouse comparing notes and progress, or rather the lack of it. "It was the most revolting encounter I've ever had with the most revolting human being I've ever met."

"I can imagine. But look at it this way, if he does fancy you, it might be useful. You could see if he takes you into his confidence."

"Even for my country, I'm not prepared to prostitute myself to elicit information from anyone."

"Many women have done so in a similar situation."

"That's their choice. This is mine."

"Think about it."

"Absolutely not!" Robert was stung to anger. "Would you do it?"

Richard hesitated. "No," he replied quietly.

"Then don't suggest that I do," he snapped, turning his back on Richard and abruptly ending the conversation.

All the next day, still troubled by his encounter with Abetz and his disagreement with Richard, Robert avoided going into Port le Bac, preferring to remain in the vicinity of the farm, taking a day off to cool his anger, letting Richard continue with his investigative work.

He remained in the cellar until he could stand its airless, claustrophobic environment no longer and, after ascertaining that it was safe to do so, wandered outside where not far from the farmhouse, he stood on a stone bridge that traversed the bubbling stream that led down to the cove, leaning against the parapet, staring down at the fast-flowing water.

After a while, feeling a little calmer, he saw Edna walking along the tree-lined lane towards him.

"Do you mind if I join you?" she asked pleasantly.

"Not in the least, although I'm not very good company at the moment, I'm afraid," he replied.

He had grown fond of Richard's aunts in the short time he had known them. Edna, calm and practical but with hidden emotional depths; Mae, self-absorbed and charming; fragile with a hidden resilience – both of them caring and warm.

They were taking a great risk in harbouring himself and Richard as well as itinerant Russian and Polish escapees from the fortifications.

"We are what is known as a 'safe house'," Edna had replied when he questioned the wisdom of their actions. "The poor souls go from house to house, only staying long enough to be given food and shelter but not putting their hosts at risk, managing to survive as best they can. There are about twenty 'safe' houses on the island and we've all of us had some narrow squeaks, I can tell you. Once, Sergei, our favourite, the one you met the night you arrived, just managed to evade capture by jumping out of the sitting room window and disappearing into the woods just as the Germans came in the kitchen door!"

Robert smiled at Edna's intentionally light-hearted rendition but said, in all seriousness, "You're taking a terrible risk."

"Of course we are, but Mae is adamant that we do this. She says that she couldn't bear to stand by and do nothing. So we do the best we can. Oddly enough, the greatest danger comes not from the soldiers, but from informants, residents of St Nicolas who either want to curry favour with the occupying forces or have some grudge against someone. So, we keep very quiet about what we do."

They stood silently together, Edna regarding Robert closely.

"If you don't mind my saying so, you look as though you have the weight of the world on your shoulders," she said, patting his hand.

Robert exhaled. "That's exactly how I feel. It all seems too much at the moment. I've been standing here wishing that it would all go away; that the war would finish tomorrow and we could go home and lead ordinary, normal, rational lives again."

"Richard told me of your encounter on the cliff top. Perhaps he shouldn't have done, but he was most upset that he had upset you last night."

"Was he?"

"You're close friends, aren't you?"

"Very much so. I don't like being out of step with him either. It's the first time we've ever had any sort of disagreement since we met."

"I'm sure you'll resolve things. But you're much troubled by this man, this Theodor Abetz?"

"That's an understatement."

They stood in silence again for a while.

"Not all German soldiers are bad," observed Edna, thinking of Albrecht von Witzenhausen. "The first *Kommandant* here on the island was a splendid man. He became a... a friend. Everyone had, and still has, a high regard for him. He was fair and just and hoped to do good things here despite being part of the occupying force. Unfortunately, he never got the chance."

"I can appreciate that. I know of many fine German men in high places; brave men who are opposed to Hitler's evil regime and do their best to counteract its excesses."

"Unfortunately, they are in a minority."

"Perhaps. Or is it that the Nazis have such a stranglehold that it's difficult for the moderates, and there are many, to gain a foothold in changing things or to influence those who wield the power or commit crimes against humanity?"

"Like Herr Abetz."

266

"Just like Herr Abetz." Robert looked at Edna. "How much did Richard tell you?"

"Everything you told him."

Robert expressed surprise.

"Perhaps he shouldn't have done?" asked Edna.

"It's not that. We trust you, but the less you know the better."

"Dear boy, I'm in it up to my neck anyway!" Edna tried not to think of the promise she had made to Albrecht about keeping out of trouble.

"I am concerned that you will have found it shocking. I did."

Edna frowned. "I'm not that easily shocked, but I have to confess what he told me did disturb my equilibrium somewhat. But I'm pretty robust. I'm a farmer. You'd be amazed at what animals get up to sometimes."

Unable to help himself, Robert smiled before saying: "However, they're not called Theodor Abetz with close links to the *Gestapo* and Adolf Hitler. Nor, like us, have they been sent on a mission by British Intelligence to uncover certain information and expose it so that its enactment no longer becomes a viable option."

"Perhaps we should send some bulls in your place. They'd bellow threateningly and trample over obnoxious people who'd be so overcome with fear that they'd beg for mercy and reveal their deepest darkest secrets to all and sundry. Or we could send in the geese. That would really sort them out." Edna looked at Robert's bemused expression. "Sorry," she said. "I do realize it's a serious matter."

"Please don't apologize. I appreciate the levity." He smiled again.

"You really do have a dilemma though."

"I know."

"Principles are all very well…"

"This doesn't come under the heading of principles. It's whether one can live with oneself afterwards."

Edna was shocked. "You're surely not considering even for a moment…?"

Robert was equally horrified. "Good God, of course not!" He shook his head. "No, but the merest thought of leading anyone on in that way in order to gain information is an anathema to me even though it is for the good of my country. With Abetz, it's dangerous as well. I can't afford to find myself in any situation where we're likely to be alone. He's physically very strong and mentally vindictive. He'll stop at nothing to get what he wants. And in this case, that would appear to be me."

"But you're just as strong. And quick. And resourceful. I daresay you've had combat training of some sort?"

Robert sighed. "Yes, but we need Abetz alive to lead us to where the plans we're after might be hidden. Besides, I'm an amiable soul who would prefer not to use those particular skills even if he is an amoral, evil…" and he stopped mid-flow, leaving the sentence unfinished out of courtesy.

"…villain," finished Edna tactfully. "Of course, I quite understand. In that case, perhaps you should take Abetz back to England with you."

"Back to England?"

"Because there, you can hand him over to the people who'll do the job for you without you having to put yourself in peril or suffer any indignities." Edna became suddenly enthused. "When are you being picked up? I presume it's by submarine?"

Robert frowned. "How *much* has Richard told you?"

"I wasn't born yesterday, my dear. You must have got here somehow and it's much too far to swim." She glanced sideways at Robert, who smiled and shook his head. "I also read a lot of thrillers," she added.

"Ah," he replied. But he was thinking, rapidly. "We've another five days before the sub is due to pick us up. It might be possible…"

"You could smile at him a bit in the meantime, without compromising your honour in any way…"

"And then entice him to some remote spot…"

"Where Richard will be waiting to render him unconscious and you can transport him out to the waiting submarine and whisk him off to Blighty!"

"There's just a slight fly in this devious ointment. We only have two canoes."

"He'd probably topple over in a canoe anyway if he was unconscious. No, I have a much better suggestion. Mae and I have a little sailing boat hidden in the barn. All vessels were supposed to be declared at the beginning of the occupation, but Sophie and I dismantled this one inasmuch as we could and distributed it in various places in the barn. Mae has no idea."

"Well, we'll need to put it back together. Is it seaworthy?"

"Of course, dearest boy, I wouldn't have suggested it otherwise. You might find it leaks a bit at first because it's been out of the water for so long, but the wood will soon swell up. Take a baler with you."

Robert looked directly at Edna, hope replacing despondency. "We'll also have to deal with the guard on the cliff path."

"A sachet or two of Mae's sleeping powders should knock him out for several hours. They're very potent. I'm sure you can find some way of administering them."

"You've been thinking about this already, haven't you?"

"I've been thinking about it all morning, my dear. Richard tells me you like acting?"

"I do."

"Therefore when you're with Abetz, imagine you're playing a role on stage. That should salve your conscience."

"True."

"But you must avoid being alone with him," she said sternly.

"Yes, Aunt Edna," replied Robert dutifully and grinned at her. "You'd make an excellent secret agent."

Edna smiled back at him, her face alight. "I don't know about that, but if it wasn't so dangerous, this could be quite exciting."

Robert looked at her again and laughed.

He liked Edna. He admired her courage and no-nonsense resourcefulness.

"So, let's go indoors and have a cup of tea before someone sees you. Richard should be back soon and you two can discuss the finer details. Let me know if you need anything."

With a combination of companionship and purpose, she linked one of her arms into Robert's and the two of them went into the farmhouse.

If we all survive the war, thought Edna, *this man would make a wonderful husband for Sophie. He's brave, caring and handsome. And intelligent. A perfect combination.*

She sighed. If only.

CHAPTER 34

Seeblick

The next morning, Sophie awoke with a raging sore throat. Her cheeks were flushed and she was shivering uncontrollably. She said nothing to anyone, but went along to the infirmary after breakfast to seek the doctor's advice. However, when she saw that Dr Reynolds was fully occupied dealing with a queue of poorly children and adults, she went away, deciding to come back later.

From a distance, she saw Heinrich on his morning inspection but made no attempt to speak to him although, had she felt better, she knew she would have wanted to do so.

Despite her best intentions, she found herself drawn to him.

Like a fly to the fly paper, she thought.

Instead, Sophie went to lie down on her bed, where she slept for a couple of hours. She woke up feeling no better; by now, her glands were swollen and she felt very sick.

She struggled on through the rest of that day, attempting to complete her usual tasks in the library, but without success. She kept having to put her head down on her arms, unable to keep awake, unable to keep warm, although she had on enough clothes for the depths of winter.

Giving up on her tasks, she returned to her bunk but there was too much noise and too many people around, the room feeling even more overcrowded and stifling than usual. Then someone came in with a message for her from the Commodore to say that she was needed for a crisis meeting in the *Kommandant*'s office. So Sophie dragged her weary and shuddering body back across the compound.

"We have scarlet fever in the camp," said the Commodore regretfully and without preamble, after Sophie had sat down.

"This is a serious outbreak, I'm afraid," added Dr Reynolds, "and it's spreading like wildfire given the close proximity of everyone here. We're so overcrowded at the moment," he added, "that it's making things much worse."

"What can be done?" asked the Commodore.

"We need to keep those infected in isolation," replied the doctor. He looked at Heinrich. "With your permission, I'd like to turn one of the huts into an isolation ward. The people currently living there can bed down in the theatre for the time being until the epidemic has passed. It would be useful if it was the one nearest to the hospital hut, then I can move easily between the two. Some of the cases are very severe. It seems to be a particularly virulent strain. I can only think that the nurse brought it with her from the village, as she is ill with it."

"Do whatever you need to do, Doctor," replied Heinrich. "If you give me a list of any special medicines, I shall do my best to obtain what you require. Though it may prove to be difficult, as any medicines are in short supply."

"I'd appreciate it if you tried. There's nothing we can do for the scarlet fever itself, which just has to take its course, but some patients may experience complications or secondary infections. It's for these that we may need the medicines. Thank you, *Herr Kommandant*."

They discussed options, concerns and obstacles for a few minutes before the Commodore said, "Well, if there is nothing further, I suggest we get on with what we have to do."

Heinrich watched Sophie as she walked out of the room, concerned that she had not acknowledged him in any way; concerned that she looked very unwell. He was surprised the doctor had not noticed, although perhaps he was too preoccupied with his immediate concerns to do so.

That evening, with everything completed and the men's section of the new isolation ward more or less established, Sophie returned to her room.

"Tommy's got the scarlet fever," announced Gert. "'e's right poorly, 'e is. Doc said I'd better keep away from the lad. 'E didn't want me to catch it neither, though I really don't feel very well. You'd better watch you don't go down wiv it, Miss Sophie. You an' 'e's been spending a lot of time wiv each other of late. Come to think of it, you do look a bit peaky, like; a bit pale round the gills if you ask me."

"I'm fine," said Sophie. "I'm just tired after helping people move their belongings into the theatre, that's all. I'll be all right in the morning after a good night's sleep."

"Well, just you check you ain't got no rash. Tommy's body was covered this mornin'," warned Gert.

"So was my eldest," said Mabel.

That night when she went for a wash, Sophie checked herself over but as there were no spots, she assumed that whatever she had was not connected to the outbreak of scarlet fever. She decided not to trouble the doctor. He had more than enough with which to contend.

After breakfast the next morning, she struggled across to the library and after he'd seen her make a slow and painful journey across the compound, Heinrich found her alone in the library, fast asleep at her desk with her head on her arms, unresponsive to his gentle efforts to awaken her.

Fear made his heart race and taking several deep breaths to calm himself, he somehow managed to rouse her enough to guide her into his office where she immediately collapsed onto the floor.

With panic overriding his usual care in not overexerting himself physically, Heinrich lifted her into one of the easy chairs and went to fetch the doctor, who came back with him almost immediately. Discreetly, Heinrich left the room while Sophie was examined and also to conceal from the doctor his own struggles to regain his even breathing.

"It's scarlet fever, I'm afraid," said Andrew Reynolds, when Heinrich was allowed into the room again. "Looks like she has a nasty bout of it. Her rash is extensive and she has a very high fever. She must have been feeling unwell for a while. I'm really surprised that she didn't come to see me." He regarded Heinrich closely. "Have you had scarlet fever? It's highly contagious."

"Yes, it almost killed me. I had it as a small child."

"Good. But I've got a real problem with where to put her. The female section of the new isolation ward is not yet ready, the hospital is full and she most certainly can't go back to her hut. Besides which, she's very poorly and far too ill to move." What was he to do? Andrew ran the back of his hand across his forehead.

Seeing the doctor's despair, Heinrich said quickly, seizing upon this opportunity to keep Sophie near to him. He would care for her himself. "Then until there's a space, she must stay here. I shall move my things and sleep elsewhere."

Dr Reynolds looked at him uncertainly for several moments, any number of considerations going through his mind, before reluctantly agreeing. "Thank you, *Herr Kommandant.*"

Between them, the two men carried her into Heinrich's adjoining bedroom, where they laid her on the bed.

"I shall send Marian along with Sophie's things. She can see to her and er... make sure that she's comfortable. Until she comes round, keep the room warm. If you could light that fire, it would be helpful."

"There is no coal left as we have not had our scheduled delivery, but I shall order my men to find wood in the forest."

It was a couple of hours before Marian could be released from her emergency duties. She looked tired and wan as she went into the *Kommandant*'s room, muttering that this was all highly improper and the doctor should never have agreed to such an unorthodox solution to Sophie's isolation problem.

Heinrich remained silent. What could he say? He saw no need to defend his honour; Mrs Maundell would have to accept the situation as it was.

Leaving her to deal with Sophie, Heinrich closed the door of the bedroom and returned to his desk, resuming his paperwork until the older woman had finished.

Sophie woke briefly while Marian washed her burning face and hands and helped her into her nightgown. She sank gratefully into the bed after all was done and fell asleep immediately.

"The doctor says that she must have a cold compress on her forehead to bring down her temperature, though the room must be kept warm, and she must have lots of cool water to drink," said Marian, as she returned to the office.

"I shall do these things myself."

Marian hovered uncertainly, reluctant to leave. This was not right. Sophie should not be left on her own at the mercy of any man, trusted or not, let alone a *German*. Really, it was too much. She would have words with Andrew later.

Impatiently, Heinrich said, "You may leave now, *Frau* Maundell. Rest assured that I shall care for *Fräulein* Langley to the very best of my ability."

And Marian went on her way, her concerns unassuaged, still muttering about the world being turned upside down.

When Sophie awoke, her nose was pressed up against something warm but slightly itchy. Slowly, with great effort, she opened her eyes and saw *Hauptmann* Hoffmeister lying next to her in the bed. His expression mirrored her fevered shock.

Hesitantly, he said by way of explanation, "It was very cold last night. The doctor said that you must be kept warm. There was no coal. It was too late to gather any more wood. Therefore, the only way of keeping you warm was to use myself.

272

Forgive me." He lifted the covers an inch or two. "As you can see, I am fully dressed."

For some reason, Sophie didn't mind that he was there. She closed her eyes for a moment and when she opened them again, she glanced down at her own body and said, "We are wearing similar jumpers."

"*Ja.* That is so. I put this one on you for added warmth. It is my favourite one."

The unexpected drop in temperature outside had been severe and there had been a heavy frost during the night, belaying the earlier promise of warmer weather. Heinrich had had the dilemma of whether to keep her warm or work at reducing her fever. In the end, he decided to keep her warm.

"I seem to be always wearing your clothes."

"That is true. You have socks this time as well."

She felt one foot with the other; a small movement, all that she had the energy for. "So I do. Can I keep them?"

Heinrich smiled. "I shall have none of my own clothes left at all very soon."

"When I am better, I can knit you some more."

"I shall look forward to it."

She closed her eyes again and drifted away briefly. "Am I very ill?"

"You are, I'm afraid."

"Why am I here with you?"

He wanted to tell her that he had seized this one chance to keep her near to him so they could be together in total privacy. However, Heinrich knew he could not say this because in her present condition it would not be right; it would be to take advantage of her and that was not his intention.

So, instead he replied, "Because there was nowhere else for you to go. The new isolation ward was not yet ready and now, you cannot be moved as you are not well enough."

"Oh."

Did he see relief and joy in her reaction or was that just wishful thinking on his part?

"Also…"

"Yes?"

"I wanted to look after you myself." There, he had said it.

Sophie opened her eyes wide.

What could he see in them? Fear? Mistrust? No, neither of these things. Just confusion.

"It is all right, I shall take good care of you."

She smiled, relieved, and closed her eyes. "I'm very glad to hear it."

She was warm and she felt safe. And there was something else… what was it? Of course, there were no other people. Only herself and the *Kommandant*.

It was so quiet; so peaceful.

Gradually, she drifted off again into her fever-induced sleep.

When Sophie awoke next, there was a fire burning in the grate and the room felt cheerful. Heinrich was sprawled out fast asleep in the arm chair, his uniform jacket slung over the back, his shirt partially undone, his braces pushed down from his shoulders and his boots off.

His features were reflected in the glow of the fire and Sophie studied him for a while.

He had a kind face. He was a good man. And she liked him. Very much. Too much. Her heart beat faster and she closed her eyes again but sleep would not come. She felt thirsty.

"*Hauptmann* Hoffmeister," she murmured.

Heinrich was alert and beside her in an instant. "Yes?"

"How long have I been here?"

"This is your third day."

He did not add that he had been up with her for the two nights previously, bathing her face, hands and upper body with cool water, trying to reduce her fever; that the doctor and Marian had come as often as they could, that all of them had been anxious and concerned that her temperature had not yet come down.

"Might I have a drink? My mouth is so dry."

"Of course."

He poured some water into a cup and sat on the bed beside her, helping to support her while she took a few sips of the precious liquid. Sensing her exhaustion after this minute effort, Heinrich lowered her back onto the pillows and gently extracted his arm.

"You should have more."

"In a moment." She looked up at him. "Can you stay for a little while?"

"Yes. My duties are finished now until tomorrow. You have slept all of today. The doctor has been several times. We have been very worried." He did not tell her just how worried. "But you must rest again."

"I shall, very soon."

She was asleep again almost before she had finished the sentence.

"Are you hungry?" Heinrich asked her.

"A little."

He felt her forehead with his hand. It was still cool. During the night he had drawn up his chair and sat beside the bed, holding her hand, bathing her burning body. Exhausted, he had fallen asleep with his head resting on the counterpane and their hands joined.

When he awoke, the crisis had passed; her fever had gone.

"Would you like some broth?"

"Do you have any?" She was surprised. "You won't have to go away to fetch it?" She didn't want him to leave.

"No." He was reassuring. "I have some on my little primus stove, see? Here in my private quarters where you are. Sometimes I prefer to eat here, alone, rather than with the others. I shall heat you up some straight away." He found a small saucepan and poured some soup into it.

Sophie relaxed. "*Hauptmann*..."

"Please, while we are here together, my name, it is Heinrich."

"Heinrich." She said the name and felt comfortable with its syntax. "Heinrich?"

274

"Yes?"

"Is it all right that I am here? I mean, you won't get into trouble with the *Oberkommando der Wehrmacht*?"

He smiled, amused. "No. Only my most trusted senior officer, the *leutnant* of the police guards, is aware that you are here. He is loyal. Therefore, all is well. Unless, of course, the *Gestapo* decide to pay us a visit unannounced."

Sophie was suddenly afraid. "Is that likely?"

"No. But I have a contingency plan. You can hide in the wardrobe." There was a twinkle in his eyes.

"You mustn't joke about it. I have seen the *Waffen-SS* and the *Gestapo*. They're inhuman. Sorry." Hastily, she apologized.

"Please, don't be. I agree." He turned off the primus. "Your soup, it is ready. Let me help you to sit up... I will put the pillows here, like so... Now, drink it slowly."

He supported her while she sipped the nourishing liquid from the spoon. When she had had enough, he laid her back onto the pillows. She closed her eyes and rested while he put the bowl and saucepan to one side.

"Have you eaten?" she asked.

"Yes."

After a moment or two, she said, "Heinrich?"

"Yes?"

"Please will you sit beside me. On the bed."

He was surprised by her request but did so without hesitation, making himself comfortable beside her.

"It's less effort to talk to you if you're nearer. Besides, I trust you."

"Thank you." He swallowed hard. He didn't trust himself.

"What did you do before the war?" Sophie asked.

"I was a schoolmaster."

"Yes, of course. I'd forgotten."

"And before that?"

"I studied English at Heidelberg University."

"So that's why your English is so good."

"Yes. Also, my parents and I came to England on many holidays." He hesitated. "It is one of the reasons I find this war difficult. It is as though Germany, the land of my birth, is fighting against my friends."

"Oh, Heinrich. I know exactly what you mean and I feel the same. You see, my grandfather was German. He came from Freiburg."

"That is why you can speak such good German."

Weak as she was, Sophie smiled up at him in such a way that Heinrich had to fight the urge to kiss her.

"If you were a teacher before the war, how is it that you can hold the rank of *Kommandant* in the army?"

"The organization of the *Wehrmacht* is a strange beast. I am classed as a *Beamte*, a civilian employee in military service. I am not a soldier nor am I trained as one, but I wear a uniform. I have the title of *Intendanturassessor* which carries the rank of captain."

"An 'administrative services official'," interpreted Sophie.

"Yes. I can be sent anywhere to do any job where my particular skills might be suited. Immediately after I was conscripted, they needed someone to teach English to the soldiers in preparation for…" he stopped.

"The invasion of England."

"*Ja* that is so."

"But it never happened. Apart from the Channel Islands."

"*Ja.*" He paused, unsure whether Sophie felt awkward at the mention of this. When she gave no apparent indication of being so, he continued. "When that requirement no longer existed, I was given other roles."

Sophie felt herself becoming drowsy. "Such as?" she managed to say before her eyes closed.

"In Berlin in the Ministry of the Interior and Karodice in Czechoslovakia as an *Intendanturassessor* in the office of…"

Suddenly, Heinrich stopped. He did not wish to continue with this line of conversation.

He glanced down at Sophie. She had fallen asleep again.

That was good, he thought, both for her wellbeing and for his own protection. He did not wish to remember the time of Berlin or Karodice.

"What did you like most about being at Oxford?" asked Heinrich.

Sophie was sitting up now. Several days of sleep and rest had passed. Her rash had disappeared and she was beginning to feel a little better, though the doctor, regretfully on his part because he wanted her back under his wing as soon as possible being anxious for her virtue and reputation, had said she was too weak as yet to be moved.

Secretly, Sophie was glad. She had grown used to being with Heinrich; had grown used to hearing the business that went on in his office next door, secure in the knowledge that very few people knew that she was actually there. She had become accustomed to his close proximity and their undemanding evening conversations when he would come and sit beside her on the bed, as he was doing at that very moment, or in his easy chair.

It seemed natural for Heinrich to be always near to her in the seclusion and quietness of his room.

She shifted her position slightly, moving closer to him so that he could support her. "What did I like the most? All of it. The course itself; the friendships; the drama society. I loved it!"

And she spoke of her life at Oxford for a little while until she fell asleep.

After days of exerting great self-control, one evening, unable to contain himself any longer, Heinrich kissed her.

Sophie made no protest but looked up at him, her eyes wide with surprise. He drew her into his arms and kissed her again.

"Forgive me. I should not have done that."

"There is nothing to forgive." Guiltily, Sophie remained within his arms. "Heinrich?"

"Yes?"

"You have been so kind to me."

"Have I? I hope so."

"You have cared for me and behaved like a perfect gentleman."

"Until this moment." His heart started to somersault. He took some deep breaths to calm himself.

Sophie smiled. "Until this moment."

He kissed her again and explored the softness of her body.

He came into the room after his work was finished to find Sophie asleep. After a moment's consideration, he undressed and got into bed beside her.

Drowsily, Sophie stirred and turned towards him. He took her hand in his, guiding it over his body. When she expressed no fear and offered no resistance, Heinrich reached beneath the covers and pushed up the folds of her nightgown before lifting it over her head. Although she lay passive and accepting of his caresses, he sensed an inner responsiveness to his increasingly intimate touch.

Eventually, he stopped and drew back, knowing she was not yet well enough nor did he possess the energy that night for them to continue.

They had come this far. He could wait a little longer.

He helped her back into her nightdress and held her in his arms.

"Heinrich?"

"Yes, *Liebchen*?"

They were lying together in the bed. He knew she was no longer shy with him but he had refrained from making love to her until he knew she was ready.

"Soon, I shall be better and then I shall have to go back to being with everyone else. But there is something I need to know; something I'd like to know very much." Sophie turned towards him and rested her head against his shoulder, hesitantly stroking his chest. "If we had met under normal circumstances, I mean if there hadn't been a war and we'd been introduced to each other or met at a dance or while we were on holiday, what would we have done?"

He looked at her, considering. *So*, he thought, *she no longer reacts passively to our growing closeness nor can she deny the deepening bond between us. She now finds the courage and desire to acknowledge possibilities and speak of them, openly.*

It was time. Before they lost their privacy; before things became difficult and the danger of discovery too great.

He felt fit enough today and she had now recovered sufficiently.

Heinrich smiled. "I would have made sure I spent every moment with you that I could. Then, I would have asked to see you again. Often. Then, I would telephone you many times just to hear your voice and to make sure you were real. Then, I would have courted you just as I am now… and then…" he paused.

"Yes, Heinrich?"

"I would have asked you to be my wife."

He looked deeply at her, searching out her feelings. "And what would you have answered, my lovely Sophie, to this proposal?"

"My answer would have been 'Yes', Heinrich. I would have accepted your proposal."

"But now, as a German officer in the middle of a war, in our present situation, to make such a proposal, it is impossible."

"But the war will not last forever. It cannot possibly last forever."

"That is true. But where shall we be, you and I, when the war is over?"

Sophie was silent. She could find no answer.

"No matter. We therefore have to make the best of what we have and let the future take care of itself." He held her face between his hands for a moment and looked enquiringly into her eyes. "So, my Sophie, I ask you this: will you give yourself to me freely and unreservedly, now, this moment?"

And Sophie, closing her eyes, seduced by the warmth and comfort of their closeness and by his constant, intimate caresses, murmured, "Yes, Heinrich. I will."

"And in the future, whenever I wish?" She was his now.

"Yes, Heinrich."

Sophie's heart beat quickly and she trembled with nervousness and something else she couldn't define as he moved on top of her.

She was committed now. There could be no going back.

CHAPTER 35

St Nicolas

Robert leant nonchalantly against the doorframe of Theodor Abetz's office in *Geheime Feldpolizei* headquarters and watched him as he opened his attaché case, methodically checking and counting each piece of paper contained in each cardboard folder before replacing them inside, closing the clasp and snapping on the padlock.

It was late evening.

"You could always come inside the room," said Abetz, looking up from his precious attaché case. "Don't be shy. You know me quite well now."

Perhaps if Robert imagined Abetz to be an attractive girl, then he might find the right facial expressions to carry out this, the most necessary and difficult part of his mission – enticing Abetz to meet with him.

He tried and failed miserably with this imaginary scenario. Abetz no more looked like an attractive girl than one of Edna's cows. And even they were preferable with their long eyelashes and soulful expressions.

"I'm quite happy here," he said evenly. "I can see you well enough."

Abetz raised an eyebrow. "You could see me even better if you came closer."

Said the spider to the fly, thought Robert. "I'm fine," he replied and, taking Edna's advice, he flashed what he hoped would be a charming and irresistible smile.

This man really is attractive, thought Abetz. He was bored now with verbal sparring. It was time to cut to the chase. "If you come inside the room," he said, lowering his voice, "we wouldn't be disturbed; it would be perfectly safe."

"I'm sure it would be but I have an alternative suggestion. How about we meet tomorrow night? But not here. I've arranged a surprise for you," said Robert, also raising an eyebrow, "something you will enjoy."

At last! thought Abetz. He gave a smile of triumph and forgot to be cautious in the heat of his carnality. "Where shall we meet?"

"The little cove not far from that old farmhouse on the far side of the island."

"You've been snooping." Abetz was suspicious for a moment.

"Only on your behalf."

Theodor relaxed. "So, you have it all planned?" This was something different. *He* was the one that usually instigated this sort of session. To have it arranged for him was most refreshing and stimulating.

"Oh yes. Down to the last detail. I've invited a friend. I owe him a favour," replied Robert, using the same words Abetz had used with Erika, knowing that it was payback time.

Abetz's face was a picture of unadulterated salaciousness. Robert could see he was almost drooling.

This was something he'd never tried before, mused Theodor. He'd done just about everything else. Why hadn't he ever thought of it himself? He'd obviously underestimated this officer. Perhaps he'd keep him around a little longer.

In any case, after tomorrow night, both men would belong to *him*. The threat of exposure and court martial would be enough to keep them in his thrall to do with exactly as he pleased.

With the thrilling prospect of a dual conquest filling his mind and hungry for the initial experience, Abetz readily agreed to Robert's suggestion; casting aside ingrained suspicion, throwing caution to the wind.

"I'll see to the patrols," he said recklessly, his excitement mounting. "There's no need for them to come near the cove. I'll make sure we won't be disturbed."

"I'll see to the guard at the top of the cliff path. He's a corpulent fellow. A large meal should send him to sleep nicely." *Especially as it will be washed down with a generous quantity of alcohol laced with two of Mae's strongest sleeping draughts,* thought Robert.

"I have some interesting pictures we could look at," said Abetz. "I keep them in my attaché case."

"We won't need any pictures," replied Robert, wondering what else was in the attaché case that never left Abetz's side.

Could it contain the documents he and Richard had searched for in vain over the past few weeks; the important, incriminating documents which should have been, according to the decrypts at Bletchley House, concealed in some secret geographical location on the island until such time as they were needed?

Trying to sound encouraging, he added, "But, by all means bring them if you wish. I should like to see them." He smiled again. "Until tomorrow night?"

"Tomorrow night. What time shall we meet?"

"Midnight."

"Ah, the witching hour! How perfect. I shall be there."

"So shall we," said Robert. *But not in the way that you are anticipating,* he thought.

He flashed his smile again and went, leaving Abetz weak at the knees.

The sentry was easy prey. He readily accepted the offer of food and sat on the edge of the cliff, a fair distance from the path to consume the delicious meal. He didn't have the nerve to ask where this officer had managed to find such a repast when everyone, civilian and soldier alike, was struggling with meagre rations.

The prospect of hours and hours of lonely duty had stretched before him interminably. To have food inside his belly would sustain him and make his task less onerous. Besides, it would be churlish to refuse such a kind offer, wouldn't it? He couldn't possibly see all that wonderful food go to waste or worse still, find its way into someone else's stomach.

The sentry ate his meal with relish and when he was offered wine, he drank this also with alacrity. After a very short while, he began to feel woozy and disorientated. Suddenly, he keeled over and began to snore. Very loudly.

Robert and Richard nodded to each other and, after giving him a good prod and shake, could see that he was out for the count.

With difficulty, they dragged the sailing dinghy (previously reconstructed and rescued from Edna's barn and lugged from the farmhouse to a transitory hiding place in a nearby wood) down the cliff path, using a branch to brush away any tracks in the loose soil.

They hauled it across the sand, concealing it at the entrance to the grotto, and began work lifting the kayaks from inside the depths of the pool. This proved to be a time-consuming, energy-sapping task. The little canoes, light and buoyant when they were on the surface, were extremely difficult and heavy to hoist upwards when saturated with water.

So Robert stripped off and dived into the pool, gasping as the icy depths covered his body. Briefly, he remembered the day when he had last swum here. Back then, it had been a warm and sensuous experience. Now, it was freezing and devastatingly unpleasant despite the mildness of the April night.

Coming up to the surface gasping for air, he then disappeared beneath the water again, pushing the first canoe upwards while Richard hauled on the rope before manoeuvring it over the flat stones.

They repeated this routine until both kayaks were once more on dry land, Robert's actions becoming slower and slower as the cold numbed his body.

Shivering and shaking and barely able to move, with Richard's help, Robert climbed out of the pool and attempted to dry himself, but could make no progress as his hands and arms would not respond to his needs.

Seeing his plight, Richard rubbed him vigorously with a towel, going some way to restoring his circulation and his ability to move freely.

Still trembling with the cold and his exertions, his teeth chattering, Robert fumbled with his clothes and once again needed Richard's help.

"Didn't your mother teach you how to get dressed?" he quipped.

Robert narrowed his eyes at his friend. "N-no, only h-how t-to g-give s-someone a c-clip r-round th-their ear."

"Can you stutter that again?" replied Richard, neatly sidestepping Robert's feeble attempt at a swipe in his direction.

They retrieved the oars and stuffed the bags of mildewed clothes from their original journey into Robert's kayak. They put their weapons aside in readiness and waited for Abetz to arrive.

He appeared at the top of the cliff path a few minutes before midnight; his form a solitary, moonlit silhouette above them.

"Thank goodness he didn't come earlier," muttered Richard.

"I was praying that he wouldn't," replied Robert, beginning to feel somewhat warmer again, "and that he wouldn't bring anyone with him."

"Well, it certainly looks like he's alone."

"Damn," said Robert, peering through the silvery darkness. "He doesn't seem to have brought his attaché case with him."

"You've been pinning your hopes on the secret plans being in there, haven't you?" observed Richard.

"I have a very strong hunch that's exactly where they are."

Theodor Abetz paused at the top of the cliff and took a deep, invigorating breath before beginning the descent.

Just as he used to whenever he was with Reinhard, he cast aside his world-weary cynicism, banishing to the recesses of his mind his overwhelming need to dominate and control. He allowed himself to feel the first stirrings of the anticipation and expectation that had so consumed him whenever he and Ziegler were alone together.

He saw the two men waiting below; waiting for *him*, Theodor Abetz. He walked rapidly towards them, discarding the towel he had brought, unable to contain himself any longer.

"I am here," he declared, opening wide his arms and closing his eyes. "Do with me as you will!"

He felt a blindfold being placed across his eyes and tied tightly behind his head; he felt the sweet taste of brandy on his lips, feeling warmed as the aromatic liquid slid easily down his throat; he felt his coat and jacket being removed and his Luger unstrapped. He waited with increasing excitement as his tie was unknotted and his shirt taken off.

But why was everything so clinical and detached?

No matter. Soon it would be *the* moment; *his* moment of sublime experience.

But why couldn't he respond? Why couldn't he feel anything? Why was he sweating? Why was the world going round and round in such a peculiar way?

The truth dawned just as everything went black.

Robert and Richard smiled at each other as Theodor Abetz collapsed onto the sand. It had been far, far easier than either of them could have anticipated.

Quickly, they pulled off his boots, trousers, underwear and socks and folded them neatly in a pile together with the rest of his clothes and his towel, high above the tide line on the flat stones of the grotto pool, making it look as though he had gone for a midnight swim – a swim from which he would never return – so that no blame could be attached to the islanders. They also left his identification papers in the inside pocket of his jacket for the same reason, placing his gun underneath the clothes.

They dressed Abetz in an old jumper and pair of trousers that Edna had provided, before turning him over onto his stomach and tying his hands and feet tightly and securely behind his back.

They dragged the dinghy and the canoes down to the water's edge and placed their remaining equipment into what had been Robert's canoe, ensuring everything was secure and watertight, before tying it behind Richard's.

They carried Abetz to the shore and with great difficulty, lifted him up and over into the dinghy.

They checked they had left nothing behind. They knew that the incoming tide would wash away their footprints before morning.

They looked at the growing surf with concern but knew they had no choice. It was now or never.

Twice they tried to launch the dinghy. Twice they were beaten back by the waves. Once they had to lift Abetz out and upend the boat to tip out the water.

Worried that the tide would soon be coming in and render their task impossible, they made one final Herculean effort and launched the little sailing boat through the waves. Clinging on for dear life and soaked to the skin, Robert managed to climb in, almost tipping it over in the process.

He grabbed hold of the oars and struck out for the open sea, watching as Richard finally succeeded in launching his canoes, seeing him paddling doggedly away from the shore.

Robert waited for his friend and together, they rowed in the direction of their rendezvous with the submarine.

At the farmhouse, Edna lay awake, tossing and turning, wondering how they were faring; worrying about them.

She had grown fond of Robert. There had been moments when he reminded her of Ralph.

That afternoon, she had found him in the sitting room looking at some of the trinkets.

"There's nothing of real interest here," she'd said. "We buried our most valuable possessions a long time ago in the garden; all our most precious books, photographs, jewellery and ornaments. Albrecht told us to do that before he left."

"You really liked him, didn't you?" It wasn't the first time that Edna had mentioned him when she and Robert had talked, as they had often done since he and Richard had been on the island.

"Oh yes. He was a dear, dear man. Look," and she went over to her bureau and opened the secret drawer. "I have his address here and he has mine." She showed this to Robert before bringing out an envelope from her pocket. "If it's not too dangerous for you to do so, will you take this? If when the war is over and we perhaps haven't been liberated here, please will you send this letter to him? We promised to keep in touch after the war, and I wanted to show him I had not forgotten his kindness towards us. Would you send it to him for me? It's in German."

Robert had looked at her. "If we're caught, this note will link you to us. That could be fatal for you and Mae."

"Then destroy it before you're searched."

"What if things happen too quickly and there's no chance?"

"Don't speak like that, dear Robert, please!"

How could he refuse? He tucked the note in the inside pocket of his tunic.

"I've a letter for my sister for Richard to take. Margot will be grateful to hear from us."

Robert smiled. "Yes, she will," he said, "though perhaps, I'd better take both, you know…"

Edna understood.

"I'll give it to her myself."

"Thank you." She took out the photo of Ralph. "This was my Welsh Fusilier."

"So you didn't bury all your most precious photographs," observed Robert with a smile.

"I couldn't bear to part with this one." She showed him the photo. "His name was Ralph Llewellyn." And briefly, she had told him the story of her and Ralph, just as she had to Sophie the first time they toured the farm together.

It seemed natural and right to do so.

When she had finished, Robert said thoughtfully, "My middle name is Llewellyn and I have an uncle called Ralph. And my regiment, before I was seconded into British Intelligence for the duration, is the Welch Fusiliers."

Edna looked up sharply. "Is it possible…?"

"It's always possible, but unlikely I think. I don't recall anyone in the family mentioning a relative who served in the Boer War and as far as I'm aware, my father and I are the only two family members who ever belonged to the Welch Fusiliers."

She handed the photograph to Robert, who studied it carefully.

"You might just recognize him…?" she said hopefully.

"I'm afraid I can't see any family resemblance, but that isn't to say it doesn't exist." He turned the photo over, noticing the spelling of 'Welsh'. "We don't spell the name like that anymore," he observed. "'Welch' now has a 'c'."

"Why?"

"The powers-that-be decided in the 1920s that the regiment should revert to the ancient form of spelling." He smiled affectionately at Edna. "It would have been a wonderful coincidence though, wouldn't it, if we'd found a family connection?"

"I would have enjoyed that."

"So would I."

They stood in silence for a moment before Robert yawned suddenly.

"Tired?"

"I didn't sleep very well last night. Or the night before that."

"I'm not surprised. Look, why don't you go upstairs and have a browse through a book or two? It might help to take your mind off tonight. I'll shout if we have any unwelcome guests."

"Thank you."

Later, when Edna came upstairs to check on Mae, she saw Robert fast asleep in Sophie's room. She didn't disturb him; there was time before he and Richard needed to begin their 'adventure' as she euphemistically called it. He needed the rest. Who knew what he might have to contend with?

She had studied him for a moment thinking, not for the first time, that he was a very special man and how right he would be for Sophie, before covering him up with the counterpane and leaving him to sleep.

As she quietly drew the curtains, she prayed for his and Richard's safe return to England.

There was no sign of the submarine.

"You're sure this is the right place?" said Robert, holding onto Richard's canoe as he came alongside.

"Absolutely sure. Even allowing for the tide and any leeway we might have made, these are the right coordinates. And we're on time, amazingly enough."

"Then where on earth are they?"

"I've no idea. What do you think we should do?" asked Richard.

"Hang around for a while, though we're sitting ducks if we're still here once it gets light. I'm surprised we haven't been picked up by the night patrols as it is." Robert shivered involuntarily.

"Cold?"

"Only with fear."

"I know the feeling. How's our passenger?"

Robert felt the pulse in Abetz's neck. "Still alive, but he won't be if we don't get him warm and dry very soon. It's all right for us for the time being, because we've been rowing." Gingerly, he massaged his hands. They were sore despite the protection of leather gloves. "My hands are giving me what for. I hope this sub makes its appearance soon."

They remained where they were for a while, using the oars occasionally to maintain their position. After about half an hour, Robert had had enough.

"Can you navigate us to England?"

"Bloody hell, Robert, that must be at least eighty-five miles! We wouldn't stand a chance."

"How do you mean – reaching there from here or going that distance without being picked up?"

"Both, but mainly being picked up."

"Well, we'll definitely be picked up if we stay here any longer. Can you get us there?"

"Yes, but…"

"Do it."

Sensing the urgency in Robert's voice and trusting his friend's instinct, Richard took out his little chart from his knapsack and, keeping his torch shaded and checking the compass, said that if they headed nor-nor-west, though it was difficult to be completely accurate without being able to plot the route properly on the chart itself with parallel rulers and a pencil or taking bearings with a sextant, they should make landfall somewhere on either the Devon or Cornish coasts. "If we're lucky," he added.

"Is it possible to hoist the sail now? You said there was no point earlier because the wind was completely in the wrong direction."

"It was on the nose. We wouldn't have made any headway at all. However, the wind's come round now so we should be fine. Anything is better than rowing all the way!"

"Do you know how to sail a dinghy?"

"They taught us at *King Alfred's*."

"Can you remember?"

Richard looked disparagingly at Robert before saying, "Of course," and carefully climbed on board.

Robert tied the canoes at the stern and Richard prepared and then hoisted the little square sail. The rising wind filled the canvas and they set off on what they knew could be an epic voyage.

If they managed to complete it.

Some hours later, Robert took his turn at the tiller.

He checked Abetz again and lifted his head, pouring some water down his throat. He didn't stir, so Robert untied his blindfold a little and further loosened the ties that bound his hands and feet together. There was no prospect of him waking up and Robert didn't want him to expire because his circulation was cut off. They needed to take him back alive, although they'd probably all die of exposure anyway before they reached England even if the regular E-boat patrols, mines and U-boats didn't get them first.

He shut the thought out of his mind.

He thought instead of his friends in the Breton fishing fleet, wondering if they were still plying their secret trade and whether he might just encounter them on this journey.

He thought of his girl on the beach; the beach in the little cove from where they had just come.

He'd looked for her on St Nicolas, of course. He'd looked for her in the streets of Port le Bac; along the country lanes and in the villages and hamlets as he and Richard went about their secret quest.

But he had not seen her or anyone who resembled the grownup version: she who was his imaginary vision of pure loveliness.

Sadly, he had come to the conclusion that she was no longer on the island and that perhaps he might never find her.

Because of its proximity to the farmhouse, he wondered whether Sophie had ever been down to the cove when she was younger but Richard had assured him when he had asked (just as a casual question without revealing exactly why he wanted to know – that was too personal and private to share with anyone) that she had never been allowed down there on her own because the path was too steep and slippery and Aunt Mae had deemed it unsafe for either of them to go without grownups being present, especially as the surf could be quite rough as well.

Just as he, Robert, had discovered earlier.

He sighed, thinking of Sophie again and how he had fallen asleep in her bed before they had left the farmhouse, unable to resist the temptation of resting on the softness of a real bed after the lumpy straw mattress on the floor of the cellar. He had not read anything, having been much to tired, and had slept deeply, his anxieties soothed by the same sweet-smelling scent on her pillow that he had discovered the first time he had spent the night in the house at Maybury.

He recalled how Edna had awoken him at the appointed time and Aunt Mae had bid them a tearful farewell and kissed them both on the cheek, entreating them to come back as soon as the war was over.

"You must," said Edna, looking directly at Robert.

He had nodded and they had hugged as well.

Robert wanted to return to St Nicolas. He wanted to see the island freed from occupation. He wanted to see sanity and beauty restored, not the madness and cruelty that now overwhelmed the peaceful land it must once have been.

He looked up at the stars and held onto the little tiller.

Steer north, Richard had told him before he had closed his eyes and slept. So far, he had managed to keep them on course. Robert checked the compass. Still heading north.

Off to his right he could see the first grey light of dawn appearing.

How far had they travelled? He had no idea other than he could see no land, so he presumed they were now beyond the coast of France.

What speed were they doing? No more than a few knots, he imagined, though the wind had picked up steadily and the little boat was tripping along briskly.

Richard had mentioned something about being carried along on the tide at some point. Perhaps they had reached that point now. Robert decided to wake him up soon for him to check and take his turn at the tiller.

Robert took a sip of water from his canister and rubbed his eyes, arching his back and stretching out his cramped legs.

He went through the routine he had devised to keep himself awake.

Check the compass. They were still on course.

Check the water for mines. They had been lucky so far.

Scan the horizon with the binoculars…

And what he saw this time made his heart pound.

He roused Richard from his slumber, who was awake and alert as soon as he felt Robert's hand on his shoulder.

Together, the two men watched in horror as, heading rapidly towards them from the direction of the now distant Channel Islands, growing larger as it drew nearer, and more distinct as the light increased, was the unmistakable shape of a motor torpedo boat.

And at their feet, Theodor Abetz began to stir.

CHAPTER 36

Seeblick/The English Channel

When Sophie was well enough to leave Heinrich's room in the Big House, she spent another seven days in the infirmary before being deemed fit to return to her hut. She found it very strange to be away from the all-enveloping cocoon her illness had created and not to be with Heinrich in undisturbed seclusion.

She felt different, there was no doubt about that. She had felt different as soon as Heinrich had moved away from her after they had made love. She knew she had lost something – not just her virginity, but something more, something indefinable that was intrinsic to herself as a person, to her innermost private self.

She hoped that this change wouldn't show in her face, as she had read that it often did; she hoped that the residual tiredness from her illness would mask any difference or loss of innocence in her expression.

In private, Marian had quizzed her several times after Sophie first arrived in the infirmary: concerned for her purity, concerned for her reputation; making sure that she had survived her unorthodox sojourn intact.

Sophie had parried the questions carefully. She was genuinely so exhausted from her illness that she hoped, once again, that this would hide any guilt she might inadvertently reveal had she been well; guilt she was now experiencing both for what she and Heinrich had done, but also that she had had to lie to her well-meaning friend.

However, apparently satisfied with her answers, Marian had not pressed her further.

Sophie went around in a dreamlike state – debilitated from her illness (a condition not helped by the fact that she was unable to sleep properly, back in the constant noise and claustrophobic proximity of so many other human beings sharing the same space) and carrying out her duties as librarian listlessly and without enthusiasm.

Heinrich seemed sympathetic to her imperfect state of physical health and she was grateful that he did not insist that she fulfil her promise to him immediately. Indeed, once back in the reality of camp life, she began to wonder about the wisdom of having made such a promise.

In the privacy of his room, given the circumstances that had necessitated her being there, it had seemed very natural to allow him to make love to her but she knew that should their liaison become public knowledge, she would be ostracized by her fellows, shunned and insulted.

Were her feelings for Heinrich strong enough to enable her to fulfil both her promise to him and withstand such castigation? What might happen to her if she reneged on her promise and refused to sleep with him the next time he asked?

For the first time, she became starkly aware that Heinrich was the *Kommandant*; that he belonged to a nation that was at war with hers; that she was his prisoner; that he was in a position of absolute authority over her and that, having given her consent, she would be powerless now to resist his demands should he wish to exert his promised right to her body.

But he was not like that. She knew him to be a kind and considerate man who had lovingly looked after her and she was infinitely grateful to him for that. He genuinely cared for her and she could not deny the deepening bond between them formed through their time together and their physical acts of intimacy.

And he had asked her, albeit theoretically, to marry him. And she had, theoretically, accepted, after all.

But was it too risky; too dangerous for them to continue as lovers? What if they were found out? What would happen if she became pregnant?

Sophie experienced a deepening sense of anxiety and insecurity as she lay on her bunk, endlessly rereading *La Chaleur de la Mer*, trying to find an answer in its familiar fictional story of profound love.

However, it provided no solutions to her dilemma. It merely served to underline the fact that she had not known with Heinrich the same inescapably overwhelming and passionate relationship as the lovers in the book: a love affair she had always dreamed of experiencing.

Which, of course, added another layer of uncertainty to her considerations.

They say that in times of extreme peril, your whole life flashes before your eyes.

For Robert that didn't happen after he had spotted the motorboat but for some inexplicable reason, the profound love and inescapably overwhelming and passionate relationship of the fictional lovers in *La Chaleur de la Mer* – a love affair he had always dreamed of experiencing but had not known with either Erika or his long-ago fiancée – sprang into his mind, immersing him in its strength and beauty as he helplessly watched the motorboat come nearer and nearer.

Thinking the very worst, his heart beat faster with an acute sense of anxiety.

At his feet, Abetz was now fully awake, squirming with discomfort, trying to free himself from the bonds that kept him prisoner, making muffled noises through the gag that Robert had put on as a precautionary measure.

Robert retightened their captive's blindfold and checked the security of the constraints on his hands and feet.

"Shouldn't we release him?" asked Richard.

"Absolutely not!" replied Robert. "We don't yet know whether that boat is friendly or not."

"Cyanide pills?" ventured Richard nervously. "Should we get them ready just in case?" The significance of the thought frightened him.

"No!"

Robert thought of the letters from Edna tucked in the inside pocket of his tunic. There was still time to dispose of them before they were arrested. If they were arrested. If only he could identify the motorboat…

Silently the two men watched as it came ever closer.

Any moment now their fate would be decided.

He watched, fingering the letters in his pocket and the little package with the pill inside as Richard took the binoculars and put them up to his eyes…

Feeling restless and with her dilemma still playing on her mind, before breakfast Sophie quietly climbed out of her bunk and dressed. Carefully, she let herself out of the hut and, taking with her *La Chaleur* and its accompanying inserts, found the most secluded, sheltered place in the camp that she could find.

Was she in love with Heinrich?

Of course she was, she persuaded herself, otherwise to have allowed a man to do what he had done would make her a… She shied away from the unpleasant thought.

Perhaps she was asking too much; perhaps real life was not like fiction and therefore she should just put every other consideration aside – the issue of sexual morality included – and allow Heinrich to become her lover on a regular basis, no matter how remote from her dream the situation with him might be and no matter what the risks were.

She turned to the poem that RLA had written on the flyleaf of *La Chaleur*. Not for the first time did she wonder what emotion had prompted the choice of that particular verse:

There swims within my life a fish
Which is the deep and glittering wish
Evoking all the hills and waters
Of sensual memories.
Your image and those days of glass
Being lost become no loss
But change into that image
At the centre of my thought,
Itself no less precious
Than the original happiness.

Sophie knew that if she had chosen it, for her it would have been prompted by her memories of the boy on the beach; of meeting and losing him and how his image, the strength of which could not be denied, still remained within her soul even after all she had experienced with Heinrich.

Therefore, it begged the question – was Heinrich the centre of her thoughts? He dominated them at the moment, certainly, but was he the *centre* of them?

Silently, clasping RLA's writing and his words to her chest, she communed all that was in her heart and mind to him who, alongside the boy on the beach, had become the natural centre of her thoughts. If only she could meet him; if only she could talk to him in real life. She knew he would understand; she knew he wouldn't judge her or think ill of her.

Sophie felt so deeply convinced of this that she could not be certain from whence the thought originated. But it was so vital and so powerful that she felt comforted and strengthened by the knowledge of its absolute truth.

"It's an M.T.B.!" exclaimed Richard, unable to conceal his relief and exhilaration.

"And we're in German uniforms," observed Robert dryly.

"Oh God!" Richard's excitement evaporated. He'd forgotten about that. "What happens if they fire on us?"

"They'll wait until they've ascertained who we are. Think about it – the British don't tend to blow unarmed sailing dinghies out of the water."

"Even so, if only we had a Union Jack or something."

"Well, now would be the time to hoist it if we had," said Robert, as the power boat throttled back and came alongside.

"Boy, are we glad to see you!" exclaimed Richard, his legs suddenly weak with relief as he immediately recognized the officer who greeted them.

"What took you so long?" said Robert, experiencing a similar reaction to that of his friend. "And what happened to the sub that was supposed to rendezvous with us?"

"Called away elsewhere I'm afraid. So we came by M.T.B. instead. Had a devil of a job to find you, especially when you weren't at the appointed coordinates."

"We couldn't afford to hang about. We had no way of knowing whether anyone was coming for us at all," said Robert.

"No, I suppose not. Were you intending to sail all the way home?" There was the slightest hint of amused admiration in the man's voice.

"Yep, if we'd had to."

"They said you chaps were resourceful. I can see why now." He smiled at them. "Anyway, do you have the package?

"In a manner of speaking," and Robert indicated Abetz on the floor of the dinghy, now writhing in both fright and agony.

"I say, good show! The beast himself no less! Well, well, well!" The officer grinned. "The powers that be are going to be mighty pleased with you chaps. There might even be a medal in it for you both!"

"Well, let's hope this has done the trick. He's a slippery customer. Once we're back on *terra firma*, I suggest most strongly that you chuck him in solitary confinement and throw away the key."

"But not before we intelligence chaps have had the chance to interrogate him. He's a valuable commodity and this is a real triumph!" He smiled again. "Well, let's get you and the bonus package on board and then we'll hightail it back to Blighty. The colonel's going to be chuffed to bits to see you two again. He's been plaguing us constantly while you've been away. Thought he'd made a ghastly mistake in sending you across."

"There were times when we thought so too," remarked Robert.

After transferring their prisoner onto the boat, taking the dinghy in tow and hauling the canoes on board, the coxswain opened up the throttles of the M.T.B. and set off for England.

"I tell you something, Robert," observed Richard, as they neared the coast. "It's a nice, safe office job for me from now on."

"You and me both. But as we're in the wartime service of our country, unfortunately we have no choice in the matter. We're obliged to go wherever we're sent."

Richard was silent. He'd had enough of this secret service stuff. All he wanted to do now was to have a bath and a shave and a decent meal and be with Caroline in the safety of her arms.

For ever.

Taking a deep breath filled with the sweet, invigorating air of home and a sense of relief and relaxed wellbeing after a successful mission, Robert watched the approaching coastline of Devon, with its hills and harbours, its multi-coloured cliffs and numerous sandy beaches.

His heart stirred at the sight.

This was what he was fighting for; *this* was what he believed in: defending the freedom of this beautiful island with its individualistic peoples; fighting for justice and peaceful humanity; for tolerance, acceptance and understanding; for his family and friends both here and in Germany; even for his mysterious girl on the beach, wherever she was.

Was this too idealistic? Was he, even after all he had experienced, a naïve idealist? Perhaps. But he knew that without idealism, the world would be a dull, unimaginative and uncaring place. However, alongside this, he also possessed a strong sense of pragmatic realism – a realism that gave him the balance, and an appreciation of the broader picture.

Robert felt the stirrings of a poem, the first for a very long time. Tired as he was, he found a pencil and a couple of sheets of paper and began to write.

When Abetz failed to turn up at *Geheime Feldpolizei* headquarters in Port le Bac the following morning and was not to be found in his living quarters, island-wide search parties were organized.

Every house in Port le Bac was investigated; notices were pinned up in prominent places demanding information as to the whereabouts of Theodor Abetz.

The patrol sergeant came forward and said that Herr Abetz had cancelled all regular patrols for the previous night along the cliff by the little cove on the other side of the island. The corpulent sentry (having previously found out from one of his friends about Abetz's cancellation of the patrols) when questioned (in order to hide the fact that he had fallen asleep yet again while on duty) lied to his superiors and said that Herr Abetz had told him to go home and sleep or find some girl to er... and he cleared his throat meaningfully at this point. (Everyone knew about Herr Abetz and his frequent excesses in that direction, didn't they?).

His superiors understood the inference and the sentry congratulated himself on his ingenuity in adding that little fabrication to his story to make it more authentic.

Continuing with his statement, the sentry declared that he had indeed returned to his billet as directed by Herr Abetz, but that he had returned to duty on the cliff top early in the morning in good time to hand over to his relief. (By this additional fiction, he covered his tracks completely. He had in actual fact woken up before the handover, fortunately).

The sentry was dismissed without further interrogation and went away feeling very pleased with himself.

No one questioning him sought confirmation from anyone that he had indeed gone back to his billet. Nor did his superiors ask why he had obeyed Abetz's orders

292

without question. It was widely accepted that since his arrival, everyone of inferior rank obeyed Herr Abetz. His reputation preceded him and his vindictiveness if his orders were disregarded was renowned.

This acquiescence to Abetz was, very naturally, bitterly resented by the *Wehrmacht* hierarchy who regarded it as an undermining of their authority which, of course, it was. However, in order to keep the peace with the *Geheime Feldpolizei*, they turned a blind eye to his frequent incursions into their territory.

After the questions had been asked and answers ascertained, a large detachment of *Wehrmacht* soldiers was immediately despatched to search the area around the cove, including the farmhouse, bursting rudely into the kitchen just moments after Sergei had leapt, once again, out of a side window and melted away into the surrounding woodland.

Edna and Mae exchanged the briefest of glances as the soldiers entered the premises unannounced; the former relieved that she had tidied away all traces of Robert and Richard ever having lived in the cellar; the latter scared that the soldiers might be looking for her 'two dear boys'.

She *had* to know. But Mae knew she also had to be careful.

Before he left, Robert had told her that if she ever needed to ask a question, she should phrase it in an oblique way so that she would get the answer she wanted but "the person of whom she asked the question would never be able to identify what it was she needed to know".

Those were his exact words and Mae now put into practice one of the things that Robert had taught her – for her own protection, he'd said.

"What are you looking for, sir?" she ventured bravely, wondering if she was being oblique enough. She had to know about them but, mindful of Robert's advice, she didn't ask 'who' she said 'what'.

The officer looked at her, an impatient, anxious scowl on his face. "For your information, old woman, and it is important that everyone knows this, a high-ranking *SS* officer is missing. We, the *Wehrmacht*, as well as the *Geheime Feldpolizei* are searching the island. If he is not found alive, it will go badly for the people of St Nicolas."

"Ah."

Inwardly, Mae experienced a huge sense of relief while maintaining a neutral outward expression. Robert had taught her how to do that as well. He said it was a useful trick to learn. They had had such fun while she had been practising but he had impressed upon her the seriousness of being good at it.

The officer sent away his soldiers to search the house, the outbuildings and farmyard.

"Have you seen him?" he demanded. "It is better that you should tell us rather than the *Geheime Feldpolizei*. They will not be merciful."

"Who, my dear? Who is it that's missing?" she asked innocently.

"Have you not seen the notices?" he snapped.

"I have not been anywhere this morning apart from my bedroom and the kitchen. I suffer with my chest, you see, so I rarely go out." She smiled at him.

The officer could see that she was a kind, innocuous old lady and now that his soldiers, having been ordered to search upstairs, were not in the room, he felt able to soften his manner and be himself. He was tired of having to pretend that he was tough all the time.

"We are looking for *SS-Oberführer* Theodor Abetz."

"And who is he, my dear?"

He wanted to call him a rude name but he stopped himself. "The person we're looking for."

"Ah," said Mae again. "Would you like a cup of tea?"

The young officer had to smile. She reminded him of his favourite aunt. "Another time, perhaps. But thank you."

"You're welcome."

He was reluctant to leave the warmth of the kitchen. His missed his home and his family.

"Will you let me know if you see anything?"

"Of course. And don't forget about the tea," she called out as he went out of the door, his soldiers having found nothing.

"I won't."

"Good boy."

After they had gone, Mae staggered backwards and sat on one of the kitchen chairs looking slightly stunned.

Edna said to her sister, "You did that very well, dear."

"Thank you," replied Mae. "At least we know they got away."

"I hope to goodness they covered their tracks successfully."

And both sisters looked at each other.

The soldiers next made their way to the cove. They found nothing except for a neat pile of clothes, boots, Luger and a towel placed on some stones in the grotto.

A quick search of his wallet revealed the owner's identity. Everything seemed to be intact – his identity papers, his Nazi party membership card and a large quantity of money. The inside pocket of his jacket contained several photographs of a pornographic nature.

The young officer grinned at his sergeant.

"What shall we do with these?" he asked, looking through them with guilty fascination.

"Put them back, young man," said the old sergeant firmly, "and forget you ever saw them. They're not for the likes of you or I and you don't want anyone to see you looking at them."

The *leutnant* did as he was told. He had great respect for the older man, who had guided him with care and tact since his recent arrival on the island.

"Looks like he went for a midnight swim and never came back," the officer remarked, "or else had some kind of assignation on the beach and then went for a swim afterwards. Otherwise why would he have cancelled the patrols?"

The sergeant raised an eyebrow. "And if it was as you suggest, *Herr Leutnant*, then whoever the assignation was with, we shall never know as they're not going to admit to it are they?"

"No, not if they value their life."

294

There was no sign of any struggle, no blood on the clothes, no footprints in the sand, no discarded weapons. Just the neatly folded garments, footwear, weapon and the towel.

"It's a shame he's gone," said the officer, not meaning a word of it. "We'll miss him."

"Like hell," muttered the sergeant.

And they exchanged a quick smile.

The M.T.B. arrived safely in Devonport and disembarked its passengers onto the quayside.

Abetz's feet were untied to enable him to hobble into the waiting military prison van and his gag removed for his own wellbeing but he remained blindfolded. No one was about to let him see the Royal Naval base.

He struggled and kicked and squirmed and made life very difficult for the M.P.s charged with transporting him to Grange Manor as they attempted to put him into the vehicle. He assumed Robert was somewhere close by, though with the blindfold on, he couldn't see him.

"Sie sind ein verräterischer Bastard! Ich werde mich rächen!" he shouted out over and over again as they pushed him into the van.

"Oh do shut up," said the M.P., "otherwise I'll knock your block off. What's he saying anyway?"

"He says I'm a treacherous bastard and that he'll have his revenge," interpreted Robert.

"Sounds a nice sort of bloke," remarked the M.P. "Come on then, sunshine, let's take you somewhere where you can cool off for a bit. Then the nice intelligence chaps can have their wicked way with you."

"I pity the poor devils who have to question him," remarked Richard.

"As long as it's not us," said Robert with deep feeling as the van drove away. "I've had enough of Theodor Abetz."

The investigation into Abetz's disappearance remained inconclusive but a verdict of accidental drowning was returned at the inquiry.

The *Wehrmacht* and the *Geheime Feldpolizei* on St Nicolas were glad to be rid of him so were happy with the decision. For once they actually agreed on something.

The Military Government in Paris accepted the verdict as accurate and dismissed it from any further deliberations concerning the island. Neither did they recommend that any action should be taken against anyone on St Nicolas, German military or civilian locals.

The authorities in Berlin remained outwardly noncommittal. However, they were persuaded by Admiral Siranac not to select a replacement to carry out the daring and possibly war-changing mission with which Abetz had been originally tasked. He said, quietly and firmly, that it should be left to his department to investigate its feasibility rather than just sending someone randomly across to England in the hope that the mission might be successful, no matter how zealous they might be and anxious to prove their worth for the glorious Fatherland.

So, Siranac 'sent' a non-existent *Abwehr* agent 'across' to England, informing the Nazi hierarchy that everything concerning the plausibility of this most brilliant scheme was being investigated, that no stone was being left unturned.

Later, much later, he informed them that after extensive study, most regrettably it would be a complete disaster: King George VI and his family were too well protected by the British Government and therefore, invulnerable to assassination. It was recommended that the idea be dropped immediately as the inevitable failure would reflect badly on the Third Reich and achieve nothing.

Admiral Siranac then sent a nonspecific coded message out on the *Abwehr* Enigma 'airwaves' that the scheme had been discarded and that the safety and security of 'very important personages' was assured. He used the same letter sequences that he had used before – presuming that someone, somewhere in England, would pick it up and make sense of the decrypts.

It was Robert who did, sitting at his desk in Bletchley Park, just as he had done when interpreting the warning contained in the *Abwehr* decrypts before he and Richard were dispatched in such haste to St Nicolas.

He smiled as he read the meaning.

Perhaps, after the war was over and peace in Europe had been restored, he would visit his friend the admiral and renew his acquaintance of this brave and honourable man, but in more congenial circumstances.

PART FOUR

APRIL – NOVEMBER, 1945

CHAPTER 37

Frankfurt/Seeblick

"Bob, can you deal with this one on your own?"

"Which one's that?"

"We've been given some ancient Kraut to interrogate. He's so old he should have been put out to grass years ago. No wonder the Germans lost if that's all they could field against us Yanks."

Robert sighed. He disliked this brash, cocksure young American intelligence officer with whom he'd been working after being seconded to Supreme Allied Headquarters Expeditionary Force (S.H.A.E.F.) in Frankfurt towards the end of April.

The war couldn't be won without their American Allies, that was a given, but it annoyed him when so many of them went around declaring that they were the 'goddamn saviours of Europe', seeming to imply that they were winning the conflict singlehandedly.

Robert sighed again. After returning from St Nicolas and before being assigned to S.H.A.E.F., he'd spent his time with Richard firstly at Bletchley Park and then at Grange Manor where they had interrogated high-ranking German prisoners-of-war, trying to extract information that might be valuable to the Allies, as well as assessing the extent of their captive's allegiance to the Third Reich.

With the prospect of defeat looming on the horizon, most German officers were very cooperative. There were some who remained stubbornly intransigent and took longer to renounce their Nazism or to reveal anything of significance, but these were few and far between, mainly because he and Richard were very good at their job.

Both of them had been relieved to find that Theodor Abetz was not among those whom they had been expected to interview.

So, now, Robert found himself here in Germany alone. Having been given the option, Richard chose to remain in England so that he could be near to Caroline while Robert had opted to come across to Europe wanting to finish the war in the place where it had begun. He also wished to discover the whereabouts of some old friends and to trace his children's Belgian relatives.

He missed working with Richard and was beginning to wish he'd stayed in England. He consoled himself with the prospect of being best man at Richard and Caroline's wedding, the date of which had been set for July.

"We should be off-duty now," said his American colleague, "but they've just landed this one on us. I gotta a hot date with a swell looking blonde from the typing pool so I'm outta here. If you do this one for me, Bob, I'll pay you back. I swear!"

"You don't have to do that, Marv." (*What a name!*) "It's okay. I'll see to this one. You go and do whatever it is you want to do. I've got nothing else lined up."

"You oughta get out and about more, Bob. See the sights. Enjoy the nightlife. Relax. Let your hair down! Some of you Brits are so…" He was going to say 'stuffy' but thought better of it. "Well, I'll be seeing ya!"

Robert nodded noncommittally and his erstwhile colleague disappeared down the corridor.

He picked up his briefcase, a new cardboard folder and some paper and went across to the interview room. There, sitting under close guard, was a sad-looking man, shabbily dressed in a dilapidated uniform.

The man stood up and saluted as Robert entered the room and he returned the courtesy. The guard left the room to take up position behind the closed door and Robert indicated that the man should be seated.

In silence, Robert briefly appraised him. He looked tired and wan and his eyes held an expression of resignation and defeat. Robert had seen it so often recently: an attitude of mind superseding the arrogance that had predominated at the beginning of the war, or the more conciliatory stance adopted during the middle years when things were not going so well for the Germans.

Yet there was a difference here. Despite his facial expression, this man still held himself proudly as though he was someone of stature and bearing. It was not arrogance but something inborn.

An aristocrat, thought Robert.

He smiled and the soldier, taken by surprise, smiled back, his eyes revealing a hint of unexpected humour.

This was how Robert worked. He was very skilled at appearing genuinely pleasant (the latter being his natural demeanour anyway) to his interviewees, setting out to win their trust and confidence but at the same time, letting them know he would brook no nonsense nor would he be taken for a ride. In this way, working as a finely honed team, he and Richard had succeeded in gaining valuable information where others had failed.

"Hello," Robert began amiably. "Do you speak English?"

The man nodded.

"Good. Let me know if there's anything you don't understand, because I speak fluent German so we will be able talk to each other freely and easily." He smiled again. "Name, please?"

"My name is Major Albrecht von Witzenhausen."

Caught completely by surprise, Robert stared at him.

In the months following D-Day, food and provisions had gradually become scarcer in Seeblick as the Allies advanced and lines of internal communication in Germany gradually broke down. Allied bombing of cities and factories also played its part in creating shortages, not just for the internees but for the civilian population as well. Coal became an unheard of commodity and Seeblick shivered through the cold and prolonged winter months. Letters and post gradually dwindled until they ceased to reach the camp altogether and Red Cross deliveries also became sporadic until they too disappeared.

The internees would have been in serious difficulties had it not been for the farsightedness of Heinrich and the organizing committee in stockpiling and rationing Red Cross parcels in anticipation of future shortages. In fact, they had accumulated so much, they even tried to send a couple of boxes to St Nicolas where they had heard, in one of the last letters to reach them, that because there were now no direct imports from France to the island and because the recently appointed *Kommandant* refused to allow any Red Cross ship to bring in provisions, the inhabitants – soldiers, prisoners and residents alike – were on the point of starvation.

Despite the shortages, everyone in the camp (with predictable exceptions) strived to maintain their routine. The drama society continued to flourish, classes were still held. Long walks in the nearby forest and the little town (where strong friendships with the villagers had developed over the years), instigated and organized during the first summer that Heinrich had been *Kommandant*, continued to be very popular. And although the two accompanying guards were armed with pistols, they complied with the Geneva Convention and kept their weapons covered. They were relaxed and friendly and everyone who was able, young or old, working on a rota system, partook of this regular and stimulating exercise.

Tommy especially revelled in these outings, finding in Fritz, their regular guard, a kindred spirit in all things to do with the natural world.

Despite the shortages, the general health and wellbeing of the inmates remained stable and, apart from a quickly contained outbreak of diphtheria when some Jewish prisoners released from a concentration camp brought the illness with them to Seeblick, there were no serious epidemics like the scarlet fever one of a couple of years previously.

Sophie's health gradually returned to normal and she remained as librarian, fulfilling her duties conscientiously. If he found her to be alone, Heinrich would seek her out and, if no one was around, take her to bed with him. However, these occasions were rare and secretly, Sophie was glad of this. She cared for him, certainly; had come to love him perhaps because of their continuing intimacy, but she was not *in* love with him. She knew that now.

They were very discreet and managed to maintain the secrecy of their liaison. Nor had she, so far, become pregnant. Using a couple of very useful biology books from the library, Sophie had researched the times to avoid and, after explaining this to Heinrich, he agreed not to press her when it was not safe. She never used it as an excuse but allowed him access to her body whenever he so desired just as she had promised and which, from her perspective, was fortunately not very often.

Gradually, over time, Heinrich became absent from the camp with increasing regularity, sometimes for a couple of weeks or a month at a time, on one occasion for two months. Prior to these absences, he would look tired and drawn, his complexion grey; his gait slow and his breathing laboured.

Concerned for his wellbeing, whenever Sophie asked him what the matter was, he would avoid giving her a direct answer but after each return to Seeblick, he seemed more cheerful and possessed of more energy. It was only then that he wanted to make love.

Eventually, however, he seemed less well permanently, even after his return. He refused to talk to Sophie about his absences or the reason for his periods of listlessness and lack of energy. He spent a great deal of time with Dr Reynolds and, in the spirit of patient confidentiality, the good doctor gave away nothing, not even to Marian, with whom there was something of a serious romance going on – so serious, in fact, that they announced their intention of being married after liberation and they had returned home. Everyone in the camp was delighted for them – even

Gert and Mabel held their acerbic tongues for once – and the couple made preliminary preparations for their future life together.

Following D-Day in June 1944, the internees knew it would only be a matter of time before they would be free. Liberation came to Seeblick Internment Camp on St George's Day, 23rd April, 1945. It was not a moment too soon; yet nor was it without its near tragedy.

Three weeks prior to their liberation the reality of war came closer to them. They saw streams of Allied aircraft flying overhead and the ground shook with the explosions as nearby towns and cities were heavily bombed. They heard machine-gun fire and the sounds of mortars as the vanguard of the Allied advance drew ever nearer.

Hundreds of refugees streamed through the village of Seeblick and up the hill past the camp gates: a pitiful sight as they trudged wearily past with their belongings piled high on prams and pushchairs, on overloaded carts pulled by thin exhausted ponies.

Following this, they witnessed the full-scale retreat of the German armed forces heading in the same direction: lorries filled with troops, armoured vehicles, staff cars crammed with officers, all closely followed by the Red Cross.

Sophie looked with consternation at Heinrich as they went by but he made no move to join the retreating forces.

"I shall stay here with all of you," he declared, a statement that earned him the admiration of all the inmates, including Sophie.

Following the *Kommandant*'s lead, although it was not a direct order, some of the police guards decided to remain. They felt they would be safer in the camp. Those who lived locally went home to their families, being anxious for their safety.

One day, soon after this, French tanks lumbered their way through the town and up the hill past the camp and although they didn't stop, the internees knew that it would only be a matter of time before they were given their freedom.

That night no one in the camp slept. The curfew was ignored and, taking advantage of the general excited melee and lack of cohesive order where no one knew what anyone else was doing or where they were, Sophie, under cover of the blackout went across to Heinrich's office in the Big House.

She knew she had to go to him; that he would need her this one last time. She was very aware that it was not a safe time for her to do so, but even so, she had no hesitation in taking that risk. She owed him that much for the undoubted love he held for her and the care and consideration with which he had always treated her.

Quietly, she opened the door and went inside.

Despite the lateness of the hour, Heinrich was still at his desk finishing off his final paperwork: a blackout curtain up at the windows, a dim oil lamp (the electricity supply had been cut three days previously) the only means of light.

He stood up as she entered the room and immediately went across to her, holding her to him and looking at her with love and gratitude.

He buried his face in her neck, saying *"Danke, mein Liebchen,"* over and over again. Then he put his arm around her shoulders and guided her to his bedroom.

For the last time, Sophie shared with her lover the intimacy they had known during the preceding years; for the last time, she allowed him to make love to her.

"When the war is over," he whispered into her ear, "I shall come to England and find you," he promised. "Will you wait for me?"

And Sophie, lying in his arms, found herself unable to reply; unable to make a promise she might not be able to keep. Instead, she kissed his cheek and smiled through her tears as the pain of separation wrenched at her heart.

Somewhere nearby a bomb dropped, shattering the night with a reminder that they were not yet safe.

"Major von Witzenhausen!" exclaimed Robert, a smile of pleasure lighting his face.

"*Ja,*" the older man replied, surprised by such a friendly reception at his interrogation. "That is my name."

"The first *Kommandant* of St Nicolas in 1940?"

"*Ja* that is so." He regarded Robert for a moment. "You know the island?"

"Yes."

"It was a good place to be," he said quietly. "I should like to have stayed. There was someone to whom I became very close. I wished to stay with her. I intend to return to her as soon as I can."

"Her name?" Robert had to be sure.

"*Fräulein* Edna Weissman."

Robert smiled again and lifted his briefcase onto the desk. "I have a letter for you."

Albrecht was mystified. "For me?"

"Yes. Edna gave it to me while I was on the island in the hope that I would be able to post it to you once the war was over."

"You know her?" the major said in amazement. "You have been to the island?" He gave Robert a shrewd look. "Since the occupation?"

"Yes." There was no harm in saying so now.

The older man chuckled. "Perhaps one day you might be able to tell me."

"Perhaps."

Although his reply was noncommittal, Robert, inexplicably, felt a sudden surge of optimism. Was it because he could do something positive for Edna, whom he liked and respected, or was it the prospect of one day holding an ordinary conversation with this man who was ostensibly his prisoner, bringing the light of normality to what had been a dark tunnel of abnormal contact with fellow human beings?

Robert took out the letter from his briefcase and handed it to von Witzenhausen, who took it from him and opened the envelope with care.

What he read inside transformed his expression and he suddenly appeared younger, more sprightly and dapper.

Watching him, Robert discerned the genuine feeling and hope the letter had obviously given this man.

"At last, I can now look forward to the future," said Albrecht, smiling with barely contained joy. "Now I can look forward with confidence and certainty to meeting her once again."

Robert smiled. "I'm glad," he said. "Edna spoke of you many times during my short stay on the island. She kept your address hidden in her bureau. She couldn't bear to bury it in the garden with her other precious things."

"Ah, so she took my advice about hiding her valuables?"

"She did indeed."

"And does she keep herself free of trouble as I requested?"

"We-ell. Not exactly."

Albrecht was immediately concerned. "What does she do?"

"Nothing that she's been caught doing," replied Robert enigmatically. No doubt Edna would tell this man herself, one day.

"So far."

"Yes, so far."

"Still, the Channel Islands should be freed from occupation soon, yes?"

"Maybe. However, the present incumbent is refusing to surrender."

"Then whoever it is, he is a very stupid man."

"Where was your next post after St Nicolas?" asked Robert conversationally, subtly beginning the interview.

"I was sent to Dresden to take up an administrative position. The bombing was terrible, terrible. Such a fine, historic city reduced to nothing but rubble. So many women and children killed." He shrugged his shoulders. "But that is the tragic nature of war. London is no doubt much altered by this calamity which befell our two great nations and which now, thank God, is nearly over."

"I agree, absolutely," replied Robert. "And we have to do all we can to prevent its repetition once the war finally does come to an end."

"Well, that will be for you young people to carry out, I'm afraid, for I have had my day. My only wish now is for a peaceful, quiet existence."

"What happened after Dresden?"

"I was side-lined into running a small army clothing department in Frankfurt not far from here. I was to be retired from the army on the very day the Allies arrived."

"Then why are you here now? Surely, you could have lived out the rest of the war in relative safety?"

Albrecht shook his head. "On that day, I decided to surrender to the British."

"Why?" Robert was mystified.

"Ah, but you see, I wanted to get to England because I reasoned that if I was there, I would be better placed to reach the Channel Islands. I did not know how many years it would be before German citizens would be allowed into your country. At my age, I could not wait for whenever that might be. To surrender and become a prisoner-of-war seemed to be the quickest way for me to get there. You see, at the end of the Great War, German prisoners were given the choice of repatriation or remaining in England. I reasoned that it will be the same after this one. I would then opt to stay and go to St Nicolas to be with Edna."

Robert had to admire him for his ingenuity and determination.

"I also discovered that once I revealed I had been *Kommandant* of St Nicolas, as a high-ranking officer having held an important post, I would be brought here for interrogation with the other high-ranking officers and thus increase my chances of being sent to England."

Robert smiled at him. "Perhaps," he replied, thinking carefully. "However, prison camps are not exactly a holiday destination of choice."

"No, but if I came under British jurisdiction, then I could be reasonably confident of being well treated. And I assumed that all captured German officers would be sent to England."

"Or Canada."

This information shook Albrecht. He had not heard this and was suddenly full of concern. "I have no wish to go there," he said quietly.

Robert wrote something down on a piece of paper and passed it across to the Major, who nodded gratefully, his former buoyancy restored.

"Is this possible?"

Robert nodded. He'd be sticking his neck out but he would do this for Edna and the man she cared about.

He then proceeded with the rest of the interview, which was easy and straightforward. At its conclusion, the two men shook hands.

"I really hope that you and Edna fulfil your dream."

"Thank you. And if by some stroke of good fortune we do, I trust that one day when all this madness has been put aside forever that you will come and visit us."

"You can count on it," replied Robert, thinking that his report of this interrogation would make an interesting study for his superiors.

He hoped that they would be sympathetic to Major von Witzenhausen's needs and that they would take on board the recommendation he was going to make that the former *Kommandant* should be transferred to a P.O.W. camp in England pending being able to stay in the country.

In Seeblick the next day, a radio message was received from S.H.A.E.F. concerning all P.O.W.s and internees stating that they were '*to remain in their camps, obey their leaders, and wait patiently for further orders*'.

Heinrich also received a message to say that the liberating French troops would be at the camp by three o'clock that afternoon and that Seeblick had been declared an open town.

On hearing this, there was great excitement and no little anxiety among the internees as no one knew exactly how events would unfold. It was expected that the French would be able to enter the area peacefully, but to everyone's dismay, retreating German soldiers began shelling and machine-gunning the French tanks and armoured personnel vehicles as they came up the hill towards the camp.

Quickly, Heinrich shepherded the watching children to safety before he and other adult internees and the police guards rushed around the camp putting up white flags and white sheets on the barbed wire fencing. Someone even managed to find a St Nicolas flag, which they hung from the balcony of the Big House, and a Union Jack, strategically placed on one of the guard towers at the entrance to the camp.

A series of terrible explosions rent the air as shells whizzed overhead, landing nearby and sending great clods of earth raining down into the compound.

Sophie looked at Heinrich in horror as they crouched with the others between the huts for safety.

However, under ferocious returning fire, the Germans soon ran out of ammunition and could be seen running away in all directions, abandoning their weapons, trying to escape across the ploughed fields, pursued by the French.

After an hour of uneasy silence as the noise of battle receded into the distance, a couple of tanks and an armoured vehicle rolled up to the entrance of the camp. Without ceremony, one of the soldiers viciously kicked at the padlock and once it had been broken, the officer in charge was first to enter through the gates.

Slowly the internees emerged from their hiding places, gathering in the compound staring silently at the heavily armed French soldiers; the smaller children clinging onto their mothers, the older ones wide-eyed with apprehension.

Their liberators were a coarse-looking group: swarthy-skinned, unshaven; their uniforms ill-kempt and dirty; their manner aggressive and impatient.

The Commodore greeted them cautiously.

"Hello," he said. "Thank you for coming. You are most welcome."

"Je ne parle pas anglais."

"Je parle français," said Sophie, stepping forward.

"Bien. Où sont les gardiens de prison ?"

However, before Sophie had had the chance to reply, the officer spotted the guards standing with Heinrich next to the steps of the Big House.

Without hesitation, the Frenchman rounded them up and ordered their execution.

Sophie and several other women screamed out for them to stop as Heinrich and their kindly German policemen were roughly and unceremoniously pushed, shoved and dragged to stand against the wall. The officer gave another command and half a dozen of his men lined up in front of them, raised their rifles, waiting for the order to fire.

The world went into slow motion and for a fraction of a second, the internees stood there in stunned immobility.

But Tommy was having none of this. He wrenched himself free from his mother's grasp and ran across the compound to stand bravely and resolutely in front of Fritz, his favourite guard.

Without speaking or communicating, every single child in the near vicinity rushed forward and did the same as Tommy until Heinrich and all the guards were completely protected.

"Ne tirez pas ! Ne tirez pas !" shouted Sophie, confronting the officer. *"Don't shoot! Don't shoot!"*

"It is what we have to do. Tell the children to stand aside."

"Non ! Je refuse ! These men are not fighting soldiers. They are policemen, some of whom live in the village. They go home to their families every night. You have no right to shoot them. It would be… murder."

"What about him?" The officer indicated Heinrich with his head. *"Is he the one in charge?"*

"Yes, but he is a civilian."

"I do not believe you. He is wearing a uniform."

"In the German system, civilian men and women drafted into the Wehrmacht wear a uniform. But they do not fight. They do not carry weapons. They are not trained to be soldiers. He does…" Sophie was pleading desperately for Heinrich's

life. How could she make this man intent on violence understand and see reason? "...*administration. Paperwork.*"

But the Frenchman remained intransigent.

"*Tell the children to move out of the way.*"

"*Non !*"

And Sophie went to stand with the children, quickly followed by their parents until Heinrich and the guards were completely hidden from view.

"*Stand aside!*"

"*Surely you would not allow women and innocent children to witness the horrors of a firing squad? You have come to liberate us so that we can go home. We know you will not kill us and we cannot allow you to kill them.*" Sophie walked forward towards the Frenchman and resolutely, stood before him. "*Is this what you have become, is this what the war has made you – animals so that you would murder civilians without stopping to think about what you are doing? We will not stand by and let you do this! Tell your men to put away their guns!*"

Faced with such implacable determination, with great reluctance, the officer ordered his men to lower their weapons.

"*We are from French Morocco,*" the officer said to Sophie, as the tension eased. "*The ways of the British are strange to us. You would spare your enemy?*"

"*These men are not our enemy. The war is over,*" said Sophie.

"*For you, perhaps, but not for us. These men are now our prisoners.*"

"*I understand.*" Sophie bowed to the inevitable. However, there was one more thing she wanted to say. "*These men have treated us well. Promise me you will treat them in the same way.*"

The officer acquiesced. "*We shall treat them in accordance with the Geneva Convention.*"

"*Merci beaucoup, Monsieur.*" Sophie knew she could do no more.

Heinrich and the guards were allowed to collect their personal belongings, before being lined up in the compound.

The Commodore shook Heinrich's hand. "Thank you," he said, his voice gruff with emotion, "from all of us. You have been good to us and your consideration towards us has made our lives here civilized and more bearable. I wish there was something we could do to help you."

Heinrich nodded, accepting the Commodore's words and grateful for them.

Her eyes filling with tears, unable to say goodbye in the way that she would have wished to the man who had become her lover, Sophie could only stand by and look at Heinrich. He returned her gaze, his face ashen and his stance uncertain.

"*Danke,*" he said quietly, wanting to hold her for one last time.

"*Bitte,*" she replied.

Then Heinrich was marched away with the others and the last view that Sophie had of him was sitting in the open back of a lorry being driven out of the gates to an unknown destination and out of her life.

He did not look at her again and the tears streamed down her face.

"Bob! Where's Bob?" said the American intelligence officer to Robert's secretary. "I need to find him because some of us from S.H.A.E.F. have gotta go to some place called Seeblick in Baden-Württemberg because there's a load of Limeys who've just been liberated by the French. Apparently, we've gotta interview them and issue passports and identity cards so they can be sent home. Been interned there for years it seems. It's gonna forever to do all that, I guess, as there's hundreds of them. Women and children as well. I want Bob to come with me as this lot are English. I ain't doin' it on my own."

"But Bob's not here. He's gone – this afternoon in fact. You've just missed him." She didn't add that they would all miss him. "He's gone on leave before taking up his new posting."

"Shit. He never tells me squat. I guess I'll have to find someone else." He pulled at his ear lobe. "Our beloved colonel's asked me to arrange a welcome for them in a few weeks' time at the U.S. Air Force Base at Mengen. See to it, will you, sweetheart? Then get old Lieutenant-Colonel Hotchkiss to find a Dakota or something so's they can be flown to Hendon in England straight afterwards."

"What happens to them then?"

"Oh, there's going to be some kinda reception for them at some place called Stanmore before they're given final clearance."

"Sounds like a bit of a long haul."

"Better than being holed up in a prison camp, I guess."

Robert's former secretary agreed and, after speaking to their colonel, made the necessary arrangements.

CHAPTER 38

Maybury

In July, 1945, having outlived its particular usefulness, S.H.A.E.F. was finally dissolved and new organizations were put in place to deal with the rapidly developing European situation.

Robert was not required to be a part of this and, after returning to England and finding himself promoted to major, was told what his next posting would be: back with his old regiment the Royal Welch Fusiliers as the senior officer charged with organizing and running the newly created Meridian Prisoner of War Camp in Bridgend in Wales, as well as overseeing a small team of intelligence officers to be stationed at the camp.

"I feel as though I've spent the best years of my life interviewing German P.O.W.s," he remarked to Freddie Ashton on being given his orders.

"That's because you're damned good at it, old chap!" came the immediate reply.

"What about Richard?" asked Robert. "What's he going to be doing?"

"Oh, as he's R.N.V.R., he'll be getting his demob very soon, so you're on your own, I'm afraid. Getting married soon, though, isn't he? To Travis's secretary. He'll be sorry to lose her."

Robert smiled. "She'll be sorry to leave Bletchley Park. But yes, they're getting married in a couple of days' time."

"And I gather you're to be best man. Good show. And his little sister has just got back from Germany in the nick of time for the wedding, I gather. Have you ever met her?"

"No, sir, I've not had that pleasure yet."

"No doubt you will. Richard was always going on about her. Took 'em long enough to get the internees home from Germany, though. Nearly a month after liberation, wasn't it?"

"Something like that."

"Well, they none of them'll be able to get back to the Channel Islands for a long time. Damn fool of a *Kommandant* didn't surrender until June, a whole month after the Germans finally surrendered in Europe. Wouldn't let the Red Cross ship in until the last minute either. Everyone was half starved to death. And to cap it all, no one's being allowed into England from there at the moment until everything's been sorted out. Hell of a mess."

"I know. Richard's aunts are very disappointed that they can't come across for his wedding. But they understand and Richard has promised to visit them as soon as he can."

"Good show. Well, enjoy what's left of your leave. You deserve it. Sorry it's not longer than a few days, but these high-ranking Nazis need to be sorted out and it needs an experienced man like yourself to set the whole thing in motion."

"Yes, sir," said Robert.

Freddie Ashton stood up and they shook hands.

"Well, good luck, old man. I've enjoyed working with you in our wartime capacities."

"Likewise. Thank you, sir."

"Don't mention it."

When he arrived at the house in Maybury, Robert was ushered into the hallway to be greeted by raised voices emanating from the first floor landing. The maid (who was new and unknown to Robert) disappeared discreetly after saying that he should wait until someone came as Sir Edmund and Lady Langley had not yet arrived home.

Standing at the foot of the stairs, having put his suitcase down on the floor and thrown his coat on top, Robert was at a loss as to know what he should do next. He was just about to go upstairs to find Richard, when the voices above him reached a crescendo.

Transfixed, he remained where he was, unable to avoid overhearing the argument.

"You have absolutely wrecked my wedding day!" exclaimed a voice shrill with accusation that he recognized as belonging to Caroline. "How could you?"

"How could I do what?" came the gentler tones of a voice he did not recognize but the timbre of which he found rather attractive.

"Do what you've done!"

"It's no more than you and Richard did!"

"Yes, but I didn't get pregnant! We were careful. And besides, this is completely different. I didn't go to bed with the enemy and I'm not expecting some *Kraut*'s illegitimate child."

"He's not just some *Kraut*," retorted the second voice. "He's the kindest man I've ever met. I wish now I'd never confided in you," additional words spoken in such a way which to Robert's ears sounded as though their owner was now close to tears. "I thought you were my friend."

"What's going on here?" said Richard, coming out onto the landing which Robert presumed to be from his bedroom.

Ah, thought Robert, perhaps Richard will make Caroline see sense and stop attacking whoever it was.

"Your sister is pregnant!" declared Caroline, sparing nothing.

Sophie, Richard's sister! Pregnant? By whom? wondered Robert.

Richard was stunned. "How could you be so stupid?"

"You don't understand."

"You're damn right I don't understand!" He was angry now; furious. "Mother and Dad will be distraught. How could you bring such shame on all of us?" He paused for breath before adding, "Who is he, the man you've allowed to do this... this thing to you?"

"Someone whom I care about very much," Sophie was bravely defiant; holding her own.

Robert admired her for that. He hoped that her feelings were returned by this man, whoever he was.

"It's the *Kommandant* from Seeblick, that's who it is; the man she hasn't heard anything from in three months and probably never will again," said Caroline, re-entering the fray.

Richard was horrified. "When you told me about him, I only imagined it to be something innocent; a crush on your part perhaps. Good God, Sophie, I never for a moment realized you were his mistress."

"I wasn't. We were lovers. But why are *you* turning against me? I would have thought you would have been on my side," she said imploringly to her brother.

"Not in this case, I'm afraid," retorted Richard, uttering words that shook Robert profoundly. "I'm with Caroline on this one."

"To hell with both of you," muttered Sophie, who ran frantically down the stairs, tripping in her agitation and losing her balance as she neared the bottom of the staircase.

Reacting swiftly, Robert caught her before she fell, supporting her in his arms. Shocked by how close she had just come to disaster, Sophie remained within his protective embrace, regaining her breath and her equilibrium.

A feeling of comfort and safety washed over her and as she looked up at him, Robert smiled, his eyes warm and kind.

"That was a close shave," he said softly, his heart melting as he held her. *This is ridiculous,* he told himself. And yet somehow, it wasn't.

Upstairs, Richard and Caroline were now embroiled in their own argument. Sophie and Robert exchanged a wry expression.

"I'm Robert, by the way, the best man. I'm afraid I've been standing here for a while and couldn't help but overhear."

"Don't worry. I'm very glad you arrived when you did. Thank you, Robert, for rescuing me."

"You're welcome."

"I'm Sophie, Richard's sister."

"I'd guessed as much." He smiled at her again, neither of them making any move to be apart. "Are you all right?"

"I'm fine, honestly."

"Good. So now that we've introduced ourselves and got all the formalities out of the way, I presume that you weren't intending to have an accident?" he asked, gently brushing a few stray wisps of hair back from her forehead.

"Of course not! I want this baby."

Despite her expression of defiance, Robert perceived a hint of regret and guilt below the surface; her bravado as much trying to convince herself as everyone else.

Still supporting her carefully within his arms, he said, "Forgive me, but I have to ask this question. Did he love you, the father?"

For some reason, this now mattered to him. Very much.

"Yes."

"You weren't coerced in any way?"

"No. It was nothing like that. He really did love me. Still does, I imagine." Her eyes filled with tears.

They always seemed to be doing that at the moment. Every time she thought of Heinrich; every time she spoke of Seeblick. She had received sympathy for the latter and had kept quiet about the former (until just now) but no one at home really *understood* her experiences: what it had been like to be *there*. Because of these things and because her years at the camp had profoundly changed her, since coming back to England and no longer in contact with the people with whom she had shared the past four years, she had felt utterly, completely *alone*.

"But you have no idea where he is?" asked Robert, after a few moments, seeing the pain in her eyes. Without thinking, he stroked her hair in a gesture of comfort, its texture and softness and his reaction to it catching him off-guard.

She smiled up at him, warmed by his concern; a frisson of delight going up her spine at his touch.

All at once, Robert wanted to kiss her.

"No, none. He said he would find me after the war was over."

"And is he a man to keep his promises?"

"Yes, but..."

"...you've given up hope of ever seeing him again?"

"Yes."

"Do you want to see him again?"

"I'm not sure," she replied honestly, "despite being pregnant. I was never in love with him, you see."

With sympathy, understanding and an unexpected feeling of relief at her words, Robert released her gently as Caroline and Richard came down the stairs.

"And what about your bridesmaid's dress?" demanded Caroline, launching into the attack once again. "It was specially made for you. It won't fit now. You'll look dreadful in it! As I said before, you've completely ruined my wedding day." Then, hardly stopping to draw breath she said, "Oh, hello, Bob."

Sophie shrank back towards the safety of Robert in the face of this renewed onslaught. He responded by supporting her body with his; putting one arm round her waist and the other diagonally across to her shoulder, enclosing her within a cocoon of safety; creating a sanctuary from the verbal fury raging in front of her.

"Caroline," acknowledged Robert placidly, "it's nice to see you too. Things can't be that drastic, surely. If you and your retinue have had any fittings recently, I imagine that any dress that looked perfect on Sophie yesterday will still look perfect on her at the wedding the day after tomorrow. Babies take a while to grow, you know."

"Why should you take her part? You haven't even been introduced to her." Caroline seemed put out by Robert's immediate defence of Sophie and not slow to take in their close proximity to each other.

"Oh, we're old friends," said Robert, looking down at Sophie and feeling gratified to see a smile of acknowledgement reach her eyes.

"We are," she agreed, her confidence returning.

"I'm not sure I want her as a bridesmaid now anyway," said Caroline sullenly, as though Sophie was no longer in the room. "What will my parents think?"

"Nothing, if you don't tell them," said Robert.

"But she's a traitor. She's carrying the enemy inside her."

Robert became impatient. "Don't be ridiculous. In case you hadn't noticed, the war's over."

"But the baby will still be German. You can't just suddenly switch off from regarding them as the enemy, just like that."

"Why not? As far as I'm aware, we were fighting to destroy an evil regime not the German people themselves."

"Weren't they one and the same?"

"You and I have had this discussion many times," said Robert, now thoroughly exasperated. "Of course they weren't. The Nazis brought about the destruction of a very fine and proud country and we were fighting against *them*, not the good German men or women who hated everything that Hitler and his cronies stood for and who, because of the all-pervasive nature of the system, were powerless to bring down Nazism."

Sophie, still leaning against Robert, reluctant to leave the shelter of his arms, began to feel the glow of having discovered a kindred spirit: someone who understood, someone who *knew*.

Strengthened by his strength, she said, "Heinrich was a good and special man. And what's more, I'm proud to be carrying his child."

"By allowing him to do what he did to you, you've become nothing more than a slut."

"That's enough, Caroline," said Robert firmly. "Let it go."

"No, I won't. What right have you to tell me what to do anyway? She's tarnished her reputation and by association, everyone else's in Richard's family. And the wonderful exquisite purity she always had will be gone forever." Caroline's bottom lip was beginning to tremble.

"That seems a very strange thing to say," said Robert, glaring at Richard for not stopping his fiancée's diatribe or defending his sister, "especially as we none of us are as pure or innocent as we were before this war began, are we?" and he looked pointedly at Richard and Caroline. "All of us will have been changed by our experiences and to say that one is right and another is wrong seems to me to be the height of arrogance. Who we are fundamentally will never change. That's always within us somewhere, adapting and maturing to circumstance."

Oh yes, thought Sophie, experiencing overwhelming relief and joy. *Where on earth did Richard find this man? He's quite, quite wonderful.*

They heard the turning of a key in the front door, and further discussion was forestalled as Edmund and Margot came into the house. With reluctance, Robert carefully released Sophie from his arms.

"Dear, dear boy," exclaimed Margot, immediately coming over to him and kissing him on both cheeks. "It's so good to see you again. I think it's absolutely splendid that you're able to be here to fulfil your best man duties! Richard would have been so terribly disappointed if you hadn't been able to extend your leave. We all would have been! You've become such a part of the family now."

"And I expect your old nag is impatient for you to exercise him," said Sir Edmund with a smile, shaking Robert's hand. "Especially as he doesn't want to know me since Sophie's been riding him. He seems to prefer her. I can't think why. Whinnies whenever he sees her!"

"Well, I'm most grateful to both of you for continuing to look after him for me. It's been a weight off my mind, I must say, especially as my parents weren't able to find a home for him."

"That's all right, old man, don't mention it. It's a pleasure."

"Sophie, dear, you do look pale," observed Margot, seeing her daughter's faraway expression. "All this pre-wedding excitement is too much for you, perhaps, with everything you've been through. After all, you haven't been home for very long."

"I'm fine, Mother, honestly. Please don't fuss."

"Well," said Margot, not quite knowing where her daughter's thoughts were these days.

Because Sophie had been so withdrawn and irritable since she'd been home, Margot felt she was treading on eggshells every time she spoke to her. Still, she supposed, she needed time to adjust. It must be difficult for her after spending all that time in the camp. Not for the first time, Margot was secretly proud and gratified to think that the Red Cross had gone such a long way to making Sophie's and the other internees' lives bearable and sustainable. It made all that hard work worthwhile and in a deeply personal way too.

"Well, I need to bathe and change for supper tonight," said Margot. "Edwin and Cicely and the families are coming at seven. I must see Cookie first and make sure that everything's under control. This new housekeeper hasn't a clue." She shook her head in despair. "It's impossible to find good servants these days; the war's put paid to that – everyone seems to be off doing their own thing," she added, before disappearing in the direction of the kitchen, leaving Sir Edmund to mumble his excuses and escape to his study for a cigar.

"I expect you'd like to unpack," said Richard, coldly polite.

"That would be great, thanks," replied Robert courteously. "Am I in the newly emptied cream guest room?"

"Yes."

"I'll show you," said Sophie, seizing upon the excuse to extricate herself from further conversation with Caroline and Richard. "Although I expect you know exactly where it is."

"I do. But that doesn't matter."

"Have you stayed here often?" she asked, as they reached the top of the stairs.

"Many times," confirmed Robert.

"Where did you sleep?" she asked conversationally. "From what I can gather, the whole house was taken over by Red Cross boxes."

"It was." Robert hesitated. "I'm afraid that I slept in your room."

"My room!" Sophie looked at him askance.

"It's all right, it survived. I treated it carefully."

"I'm sure you did." She smiled, a dimple appearing in one of her cheeks. "Perhaps that accounts for us being old friends."

"Perhaps it does."

Suddenly, Robert felt a tremor go through him. How much comfort had he gained from her imagined presence throughout the years of intermittently sleeping in her room; how much solace had he found within the warm softness of her bed; how curious he had been to meet her.

And here was Sophie *now*, standing before him, having already been in his arms – very, very real and as unassumingly beautiful as he had imagined her to be.

For her part, Sophie stood before Robert, experiencing the same comfort and security in his presence as she had always found in the imaginary RLA at Seeblick. Of course, she made no connection with this man who had moments ago held her in his arms and her unknown confidante – that would be ridiculous – but here, in this very real and compassionate man, was the same ability to console and reassure that she had so often sought and found with her RLA during her loneliest hours at Seeblick.

Both of them hesitated on the threshold of the guest room for a moment: neither not knowing quite what to say; both of them aware of an underlying potential for much to be said, for much that might be shared.

Eventually, Robert smiled at her. "Well, I guess I'd better go and unpack."

"Yes." Suddenly, she was reluctant to let him go. "Thank you for... rescuing me back there."

"It was my pleasure."

"I didn't mean just stopping me from falling."

"I know."

"Why did you defend me?"

"I don't know. It was instinctive and I just went with my instinct."

"I'm so glad that you did. I feel happier than I did because of it. And safer."

He smiled. "Perhaps you'll have to come to me every time you need protection and cheering up."

"You can be my knight in shining armour and rescuer in my hour of need."

Robert smiled. "I'd rather be your friend."

"I'm sure that can be arranged," said Sophie, tiny spots of red appearing in both cheeks.

Robert found this most becoming. "That's settled then."

"Shall I see you at supper?"

"I'll look forward to it."

"I'm not particularly."

"What, not seeing me? Oh no, please don't tell me our friendship is over so soon!" He put his hand to his chest, feigning dismay.

Sophie laughed. "Not you. The others."

"I understand. Well, I'm here for a few days, so we can ride out any storms together."

"You're very kind."

"That's what friends are for."

"I thought Caroline was my friend," observed Sophie regretfully.

"Caroline needs her head examining. And Richard," declared Robert emphatically. "I'd like to knock some sense into both of them."

"Their reaction will be nothing to that of my parents. I'll probably be sent away in disgrace."

"Like some heroine in a nineteenth-century romantic novel – away to the countryside for her confinement, safe from prying eyes?" Robert smiled at her.

"It's no joke."

"I know. Well, if you are cast out on your ear, I've just been posted to Bridgend – not the most salubrious of locations I admit – but Wales is as good a place as any to hide away in seclusion. I'll look after you." His words surprised him.

"Seriously? You'd do that for me?" Sophie was amazed. "Even though we've only just met?"

"Yes," said Robert quietly. "I would actually, strange as it may seem."

They stared at each other for a moment in mutual astonishment.

"An unmarried mother with a child?" asked Sophie.

"I already have three children and I'm not married, so I'm hardly in a position to make any fuss about sheltering you and your one offspring." He smiled at her again.

At first, Sophie looked at him in surprise. "You have three children without being married?" Then, sensing something else, she narrowed her eyes at him.

Robert chuckled. "I do, actually. The children are orphans. I rescued them from Belgium after the Germans invaded. They go to my father's school and live with my parents in Oswestry during the holidays. I'm afraid that because of my war service, I've seen very little of them even though I'm their legal guardian. They're more or less grown up now and will be fleeing the nest soon."

Sophie smiled, feeling her spirits lift. "I'd like to hear more."

"You shall, and you must also tell me about your *Kommandant*," said Robert gallantly, though in reality now not wishing to know.

"I'd like that, thank you." She hesitated. "It's been difficult."

"I can imagine."

"See you later then."

"Yes."

Supper that evening was awkward. Margot, being the excellent and experienced hostess that she was, kept up a bright flow of conversation while all the time minutely observing the people around her table.

She sensed that things were not right, though she couldn't exactly pinpoint what was wrong, nor did anyone say anything that could shed any light on what might be amiss.

She perceived that there was none of the usual banter between Richard and Robert; none of the usual giggly girlish conversation between Sophie and Caroline. Only Edwin and Cicely and the others – Caroline's and Edwin's respective parents – chatted away easily, maintaining the anticipated sociability of the evening.

Sophie looked very pale and toyed with her food (Margot hoped that she wasn't coming down with something). Robert was being rather solicitous towards her and the two of them couldn't stop smiling as they talked quietly and exclusively together. (Margot was pleased by this. She'd always thought that Robert would be perfect for Sophie).

Caroline didn't say a word to anyone (which was odd, thought Margot as this was supposed to be a family supper to celebrate hers and Richard's wedding).

And as for Richard – and here Margot experienced both exasperation and concern – her son either stared morosely at his plate, glancing at Sophie every so often with a pained expression on his face, or kept refilling his glass and downing it far too quickly, drinking more wine than was good for him. (Perhaps they'd had some kind of disagreement. Margot considered this for a moment and decided that this was more than likely).

At the end of the meal, Sophie excused herself after saying goodnight to Robert and went upstairs to her room. Robert, Richard, Edmund, Edwin and the other men went into the drawing room for an after-dinner brandy and Margot led the ladies into the sitting room before Caroline also excused herself and went to bed, claiming a headache.

After Edwin and the others had gone home, Robert took Richard, who had drunk far too much brandy after the wine and was decidedly unsteady on his feet, outside into the garden for some fresh, sobering air, determined to talk to him despite his friend's inebriated state and try to make him see reason.

They stopped some way from the house, away from prying ears.

"You have to be more supportive of Sophie," Robert began without preamble, surmising that Richard would have limited concentration. "You are her brother."

"And Caroline's going to be my wife. My greatest loyalty has to be with her now," he replied coherently but with a distinct slur in his voice.

"Not necessarily." Robert was being tactful, though it would be all too easy not to be so. "I could understand it totally if you said that you felt caught between the two of them and didn't know which way to turn. But this outright condemnation and rejection of your sister, who you've always said you were so close to, I find impossible to comprehend. During the war, you talked about her the whole time, sometimes more often than Caroline. It was obvious to me that you cared for her deeply and thought very highly of her."

Richard was silent for a moment, then he said bitterly, "But that was before Sophie shamed and disgraced the whole family. Before she brought dishonour to the family name."

"Oh come on, Richard. That's a very old-fashioned, stuffy thing to say."

"Is it? What if it was your sister?"

"Then I'd try and bring my fiancée round to my way of thinking, especially if they'd always been the best of friends. You can't cast someone out just like that because they've done something of which you disapprove."

"How dare you tell me what to do? You're not my keeper!" Richard's drunkenness turned to rage and he teetered unsteadily on his feet. "And where do you get off having this holier-than-thou attitude?"

"I thought it was you who was having the holier-than-thou attitude. I think you're confused."

"You're damn right I'm confused. I'm confused because my sweet, virginal sister has allowed some German bastard to get her pregnant. Caroline's right, she's behaved like a slut."

Robert was shocked. "Of course she hasn't! That's a monstrous thing to say."

"Well, you would think that, wouldn't you? After all, you slept with Erika without a backwards glance. Maybe you and Sophie are two of a kind."

316

"How dare you!" Robert was angry now. "If I wasn't a guest in your parent's house, I'd punch you on the jaw for that remark." He turned to go before his anger got the better of him. "Goodnight, Richard. I'll talk to you in the morning when you've sobered up and had a chance to think about how much pain you and Caroline are causing Sophie."

"Sophie's the one that's causing the pain."

"No, she isn't. Perhaps before you continue to condemn her, you might like to look beyond your sanctimonious, hypocritical little mind-set and consider her wellbeing before you and Caroline create a permanent rift in your family and destroy our friendship into the bargain, which I might add, I happen to value profoundly."

And Robert strode off towards the house, leaving Richard wobbling uncertainly on the lawn, physically unsteady on his feet but mentally sobered by Robert's parting words.

CHAPTER 39

Maybury

Robert tossed and turned for most of the night, unable to sleep; unable to stop thinking of Sophie; upset by his row with Richard.

As the first light of dawn appeared he got up, washed and shaved, dressed in his riding clothes and crept down the stairs to the stables, deciding that an early morning ride might help soothe his troubled spirit.

He found Sophie there, pale but cheerful, stoking the nose of his horse.

She smiled as he approached, her heart giving an unexpected lurch at the sight of him; mindful of how close they had become during supper and of how she had thought about him constantly during the night.

"Good morning," she said, tiny spots of red appearing in both cheeks.

"Hello." Robert smiled and came to stand beside her.

With difficulty, Sophie turned her attention to the horse. "He's a thoroughbred, isn't he?"

"Yes."

"He's a wonderful animal. I've been riding him every day during the past few weeks since I've been home, do you mind?"

"Of course not. I can see you've taken to each other."

"We have."

"I've ridden your horse, too. Many times. She's lovely."

"In that case, it's just as well you and I are friends," she said. "You've slept in my bed, ridden my horse…"

"And it's been my privilege to do both," he replied graciously. "So, how did you sleep last night? In *our*…" clearing his throat deliberately to convey that there was no intention of anything suggestive, "…bed," though the remark conjured up a vivid picture in his mind that he knew should not have been there – it was too soon; much too soon.

Sophie smiled. "Badly, I'm afraid."

"Me too."

"I kept turning things over and over in my mind."

"Likewise." They exchanged a brief smile before he sighed. "I had a short but blazing row with Richard after everyone had gone last night. A rather damaging one, I'm afraid."

"What about?"

"You. Me. He said some despicable things about both of us. Richard and I have become so close that I thought I knew him inside out and back to front. But yesterday, I felt I didn't know him at all. I can't believe that he has such a priggish and hypocritical side to his nature, one that overrides his affection for you."

"Not everyone has your generosity of spirit and tolerance, I'm afraid." Sophie's expression changed to one of anxiety. "I wouldn't want you to lose your friendship with Richard on account of me."

"I won't, but the row wasn't just about you."

"What did he say?"

"That you and I were two of a kind."

"That isn't so terrible because I have a feeling we might be," replied Sophie with happy sincerity.

"So do I." He contemplated her for a moment before saying, "It was the inference behind his words that I found upsetting."

Seeing the sudden pain in his eyes, Sophie changed the subject. She would ask him later, perhaps, exactly what it was that had been said but for now, she became practical. "Have you had any breakfast?"

"No. Too early. How about you?"

"No. Too queasy."

"That must be difficult."

"It is but it's bearable. I like to think of it as being all in a good cause."

"I suppose it is. I imagine that you're a rare woman to have such a positive attitude to morning sickness."

"Have you known many with that condition?" she asked pertly.

Robert chuckled. "Only through hearsay."

"I'm glad to hear it. Despite the three children."

"Despite them."

They smiled at each other.

"Shall we ride?" she said.

"Do you think you ought to?"

"Gentle exercise won't do me any harm. I wasn't planning on doing any steeplechasing."

"That's a relief. Gentle exercise first thing in the morning is always preferable to steeplechasing. Or polo. Much too energetic!"

"Have you played a game or two with Dad? He's rather passionate about it."

"We've played many times."

"Who wins?"

"Me mostly, I'm afraid, when it's just the two of us."

"Don't apologize. He'll just be glad he can knock a ball about with someone. Mother takes exception every time he goes off to Windsor Great Park to play in the all-comers matches they sometimes have at the club. At least she did, before the war."

"The war has changed a lot of things."

"Yes." Sophie took a deep breath as the reality of her situation intruded. It seemed all too easy to cast her burden aside while she was with Robert.

Together, they readied the horses, with Robert lifting the heavy saddle onto Sophie's mount, tightening the girth and helping her fetch the bridle from the tack room before seeing to his own. They chatted easily about horses and riding as though they had been doing this for all of their lives. Naturally and without embarrassment, they both said as much and then stared at each other for several moments before Sophie blushed and looked away.

As they set off, after Robert had helped her into the saddle, Sophie admired the easy way he sat astride his horse; appreciating the sensitivity of his hands on the reins, liking the way he exerted gentle control over his mount.

319

Robert thought how attractive she looked: her body relaxed and at one with her horse; how he wanted to hold her in his arms again.

In companionable silence, they rode along the towpath beside the Thames, the sunlight casting dappled shadows on the river; the early morning birdsong and gentle lapping of the water in perfect harmony with the placid clip-clopping of the horses' hooves.

The tranquillity was suddenly disturbed when a couple of coots careered out from the reeds, shrieking and flapping in alarm, causing Sophie's horse to skitter, something that gave Robert a moment of consternation; a moment that quickly turned to admiration as she deftly and calmly controlled her animal.

"You ride well," he observed.

"So do you," she replied. "And our horses seem very companionable together."

"They are. In the old days, they would have been put together as carriage horses. They're a well-matched pair."

For a moment, they glanced at each other again.

"Richard says that you studied German at Oxford."

"I did. Richard says that you studied English at Oxford. I worked out that we overlapped by a year."

"Yet we never met," she mused.

"No," he replied, a hint of regret in his voice. "But then Oxford colleges do tend to be separate entities."

"And at Somerville, we were chaperoned to within an inch of our lives."

They grinned at each other.

"What else did Richard say about me?" Sophie was curious.

"He talked about you incessantly during the time we worked together. More than enough to make me want to meet you." He smiled at her.

"I hope you're not disappointed." Suddenly, it mattered to Sophie what this man thought about her.

Robert turned to her. "Surprised perhaps about your condition but I'm not disappointed at all in you…" He paused.

"And?" She sensed an 'and'.

He realized that if he said exactly what he was thinking, he would be treading dangerous ground far too quickly – he didn't want to scare her away.

"What did he say about me?" Robert asked quietly, deflecting the subject.

Sophie, sensing his reluctance to say exactly what he thought yet picking up enough in his tone to know that if he did, she would not be disappointed.

"A great deal since I've been home," she replied, feeling her cheeks grow warm. "Nothing about what happened during the war, which I guess must be very secret, but it's been 'Bob said this' or 'Bob thinks that'. He really respects you."

Robert sighed. "I wouldn't have believed he had any regard at all for me last night."

She paused for a moment and looked at him. "Incidentally, which do you prefer to be called Robert or Bob?"

"Robert, but I seem to have been called Bob throughout my army career, so I really don't mind."

"Then I shall call you Robert. So, what did he say last night?"

"How honest would you like me to be?"

"Completely honest."

"He said that you were a slut and that I only defended you because I was the male equivalent, or words to that effect."

Robert could see the tight line of anger on Sophie's lips.

"I'm so sorry," she said.

"It's not your fault."

The sun was becoming very warm and soon they had reached a wood where Robert suggested they find a comfortable place to sit and talk properly, knowing they would find welcome shade.

They dismounted and after settling the horses, sat down next to each other on an ancient mossy tree trunk, long since abandoned to the forest floor.

"Tell me about your time at Seeblick," he said, deciding not to disclose, for the moment, that he had been there also. He wanted her to reveal her story to him in total clarity without clouding the picture by adding his own reminiscences. There would be time enough for that.

This first conversation had to be about Sophie.

So she told him about the early days at the camp; how Heinrich's arrival had changed everything for the better; about their attraction for each other; how he had nursed her through scarlet fever; how they had become lovers.

She poured out her feelings to Robert openly and instinctively without restraint; concealing nothing, revealing everything; relieved at last to be able to speak freely to someone without fear of judgement or condemnation.

And Robert lived with her through her emotional journey: sharing the intimate details of her relationship with Heinrich; how she had thrown caution to the wind and sought him out, allowing him to make love to her that one last time because they knew that the camp was about to be liberated. He shared the circumstances and pain of their parting; learned how foolish she knew she had been.

"No, not foolish," Robert told her, gently stroking her hair, just as he had done on the stairs the previous day. "Just emotionally involved."

She touched his hand in acknowledgement of his support and understanding, allowing it to rest on his. Spontaneously, he lifted it to his lips.

Keeping hold of her hand, he asked what else she had done at Seeblick.

She told of how she had looked after the library in the Big House; how she had been so involved with the amateur dramatic society; how she could read to her heart's content; how happy she had been before her involvement with Heinrich, doing all the things she loved the most, except for riding and being on the farm with her aunts.

And watching her expressive face as she told her story, because he had been there, Robert was absorbed completely into the world in which she had lived.

He knew in minutest detail the places she described. He had admired the same stunning scenery; shivered in the same freezing cold; breathed the same clear mountain air; washed in the very same shower room; acted in the same theatre. He had experienced the lack of privacy; endured similar deprivations; moaned about the terrible food and relished the lifesaving Red Cross parcels with the very same emotions that she had.

Through her words, Seeblick came back to him vividly and poignantly; his feelings rekindled and brought back to life by this lovely woman with whom he unwittingly shared so many memories and so many similar thoughts and observations.

"Was I wrong to find happiness and security in somewhere that was surrounded by barbed wire and patrolled by guards?" asked Sophie. "After all, we were prisoners in what was to most people a foreign land and parted from our families and friends but…" and she hesitated, uncertain.

"There were other things that compensated for that," he continued for her. "Making new friends; acquiring new skills; inventing ingenious things out of nothing; discovering a vibrant community spirit. Knowing a feeling of complete security."

"Oh yes, all of those things."

She looked up at Robert earnestly. Somehow, he *knew*; he understood.

They sat in reflective silence for a long time still holding hands; subconsciously absorbing the sounds of the woodland: the rustling leaves, the soothing drone of insects, the sweet sound of bird song high up in the protective canopy – drawing ever closer to each other in body, mind and spirit.

"I'm not really some kind of slut am I?" she asked after a while, looking up at him, anxious for reassurance.

"Oh no," declared Robert, putting his arm around her. "There is absolutely no question of that."

"Heinrich is the only lover I've ever had."

"And because you cared for each other, what followed was very natural despite the obvious barriers."

His words revealed his innate generosity of spirit but Robert also knew that his jealousy of Hoffmeister was growing.

"I suppose so, but I regret now what happened."

Prompted by some inner longing, perhaps without being conscious of her actions, Sophie turned the palm of Robert's free hand upwards and gently caressed it with her fingers, minutely exploring its contours.

"Why did Richard say to you what he did?" she asked, interlocking his fingers with hers.

Robert, taking an inward breath as his palm tingled and his body responded to her touch, said that at one time during the war, he had been deeply involved with a German girl, except that she didn't match his commitment.

"Did you love her?"

"In a way, at first. I allowed myself to be completely seduced by her. She was very persuasive."

"I'm not surprised. You're a wonderfully attractive, caring and considerate man."

"And you are a very beautiful, desirable woman."

Robert pulled her towards him and Sophie responded without hesitation to his kiss, both of them immediately lost in the passionate beauty of an embrace that was all at once deeply familiar yet at the same time, held the promise of infinite renewal and refreshment.

After a while, they drew back and looked at each other in amazement.

"Wow!" said Robert, his eyes alight. "That was unexpected!"

Feeling extraordinarily alive and safe, Sophie nestled up against him and protectively, he put his arm around her. They sat in stunned silence until Sophie asked what had happened next with Erika.

Swallowing hard, wondering what was going to happen with Sophie, Robert continued. "It turned out that she was using me to try and get information."

"Oh, but that's terrible!" Indignation made Sophie sit upright.

"I also found out that she was sleeping with someone else; several people in fact. It was part of her job."

"How awful." Sophie stroked his cheek, offering him comfort.

He took her hand in his and kissed the palm before, just as she had done, placing his against hers, interlocking their fingers.

After a while, he said, "It was and I bitterly regret what happened between us."

"I can imagine. But more fool her for not recognizing your qualities despite her 'job'." She thought for a moment. "Has there ever been anyone else in your life?"

"Before the war, I met a French girl then I became engaged to someone of whom I was very fond, but who decided in the end that marriage to me was not for her, despite our intimacy. So, you see, I've had experience, but no luck in love. Hence the equivalent slut label from Richard."

"But that's grossly unfair and untrue." Sophie defended Robert as vigorously as he had her. "You'll meet someone one day who'll love you and whom you'll be able to love freely."

"Perhaps," he replied almost inaudibly, seeking out her lips again, unable to contain himself; their renewed embrace powerful and overwhelming.

And Sophie knew that she didn't want him to love anyone else. She wanted him to love *her*.

"What's happening to us?" she asked, her voice tremulous with excitement and awe.

"A great deal," replied Robert, his heart pounding.

Perhaps he should put the brake on; perhaps he should slow things down. But he didn't want to do that. At all.

"Robert, I don't want you to find someone else to love," she gasped, as he kissed her lips, her cheeks, her neck, his touch vital and alive on her skin. "I want it to be me."

"So do I," he murmured and gave in to his feelings.

After a while, Sophie took his hands in hers and looked up at him, her expression full of wonder. "I've never felt anything like this before."

Robert smiled with relief at her words and her frankness in speaking them.

"Nor have I," he replied with absolute honesty.

And Sophie was glad, oh so glad.

"Perhaps," said Robert, eventually, "we should step back for the moment and gather our thoughts. Not that I want to."

Filled with joy, Sophie said, "Nor do I, but perhaps that might be wise."

"I don't know about you," he said, thinking of something that might stem their ardour temporarily, "but I'm in need of refreshment after all this excitement."

Sophie smiled at him, and now that she thought about it, her early-morning feeling of nausea had been replaced by a surprising need for food.

"What if we find some breakfast somewhere? It'll take us a long time to get home and the horses need a drink."

Robert agreed and after standing up and making themselves presentable again, together with one final lingering, spine-tingling embrace, he helped her remount and they resumed their journey, soon finding a farm, where a friendly farmer's wife offered them fresh milk, eggs and thick slices of oven-warm, freshly baked bread, as well as a nosebag of oats and water for the horses.

She insisted Sophie and Robert ate at the kitchen table, refusing to accept a penny in return for her hospitality, saying that it was a pleasure to help a young couple who looked as happy together as they did, especially now she had found out from them that Robert was a major in the British army. The least she could do was feed one of the brave fighting men who'd won the war in Europe, even if "those pesky Japanese were still refusing to give in."

Sophie and Robert exchanged the briefest of amused smiles and having finished a substantial breakfast, thanked her sincerely for her generosity.

"You're welcome, dearies," she said, standing at the kitchen door and waving to them as they left the farmyard. "And don't forget to come back soon if you're ever passing this way again!" she called out after them.

It was late afternoon by the time they arrived home. Robert offered to see to the horses. Grateful, and feeling tired after the exertions of the day, Sophie decided that she would go up to her room to rest and read.

She touched his arm. "Thank you," she said quietly. "It's been a wonderful day, and given everything that preceded it, unexpectedly so."

"Oh, yes," he responded, understanding her meaning.

He smiled and Sophie was lost in the warmth of his eyes.

"See you at supper," she said, her cheeks burning; reluctant to be apart from him even for a moment.

"Yes," he replied, seeing her colour rise, wanting to take her in his arms.

But Robert knew that if he kissed her again, he would not be able to stop this time and the danger of discovery in the stable was too great.

He watched her walk across the yard to the house, where she stood for a while before disappearing inside.

Oh God, he thought, *what have I gone and done, now?*

Fallen in love, came the immediate answer to his question. *Absolutely and irrevocably.*

The next day was the day of Richard and Caroline's wedding. To ensure the happiness of the occasion, everyone remained civilized and cheerful; the contentious issue of Sophie's pregnancy temporarily forgotten; all arguments and recriminations put aside for the time being.

The church service went according to plan, with the interior full of fragrant flowers, the organist, choir and congregation on good form. The speeches and congratulations at the reception, held at Sir Edmund and Lady Margot's capacious house, were heartfelt and genuine.

Robert gave a witty and eloquent speech praising Richard's bravery and resourcefulness in his war service; sharing funny anecdotes; beginning several sentences with: "When we were in..." or "When we did..." both statements always interrupted by an exaggerated scrutiny of his notes before saying, "Oh, but I'm afraid I can't tell you any of that. It's classified, you know!" phrases that evoked much laughter and applause.

When Robert asked the guests to be upstanding and toast the "three beautiful bridesmaids", there was only one to whom he directed his own glass of champagne.

After the tables had been cleared away, the bride and groom took to the floor in time-honoured tradition, closely followed by the chief bridesmaid and best man: the onlooking audience appreciative; the room dimly-lit and the mood romantic.

For the rest of the evening, Robert and Sophie never left each other's sides, dancing closely, talking intimately, sharing their food, completely absorbed in each other.

At the end of the celebrations, Richard and Caroline were dispatched on their honeymoon amid much homemade confetti and the clanking of several old tin cans tied to the back of Richard's car with the words 'Just Married' written in bright red paint emblazoned across the boot on an attached cardboard sign.

As the sports car roared on its noisy way, its taillights soon disappearing into the darkness, the assembled waving guests gradually dispersed inside or to their respective homes.

Eventually, Sophie and Robert were left standing alone on the driveway, unable to keep their eyes away from each other; she, beautiful in her pale blue, full-length bridesmaid's dress; he, handsome and debonair in his uniform.

Without saying a word, he took her hand and they walked together across the lawn into the velvet night.

Looking out of their bedroom window, having observed Robert and Sophie's unmistakable closeness, Margot called her husband over and said, "Look at this, before they disappear into the trees. If I'm not much mistaken, those two have fallen in love with each other."

"I do believe you're right, my dear," said Edmund, as he saw where she was looking. "It's just as well, if you ask me."

"Why's that, dear?"

"His horse has already moved in!" Edmund took his wife's hand in his. "Come on, old girl, let's get into the marital bed. I prefer the comfort of a soft mattress to prickly bushes for our romantic assignations these days!"

Concealed from the house by the all-enveloping darkness, Robert took Sophie into his arms and they kissed once again with the unbridled desire and intense hunger that his soul had always craved and of which she had always dreamed ever since she had first read *La Chaleur de la Mer*.

But their embrace was much, much more than the evocation of words from a work of fiction; this was beyond anything either of them had ever imagined. It was vibrant and alive; more profound and irresistibly powerful than anything Sophie had ever experienced and she responded to Robert with all her heart and soul, just as he did to her.

"This makes things complicated," he said, his heart racing as he undid the buttons of her dress.

"Very," she replied, fumbling in her haste to remove his clothes.

"We shouldn't be doing this," he murmured, holding her to him.

"No, we shouldn't," she gasped, throwing back her head in ecstasy as he kissed and caressed every part of her with tender urgency.

"I love you," he said, pulling her down onto a soft bed of mossy grass.

"I love you too," she replied, trembling with pleasure and anticipation as he came to her without hesitation, their reactions fuelled by mutual passionate desire.

And in the spine-tingling exhilaration of their climax, Robert and Sophie found in each other everything they had ever needed or wanted.

Eventually, reluctantly, they dressed before they became chilled and, arms wrapped round each other, walked in dreamy, satiated silence towards the house where they crept upstairs to Sophie's bedroom.

Quietly and discreetly, they spent the rest of the night together in the warm softness of her bed, rejoicing in their closeness and intimacy and then, just before dawn, sharing further ecstasy and delight in each other.

"At least I can't get pregnant," murmured Sophie drowsily, as she lay contentedly in Robert's arms.

"There is that, of course," he responded sleepily, closing his mind to anything beyond their immediate blissful happiness.

CHAPTER 40

Bridgend (1)

In a stark return to reality, the very next day, Robert's leave was over.

He made a cold and lonely train journey to Wales: a heavy summer downpour lashing against the carriage window that combined with smuts from the engine smoke to create an obscuring haze of grime.

Confined within his compartment, images of Sophie dominated his thoughts.

They had awoken that morning about seven o'clock and Robert had made a discreet return to his room without embarrassing discovery, to wash, shave and pack, relieved to have successfully concealed the fact that they had spent the night together.

After a latish breakfast, he had expressed his thanks and taken leave of Margot and Edmund, with a promise to return as soon as he could, all too aware of their subtle but keen observation of himself and Sophie as he spoke.

Robert surmised they must both have looked rather tired.

Sophie had driven him to the station in Maybury and they had said very little on the journey, both of them dreading the parting that was to come, their joint mood suffused with uncertainties and longing.

As they stood together on the windy platform waiting for his train, he held her tightly in his arms, desperately wanting to ask her to be with him for always.

But something made him hesitate, hold back.

What was it? His own fear of rejection, perhaps? Or a slight doubt, that despite her declarations of love the previous night and again that morning, she still cared for the father of her child and should he return, this would be for her an even greater consideration than the depth of feeling and height of passion they had shared in what could only be described as an astonishing and overwhelming emotional whirlwind.

They needed time to take stock and talk about things properly; time to discover what they really wanted; time to work out what was really happening and time to overcome any confusion Sophie might well experience once their immediate and urgent physical needs had subsided. If they ever did...

For his part, without Hoffmeister entering the picture, it would be very simple. Robert wanted to spend the rest of his life with Sophie and would have no qualms whatsoever about bringing up her baby as his own, full of optimism that he would experience no jealousy or resentment in nurturing another man's child because that child was also part of the woman he loved and had been conceived before they had known each other.

He would stand by her, not out of any sense of duty or honour (though he would have done that anyway were she to be rejected by her family, an occurrence which, knowing Margot and Edmund as he did, he thought unlikely) but because he really did love Sophie with all his heart and soul and wanted her as his true and loving wife.

He hoped that Heinrich Hoffmeister never reappeared and that he, Robert, would one day *very* soon, given the inevitable advances of her pregnancy, be able share his life with Sophie.

As the train drew into the station, she had clung to him.

"Write to me," she had said, her eyes full of tears, her expression full of misery.

"Oh yes," he had promised, enfolding her in his arms. "I love you," he'd said, kissing her.

"I love you too," she'd replied, returning his embrace,

"But we do need time to talk."

"I know we do. And it must be soon."

"Yes."

He'd been about to say, "come to Wales with me" when the guard had blown the whistle and all around them, in a flurry of urgency, last minute passengers entered nearby carriages amid great slamming of doors.

Hurriedly, Robert had found his own compartment and had leaned out of the window, holding Sophie's hand as the guard blew his whistle again and waved his flag.

"Come back to me soon," she'd said but his loving reply was lost in the hissing of steam and powerful exhaust beats as the engine drew away from the platform.

He'd stayed at the window until he could no longer see her.

So, here he was now.

In love, in a way that he had never known before. He saw his two previous relationships as mere specks in the deep ocean of feeling that he now knew existed because of his love for Sophie. She was a reflection of his soul just as he was a reflection of hers and Robert knew with absolute certainty that he would never be able to care for anyone else ever again.

But it had happened incredibly fast.

Just as it had for the characters in *La Chaleur de la Mer*.

That evening in his solitary room, he wrote to Sophie, penning a long letter, telling her how much he loved her; how much he missed her; how much he wanted them to be together for always: setting out on paper his hopes and fears and dreams for their future.

He didn't know when he could next get leave, he said. But if she could come to him…? He would find somewhere discreet for her to stay; a cottage, perhaps, where they could be together whenever he could get away. It wasn't ideal or perfect (and how he longed for the ultimate perfection of marriage) or what he wanted for them both but in the circumstances, it was better than nothing. At least they would be together and that was all that mattered.

He also described his job so that she would know what he was doing while they were apart:

I'm responsible for overseeing the arrangements at Meridian Camp here in Bridgend, he wrote, *in preparation for receiving high-ranking captured German officers (the first batch of whom arrive tomorrow).*

328

My job will also then involve investigations into whether (a) a particular officer is innocent of war crimes but needs shipping off to a psychologist for 'de-Nazifying' if they pose a threat to the stability of Germany by refusing to let go of their ideology or (b) there is enough evidence to convict them of war crimes or (c) whether they might be able to act as witnesses to others who committed such crimes. Those deemed to be innocent will be given the choice of repatriation or becoming resident in Britain.

I've been investigating captured German military personnel both in England and abroad for a while now so I'm well experienced at this sort of thing. It is perfectly possible, as I said to you during one of our conversations at the wedding reception yesterday, that I may be able to uncover the whereabouts of Heinrich Hoffmeister. I certainly know the right people to ask.

We do have to resolve this, dearest Sophie, so that any lingering feelings of obligation you might be subconsciously harbouring, despite everything we have shared, can be put aside for ever. All I want is for us to be together always.

Write soon, my darling,

And Robert signed his name: his handwriting distinctive, the phrasing eloquent.

Sophie, as soon as she saw the envelope addressed to her (having rushed downstairs the moment she heard the post being delivered in anticipation that Robert would have written to her straight away), unable to wait a moment longer, tore it open.

She unfolded the letter and with her heart hammering in her chest, stood in shocked surprise even before she began to read the words for which she had longed.

She *knew* this handwriting. It was as dear and familiar to her as the very room in which she and Robert had spent the night.

Quickly, she ran back upstairs with the letter in her hand and took out the leather pouch from the locked drawer in her bureau and extracted *La Chaleur de la Mer*, opening the flyleaf and carefully removing the handwritten note from inside.

She laid Robert's letter, the poem and the note side by side, examining the handwriting minutely.

She couldn't be mistaken, surely.

Sophie looked again to make absolutely sure, tracing the letters with her fingers. It *had* to be the same.

It *was* the same.

Her beloved RLA was her beloved Robert.

He'd reached England; he'd survived the war and they had made the most wonderful love.

She stood by the window, stunned by the revelation.

Why hadn't Robert said anything when she'd told him about Seeblick? Why had he kept quiet? Was it part of his intelligence work and therefore he couldn't tell her?

She would ask him.

No wonder he had understood so absolutely; no wonder he could empathize with her so completely.

He had been there, had really known what it was like. All the things she knew, he had known as well. They really did share the same memories.

Now, even in the absence of Heinrich, she would never have to worry about being misunderstood ever again; now, she would be with someone who would always know in the minutest detail exactly what she was talking about.

Agitatedly, Sophie paced the room.

He had to know that it was she who now possessed the leather pouch. He had to know that it was she who had slept in his bunk…

She stopped mid-thought.

She had slept in his bunk, comforted by the feel and sight of his initials and his words in the note and the poem… He had slept in her bed, feeling comforted and safe in the ambience of her room, surrounded by her things… And last night, they had slept together in that very same bed, warmed and comforted by their love for each other.

The wonder or significance was not lost on her.

The very real man with whom she was in love and who loved her *was* RLA. They were one and the same.

She and Robert *had* to be together now, for always. But what about Heinrich?

She stopped again, mid-thought.

He had loved her too and had cared for her when she was ill. She knew it would be difficult to let go of her feelings for a man with whom she had once shared so much and whose child she now carried, even though she had not heard from him in three months and had given up hope of ever doing so.

But, came a nagging inconvenient thought, with the vagaries and uncertainties right across Europe, not to hear from him was not necessarily of any significance.

What would happen if he *did* contact her?

Sophie sat down on the bed, the unread pages still in her hand; the euphoria of joyous discovery evaporating.

Taking a deep breath, she began to read Robert's letter and knew instantly that there was no contest between Robert and her former lover.

Energy and excitement flooded through her again.

This was the man with whom she was in love; *this* was the man she wanted to be with more than anything; *he* was the man who would stand by her (although she didn't doubt for a moment that Heinrich would have done the same) and Sophie knew she would never have to worry about bringing disgrace upon anybody ever again.

He was her present, her past and he would be her future.

They could be married quickly and then, apart from themselves, Richard and Caroline would be the only other people who would ever know that her child was not Robert's.

She would tell Aunt Edna the truth because she was wise and would understand and because she wanted her to know, free of deception, how truly wonderful Robert was.

No one else needed to know. Ever.

In that fleeting moment, Sophie made her decision. She would go to Wales the very next day.

She would tell her parents that she was going to see Robert. They would understand that. She had a feeling that her mother knew exactly what had happened between them and because she approved of him and wanted to see Sophie settled and happy, would make no fuss.

Yes, that's what she would do. She'd send a telegram to Robert once she knew her train times and then she would set off to be with the man she truly loved.

Lost in the busyness of her thoughts, Sophie suppressed the memory of Heinrich's caresses and the blueness of his eyes and the fact that it was only three months ago that they had last made love: the remembrance of that act still alive somewhere within her subconscious.

Sophie tried to forget that the child she carried was his or that Heinrich might possibly assert his right that she should be with him, just as, in theoretically accepting his proposal, she had promised she would be, even before she had conceived, even before he had promised to find her.

Frustratingly, she was not very successful in channelling her thoughts away from her former lover, knowing that it would only be fair to tell Heinrich about her baby, his child.

Sophie got up from the bed and stared out of the window. She was not made for this kind of emotional trauma or prolonged indecision; she was not cut out to have to make a choice between two kind men who loved her. She preferred peace and quiet over chaos and uncertainty.

Yet, she knew without a shadow of a doubt that in Robert, even though they had known each other for such a little time (and here she wondrously drew a parallel with the characters in *La Chaleur*) she had found the greatest love of her life. Her feelings for Heinrich carried no significance beside the passion she held for her RLA.

Joy bubbled up inside her again.

She had to go to him. She had to tell Robert – her friend, her confidante, her lover – of her discovery.

She had to tell him that she wanted to be with him for always, whatever happened.

But in her haste to make her travel arrangements, Sophie forgot to send the telegram to say she was coming.

Robert, accompanied by the usual escort of an intelligence officer, interpreter and a couple of guards, stood on the platform of the station at Bridgend awaiting the next batch of high-ranking German officers to arrive and be taken to Meridian Camp.

Idly, he watched a train arrive on the opposite platform, thinking of Sophie. As it drew out and the residual smoke disappeared, he looked across the empty tracks.

And there she was, vulnerable and alone: returning his gaze with her exquisite smile and beautiful, expressive eyes. For a moment, an evanescent memory of bright sunlight flitted its way across his mind but dissolved without form or substance before he could capture its essence.

In a heartbeat, Robert was running along the platform, up the steps, across the footbridge, down the other side, taking her into his arms and throwing propriety to the wind by kissing her – to the accompaniment of friendly wolf-whistles from the soldiers on the opposite platform.

He grinned across the rails at them and put his arm around Sophie, picking up her suitcase, which he was relieved to see was neither too large nor too heavy as she would have had to carry it throughout the journey, and guiding her towards the footbridge.

"Why didn't you tell me you were coming?" he said, his expression alive with joy and delight as they walked slowly up the steps.

"Didn't you get my telegram?"

"What telegram?"

It took a moment for realization to dawn.

She put her hand over her mouth. "Oh no, I forgot to send it! I was going to ask you to find me somewhere to stay."

"That's such a shame." He smiled at her. "You'll have to stay with me."

"That's terrible. I'm so upset."

"I can imagine."

They grinned at each other.

"Can I really?"

"Yes. They've given me a whole house to myself. It's wonderful and ridiculous at the same time. We officers have all been billeted out in the town because there aren't enough decent facilities at the camp and there are no army barracks nearby. They've all been feeling sorry for me because I have to do my own catering as I have no landlady nor yet been assigned an orderly. I said I was quite happy to look after myself, but no one believed me." He grinned at her again. "The other ranks are sleeping in a hastily erected Nissan hut just outside the perimeter fence and are moaning like stink because they say the German officers have got better facilities than they have. There's been some almighty cockup somewhere and I've got to try and sort that out, along with everything else." They had reached the bottom of the footbridge steps on Robert's platform. "But don't worry about that now. Look, I'm on duty at the moment. The train we're supposed to be meeting will be arriving in a couple of minutes."

Robert had to think quickly before they reached the others. He laid his hand on her arm to stop her from going any further.

"For propriety's sake, we may to have to offer up some kind of explanation as to why you're here and about to stay in my house with me."

"Why don't we say that we're married?" declared Sophie brightly. "Does anyone know you're not?"

"No-o. These chaps I'm with, although they're 1st Battalion Royal Welch, I've never met any of them before. Even the colonel doesn't know me. It'll be on my file that I'm single, but I don't suppose he'll look at that if I do my job properly." Robert hesitated for a moment before smiling mischievously. "If we were to do that, we'd have to buy rings."

"Can I choose my engagement ring?" asked Sophie, full of excitement.

"Of course. We'll go into Cardiff. We're less likely to be spotted there."

"Will you get into trouble if they discover we're not married?" asked Sophie with sudden concern.

"Yes, so it's best if we don't say anything unless we absolutely have to. In any case, we really ought to be married as soon as possible."

"Before the baby begins to show."

"Exactly. In the meantime, it might be wise to find you alternative accommodation, despite the obvious temptation to be together. But we'll worry about that later. Tonight, as long as we're incredibly secretive, you can stay with me."

They heard an engine whistle in the distance and moved towards the station exit.

"Look, here's my key," said Robert, handing it to her discreetly. "There's a taxi rank just over there." He told her where he was staying. "I'll see you when I get off duty – probably about seven, but don't worry if I'm a bit later."

"You see, we're beginning to sound like an old married couple already!" and Sophie gave him a peck on the cheek. "Bye, bye dear, see you at home," she said impishly, as she took her suitcase from him and gave her new address to the taxi driver.

That evening, he was home later than he thought. Tired and hungry, he threw his uniform jacket over the settee and called out quietly to Sophie. When he received no reply, he went upstairs to find her fast asleep in his bed; *their* bed.

He didn't disturb her but went downstairs again into the small dingy kitchen to find the oven left on and inside, a homemade dinner keeping warm for him.

On the table he found a note.

Darling Robert, it ran, *thought you might like some supper. I'm not the best cook in the world (I learnt my trade at some P.O.W. camp) but at least it will keep the wolf away from the door. I used some of the ingredients I found in the larder. I hope that was all right.*

I'm so tired after all the travelling, that I really do need an early night.

In the morning, I'll tell you what precipitated my sudden impetuous flight into your wonderfully waiting arms. You'll be amazed! It's something very, very special to me and I know you'll find it equally so for you.

Come up later. The bed's big enough for both of us to share…

Your very own,

Sophie.

Curious and rereading her note several times, not least of all because he found her handwriting most attractive, Robert sat at the table and ate his food, appreciative of the time and effort she must have put into its preparation, especially after so long a journey. It was somewhat dried out, having been in the oven for a while, but he enjoyed it nevertheless, especially as it was the first meal Sophie had ever cooked for him.

He speculated as to what it might be that she had to tell him but, unable to come to any definite conclusion and, having finished his meal and washed up his plate and cutlery, he put money into the gas and electricity meters to ensure that there was enough ready for the next day, before going upstairs, where he undressed and slipped quietly into bed.

Sophie turned towards him sleepily and he gathered her into his arms and was fast asleep himself within moments.

CHAPTER 41

Bridgend (2)

They lay talking together quietly; their combined dreams for the future beginning to coalesce.

"So," said Robert, after they had covered everything they could in a most satisfactory way, "what was it that brought you to me in such indecent haste?"

Sophie smiled enigmatically and got out of bed, going across to the chest of drawers, blushing as, turning to look over her shoulder at him, she caught Robert's obvious admiration of her.

"Close your eyes," she said.

"But I want to look at you," he replied, "especially how you are at the moment..." He smiled, lifting an eyebrow. "Surely you can't be embarrassed by that? Not after everything we've been up to?"

"I'm not in the slightest, you silly goose, but there is a reason for this and it's only for a moment."

Robert studied her for a little while longer. "All right then," he said, before obediently closing his eyes.

"Don't peek," said Sophie sternly.

"No, ma'am," replied Robert.

He heard a drawer being opened and shut and presently felt her come back into bed.

"Can I look yet?"

"You have to sit up first."

He did as he was told while Sophie watched him closely, her face alight with anticipation.

"Okay, you can open your eyes now."

Her own filled with tears of joy as Robert saw the leather pouch. He looked at her in disbelief at first, then his expression flooded with amazement. For a moment he was lost for words.

"*You* found it!" he exclaimed at last. "It was you!"

"Sort of. I rescued it."

"I never..."

"Well, open it!"

It felt like Christmas morning.

Carefully, Robert undid the drawstring and there inside, was his treasured copy of *La Chaleur de la Mer*, his note and the poem, the feather and the stone.

He looked at Sophie in wondrous disbelief.

Rushing into his mind came his own memories of that time – his capture, his incarceration, his escape, Erika, the *Abwehr*; the strain, the joy, the despair – and Robert found himself letting go of the pent-up feelings he had for so long kept hidden; for, despite his early exchange of confidences with Richard and reliving his time at Seeblick through Sophie's memories, the psychological impact of what he had experienced at the beginning of the war had remained within him, deeply buried.

At last, in the arms of the woman he loved and the discovery that she had made – a discovery that profoundly affected them both – he found emotional release at the unexpected reappearance of the gifts he had left behind: the simple, deeply personal things he had valued most from that time.

And after they had both dried their tears, Sophie told the story of how she had rescued the leather pouch and its contents; how the discovery had affected her; how she came to rely on the novel and his words as a source of comfort; how she had slept in his bunk and how his initials carved into the wood had been her solace, her consolation. But, above all, how the unknown RLA had helped her to bear her darkest moments of captivity.

"Oh my darling," and Robert took her into his arms. After a while he said, with no little amusement, "So you slept in my bunk?!"

"Every night I was at Seeblick," she replied, "Well, except when I had scarlet fever…"

"Yes," he said, wanting to punch Heinrich Hoffmeister on the jaw, despite the fact that this man had probably saved her life.

"I used to trace the outline of your initials when I couldn't sleep."

"I never thought for a moment that when I carved them, it would have such an effect. I did it one afternoon because I was bored and fed up. I'm glad they found a higher purpose to their existence."

"So," observed Sophie, "at exactly the same time, we were sleeping in each other's beds and becoming familiar with each other's things," she paused and smiled at him. "Even before we met."

"How remarkable is that?" replied Robert. "But isn't it just another indication that we were meant to be together? And now, having met, we're able to share everything that has gone before."

"It's almost as though we've always known each other; almost as if we were sending messages to each other while we were in captivity." She kissed him. "Does that seem *too* fanciful?"

He held her closer to him and kissed the top of her head, breathing in the sweet fragrance of her hair. "No, my darling, it's not, because I feel it too. Very strongly."

Robert picked up the novel that belonged to both of them now.

"I've always loved this book," he said. "It's so beautifully written."

He told her then how, like her, he had been the librarian at Seeblick; how the original library had been in the storeroom where the leather pouch had been found; how *La Chaleur* had arrived one day in a consignment of books from the Y.M.C.A.

However, he refrained from saying that he had previously spent so many years searching for it; that he had longed to find the girl who had discovered him lying on the beach. He thought it best not to say that ever since then, in times of crisis, she had become a symbol of pure loveliness in his mind.

He had no wish to make Sophie jealous talking about someone he had met and lost in an instant; a girl he had never forgotten, a girl who lived in his memory even now.

No, he would not say anything about that. It was not necessary because he had Sophie now, and she was everything to him; more than he had ever wanted or desired because she was real, very real, far better than any fantasy.

"I know exactly what you mean," she agreed. "It's the most exquisite book I've ever read."

She refrained from saying that because of forgetting this book, she had discovered a boy lying on the beach and how he had grown up in her imagination, making passionate love to her in that very place.

She had no wish to make Robert jealous talking about someone she had met and lost in an instant; a boy she had never forgotten; a boy who lived in her memory even now.

No, she would not say anything about that. It was not necessary because she had Robert now and he was everything to her; more than she had ever wanted or desired because he was real, very real, far better than any fantasy.

"Why didn't you tell me you were at Seeblick that day in the wood?"

That momentous first day they had really talked; the first day she discovered she was falling in love with him.

"Because I wanted to hear your memories uncluttered by any of mine."

"But we could have shared them."

"We did, if you remember," he said, tenderly stroking her hair. "And it brought us very close in a very subtle way. I could empathize with and uphold you because I knew exactly what it was you had experienced."

"Yes." Sophie understood. It was far, far better this way. "Tell me about your time at Seeblick and what happened before," she said.

So he did. The River Dyle, the Escaut, the horrors of Saint-Venant; his subsequent injuries and capture, the indignities of the transit camp, his arrival in Seeblick – this time expressing from his perspective the myriad observations and experiences he had already shared with Sophie during the telling of her story. He told her about his involvement in the theatre productions, his love of drama and literature, his poetry. He told her about his friendship with Harry, about Oscar the dummy, about his escape.

"Oh, my love," she said, "we really do share it all, don't we?"

"Yes, darling, we do."

"And in a way that no one else could possibly understand."

"Yes."

He brought her into his arms, just holding her close to him, each silently communing love and joy in mutual shared discovery and realization to the other.

"What happened to Harry?" asked Sophie, after a while.

"He never made it, unfortunately."

"Oh, I'm so sorry. What happened?" she said gently.

"About a month after I made my escape, all the prisoners in Seeblick were transferred to another P.O.W. camp in Poland where conditions were appalling. Then, as the Russians advanced, the inmates of all the camps in that region, including the eastern half of Germany, were forced to go on a long march west with very little food or water. Many more died than survived and Harry never made it back. But someone who did, brought back his personal effects. My original cap

337

badge that Harry was keeping for me must have been among them because it was returned to me via the Red Cross. My letters from home, which he also had, were presumably lost. But that's neither here nor there. I'd rather Harry had survived."

Sophie didn't need to say the obvious, that if Robert hadn't escaped when he did…

"Is that the same badge you wear on your cap now?"

"Of course."

"I wonder what happened to Seeblick after you left? I must have arrived about fifteen months later and the place was in an appalling state. Everything was derelict and filthy dirty and we had to spend a great deal of time making it habitable."

"It was more or less brand new when we arrived. It was originally built as a training camp for German soldiers but never properly utilized, so we were lucky. But I have no idea what happened after that. It would be interesting to find out, especially now."

They lay in contemplative silence for a while.

"So, if you're able to read *La Chaleur*, you must be fluent in French as well as German," said Sophie, at length. "So am I."

"I know."

"Richard told you." It was a statement not a question.

"Who else? It's just another in a long line of things that make us a reflection of each other."

"I like being your reflection," said Sophie.

"And I like being yours," replied Robert.

And there followed another passionate interlude at the end of which Robert happened to glance at the clock and the time made him leap out of bed in a panic, washing and dressing quickly before he was late for duty.

That day, as they had agreed, albeit reluctantly, Sophie found alternative accommodation for herself in the only hotel in Bridgend, the Cynhesrwydd Arms, a former coaching inn. It was not the most elegant or luxurious place to stay, but at least it was clean and reasonably comfortable.

It had the added advantage of not being too far from Robert's house and Sophie was content with its proximity. Having found her accommodation, she collected her suitcase and carried it the hundred yards or so to the hotel and unpacked. She spent the remainder of the morning exploring the town before resting and reading in her room during the afternoon, whiling away her time until Robert came off-duty.

That evening, they ate supper at the hotel and the next day, as it was a day off for him, they travelled into Cardiff.

"How long have we known each other?" she asked, as Robert placed the chosen engagement ring on her finger and she held it up to admire the sparkling emerald and diamond cluster.

She knew the answer down to the last minute, but she wanted to hear him say it.

He chuckled. "Four days and…" he named the hours and minutes.

She kissed his cheek. "A very little time. Just like the characters in *La Chaleur*. And yet it is a lifetime."

338

"I know." He looked at her. "Remarkably, there are other similarities too," said Robert as they walked out of the shop, having paid for their purchases.

Sophie blushed. "Yes," she replied, knowing that he too felt the overwhelming intensity and inescapable nature of their affair.

"So," he said, stroking her cheek, "we have the rings, when shall we get married?"

As he said the words, although absolutely certain of her feelings for him and knowing that because of her condition, it needed to be as soon as possible, he could not shake off a tiny irritating doubt at the back of his mind that somehow, some day, any latent feelings that Sophie might still have for Hoffmeister would surface: feelings that at present she might not even be aware of herself, feelings that might be hidden by the rush of sexual energy produced by their chemistry and also by her pregnancy.

After all, he reasoned, it was only three months since she had last slept with Hoffmeister; three months since the German had promised to find her and 'make her his' (even though he knew that Sophie had said that she had not made any promises herself that she would wait for him). She was also carrying this man's child.

There were a lot of powerful emotions with which she might have to contend. What might she feel if he did turn up?

Quickly, he put the thought out of his mind.

"As soon as possible, please," she said. "I want to be with you all the time. Forever. Freely. And with nothing to hide."

Even as she said it, Sophie knew there would be a lot to hide.

Robert looked at her and she knew he was thinking the same.

"Once we're married," he said gently, dealing with the obvious consideration first (they could talk about the rest another time), "it won't matter if we tell our families a few months down the road that the baby isn't mine. We will have to be honest, my darling. I don't want your parents and mine to think that this child was conceived by us, although he or she will become ours once it is born."

Sophie's eyes filled with tears in relief and gratitude at his words: her anxiety about keeping such an enormous deception hidden from those she cared about having been weighing on her conscience, despite her earlier thoughts before she had left Maybury.

He put his arms around her and held her to him, shielding her from the stares of passers-by, until her tears had lessened and she was in control again.

"It is better to be truthful," she said eventually, wiping her eyes with the handkerchief that Robert gave to her, "although we may have to withstand some censure and hostility."

"That's an understatement! But we shall weather the storm together, dearest Sophie. We are strong enough to do that and when our families see how happy we are, they will soon forget the circumstances that led us to be married so quickly, even though we would have wanted to do that in any case, without having to consider your pregnancy. You see, I couldn't bear to live with the deception of pretending the child is mine."

"Nor me, darling. To speak the truth is the best thing to do but it will be hard."

"Only at first." He smiled at her. "And we will have children of our own one day."

She laid her head on his chest and nodded. "Oh, yes. I want that so much."

"Good. So, we've decided when, or nearly when. How about where? At your home in Maybury with family and friends or quietly by ourselves here in Bridgend?"

"Quietly, please, just you and I and whatever witnesses we have to have. I've never wanted a big wedding with all the paraphernalia and fuss that goes with it. I quite like the idea of being secretive about it."

"I think I do as well. Although," he hesitated for a moment, "I'd quite like to tell my poor, long-suffering parents. First I dump three orphaned children onto them…"

"And then you bring home a wife they've never met who's pregnant with another man's child!"

"Although they're very fond of her brother…"

Sophie smiled up at him. "I'd like to tell my parents too. They're very fond of you."

"Perhaps we should invite both sets, even if they can't come as it will be such short notice."

"Yes, let's do that!" She really wanted her parents to be there.

So, having decided what they wanted to do, they made the necessary arrangements and fifteen days later, in the local parish church by special licence, Miss Sophie Langley became Major Robert Anderson's wife to the shocked delight of their respective parents, who all came, saying they wouldn't dream of missing the wedding.

Edna and Mae sent their love and congratulations, saying how delighted they were for them both; sorry that yet again because of the official travel restrictions, they were unable to attend a family wedding. They implored them to come and visit as soon as they could.

Richard and Caroline sent their regrets.

"I'm sorry about that," said Robert, hurt by their friend's continued reticence. "Perhaps they're too embarrassed to come."

"Knowing Richard," replied Sophie, "he's probably regretting his tactlessness but can't step back now without upsetting Caroline."

"The whole thing's ridiculous. I still find it hard to believe."

"He'll come round eventually," said Sophie, having experienced other instances of Richard's prolonged spells of petulance over the years.

"Let's hope he doesn't take too long on this occasion."

"That rather depends on Caroline."

"Unfortunately."

After a very happy family meal at the Cynhesrwydd Arms, the young couple set off on their honeymoon to the Gower Peninsula, where in perfect summer weather, they explored the countryside and coast, paddled in the sea and relaxed for five glorious days, the maximum amount of leave that Robert had managed to wangle out of his colonel.

On their return to Bridgend, Sophie set up home for them in Robert's house, and they settled blissfully into their first weeks as husband and wife.

CHAPTER 42

Bridgend (3)

"Well, Bob," said General Sir Freddie Ashton who, at the end of the war, had been promoted, knighted and given overall responsibility for intelligence gathering at P.O.W. camps in England and Wales, and who was now paying his first visit to Meridian Camp, "you've made excellent progress here. The Welch Fusiliers seem very happy with their Mess arrangements, the facilities outside the compound that you *insisted*," he smiled at Robert, "that I give the order to be constructed, are first rate. Our 'guests' seem settled and your intelligence chappies are doing a splendid job in separating the wheat from the chaff."

"Thank you, sir," replied Robert.

"In a month or so, once the necessary arrangements can be made, those deemed no longer to be a Nazi threat will be repatriated or given sanctuary in this country should they wish to stay. It will mean relinquishing their German citizenship, but that's a small price to pay for security and freedom."

"Of course."

Robert sensed a 'but' – he had not lost any of his sensitivity when it came to Freddie Ashton's methods.

"However, the emphasis here at Meridian will shift, along with the main thrust of your work, Bob, to the specific investigation and holding of known or suspected war criminals, including some of Hitler's nearest and dearest."

"I see," said Robert, knowing the extra responsibility this would involve.

"In addition to this, you'll also be looking after very high-ranking officers who have already been investigated and are awaiting their own trial at Nuremberg; others who are witnesses and will be expected to give evidence, and those who are waiting for extradition transfers to whichever country may wish to prosecute them." He smiled. "Whatever their situation, our German guests seem to prefer us Brits to delve into their pasts – they feel that we'll be fairer than some other countries I could mention; that we're less inclined to go for immediate and unthinking retribution. Also, that they'll be better treated here."

"I'd like to think that they're right on all counts, sir."

"Absolutely, old man." The general hesitated before choosing his next words carefully. "You're used to dealing with a mixture of *Wehrmacht* and *Kriegsmarine* officers but this time, we're going to throw some senior *Waffen-SS* and *Gestapo* your way as well. It'll be a potent mix as the decent *Wehrmacht* officers hate them."

Freddie Ashton then gave him a direct look, which also held the touch of an apology.

Robert felt sick. He guessed what was coming.

"Including, I'm afraid, *SS-Oberführer* Theodor Abetz."

"No! Absolutely not!"

"Now, now, Bob," and the general put his hand up to prevent any further protest. "I'm afraid there's no choice. I quite understand how you feel about him."

"You can have no idea."

A tremor of fear and disgust went through him. Why did he never seem able to escape from this odious man?

"The chaps who questioned him first, as well as those who've tried since, got very little out of him but, because we've discovered from other sources that Abetz was on the staff of the much hated *SS-Oberst-Gruppenführer* Reinhard Ziegler in Karodice when he was assassinated, we've reason to suspect that, in addition to the reasons you brought him across to England with you, he may be in some way linked to the Birensk massacre."

"Good grief! But there's no proof?"

"Nope, can't find any and he won't talk. If he is culpable, he's covered his tracks pretty well."

"What makes you think I'll be any more successful than the others who've tried so far?"

"I don't. But you're the last resort."

"I'm not sure how to take that." Robert grimaced.

"Take it as a compliment. I've kept him out of your way for as long as I could, Bob, knowing what you went through, but needs must, as they say."

"If I'm going to do this, I want Richard Langley with me."

Robert knew they had to work on this together, to finish the job they had begun.

"Let's see, he's due to be demobbed in a couple of weeks, isn't he? I doubt that he'll be best pleased."

"Too bad. There's no one I'd rather work with, good as the others are on my team here."

"Okay, Bob. I'll arrange for his secondment from the Royal Navy. You're married to his sister, aren't you?"

"Yes."

"He can stay with you then."

He'll hate me for this, thought Robert, *and probably never speak to me again when we're done here, not that we've heard anything from him and Caroline these last months, in any case.*

However, he could see it also as a glimmer of light: a way of restoring their friendship and healing the rift between Sophie and her brother.

"Damn you, Bob!" exclaimed Richard when he arrived a few days later. "I was just getting everything sorted out. How could you do this to me?"

The three of them were standing in the kitchen before showing him up to his room.

"Because we have a job to do."

"I couldn't care less. The war's over. I'm about to be a civilian again. I'm about to leave all this stuff behind and then you go and pull a stunt like this. I really don't give a damn about Theodor Abetz!"

"But you should, Richard," said Sophie, her eyes filling with tears at the harshness in her brother's manner. "You have to find out whether this horrible man is guilty of the crime they suspect. What's happened to you, Richard?" she added plaintively. "Where's your sense of fair play and decency?"

342

He was silent for a moment and took a deep, shuddering breath. "I really don't want to get mixed up with Abetz again, even though you, Bob, bore the brunt of his nastiness when we were on St Nicolas. I've had enough. Enough of everything, I tell you!"

Robert and Sophie exchanged a brief glance.

"How's Caroline?" asked Robert with apparent innocence, concerned that something was wrong in the marriage; concerned, therefore, that Richard might not be able to cope with the stress that would inevitably fall their way. "I hope she didn't give you too much of a hard time before you came here."

Richard shrugged. What did it matter now anyway? What did anything matter?

"Where's my room, then?" he demanded, avoiding giving a direct answer.

"I'll take you up," said Robert.

"Supper will be ready in a few moments," said Sophie, with a brightness in her voice and manner that she did not feel.

"You have no secrets then from Sophie?" said Richard, as he slung his suitcase onto the bed.

"None. I trust her implicitly, although there'd be hell to pay if the colonel found out about some of the things I've talked about. Technically, I suppose, you could argue that I'm breaking the Official Secrets Act."

"I doubt it now the war's over. Depends on how much detail you go into."

"I don't talk specifics. She knows nothing about Bletchley Park."

"Well, that's all right then. In any case, anything you find out in this place will become public knowledge once the undesirables in your tender care stand trial at Nuremberg or wherever else they're being sent. Besides, I told Edna everything that was going on when we were on St Nicolas. Neither of us were a bit concerned then."

"No, and in the end, it proved to be helpful." Robert looked at his friend. "It's good to see you again, Richard. Can't you forgive and forget? For Sophie's sake?"

Richard took another deep breath. "No," he said.

"Why ever not?"

"Because, no matter how honourably you've behaved towards my sister – and you have, incredibly so, I might add – the fact of the matter is, that she allowed herself to become Hoffmeister's mistress and is carrying his child. She's brought disgrace to the family and, although they obviously don't know the details yet, there will be huge ructions when you and Sophie tell the parents, as you will, no doubt, because you're both too damned honest."

"Surely honesty is the best thing?" Robert was treading carefully.

Caroline hadn't been very honest with him, had she? thought Richard. *Until recently, that is, when she'd been too honest.*

But he said nothing and followed Robert downstairs to the dining room, where the three of them ate their supper in strained silence.

Theodor Abetz arrived at Meridian Camp on a damp, dismal autumnal day. Security was at maximum as Robert had impressed on the guards the need for absolute vigilance.

As he got out of the lorry after being driven up from the station, Abetz took stock of his surroundings, formulating a plan in his mind.

Oh, yes. He'd be convincing in the renunciation of his Nazism. He'd make this new lot of weak and spineless intelligence men think that he was a good boy, that he had reformed, that he wanted to stay in England and give up his ideals. He'd persuade them that he could be released.

Oh, yes. It would be easy. The war was over, his British interrogators were too soft. He'd fed them little bits of information here and there since being imprisoned but they'd got nothing much out of him after two years. And why should they? He'd outfoxed them in any game they'd tried to play with him; he'd seen through their subterfuge and their wiles. They were no match for him, Theodor Abetz. He could give *them* lessons in how to interrogate a prisoner and get what you wanted. None of this namby-pamby stuff that the British went in for.

He'd gain his freedom somehow and then set out to find the man who had thwarted and double crossed him; a man whose identity remained elusive; a man he'd found so desirable, he'd risked everything and ended up paying a heavy price for his lack of caution.

Nobody had ever done that before to Theodor Abetz and lived to tell the tale. He'd find this man and get his revenge even if he had to scour every inch of the English countryside.

He'd thought of nothing else since being imprisoned other than getting even. He wanted to look upon this man one last time and then he would destroy him, ruthlessly and utterly.

Remaining discreetly in the background, Robert and Richard observed carefully while Abetz was transferred from lorry to a secure, purpose-built brick building for potentially difficult prisoners, isolated from the other inmates; away from possible escape routes or internal retribution. Although spartan, they had made sure his room had all the necessary comforts and facilities.

Robert and Richard had decided that they would lull Abetz into a false sense of security; make him think he had the upper hand, allowing him to become complacent. Then they would set out to confuse him, to upset his equilibrium.

Robert had also decided that they would not interview Abetz themselves immediately but would keep out of his way for the time being and not let him know of their presence in the camp.

For several days, they kept their distance; listening from another room to the interrogation sessions; reading the transcripts of the recordings, seeing what might be gleaned. It was obvious that Abetz wasn't even bothering with verbal sparring. By his silence, he was playing Robert's intelligence team for a bunch of fools.

Eventually, they knew they could stay out of it no longer.

There was a knock at the front door and Sophie went to answer it. She found Caroline standing in the little porch, a forlorn figure, bedraggled and dripping from the rain.

Without saying a word, she opened the door and ushered her former friend inside.

344

Abetz was taken into the interview room again. But this time, it was at night. He was seated as usual on a hard wooden chair in front of the usual table. On this occasion, a blindfold was put over his eyes by the guard and he was left on his own.

After an inordinate length of time, he heard movements: the scraping of a chair, the rustle of paper. Then his blindfold was removed. Still he could see nothing as the room was in darkness. Suddenly, the lights snapped on: bright, penetrating, and Abetz found himself opposite Robert, who stared at him silently before the room was plunged into darkness.

Stunned, Abetz failed to react and when the lights came on again, he was alone. After a while, he was taken back to his room.

The whole scenario was repeated on consecutive nights. Sometimes it was Robert; sometimes Richard; sometimes someone else.

Abetz became unnerved by this, insecure. He never quite knew what was happening. He started having bad dreams; he began to shout at the guards who brought him his food, kicking at his door with such annoying regularity that in the end, they removed his boots.

Then one night, Robert spoke. "Tell me about Birensk," he said.

Then the lights went out again and when they came back on, he was gone.

Gradually, Abetz brought himself under control and mentally prepared himself to be ready to strike when Robert next appeared.

As soon as he saw him, Abetz lunged forward across the desk at his adversary, but was stopped in his tracks when he felt the cold muzzle of a gun on the back of his neck.

"I wouldn't dream of it if I were you, sunshine," said the M.P.

"Tell me about Birensk."

The statement was always the same. Abetz, fed up after weeks of the same request being made over and over again, said finally, "I know nothing. I was not there."

"No one said that you were," replied Richard.

"What made you think that we did?" asked Robert.

Abetz realized he'd made his first mistake. What happened at Birensk was common knowledge. He should have just described the event.

"Will you release me if I tell you who was responsible?" he said hastily.

"Where would you go?"

"Wherever you go."

Robert signalled to the guard and Abetz was removed from the room.

"Wherever you go, I go!" he shouted over and over again, dragging his feet, making his exit as difficult as possible.

"You've made a friend," observed the M.P. later that evening as he went off-duty.

"Like hell," said Robert.

"I take your point, sir. Nasty type."

"To put it mildly."

"Same again tomorrow night, sir?"

"Yes, please, Sergeant."

"Tell me about Birensk."

"I know nothing. I told you, I wasn't there. But I'll tell you who was. And I have the evidence to prove it. Will you release me if I tell you? I'll be good now. I'm reformed."

"Where is this evidence?" asked Richard.

"Hidden."

"Where?"

"Wouldn't you like to know?" sneered Abetz.

"I thought you said you had reformed?" said Robert.

"I lied."

"Lying won't get you anywhere," observed Richard, standing behind Abetz.

"So where is this information?" asked Robert.

"What's it worth?"

"That depends."

"On what?"

"On whether you tell me or not." Robert smiled.

Abetz looked at him, torn between hate and remembered desire. Unexpectedly, he relented.

"On St Nicolas. In my attaché case which I hid in a safe place and which got left behind when you…" In sudden anger, he lunged across the table at Robert, who avoided his grasp.

The military police sergeant immediately restrained Abetz and took him back to his room.

"Where on earth could he have put it?" asked Richard.

"I don't know, but one of us has to go to St Nicolas and find out. He must have hidden it just before we saw him at the top of the cliff."

"A lot will have changed on the island since liberation."

"A lot will have been destroyed by the Germans immediately before they surrendered."

"It's a bit of a long shot, but we have to find out. We might even find the plans for his thwarted mission, even though they're no longer relevant."

"I'll go," said Richard. "Sophie needs you and you need to be with her."

"Yes. But she would understand if I had to go."

If only Caroline could be that understanding, thought Richard morosely. She'd hardly said a word since coming to Bridgend. He really had no idea why she'd bothered to come at all. Their continuing estrangement only distressed Sophie and created an atmosphere of tension within the house. He'd suggested they move into a hotel, but neither Sophie nor Robert would even entertain such an idea.

He envied his sister in her marriage. He and Caroline were not close in anything like the same way that they were.

Perhaps Robert had been right all along; perhaps he should have persuaded Caroline not to be so intransigent and judgemental about Sophie's pregnancy; perhaps he should have stood up to her and defended his sister. Perhaps it would have shown his not-so-loving wife that he could be strong and decisive when the situation demanded it and that he would brook no nonsense from her.

He did try to be decisive, but his natural indolence always seemed to get in the way.

After the necessary arrangements had been made, courtesy of the R.A.F., Richard flew to Guernsey and then travelled onto St Nicolas by M.T.B. He paid a fleeting visit to Edna and Mae, sent love from Sophie and Robert, avoided talking about Caroline and enlisted help from the soldiers stationed at the now restored British garrison.

Together, they scoured the countryside yet again: farm buildings, hay lofts, the old silver mine workings, even the ruined Château sur la Colline – all without success.

And Richard added yet another layer of association to his memories of childhood holidays and secret missions on the island.

He was on the point of giving up when Edna was shown into the commanding officer's room at the garrison, breathless and excited.

"Dear boy," she said to Richard, a broad smile of triumph on her lips. "Is this what you're looking for?"

"Yes!" he exclaimed, seeing the familiar attaché case. "That's the one. Where on earth did you find it?"

"Tucked away behind an old rusty plough that we don't use anymore. We have a hen who likes to lay her eggs in strange places and she'd gone right to the back of the barn where we store old bits of equipment that are no use to us anymore but which Mae won't let me throw away as she says they might come in handy."

"You are an angel!" said Richard and gave his aunt an enormous hug, much to the amusement of the onlooking garrison commander.

Later, when Richard had left Guernsey airport and was on the R.A.F. plane winging his way homewards, he opened the attaché case and read through the contents.

What he found made him livid with rage.

"You won't like it," warned Richard, as Robert removed the documents from the attaché case.

They were alone in the latter's office at Meridian Camp.

"Why?" he said, looking at his friend, the unopened files poised in his hand.

Richard hesitated for a moment, doing his best, despite his anger and revulsion, to delay the inevitable moment of pointing out to Robert the disturbing material contained within, avoiding the issue by not giving a direct answer. (He seemed to be doing an awful lot of that these days, especially with Caroline.)

"There's a whole bunch of stuff written in code that needs decrypting," he said.

"That's not so terrible. We'll just get the Bletchley Park boffins to sort that out. It'll make a change for them after listening to the Russians all day every day. Edwin might like to take up the challenge."

Richard watched agitatedly as Robert sorted through the papers. Unable to resist the temptation, he jabbed his fingers at specific pages and said, "Look at this,

Robert …and this…" regarding his friend with an 'I told you so' expression on his face.

Even a cursory glance made Robert go pale with shock.

"No!" he said. "Shit!"

"Yeah." Richard nodded his head, his expression grim. "It's like that, isn't it? I told you months ago that he was a German bastard but you wouldn't believe me, would you?"

"We don't know for certain that these documents are genuine." For Sophie's sake, Robert had to clutch at straws.

"I do. Look at them. They're official, headed, signed documents giving the authorization to carry out a reprisal attack on Birensk – a reprisal that turned into a massacre where innocent women and children were murdered and the men forced to dig their own graves before being shot." He thumped his fist on the table. "And your wife, my sister, is carrying this man's child: the man whose name is on the papers giving the orders for this atrocity. So when are you going to tell Sophie what kind of man she slept with?"

Robert took a deep breath, trying to keep his anger and shock under control. "Not yet. We've got to locate him first and hear his side of things before taking any action. You know the drill and I'm not going to approach this any differently. Besides, we have no other proof."

Richard grabbed the pages still in the folder and held them up to Robert's face. "All the proof you need is right here, right in front of your eyes!"

And Richard flung the documents back onto the desk and strode angrily out of Robert's office.

CHAPTER 43

Bridgend (4)

Sophie was beginning to regret allowing Richard and Caroline to stay with them. In all the weeks they had been there, she had been unable to ascertain from her friend exactly what had prompted her unannounced appearance on the doorstep of their little Bridgend house.

All she knew was that Caroline moped around in her room most of the day, occasionally going out into the town, unwilling to communicate. When Richard came home in the evening, he seemed full of anger and disappeared up to *his* bedroom as soon as he could after supper. Even Robert seemed subdued and unusually reluctant to talk about his work.

"It's like living under a black cloud," remarked Sophie one night as she and Robert lay in bed. "It's spoiling my pleasure in being at home, where I'm normally quite happy and contented to be, while waiting for you to come off duty. I have no idea what's wrong between the two of them but it's definitely something serious. They're not sleeping together and they hardly talk to each other. And yet, they neither of them want to be anywhere else. It's really odd. Has Richard said anything to you?"

"No."

"Do you think it would be all right to ask them to move out? I know we scuppered the idea when they suggested it soon after Caroline arrived because you and I both hoped we could forge some kind of reconciliation between them as well as with us. But as far as I can see, that's not going to happen is it? In fact, things seem to be going from bad to worse. And to cap it all, you and Richard seem incapable of even looking at each other at the moment."

Sophie seemed close to tears, so Robert took her into his arms and held her close.

"Things are very difficult at the moment in our work at the camp. I can't tell you exactly what's going on, but I will as soon as I can, I promise. And it's affecting Richard badly." Tenderly, he stroked her hair. "You could always go to Maybury for a few days if it's all getting too much."

Sophie snuggled deeper into his arms. "Oh, no. Not without you. I couldn't bear it if we didn't see each other, no matter how much of an awkward atmosphere our house guests are creating."

Robert kissed her, relieved by her unequivocal response to his suggestion. He switched off the light and they fell asleep, warm and secure in their love for each other.

A couple of weeks later, coming into his office, the situation with Richard and Caroline still not resolved, Robert found the latest batch of files from the previous evening's arrivals on his desk.

Before he'd had a chance to even glance at them, the doctor, after knocking, came into the office.

"I thought I saw your light on," he began conversationally. "You're an early bird this morning."

"I could say the same about you!"

"No, I'm a late bird. I'm off-duty shortly, but I waited to speak to you before I left." He sighed. "I don't suppose you've seen anyone yet or had a chance to read your latest files, Bob, but after you'd gone off-duty last night, the chap you were waiting for arrived."

"Heinrich Hoffmeister?" Robert gave a start.

So, this was it.

"Yes. But he's in a very poorly state and the guards on duty asked me to take a look at him as soon as he came in. I've only been able to give him a quick once over, but it was enough to tell me that this man has a very serious heart condition. If you've got a moment to spare, I wonder if you'd take a gander through his file and see if there's anything in there that might be of help."

"Of course. I'll come and find you when I'm done."

"Thanks, Bob. I'll be in the infirmary."

The doctor took his leave and, his heart beating fast with apprehension, Robert searched through the pile of folders on his desk.

He found what he was looking for almost at once and opened the slim buff-coloured file.

A photograph.

So, there he was. Sophie's former lover, the father of her child.

He experienced a sudden surge of jealousy.

Robert read the pages closely, although it was no more than a thumbnail sketch. It would be up to his team to fill in the detail.

Heinrich Hoffmeister b. 1911. Studied English at Heidelberg University then appointed English teacher at the Karls-Gymnasium in Stuttgart. Conscripted as a civilian into the army as an Administrative Services Official by the Ministry of the Interior 1938. Teacher of English to Wehrmacht recruits in preparation for the invasion of Britain 1938 – 1940; Administrative Services Official in Ministry of the Interior in Berlin 1940 – 1941; appointed to staff of Theodor Abetz in Karodice 1942...

Robert felt sick.

There it was. In black and white. Evidence matching the documents in the attaché case, placing Hoffmeister in the right location at the right time, and confirming beyond any shadow of a doubt his connection with Abetz.

From the undeniable evidence in front of him, with Hoffmeister also working as an administrative official for the Ministry of the Interior in Berlin – the ministry with overall responsibility for the organization and running of the concentration camps – he would appear to have been deeply involved with the National Socialist Party. He would have been in the thick of it – at the black heart of the evil regime.

This meant that Sophie might be carrying the child of a dedicated and ruthless Nazi.

However, on the surface, this picture did not coincide with anything she had told him. Sophie had said that Hoffmeister hated Hitler and his henchmen for what they had done to his country and for what they were doing to the Jews, the Poles and others; she said he hated everything the Nazis stood for.

Was it possible that Sophie had been taken in by this man?

On seeing that she liked him, and Robert had no doubt that her feelings would have shown on her face, could Hoffmeister have persuaded her that he was all the good things he said he was in a determined effort to get her into bed? After all, as *Kommandant*, he might wish to assert his power over the internees, and what better way than by taking a mistress?

But Sophie had told him they had taken great pains to keep their liaison secret and as far as she was aware, they had been successful in that. However, Robert knew that for all her belief that they were only lovers, to the coldly moralistic and judgemental outside world, the reality was that she had been Hoffmeister's mistress.

His heart pounding; his own balanced and clearheaded judgement under threat, he read on:

...Kommandant of Seeblick Internment Camp January, 1943 – April 1945 when taken prisoner by French after liberation. Transferred to British jurisdiction in tripartite prisoner exchange between the French, the British and the Americans. Arrived England October, 1945.

Robert then studied Hoffmeister's medical records. It listed several periods of hospitalization, including three lengthy stays in 1940 – 1941 followed by extended sick leave in each case; three months at the beginning of 1942, again followed by sick leave, and at least six further spells between 1942 and 1945 varying from a couple of weeks to a couple of months, each followed by a period of convalescence.

The cause of his frequent hospitalization?

A defective heart.

The report went on to list the medication he had been prescribed by the German doctors and its dosage; how it had to be taken regularly for it to be effective; how that medication had been withdrawn by the French; how that withdrawal was now seriously undermining his health.

Robert wondered if Sophie's baby would inherit the same physical weakness.

A footnote at the bottom of the page recommended that the connection to Abetz be investigated further.

Damn right, thought Robert. He also knew it would fall to him to carry out that investigation alone. He presumed that Richard would want no part of this. Perhaps it was better that way.

Innocent or guilty, Hoffmeister might be useful in shedding further light on Theodor Abetz who, after further extensive questioning by Robert's colleagues, had become sullen and uncooperative following his unexpected revelation of the possible whereabouts of the attaché case.

Whichever way his interviews with Hoffmeister went, Robert resolved that he would not share the former's arrival with Sophie just yet; nor would he reveal to Hoffmeister that his former mistress was now his interrogator's wife.

Now there's an interesting juxtaposition, he thought, as he shut the file and put it into his brief case before walking to the infirmary, *especially as I am the commandant of a P.O.W. camp.*

Robert opened the door of the hospital and gave the medical records to the doctor who, after he had finished reading, drew his lips together in a straight line.

"The first thing we have to do, is get hold of Hoffmeister's medication. I don't care what he may or may not have done – although from what I've seen of him, he's a courteous man and doesn't seem to be the typical Nazi criminal type – but he's a human being in desperate need of treatment. Naturally, he'll have the usual psychological profile done and that will tell us more about his frame of mind. However, Nazi or not, my immediate concern is his state of health. It's appalling that his medication was taken away from him. As he's awake, I'll give him a thorough examination before I go off-duty this morning and find out what sort of treatment he received in hospital. German physicians have made great strides in all sorts of ways in recent years and as usual, are probably streets ahead of us." The doctor shook his head. "Lord knows what damage has been done to his heart by his not being allowed to take his pills these past months. I suspect that unless we can get hold of this stuff PDQ, he may not survive for too much longer."

"Is he well enough for me to speak to him at the moment?" asked Robert shocked, despite himself, by this observation.

This was something he had not considered. It was also something that Sophie had not told him about. Perhaps she didn't know; perhaps Hoffmeister had never told her.

"Not really, but I know you'll be kind."

"I'll try my best," he said. "Where is he?"

"On the left there. In the corner bed."

"Thanks."

Robert walked slowly down the ward.

Heinrich lay still, his eyes closed; the weight of his lids too great to keep them open.

"Hauptmann Hoffmeister?" said Robert, as he reached the bed.

"Ja?" He opened his eyes.

"Ich bin Major Anderson," said Robert, struck by the blueness of this man's eyes.

Would Sophie's baby inherit those, he wondered?

"Wie fühlen Sie sich?" he asked.

"I have felt better."

"We're going to try and find you the proper medication for your heart."

Heinrich closed his eyes again and tried to smile. *"Thank you. I would appreciate that."*

Robert sat down beside the bed and studied him for a while. His face was very thin and pale; with deep, deep shadows under his eyes. He had remained polite, even though he was very ill.

Hoffmeister seemed to exhibit neither guilt nor bravado; his demeanour was one of complete exhaustion and total resignation.

But resignation to what? His capture and imprisonment? The trial and punishment that would inevitably follow should he be found guilty of the crimes of which the evidence seemed to suggest? His state of health?

"I do not expect to get well again," he said quietly, as though answering Robert's thoughts. *"My health has been growing worse over a number of years and I am now too long without medication."*

"Well, don't give up, just yet," Robert heard himself saying as though from a great distance. *"We'll do everything we can for you."*

"Thank you. I am grateful for that." Heinrich closed his eyes and drifted off to sleep.

Robert smoothed the crumpled sheet on his bed and returned to his office, where he stood staring out of the window for a long time.

Was it possible there had been some mistake? Perhaps Hoffmeister had been coerced in some way while giving the information contained on his prisoner-of-war file (although Robert thought that unlikely). There was no doubt that the authorization documents in the attaché case for the attack on Birensk showed his signature. Therefore, as far as Richard was concerned, this man was guilty.

Yet experience had taught Robert that things were often not what they seemed and that it was all too easy to make assumptions.

He had to be fair-minded, to retain his objectivity.

Therefore, should he tell Hoffmeister about Sophie?

If the German was indeed innocent and died before he knew about his child, Robert knew he would never forgive himself. That would be cruel and unfeeling and he was neither of those things. Whatever his personal ambivalence might be towards Hoffmeister, Robert had to answer to his conscience.

What if Hoffmeister was guilty? Robert knew the effect on Sophie would be devastating and potentially damaging to her pregnancy, even causing her to miscarry the baby, which could, in turn, threaten her own life given the stage she had reached. She might also come to hate the child she was carrying.

Robert knew he could not risk any of those things.

Perhaps, on balance, it was best that he did not tell Sophie anything just yet, not until he had gathered and verified all the evidence. In any case, because of the current non-fraternization rules, she would not be allowed to see Hoffmeister and she would find that difficult to cope with.

No, it was better that she did not know anything for the moment.

Putting aside his own feelings towards this man, Robert came to the conclusion that impossible as it might seem, for Sophie's sake and the sake of her unborn child, he had to do his utmost to try and prove Heinrich Hoffmeister's innocence.

But it would take every ounce of integrity and generosity of spirit that Robert possessed.

"Tell me about Birensk."

Several days later, Robert and Heinrich were seated in the former's office, the latter having been brought across in a wheelchair, sufficiently recovered with the medication supplied by a heart specialist in Cardiff to be able to withstand some gentle questioning. ("Take it easy, though Bob," the doctor had warned him).

There were no guards present, apart from a sentry outside the door: Hoffmeister's physical frailty was not deemed to render him any kind of threat.

Robert had arranged for the fire to be banked up and for two easy chairs to be placed in front of the hearth. Tea and biscuits had been brought in.

Heinrich had looked around the room as he was helped into the easy chair by the German orderly who then left the room.

"It is an unusual setting for an interrogation," he observed.

Robert nodded. "Available only for the privileged few."

"Then I feel honoured."

"Tell me about Birensk," said Robert.

A shadow passed over Hoffmeister's face. "Birensk was a small village some miles to the north of Karodice in Czechoslovakia. There was a terrible massacre there, carried out in revenge for the assassination of Reinhard Ziegler." He shook his head. "It was unspeakable; horrific. It made me ashamed to be German."

Robert allowed the silence.

"Go on," he said after a while, watching Hoffmeister closely as very simply and with sorrow and regret, the latter described what had taken place.

"How do you know about Birensk?" said Robert, sickened by what he had just heard.

"Everyone knew about it. It was in all the newspapers after it happened, hailed as some kind of triumph, and then, when the full extent of what had taken place was revealed, it was quickly hushed up and those suspected as being responsible removed quietly from their positions of prominence."

"The order to carry out the massacre came from the office of Theodor Abetz, did you know this?"

Heinrich shook his head, his manner one of sadness rather than the desperate denial of a guilty man. "Not directly, but it would have been the obvious place as he was Ziegler's head of security at that time."

"Tell me about Ziegler and Abetz."

Hoffmeister's expression darkened. Yet his voice and manner remained calm; measured. *Almost as though he's conserving his energy,* thought Robert.

"They were two of the most evil men I have ever encountered. They formed a close, intimate alliance. It was well known that Abetz idolized Ziegler and would have done anything for him. It made Abetz a laughing stock in decent *Wehrmacht* circles. But aside from this, he was also a ruthless killer who would stop at nothing to further his own ends and those of Ziegler."

Robert thought of Admiral Siranac and Erika.

"Would he have been capable of carrying out an act of revenge for Ziegler's death?"

"Yes. He was totally distraught when Ziegler was assassinated."

"You must have known him well to be able to tell of these things."

"No. I met him only once – at a reception to welcome new staff members into the fold."

"How is it therefore that you know of Abetz's character?"

"It was common knowledge. He was so disliked by everyone that everyone talked about him. Privately, behind closed doors, of course."

"If you were on his staff, how is it that this was the only time you met?"

"I never took up my appointment."

354

"Why not?"

"I had a massive heart attack and was hospitalized for the first three months of 1942."

"So you never worked for either him or Ziegler at any time?"

"No."

"Do you have proof?"

"I presume the record of my indisposition will be in the hospital records."

"Where?"

"In Berlin."

Robert grimaced. "These may be difficult to find."

"Yes. I would imagine that Berlin is a very different city now to what it once was. Much will have changed."

"Much will have been destroyed."

"Yes. Unfortunately."

Robert could see that Heinrich was tiring. It was time for him to return to the infirmary.

"Thank you, *Hauptmann*. Oh, just one further thing, could I have your signature, please."

"I thought I had completed all the paperwork."

"There is just one more form to complete."

"Of course."

Robert handed him a blank form which he extracted from the drawer in his desk.

"What is it for?" asked Heinrich.

"Hopefully, your advantage."

"Then I shall make it the best signature that I can manage at the present time, although my hands are somewhat shaky."

He handed the form back to Robert and smiled, his eyes very blue behind his glasses. "What about the rest of it?"

"The rest of what?" said Robert, absentmindedly as he studied the signature.

"The form. I imagine that a requisition for boot polish does not usually require the approval of a prisoner-of-war?"

Robert looked at him and had to laugh. "It's a new procedure, actually."

"And I am the first?"

"And the last."

He bowed his head. "Then I am most honoured."

Robert smiled. "You are a very astute man and your English is very good."

"Thank you. I attained the highest marks in my year when I was at Heidelberg."

Robert regarded Hoffmeister for a moment before saying, "And you are an honest man?"

"I have always tried to be so."

"And you always speak the truth?"

"I have been known to be 'tactful', shall we say, when the situation demanded it." Heinrich raised an eyebrow.

Robert smiled again. "Thank you," he said quietly.

After Heinrich had been wheeled away, Robert compared the signatures – between the form and the documents contained in the attaché case.

Although the newest one was spidery and written in an unsteady hand, there could be no doubt that they both belonged to the same person.

Having been convinced that Hoffmeister was telling the truth, Robert now began to doubt the veracity of his answers.

With a sigh, he closed his office door and made his way home with a heavy heart.

CHAPTER 44

Bridgend (5)

"Tell me about Seeblick."

"Seeblick?"

"You seem surprised that I should ask the question."

"No, it's just..."

"What?"

"I try not to think about it too much."

"Why?"

"Because of Sophie."

"Tell me about Sophie."

"She was one of the internees. I rescued her from a... situation... on the day I arrived. I fell in love with her. And then I seduced her. Slowly. Gradually. Taking my time because she was innocent and I wanted her to be completely mine of her own volition without being frightened." Heinrich looked at Robert, his eyes full of pain. "I had looked after her, you see, while she was ill. She had scarlet fever. There was nowhere else for her to go in the camp. The women's isolation ward was not yet available."

"She became your mistress?"

"Yes."

Robert controlled his jealousy. He had no need to feel that way. Sophie and he belonged to each other far more deeply than anything she had ever known with this man.

"But I should not have done what I did."

"Why?"

"Because it was unfair."

"Why?"

"Because the situation was difficult."

"For what reason? Because you were the *Kommandant* and she was your prisoner or because you were married?"

"No. None of those things. I am not married. If there had been no war and we had met, I would have asked Sophie to marry me."

"So why was it difficult?"

"Perhaps I will explain to her one day."

"Why not to me, now?"

Heinrich stared into the fire and remained silent.

Robert's curiosity was aroused but he let that question go for the moment. "Have you tried to contact her since the end of the war?"

"No."

"Why not?"

"Because I can offer her nothing. I am a prisoner-of-war. I am ill. I cannot guarantee to be able to support her."

"Did she love you?"

Heinrich hesitated. "In a way, yes. And I would have settled for that. But I do not think she was in love with me. She gave herself to me certainly of her own free will, but she was not in love with me. There was always a part of her that was not open to me."

Suddenly, Robert was not afraid anymore. He and Sophie shared *every* part of the other.

"Did anyone in Seeblick know?"

"No. It was our secret. I cared for her and did not wish her to be ostracized by her fellow internees."

Robert was silent for a moment before he said quietly, "And if it could be arranged, would you wish to see her again?"

Heinrich looked down at the floor. "Yes, of course, more than anything but I can offer her nothing. Therefore, there is no point."

"And what if she might want to see you? What if she is still waiting for you to contact her?"

"She will not wait for me. I knew that the day we parted. And that is right; it is as it should be. I can give her nothing."

That night, as Robert held a sleeping Sophie in his arms, he thought about his latest conversation with Hoffmeister – knowing that he spoke the truth; that his version of his feelings dovetailed with Sophie's own description of their relationship.

Robert remembered their time in the wood when she had poured out her heart to him with such candour, creating between them an immediate closeness and intimacy that might have taken longer to establish otherwise.

Was it because of this that they had fallen in love with each other so instantly? Or were they always destined to be together and this was just one more connecting piece in the intricate mosaic of their relationship?

"Tell me about your work at the Ministry of the Interior."

"I was only there for one day and unable to complete the registration process."

"You were ill again?"

"Yes." Heinrich smiled. "It was most fortunate, because in order to work there, I would have had to become seconded to the *Waffen-SS*. I did not wish to do that and it would have been a dilemma that I would have lost. In every way, whatever I did."

"You did not like the *SS* or the Nazis?"

"No, I despised them."

"Why?"

He looked at Robert. "Wouldn't every decent, upright citizen feel the same?"

"Yes."

And Robert knew that Heinrich Hoffmeister had indeed spoken the truth to Sophie at Seeblick. It was not just some ruse to sleep with her.

More than ever, it was imperative that someone had to go to Berlin to corroborate his periods of hospitalization and exonerate him from blame in the Birensk massacre.

358

Could Robert send Richard on his own? Could he persuade him that it was in Sophie's best interests that Hoffmeister be proved innocent? Could he trust him to do that?

Of course he could. Richard was thoroughly professional, despite his present mood and opinions about the father of Sophie's child.

But there were other things that Robert needed to ascertain first.

They had Abetz brought to the interview room.

"Tell me about Heinrich Hoffmeister."

"Who?" Abetz was evasive; wary. "I've never heard of him."

"Come now," said Richard, "you have papers in your attaché case with his signature on."

"Do I?" He feigned innocence.

Robert looked at him. "You know you do."

Abetz shrugged.

"If you've never heard of him, how come these documents are in your possession?" said Richard.

Silence.

"Why did you tell us where to find the attaché case?" asked Robert.

"To waste your time."

Robert and Richard exchanged a glance.

Silently calling the M.P. over, Robert moved round behind Abetz and whispered in his ear, "Did you give the order for the massacre at Birensk?" moving away quickly before Abetz could react.

"I know nothing."

"We think you do."

"Why do you have the documents with Hoffmeister's signature on them?" said Richard.

"I have no idea what you're talking about."

"Then you're less intelligent than I thought," said Robert dismissively.

Abetz was becoming anxious. Part of him needed Robert's regard but he could never forgive him. "You betrayed me."

"You would have betrayed me without a backwards glance."

"That was different. I was doing it for the *Führer*, for the glorious *Third Reich*."

"So you still claim your Nazism?" asked Richard.

"Yes!"

"I thought you had reformed," observed Robert.

"I lied."

"You do a lot of that," said Richard.

"What?"

"Lying."

"Are you the Butcher of Birensk?" asked Robert, once again.

"No!"

"Why do you have the documents with Hoffmeister's signature on them?" asked Richard.

"I don't. You do."

"How do you know that?" questioned Robert.

"Because I told you where to find them."

"Ah, so you admit you knew about them," said Richard.

"What were they for?" continued Robert.

Abetz realized he'd fallen into a clever trap. "I wanted to use them as evidence," he muttered.

"For what reason?"

"As evidence to prove I did not give the order."

"What order was that?" asked Richard.

Abetz began to show signs of confusion.

"I am not the Butcher of Birensk. He is! The evidence in the attaché case proves it wasn't me. You cannot accuse me. I did not give the order. I did nothing. I was not there!" He slammed his fist down onto the table.

"The order for what?" asked Robert.

"I have no idea."

"You just said you did not give the order," said Richard.

"What order?"

"The order you said you did not give," replied Robert. "Tell me about Reinhard Ziegler."

"I never knew him." Abetz felt like a traitor.

"There you go," said Richard.

"What?"

"Lying again," replied Robert.

"I am not."

"You just said you did not give the order when you did," repeated Richard. "What order was that?"

"I don't know!" His body had begun to shake.

"Did you have a homosexual affair with Reinhard Ziegler?" asked Robert.

Abetz broke down and sobbed like a small child.

"He's all yours," said Robert to the M.P. who looked askance at Abetz.

"I'm not sure I want him, sir. Still, let's take him back so he can mop up."

"You have to go to Berlin."

Robert and Richard were walking home from Meridian Camp a few days later.

"Why?"

"Because we need to prove that Hoffmeister is innocent."

"Why?"

"Because we do. It's better for Sophie, better for you, better for me. After all, I'm the one that's going to have to bring up his child. You'll be the baby's uncle."

"Never. Not in a million years."

"I'm afraid you can't escape the ties of being a blood relation, my friend. It's a foregone conclusion, no matter how much you might try to avoid the issue or ignore it. The fact remains that Sophie's child will be related to you."

Richard was silent.

"Now, wouldn't you much prefer a decent man to be the father of your nephew or niece than a ruthless Nazi? I know I would."

360

"You're unbelievable, you know. Here you are calmly trying to protect another man's child that your wife is carrying after hearing all that stuff about how he seduced her. I've been listening to the tapes, so I know."

"I'm trying to protect Sophie's wellbeing. And besides, it all happened before I knew her."

"It didn't for me."

"Be reasonable, Richard."

Richard sighed. "Okay, I'll do it."

Robert smiled. "Properly now, mind. Nothing half-hearted."

"You insult my professionalism."

"That's settled then. I'll make the arrangements."

A week later, Richard flew out to Germany.

"Tell me about Reinhard Ziegler." Robert knew now that he had found Abetz's Achilles' heel.

"He was a great man." Abetz felt himself beginning to tremble uncontrollably again.

"How did you feel when he was assassinated?"

Abetz covered his face with his hands. "It was all my fault."

"Your fault that he was assassinated?"

"Yes. I should have done more to protect him. Taken the bullet that killed him."

"How did you feel afterwards?"

"I wanted to get revenge."

"On whom?"

"The people who were responsible for his assassination."

"And did you?"

"I had to. The authorities blamed me for his death. They said I hadn't taken the threats to his life seriously and that if I had, I could have prevented him being shot."

"What did you do?"

"Why should I tell you?"

"Because I want to know."

"Why do you want to know?"

"Because it's my job."

"Will I be prosecuted if I tell you?"

It was an unusually stupid question from a man like Abetz. Robert wondered if they'd got to him at last.

"Only if you're guilty of something," he replied. "Are you guilty?"

"No!" He thumped the table with his fist but it had less impact than before.

"Tell me about Erika Kleist."

Shocked, Abetz stared at Robert. "How do you know about her?"

Quickly, he thought back to previous interrogations. He hadn't mentioned her inadvertently had he?

"I know many things about you."

"Erika Kleist. A prostitute. She was very good at getting men into bed and extracting information from them. She worked for the *Abwehr*."

"Was she in love with you?"

361

"What relevance has that got?" He sighed. It wouldn't matter to reveal that. "Yes. Stupid little fool. So I used her." He smiled lasciviously. "In more ways than one, just as I did with many women. But she was better than most."

"What happened to her?"

"I have no idea. When she had outlived her usefulness I had her sent away."

"Where to?"

"Ravensbrück. She was a Jew."

Robert called the M.P. over. "Take this piece of shit back to his quarters."

Abetz was dragged unceremoniously out of the room.

"Tell me about Admiral Siranac."

"The head of the *Abwehr*?" Abetz laughed. "I tried to have him removed from office."

"Why?"

"So that Reinhard could take over."

"Did you succeed?"

"No." He hung his head in embarrassment. "Someone found out."

"So your dastardly plot failed."

Abetz was silent.

"Tell me about Otto Stolze."

"How do you know about him?" He laughed harshly in his growing nervousness. "A weak, spineless idiot. He disappeared. If he hadn't, I would have had him shot."

"And what about the new Otto Stolze, the one that arrived unexpectedly in the Brussels *Abwehrstelle*?"

Did this man know everything? Suddenly, Abetz felt exposed and vulnerable.

"How do you know about him?"

"I know because *I* took on the identity of Otto Stolze. I worked at the *Abwehrstelle* in Brussels and I was the one who foiled your attempt to bring down Admiral Siranac."

And the M.P. escorted a stunned Abetz back across the compound.

"Tell me about Birensk."

"I know nothing."

"Have you ever been there?"

"No!"

"That is not true."

"How do you know?"

"I have two photographs placing you at the scene of the massacre."

"You are lying."

"I never lie."

"You did on St Nicolas."

"No. I just aimed to mislead."

Abetz considered for a moment. "Stupidly, I trusted you. So therefore I now don't believe you. Show me."

Robert had the photographs (wired from Berlin by Richard) brought in.

Abetz hung his head. Now he could deny nothing.

"Are you willing to make a full confession?"

"Never! I did not give the order!" and he lunged across the table at Robert.

The M.P. took him away.

"Please will you write a simple phrase – oh, I don't know, something like: 'The cat sat on the mat' and 'How do you do?' – on this piece of paper."

Heinrich smiled. "In German or English?"

"Let's have both," said Robert.

"Anything else?"

"One question. If Sophie had fallen pregnant and was now carrying your child, would you still not want to see her?"

"If that was the case, it would change everything and yes, I would want to see her again."

Robert stared out of the window after Hoffmeister had gone.

"Please copy these phrases, trying to match the handwriting." Robert had added a couple of his own to Hoffmeister's. "Make it as close to the originals as you can. Keep trying until you get it right."

"Why should I?"

"Because I've asked you politely."

"What will you do to me if I refuse?"

"Then, like the proverbial naughty schoolboy, you can sit there until you do."

"What happens if I stay here so long I die?"

"Then that will be to your disadvantage, won't it?"

Sullenly, Abetz did as he was asked.

Afterwards, Robert studied the results.

In his room, Abetz knew the game was up and he began to formulate the plan for his final act of revenge.

It was now or never.

He'd need a gun and a uniform so he made a study of the military policeman who always took him to and from his interrogations.

Robert took Sophie out for a walk. She put her arm through his and they left the town behind, ascending the grassy hillside above the church. It was overcast and cold but they were well wrapped up against the damp November chill.

Sophie chatted away happily for a few moments before perceiving that Robert was unusually unresponsive.

"What is it, darling?" she asked.

Robert took a deep breath. "Heinrich Hoffmeister is in Meridian Camp and has been for some weeks."

Sophie went pale with shock. "Why didn't you tell me?"

"I couldn't tell you, my darling, not because I wanted to keep it from you but because there were several things that needed to be sorted out first." And he explained all that had transpired.

After listening carefully and trusting in everything that he told her, she said, "So, you've proved that Abetz faked the signature?"

"More or less. I've certainly established that he's capable of imitating handwriting very accurately. We've got the photograph that places Abetz at the scene of the crime and I'm just waiting now for Richard to come back from Berlin with proof that Hoffmeister was hospitalized and couldn't possibly have been there."

"I always knew that Heinrich was a good man."

"I know and because of that conviction and for the sake of your wellbeing, I set out to prove that he was not."

"My wellbeing?"

"Yes. It would have been terrible to discover that your child's father was a committed Nazi."

Sophie nodded, full of gratitude. "Thank you," she said, holding him closer to her. "I love you."

"I know." He kissed her tenderly and looked into her eyes. "I love you too."

They continued on their way for a while.

"Would you like to see him?" Robert asked tentatively.

"Yes please, especially if he's unwell. He ought to know that he conceived a child before he... dies."

"And you can cope with that?"

"Yes." Sophie felt strong and confident in her love for her husband knowing that it superseded all else, though she felt deeply saddened that Heinrich may not have long to live. "What about you?"

"I'll let you know," replied Robert honestly.

"You have no need to worry," she said reassuringly.

"I know," he replied.

Three days later, Robert took Sophie to meet with Hoffmeister, the official pretext for her visit being that of 'character corroboration' by an eyewitness. He ensured that this initial meeting was not recorded.

Hoffmeister's face registered shock when Sophie walked into the room, both for seeing her again and by her advancing pregnancy.

For her part, she was equally shocked by his pallor and feebleness.

"My Sophie. Please forgive me, but I cannot stand to greet you."

"It doesn't matter."

She removed one of her gloves and held out her right hand to him. He took it in his own and kissed it. He looked up at her.

"The child? It is mine?"

"Yes, Heinrich."

Robert sat at his desk, trying to keep calm, trying yet again to keep his jealousy and resentment under control.

"Then we must be married."

Sophie shook her head. "No," she said, as gently as she could. "I'm afraid we can't. I'm so sorry."

"You have met someone else?"

"Yes."

364

"And he is a good man? He stands by you?"

Sophie tried very hard not to look across at Robert. "Oh yes," she said with deep and total conviction. "He is the very best."

Relieved, Heinrich sat back in his chair. "That is good. Very good. As you see, I would not be an adequate provider for your needs and those of our child. And I would not have wished for you to work in order to keep us both or to have endured an imperfect marriage where your husband was a burden."

"I understand." She kept his hand in hers, near to tears at seeing him again, despite herself.

They sat in silence for a while before Sophie said, "Did you try to contact me?"

Heinrich shook his head.

"Why?"

"I thought long and hard about you, my beautiful Sophie. I had to wrestle every natural inclination, knowing that all I wanted was for us to be together freely and without restraint. In the end, I did not write because it would not have been fair to you."

"What do you mean? Surely it would have been fairer to write to me."

"Putting my incapacity aside, I did not want your life to be tainted by association with me."

Robert's head came up. Just when he felt everything was resolving, the truth established, the pieces fitting into place, Hoffmeister decides to make a statement like this.

"I don't understand," said Sophie.

"Unfortunately, in war, things are not always clear-cut. There are varying degrees of responsibility and guilt."

Sophie was shocked. "What on earth do you mean? That you are in some way culpable for what happened at Birensk?" She looked anxiously at Robert.

Heinrich looked confused. "I had no idea I was a suspect." It was his turn to look across at Robert. "This you did not say."

"No." Robert smiled, relieved. This was not the reaction of a guilty man.

"I am not directly responsible for what happened at Birensk and other atrocities like it," said Heinrich, wondering how much Sophie knew, "but all Germans are culpable. For that, and for everything else that happened during the war."

"That isn't true! You cannot take the guilt for a whole nation onto your shoulders. Think carefully, Heinrich, about what you are saying. I know you to be a good man. You were wonderful to all of us at Seeblick. You cannot align yourself with the Nazi criminals who carried out Hitler's terrible orders knowingly and without question."

"They are my fellow countrymen and we allowed it to happen."

"Yes, and Jack the Ripper was English, but that doesn't make all Englishmen guilty of the crimes he committed."

Robert couldn't help smiling at this. "She's got you there," he said.

"That is true. Nevertheless, I stand by what I feel. Therefore, dear Sophie, I did not contact you. And now, it would seem, I have lost out because of that. For myself therefore, I will always have regrets, but for your sake it is right."

"Do you know who is responsible for Birensk?" asked Robert.

"It has to be Theodor Abetz. Many people thought they knew at the time but no one acted to accuse him. He went too far and the whole incident was brushed under the carpet, as you say in England."

"Can you prove that it was him?"

"All I have is hearsay."

"We have to have concrete evidence."

"Of course."

There was a knock at the door and without waiting on ceremony, Richard walked in.

"Got it!" he exclaimed triumphantly, his face alight. "Got the stuff exonerating Hoffmeister, so Sophie's baby is in the clear and…"

He stopped in midsentence as the three people in the room looked at him in amazement.

"Sophie!" he exclaimed, taking in Robert and Heinrich with his glance. "How…?"

"Character reference."

"Ah. Well, and here's the best bit! I've also come back with proof that Abetz is guilty. Absolute fool-proof proof."

Robert smiled, seeing a transformation in Richard's manner. The success of the trip had obviously done him good. "That's great news!"

"And you seem more like your old self as well," observed Sophie.

"I'll tell you all about it when we get home," he said, "and Robert and I can discuss the finer details later. And boy, are they fine!"

"When you get home?" said Hoffmeister, looking at Sophie in bewilderment. "He is not…?"

Sophie smiled. "No, he's not. Heinrich, I'd like you to meet my brother Richard, and this man here," she gazed lovingly at Robert, "is my husband…"

Heinrich looked across at Robert in shocked admiration and acknowledgement. He was about to speak when all at once, there was a terrific commotion from outside the room and suddenly, Theodor Abetz burst through the door.

"No one should move or I will shoot!"

For a split second, taken completely by surprise, the four of them remained immobile.

Putting the gun to Richard's head as he was nearest the door, but keeping his gaze fixed on the other occupants of the room, Abetz ordered him to shut and lock it. As he did so, Richard had a glimpse of the guard lying unconscious on the ground, blood seeping from a wound on his head.

"Over there with the others," Abetz ordered Richard. "*Do not try anything,*" he said to Robert, seeing his hand move surreptitiously as he prepared to remove his revolver from its holster. "*Believe me I will shoot. Put up your hands behind your head and lock your fingers together.*"

Robert did as he was asked. He glanced briefly across to Richard knowing that they would at any moment be acting in tandem to disarm Abetz.

But Richard moved a moment too soon and Abetz shot him. He fell to the ground, clutching his shoulder. Immediately, Sophie went to go to his aid, but was ordered back by Abetz who pointed the gun at her head and kept it there.

366

He directed wild, desperate eyes onto Robert.

"*Over here, to me,*" he ordered, keeping the gun trained on Sophie so that Robert, without any choice, came round from behind the desk.

Abetz threw Robert's gun across the room and shoved him onto the desk, pinning him down so that he was stretched out backwards, with his hands pressed hard behind his neck and his feet on the floor, his body bent awkwardly over the edge of the desk, making any escape impossible.

Abetz leant over him and put his face close to Robert's.

"*If you try anything this close up, you'll kill yourself as well,*" said Robert, squirming, trying to free himself.

"*It is no matter. If you try anything, I will kill the woman.*"

Abetz thrust his body harder against Robert's, jamming his chin up and back with his free hand ensuring complete physical restraint, all the while keeping his gun pointed at Sophie.

"*You see, you can do nothing. I am in control. Never again will you double-cross me. Nor will you send me to trial. I am in charge now and because of that, I will tell you what you want to know so you will understand.*

"*Yes, it was I who ordered the massacre at Birensk where Reinhard's assassins were holed up. It was I who carried out that glorious act of revenge for his death! Me! Theodor Abetz and not some lowly, faceless Intendanturassessor.*

"*Yes, it was I who planned the assassination of your royal family – a daring and audacious plan that would have brought glory to the Third Reich and restored me to the Nazi hierarchy. But you deprived me of the chance to redeem myself by taking me away.*

"*So now I shall take you away with me in an even greater act of vengeance and I shall be free of your duplicity forever!*"

For a brief moment, Abetz looked into Robert's eyes before putting his own head next to that of his prey, jabbing his weapon against Robert's temple and pulling the trigger.

Sophie screamed.

EPILOGUE

St Nicolas
July, 1947

A small child playing on golden sand, industrious and focused.

An elderly woman sitting in a deck chair keeps watch, a sun hat pulled low over her forehead to shield her eyes. Suddenly, the child's ball rolls away down the sloping sand.

A man, casually dressed in linen trousers and an open-necked shirt, approaches slowly.

"Yours, I think?" he says, holding out the brightly coloured object to the child who runs to the woman, standing quietly beside her while at the same time, regarding the man with wide, unblinking blue eyes.

He puts the ball down on the sand and smiles at the child before scooping her up into his arms, his movements measured and careful.

"Guten Tag, Fräulein Edna," he says to the older woman, his eyes warm and kind.

She chuckles. "Dear boy, it's so good to see you! You're earlier than we were expecting."

"Yes, I wanted my appearance be a surprise. The crossing was excellent and I was able to find a taxi straight away." He smiles again at the child who has put her arms around his neck.

"Dadda," she says.

He kisses the little girl on the cheek and hugs her.

"Where is my Sophie?" he asks Edna.

"Gone into Port le Bac on an errand for Mae. You must have missed her somehow."

"I came straight up from the harbour." He is disappointed but in a moment his expression brightens. "No matter. I expect your mummy will appear in good time," he says, addressing the child who is now squirming to be free. He sets her down gently and takes a moment or two to regain his breath.

The man feels in his trouser pocket for the photograph that has been his talisman during the long weeks of separation. It is still there. He won't need it so much now. But he will always keep it.

"How are you feeling?" asks Edna.

"Much better, thank you. The doctors in Berlin were excellent."

"Good." Edna smiles and says, "Well, I think that Gabrielle and I have both had enough sun for today." She stands up and takes the little girl by the hand. "Come, child. It is time for us to go home and see how Uncle Albrecht is getting on."

"Blub, blub."

"True, he might have caught our supper by now. Though we'll most likely find him having fallen asleep in his deckchair by the stream with his favourite straw hat over his eyes and the fish swimming in circles at his feet."

She turns to the man and smiles. "Come up to the farmhouse as soon as you are ready. I'm longing to hear your news."

The afternoon sun is hot and the man feels jaded. He stoops to pick up the book that Edna has left behind on the sand beside her deckchair. He smiles as he reads the title and takes it with him as he walks slowly across the little cove to the grotto. Stripping off his clothes, he lowers himself into the water, swimming carefully across its full extent.

Tiring quickly, he comes out and lies on the sand, allowing the sun to dry his body.

He picks up the book and begins to read.

After a while, he hears a small sound and looks up and there she is.

They look at each other for a long time in the bright sunshine. He sees the blue of her eyes and feels himself enveloped in a golden aura of purity and loveliness.

Just like the girl from his adolescence. The girl he loved and lost in an instant; the girl he has always dreamed of finding.

But this can't be her, surely?

She sees him lying naked on the sand and her cheeks grow warm and her body trembles.

Just like the boy from her adolescence. The boy she loved and lost in an instant, the boy she has always dreamed of finding.

But this can't be him, surely?

In one swift movement, she has knelt beside him and wordlessly, he takes her into his arms and they kiss with all the impassioned yearning of the lovers in *La Chaleur de la Mer*, the book that now lies beside him on the sand.

Slowly and sensuously, he undresses her and enfolds her within his arms until the exquisiteness of their caress envelops them both in the beauty of ecstasy.

Afterwards, breathless and tingling, they lay together on the sand, their closeness inviolate.

"I've missed you so much," said Sophie.

"I've missed you too," replied Robert, stroking her hair.

"Are you completely better? I've been so worried. I wanted so much to be with you."

"I know, but it wasn't possible as the situation in Berlin with the Russians was becoming very volatile." He smiled reassuringly. "But I'm fine, honestly, just a bit tired still. Shingles was a stupid thing to have gone down with. And it wrecked my final weeks of duty."

"It was all the strain of the war years and particularly..." She couldn't bring herself to utter the words, even now, even after all this time.

"Yes."

"I still get nightmares."

"So do I. But they will fade with time."

"What about Abetz?"

"He was found guilty at his trial in Nuremburg."

"So you said in your letter. Have they carried out the sentence yet?"

"Yes. He won't be troubling anyone again."

"You were so lucky." She buried her face in his shoulder.

"*We* were so lucky. If the gun hadn't failed to go off…"

"Don't!"

"I know."

"Heinrich was very brave."

"Yes. And noble," added Robert, "especially as he must have known that the effort of tackling Abetz in that split second before he could pull the trigger again would probably shorten his life."

They looked at each other, the picture in their minds as vivid as the day it had happened: both of them seeing Heinrich's unanticipated leap to push Abetz away, enabling Robert to overpower and disarm him.

"Heinrich loved you very much." Robert could speak of this now, freely and without jealousy.

"Yes, I know he did. He must have done to make that sort of sacrifice."

"I never told you, but I asked him once why he did it."

"Oh?"

"He said it was because of the way you and I had looked at each other when you introduced me as your husband. He said he realized I would give you the life you deserved whereas he could not."

Sophie smiled at Robert, tears pricking her eyes. "He was a good man," she said quietly.

"And his daughter had a good man as her father."

"She still has."

Sophie stroked Robert's cheek meaningfully and he brought her hand to his lips, kissing it, looking at her with love and gratitude.

"At least, after that second heart attack he lived long enough to see Gabrielle," observed Sophie.

"And to name her."

"Yes. That was very special for him. And we did try to make his last couple of months as comfortable and easy as we could."

"No one could have done more than you, especially given how near you were to giving birth and then afterwards, coping with a new baby."

"You were incredibly unselfish to have agreed to my caring for him."

"And in *our* house as well!" responded Robert.

"I've always said you have a wonderful generosity of spirit."

"It tested it though."

"I know." Sophie took a deep breath. "But I did have the nurse to help me and as we said at the time, Heinrich did save your life and probably mine too when I had scarlet fever at Seeblick."

"Yes. So it was the least we could do."

"I love you."

"I love you too." He smiled at her. "So tell me, what other news is there?"

"Edwin and Cicely have decided to move up to the Lake District and Caroline is expecting a baby!"

"That's fantastic news. I'm glad she and Richard have sorted out their differences. It took them long enough."

"And to think it was all to do with her not wanting to have a family."

"And with Richard wanting children," said Robert, "I can appreciate why he was so upset about you."

"So can I. Here was me, his sister, pregnant by the 'enemy' and his wife refusing to have his baby."

"Especially after having prevaricated about marrying him in the first place."

"And calling him an indolent, lazy good-for-nothing into the bargain."

"A complete recipe for marital discord! Hopefully, they can forgive and forget now that it's all resolved."

"Thank goodness," said Sophie with heartfelt relief, glad that her eventual end-of-tether outburst to her brother and his wife had been humbly accepted and acted upon. "And we might just manage to have our old friendship back again."

"I hope so. So, how's Mae?"

"Found herself a beau!"

"No! Good for her!" Robert was delighted.

"He's a few years younger than she is and a recent arrival on the island. He takes her out to the cinema or for afternoon tea in the new restaurant that's just opened in the High Street. They're quite serious about each other and it's done wonders for her health."

"I'm away for two months and the whole world changes!"

"Aunt Edna and Albrecht are really glad for Mae. I know that when the major first arrived, Edna was worried that Aunt Mae might be jealous or feel left out, especially as she had always thought that Albrecht was coming to see her while he was *Kommandant*." Sophie turned over onto her stomach. "Edna says she'll always be grateful to you for obtaining passage to England for Albrecht at the end of the war. They're so terribly happy."

"Hm. I had to pull a few strings and call in a few favours, but it worked out well in the end."

"You're wonderful."

"Flattery will get you everywhere." He kissed her gently and ran his finger slowly down her spine.

"I know," replied Sophie, trembling at his touch. "Oh, and there's a letter for you from the Mother Superior in Brussels. It came last week, but I didn't bother to send it on as I knew you'd be home soon."

"Knowing I wasn't able to visit her as planned because I had shingles, she must have written to me instead and her letter reached here before I did! Perhaps now that I'm better, we'll be able to go. I'd like you to meet her."

"So would I! Did you find out anything about your Admiral Siranac while you were in Berlin?"

Robert was silent and breathed in deeply. Immediately, Sophie could tell that something was wrong.

"He didn't make it, did he?" she asked.

"No. After I found out, I went to visit his wife and she told me that by some unfortunate quirk of fate the *SS* came across some diaries written by a close associate that not only chronicled the admiral's thoughts and feelings but those of his closest colleagues who shared his philosophy. Hitler was livid at his 'betrayal' and ordered Siranac's immediate arrest and his anti-Nazi friends. He was imprisoned, accused of trying to assassinate Hitler, then tortured by the *Gestapo* and just days before the war ended, given a bogus trial and executed."

"Oh, Robert, I'm so sorry. I know how highly you regarded him."

"Yes. He was an amazing man."

"How did his wife seem?"

"Brave. Philosophical. He'd realized, apparently, that it would only be a matter of time before they caught up with him and was glad to have been able to continue with his work for as long as he did."

"War is a terrible, terrible business."

"Yes."

"But it's over now, thank God. And we came through safely."

For several moments they held each other close knowing that, but for a stroke of good fortune, it might have been very, very different.

"Aimée and Claude are coming here from Oswestry next week," said Sophie, becoming resolutely cheerful again, "and Hélène is home from university, so we're to be quite a houseful. Tommy can't wait! He has quite a crush on Aimée. They both like nature, and if you remember, when your adoptees came last time, he and Aimée spent most of the time on long cycle rides across the island!"

Robert chuckled. "I do. I like the fact that they get on so well."

"And Aimée doesn't stand any nonsense from Gert, either, who's actually become a bit nicer since Cyril was demobbed and they decided to settle permanently on St Nicolas. Aimée confided to me that she wants to marry Tommy when they're older."

"I hope they do. He's a lovely lad, in spite of his awful mother."

"Yes." She hesitated. "Claude still wants to be a soldier."

"Unfortunately."

"What did you say to him this last time?"

"I advised him against it. Again."

"How did he react?"

"He was upset. He wants to take my place, as it were, now that I've come out of the army and thought I'd be pleased. But I'm not. I don't want him involved in any way. It's not the life for a sensitive young man like Claude." Like he had been; like he would never be again.

"Perhaps Aimée will dissuade him."

"Let's hope so."

Tactfully, Sophie changed the subject. "At the end of her course, Hélène is determined to go back to Belgium and train as a teacher."

"I'm not surprised," he said, taking deep breaths, calming the latent fears borne of bitter experience that intruded on his equilibrium these days. "It will suit her very well."

Sophie regarded Robert carefully. "Talking about teaching, have you decided yet?"

"Whether or not to take up my dad's offer at his school?" He considered for a moment. "No, not yet. You and I need to talk about it a bit more first. In many ways, I'd prefer to stay here on St Nicolas and for us to work together on the farm."

"Really?" said Sophie, feeling pleased. "Edna and Mae would be delighted if we stayed. But your parents would be equally delighted if you accepted your dad's offer, especially as they've been so kind to us and the children."

"I know." He sighed. "I suppose that what I do depends to a large extent on whether you'd be happier living here or in Shropshire."

"Darling, I'm happy anywhere as long as I'm with you."

Robert kissed her lovingly. "And I feel the same about you." Then he chuckled. "It's a funny old world, isn't it?"

"What makes you say that?"

"Being in places. Coming back to them after a long time. I've been here before, you know," said Robert, stroking her body, admiring her perfection.

"Really?" murmured Sophie, yielding to his touch. "When you came here with Richard, you mean, during the war?"

"No, before that. When I was fifteen. I came to the island on holiday with my parents and wandered off by myself for the day and discovered this very cove. I found a book here, on the beach, and began to read it. I didn't manage to finish it because a young girl came and picked it up. I never saw her again, though I wanted to, very much."

Astonished, Sophie sat upright.

"The book was *La Chaleur de la Mer*. That girl was *me*!"

They stared at each other.

"I never forgot you," he said in wonder, reaching out for her.

"Nor I you. I used to dream about you. I used to have this fantasy that you had grown up and that I would find you again and you would make love to me on this very beach."

"You did?"

"Yes."

"And I have!"

Sophie kissed him. "Oh yes!"

"Do you know, I searched for years for *La Chaleur de la Mer* as a reminder of that day, but I never found it."

"Until it turned up unexpectedly at Seeblick and, after you'd left it behind, *I* was the one who rescued it from disaster!"

"I tried to find the 'girl' here on the island when Richard and I came during the war."

"But you couldn't possibly have found her."

"No, because she was…"

"…at Seeblick!" they chorused, and held each other close.

"You were so embarrassed that day when you saw me," said Robert, his expression full of tenderness.

"I know! My cheeks must have been a picture. You made a very deep impression upon my thirteen-year-old sensibilities."

Robert smiled. "And now, here I am again. Like this…"

"Aren't you just?" responded Sophie. "And so am I! And it's *us*. *You* and *me*!"

"It would seem we've known each other even longer than we thought."

"For always."

He takes her by the hand to the smooth-edged stones by the pool and as one, they dive into the deep, sun-dappled water. They come up to the surface, gasping for air, the liquid coolness embracing every part of them as they come together, their limbs entwined, their sensuality heightened, before swimming with languid strokes across the pool, their bodies perfectly synchronized.

Leaving the water, they dry themselves and dress. It is time to return to the farmhouse.

In the glow of the setting sun, Robert and Sophie, arms wrapped round each other, walk together along the edge of the shore: the warmth of the sea lapping against their bare feet, the copy of *La Chaleur de la Mer* in her hand, and a lifetime of love before them.

OTHER PUBLICATIONS FROM
ŌZARU BOOKS

The Call of Cairnmor
Sally Aviss

Book One of the Cairnmor Trilogy

The Scottish Isle of Cairnmor is a place of great beauty and undisturbed wilderness, a haven for wildlife, a land of white sandy beaches and inland fertile plains, a land where awe-inspiring mountains connect precipitously with the sea.

To this remote island comes a stranger, Alexander Stewart, on a quest to solve the mysterious disappearance of two people and their unborn child; a missing family who are now heirs to a vast fortune. He enlists the help of local schoolteacher, Katherine MacDonald, and together they seek the answers to this enigma: a deeply personal journey that takes them from Cairnmor to the historic splendour of London and the industrial heartland of Glasgow.

Covering the years 1936-1937 and infused with period colour and detail, The Call of Cairnmor is about unexpected discovery and profound attachment which, from its gentle opening, gradually gathers momentum and complexity until all the strands come together to give life-changing revelations.

"really enjoyed reading this – loved the plot... Read it in just two sittings as I couldn't stop reading." (P. Green – amazon.co.uk)

"exciting plot, not a book you want to put down, although I tried not to rush it so as to fully enjoy escaping to the world skilfully created by the author. A most enjoyable read." (Liz Green – amazon.co.uk)

"an excellent read. I cannot wait for the next part of the trilogy from this talented author. You will not want to put it down" (B. Burchell – amazon.co.uk)

ISBN: 978-0-9559219-9-5

Changing Tides, Changing Times
Sally Aviss

Book Two of the Cairnmor Trilogy

In the dense jungle of Malaya in 1942, Doctor Rachel Curtis stumbles across a mysterious, unidentifiable stranger, badly injured and close to death.

Four years earlier in 1938 in London, Katherine Stewart and her husband Alex come into conflict with their differing needs while Alex's father, Alastair, knows he must keep his deeper feelings hidden from the woman he loves; a woman to whom he must never reveal the full extent of that love.

Covering a broad canvas and meticulously researched, Changing Times, Changing Tides follows the interwoven journey of well-loved characters from The Call of Cairnmor, as well as introducing new personalities, in a unique combination of novel and history that tells a story of love, loss, friendship and heroism; absorbing the reader in the characters' lives as they are shaped and changed by the ebb and flow of events before, during and after the Second World War.

"I enjoyed the twists and turns of this book ... particularly liked the gutsy Dr Rachel who is a reminder to the reader that these are dark days for the world. Love triumphs but not in the way we thought it would and our heroine, Katherine, learns that the path to true love is certainly not a smooth one." (MDW – amazon.co.uk)

"Even better than the first book! A moving and touching story well told." (P. Green – amazon.co.uk)

"One of the best reads this year ... can't wait for the next one." (Mr C. Brownett – amazon.co.uk)

"One of my favourite books - and I have shelves of them in the house! Sally Aviss is a masterful storyteller [... She] has obviously done a tremendous amount of research, judging by all the fascinating and in-depth historical detail woven into the storyline." ('Inverneill' – amazon.co.uk)

ISBN: 978-0-9931587-0-4

Where Gloom and Brightness Meet
Sally Aviss

Book Three of the Cairnmor Trilogy

When Anna Stewart begins a relationship with journalist Marcus Kendrick, the ramifications are felt from New York all the way across the Atlantic to the remote and beautiful Scottish island of Cairnmor, where her family live. Yet even as she and Marcus draw closer, Anna cannot forget her estranged husband whom she has not seen for many years.

When tragedy strikes, for some, Cairnmor becomes a refuge, a place of solace to ease the troubled spirit and an escape from painful reality; for others, it becomes a place of enterprise and adventure – a place in which to dream of an unfettered future.

This third book in the *Cairnmor Trilogy*, takes the action forward into the late nineteen-sixties as well as recalling familiar characters' lives from the intervening years. *Where Gloom and Brightness Meet* is a story of heartbreak and redemptive love; of long-dead passion remembered and retained in isolation; of unfaltering loyalty and steadfast devotion. It is a story that juxtaposes the old and the new; a story that reflects the conflicting attitudes, problems and joys of a liberating era.

"the last book in Sally Aviss's trilogy and it did not disappoint ... what a wonderful journey this has been ... cleverly written with an enormous amount of research" (B. Burchell – amazon.co.uk)

"I loved this third book in the series ... the characters were believable and events unfolded in a beguiling way ... not too happy ending for everyone but a satisfying conclusion to the saga" (P. Green – amazon.co.uk)

ISBN: 978-0-9931587-1-1

Reflections in an Oval Mirror
Memories of East Prussia, 1923-45
Anneli Jones

8th May 1945 – VE Day – was Anneliese Wiemer's twenty-second birthday. Although she did not know it then, it marked the end of her flight to the West, and the start of a new life in England.

These illustrated memoirs, based on a diary kept during the Third Reich and letters rediscovered many decades later, depict the momentous changes occurring in Europe against a backcloth of everyday farm life in East Prussia (now the north-western corner of Russia, sandwiched between Lithuania and Poland).

The political developments of the 1930s (including the Hitler Youth, 'Kristallnacht', political education, labour service, war service, and interrogation) are all the more poignant for being told from the viewpoint of a romantic young girl. In lighter moments she also describes student life in Vienna and Prague, and her friendship with Belgian and Soviet prisoners of war. Finally, however, the approach of the Red Army forces her to abandon her home and flee across the frozen countryside, encountering en route a cross-section of society ranging from a 'lady of the manor', worried about her family silver, to some concentration camp inmates

"couldn't put it down... delightful... very detailed descriptions of the farm and the arrival of war... interesting history and personal account" ('Rosie', amazon.com)

ISBN: 978-0-9559219-0-2

Carpe Diem
Moving on from East Prussia
Anneli Jones

This sequel to "Reflections in an Oval Mirror" details Anneli's post-war life. The scene changes from life in Northern 'West Germany' as a refugee, reporter and military interpreter, to parties with the Russian Authorities in Berlin, boating in the Lake District with the original 'Swallows and Amazons', weekends with the Astors at Cliveden, then the beginnings of a new family in the small Kentish village of St Nicholas-at-Wade. Finally, after the fall of the Iron Curtain, Anneli is able to revisit her first home once more.

ISBN: 978-0-9931587-3-5

Skating at the Edge of the Wood
Memories of East Prussia, 1931-1945… 1993
Marlene Yeo

In 1944, the twelve-year old East Prussian girl Marlene Wiemer embarked on a horrific trek to the West, to escape the advancing Red Army. Her cousin Jutta was left behind the Iron Curtain, which severed the family bonds that had made the two so close.

This book contains dramatic depictions of Marlene's flight, recreated from her letters to Jutta during the last year of the war, and contrasted with joyful memories of the innocence that preceded them.

Nearly fifty years later, the advent of perestroika meant that Marlene and Jutta were finally able to revisit their childhood home, after a lifetime of growing up under diametrically opposed societies, and the book closes with a final chapter revealing what they find.

Despite depicting the same time and circumstances as "Reflections in an Oval Mirror", an account written by Marlene's elder sister, Anneli, and its sequel "Carpe Diem", this work stands in stark contrast partly owing to the age gap between the two girls, but above all because of their dramatically different characters.

ISBN: 978-0-9931587-2-8

Travels in Taiwan
Exploring Ilha Formosa
Gary Heath

For many Westerners, Taiwan is either a source of cheap electronics or an ongoing political problem. It is seldom highlighted as a tourist destination, and even those that do visit rarely venture far beyond the well-trod paths of the major cities and resorts.

Yet true to its 16th century Portuguese name, the 'beautiful island' has some of the highest mountains in East Asia, many unique species of flora and fauna, and several distinct indigenous peoples (fourteen at the last count).

On six separate and arduous trips, Gary Heath deliberately headed for the areas neglected by other travel journalists, armed with several notebooks... and a copy of War and Peace for the days when typhoons confined him to his tent. The fascinating land he discovered is revealed here.

"offers a great deal of insight into Taiwanese society, history, culture, as well as its island's scenic geography... disturbing and revealing... a true, peripatetic, descriptive Odyssey undertaken by an adventurous and inquisitive Westerner on a very Oriental and remote island" (Charles Phillips, goodreads.com)

ISBN: 978-0-9559219-8-8

West of Arabia
A Journey Home
Gary Heath

Faced with the need to travel from Saudi Arabia to the UK, Gary Heath made the unusual decision to take the overland route. His three principles were to stay on the ground, avoid back-tracking, and do minimal sightseeing.

The ever-changing situation in the Middle East meant that the rules had to be bent on occasion, yet as he travelled across Eritrea, Sudan, Egypt, Libya, Tunisia and Morocco, he succeeded in beating his own path around the tourist traps, gaining unique insights into Arabic culture as he went.

Written just a few months before the Arab Spring of 2011, this book reveals many of the underlying tensions that were to explode onto the world stage just shortly afterwards, and has been updated to reflect the recent changes.

"just the right blend of historical background [and] personal experiences... this book is a must read" ('Denise', goodreads.com)

ISBN: 978-0-9559219-6-4

Ichigensan
– The Newcomer –
David Zoppetti

Translated from the Japanese by Takuma Sminkey

Ichigensan is a novel which can be enjoyed on many levels – as a delicate, sensual love story, as a depiction of the refined society in Japan's cultural capital Kyoto, and as an exploration of the themes of alienation and prejudice common to many environments, regardless of the boundaries of time and place.

Unusually, it shows Japan from the eyes of both an outsider and an 'internal' outcast, and even more unusually, it originally achieved this through sensuous prose carefully crafted by a non-native speaker of Japanese. The fact that this best-selling novella then won the Subaru Prize, one of Japan's top literary awards, and was also nominated for the Akutagawa Prize is a testament to its unique narrative power.

The story is by no means chained to Japan, however, and this new translation by Takuma Sminkey will allow readers world-wide to enjoy the multitude of sensations engendered by life and love in an alien culture.

"A beautiful love story" (Japan Times)

"Sophisticated... subtle... sensuous... delicate... memorable... vivid depictions" (Asahi Evening News)

"Striking... fascinating..." (Japan PEN Club)

"Refined and sensual" (Kyoto Shimbun)

"quiet, yet very compelling... subtle mixture of humour and sensuality...the insights that the novel gives about Japanese society are both intriguing and exotic" (Nicholas Greenman, amazon.com)

ISBN: 978-0-9559219-4-0

Sunflowers
– Le Soleil –
Shimako Murai

A play in one act
Translated from the Japanese by Ben Jones

Hiroshima is synonymous with the first hostile use of an atomic bomb. Many people think of this occurrence as one terrible event in the past, which is studied from history books.

Shimako Murai and other 'Women of Hiroshima' believe otherwise: for them, the bomb had after-effects which affected countless people for decades, effects that were all the more menacing for their unpredictability – and often, invisibility.

This is a tale of two such people: on the surface successful modern women, yet each bearing underneath hidden scars as horrific as the keloids that disfigured Hibakusha on the days following the bomb.

"a great story and a glimpse into the lives of the people who lived during the time of the war and how the bomb affected their lives, even after all these years" (Wendy Pierce, goodreads.com)

ISBN: 978-0-9559219-3-3

The Body as a Vessel
Approaching the Methodology of
Hijikata Tatsumi's Ankoku Butō
MIKAMI Kayo

An analysis of the modern dance form
Translated from the Japanese by Rosa van Hensbergen

When Hijikata Tatsumi's "Butō" appeared in 1959, it revolutionized not only Japanese dance but also the concept of performance art worldwide. It has however proved notoriously difficult to define or tie down. Mikami was a disciple of Hijikata for three years, and in this book, partly based on her graduate and doctoral theses, she combines insights from these years with earlier notes from other dancers to decode the ideas and processes behind butō.

ISBN: 978-0-9931587-4-2

Turner's Margate Through Contemporary Eyes
The Viney Letters
Stephen Channing

Margate in the early 19th Century was an exciting town, where smugglers and 'preventive men' fought to outwit each other, while artists such as JMW Turner came to paint the glorious sunsets over the sea. One of the young men growing up in this environment decided to set out for Australia to make his fortune in the Bendigo gold rush.

Half a century later, having become a pillar of the community, he began writing a series of letters and articles for Keble's Gazette, a publication based in his home town. In these, he described Margate with great familiarity (and tremendous powers of recall), while at the same time introducing his English readers to the "latitudinarian democracy" of a new, "young Britain".

Viney's interests covered a huge range of topics, from Thanet folk customs such as Hoodening, through diatribes on the perils of assigning intelligence to dogs, to geological theories including suggestions for the removal of sandbanks off the English coast "in obedience to the sovereign will and intelligence of man".

His writing is clearly that of a well-educated man, albeit with certain Victorian prejudices about the colonies that may make those with modern sensibilities wince a little. Yet above all, it is interesting because of the light it throws on life in a British seaside town some 180 years ago.

This book also contains numerous contemporary illustrations.

"profusely illustrated... draws together a series of interesting articles and letters... recommended" (Margate Civic Society)

ISBN: 978-0-9559219-2-6

The Margate Tales
Stephen Channing

Chaucer's Canterbury Tales is without doubt one of the best ways of getting a feel for what the people of England in the Middle Ages were like. In the modern world, one might instead try to learn how different people behave and think from television or the internet.

However, to get a feel for what it was like to be in Margate as it gradually changed from a small fishing village into one of Britain's most popular holiday resorts, one needs to investigate contemporary sources such as newspaper reports and journals.

Stephen Channing has saved us this work, by trawling through thousands of such documents to select the most illuminating and entertaining accounts of Thanet in the 18th and early to mid 19th centuries. With content ranging from furious battles in the letters pages, to hilarious pastiches, witty poems and astonishing factual reports, illustrated with over 70 drawings from the time, The Margate Tales brings the society of the time to life, and as with Chaucer, demonstrates how in many areas, surprisingly little has changed.

"substantial and fascinating volume... meticulously researched... an absorbing read" (Margate Civic Society)

ISBN: 978-0-9559219-5-7

A Victorian Cyclist
Rambling through Kent in 1886
Stephen & Shirley Channing

Bicycles are so much a part of everyday life nowadays, it can be surprising to realize that for the late Victorians these "velocipedes" were a novelty disparaged as being unhealthy and unsafe – and that indeed tricycles were for a time seen as the format more likely to succeed.

Some people however adopted the newfangled devices with alacrity, embarking on adventurous tours throughout the countryside. One of them documented his 'rambles' around East Kent in such detail that it is still possible to follow his routes on modern cycles, and compare the fauna and flora (and pubs!) with those he vividly described.

In addition to providing today's cyclists with new historical routes to explore, and both naturalists and social historians with plenty of material for research, this fascinating book contains a special chapter on Lady Cyclists in the era before female emancipation, and an unintentionally humorous section instructing young gentlemen how to make their cycle and then ride it.

A Victorian Cyclist features over 200 illustrations, and is complemented by a fully updated website.

"Lovely... wonderfully written... terrific" (Everything Bicycles)

"Rare and insightful" (Kent on Sunday)

"Interesting... informative... detailed historical insights" (BikeBiz)

"Unique and fascinating book... quality is very good... of considerable interest" (Veteran-Cycle Club)

"Superb... illuminating... well detailed... The easy flowing prose, which has a cadence like cycling itself, carries the reader along as if freewheeling with a hind wind" (Forty Plus Cycling Club)

"a fascinating book with both vivid descriptions and a number of hitherto-unseen photos of the area" ('Pedalling Pensioner', amazon.co.uk)

ISBN: 978-0-9559219-7-1

Lightning Source UK Ltd.
Milton Keynes UK
UKHW010120161118
332438UK00002B/122/P